Hermann Oldenburg, F. Max Müller

The Grihya-Sutras

Rules of Vedic Domestic Ceremonies - Vol. 2

Hermann Oldenburg, F. Max Müller

The Grihya-Sutras
Rules of Vedic Domestic Ceremonies - Vol. 2

ISBN/EAN: 9783337168438

Printed in Europe, USA, Canada, Australia, Japan

Cover: Foto ©Andreas Hilbeck / pixelio.de

More available books at **www.hansebooks.com**

THE

SACRED BOOKS OF THE EAST

TRANSLATED

BY VARIOUS ORIENTAL SCHOLARS

AND EDITED BY

F. MAX MÜLLER

VOL. XXX

Oxford

AT THE CLARENDON PRESS

1892

Oxford

PRINTED AT THE CLARENDON PRESS

BY HORACE HART, PRINTER TO THE UNIVERSITY

THE *GRIHYA*-SÛTRAS

RULES OF VEDIC DOMESTIC CEREMONIES

TRANSLATED BY

HERMANN ̆OLDENBERG

PART II

GOBHILA, HIRA*N*YAKE*S*IN, ÂPASTAMBA

———

ÂPASTAMBA, YA*GÑ*A-PARIBHÂSHÂ-SÛTRAS

TRANSLATED BY F. MAX ̆MÜLLER

𝔒𝔵𝔣𝔬𝔯𝔡

AT THE CLARENDON PRESS

1892

CONTENTS.

GR*I*HYA-SÛTRAS.

WE begin our introductory remarks on the literature of the Gr*i*hya-sûtras with the attempt to collect the more important data which throw light on the development of the Gr*i*hya ritual during the oldest period of Hindu antiquity.

There are, as it seems, no direct traces of the Gr*i*hya ceremonies in the most ancient portion of Vedic literature. It is certain indeed that a number of the most important of those ceremonies are contemporaneous with or even earlier than the most ancient hymns of the Rig-veda, as far as their fundamental elements and character are concerned, whatever their precise arrangement may have been. However, in the literature of the oldest period they play no part. It was another portion of the ritual that attracted the attention of the poets to whom we owe the hymns to Agni, Indra, and the other deities of the Vedic Olympus, viz. the offerings of the *S*rauta-Ritual with their far superior pomp, or, to state the matter more precisely, among the offerings of the *S*rauta-Ritual the Soma offering. In the Soma offering centred the thought, the poetry, and we may almost say the life of the Vasish*th*as, of the Vi*s*vâmitras, &c., in whose families the poetry of the Rig-veda had its home. We may assume that the acts of the Gr*i*hya worship, being more limited in extent and simpler in their ritual construction than the great Soma offerings, were not yet at that time, so far as they existed at all, decked out with the reciting of the poetic texts, which we find later on connected with them, and which in the case of the Soma offering came early to be used. Probably they were celebrated in simple unadorned fashion;

what the person making the offering had to say was
doubtless limited to short, possibly prose formulas, so that
these ceremonies remained free from the poetry of the
above-mentioned families of priests [1]. We think that the
character of the verses given in the Gr*i*hya-sûtras, which
had to be repeated at the performance of the different ceremonies, justifies us in making these conjectures. Some of these
verses indeed are old Vedic verses, but we have no proof
that they were composed for the purposes of the Gr*i*hya
ceremonies, and the connection in which we find them in
the Rig-veda proves rather the contrary. Another portion
of these verses and songs proves to have been composed
indeed for the very Gr*i*hya ceremonies for which they are
prescribed in the texts of the ritual : but these verses are
more recent than the old parts of the Rig-veda. Part of
them are found in the Rig-veda in a position which speaks
for their more recent origin, others are not contained in the
Rig-veda at all. Many of these verses are found in the
more recent Vedic Sa*m*hitâs, especially in the Atharva-veda,
a Sa*m*hitâ which may be regarded in the main as a treasure
of Gr*i*hya verses ; others finally have not as yet been
traced to any Vedic Sa*m*hitâ, and we know them from the
Gr*i*hya-sûtras only. We may infer that, during the latter
part of the Rig-veda period, ceremonies such as marriage
and burial began to be decked out with poetry as had long
been the case with the Soma offering. The principal collection of marriage sentences [2] and the sentences for the

---

[1] It is doubtful whether at the time of the Rig-veda the custom was established
for the sacrificer to keep burning constantly a sacred Gr*i*hya fire besides the
three *S*rauta fires. There is, as far as I know, no express mention of the Gr*i*hya
fire in the Rig-veda ; but that is no proof that it had then not yet come into
use. Of the *S*rauta fires the gârhapatya is the only one that is mentioned,
though all three were known beyond a doubt. (Ludwig, Rig-veda, vol. iii,
p. 355; in some of the passages cited the word gârhapatya does not refer to
the gârhapatya fire.)

[2] Rig-veda X, 85. It is clear that what we have here is not a hymn intended
to be recited all at once, but that, as in a number of other cases in the Rig-veda,
the single verses or groups of verses were to be used at different points in the
performance of a rite (or, in other cases, in the telling of a story). Compare
my paper, 'Âkhyâna-Hymnen im Rig-veda,' Zeitschrift der Deutschen Morgenländischen Gesellschaft, vol. xxxix, p. 83.—Many verses of Rig-veda X, 85 occur
again in the fourteenth book of the Atharva-veda.

burial of the dead [1] are found in the tenth Ma*nd*ala of the
Rig-veda, which, for the most part, is known to be of later
origin than the preceding portions of the collections [2]. If
we look into the character of the verses, which these long
Gr*i*hya songs are composed of, we shall find additional
grounds for assuming their early origin. A few remarks
about their metrical character will make this clear [3]. There
is no other metre in which the contrast between the early
and later periods of Vedic literature manifests itself so
clearly as in the Anush*t*ubh-metre [4]. The Anush*t*ubh
hemistich consists of sixteen syllables, which are divided
by the caesura into two halves of eight syllables each. The
second of these halves has as a rule the iambic ending
(∪ – ∪ ≍), though this rule was not so strictly carried out in
the early as in the later period [5]. The iambic ending is
also the rule in the older parts of the Veda for the close of
the first half, i.e. for the four syllables before the caesura [6].
We know that the later prosody, as we see it in certain
late parts of Vedic literature, in the Pâli Pi*t*akas of the
Buddhists, and later in the great epic poems, not only
departs from the usage of the older period, but adopts a
directly contrary course, i.e. the iambic ending of the first
pâda, which was formerly the rule, is not allowed at all
later, and instead of it the prevailing ending is the antispast (∪ – – ≍). It goes without saying that such a change
in metrical usage, as the one just described, cannot have

---

[1] Rig-veda X, 14-16, and several other hymns of the tenth book. Compare
the note at Â*s*valâyana-Gr*i*hya IV, 4. 6.

[2] Compare my Hymnen des Rig-veda, vol. i (Prolegomena), pp. 265 seq.

[3] Compare the account of the historical development of some of the Vedic
metres which I have given in my paper, 'Das altindische Âkhyâna,' Zeitschrift
der Deutschen Morgenländischen Gesellschaft, vol. xxxvii, and my Hymnen des
Rig-veda, vol. i, pp. 26 seqq.

[4] The Trish*t*ubh and *G*agatî offer a much less promising material for inves-
tigation, because, so far as can now be made out, the departures from the old
type begin at a later period than in the case of the Anush*t*ubh.

[5] Compare Max Müller's introduction to his English translation of the Rig-
veda, vol. i, pp. cxiv seq.

[6] To demonstrate this, I have given in my last-quoted paper, p. 62, statistics
with regard to the two hymns, Rig-veda I, 10 and VIII, 8; in the former the
iambic ending of the first pâda obtains in twenty out of twenty-four cases, in
the latter in forty-two out of forty-six cases.

taken place at one jump. And accordingly a consideration of the Vedic texts reveals a transition period or rather a series of several transition periods between the old and the new standpoints. The first change is that every other ending of the first pâda is allowed by the side of the iambic ending. The two forms of the ending, the one prevailing in the earliest, and the one prevailing in the later period of the prosody, the iambic ($\smile - \smile \overset{\smile}{\smile}$) and the antispastic ($\smile - - \overset{\smile}{\smile}$), are those that occur most frequently in the intermediate period, but besides them all other possible forms are allowed [1].

This is precisely the stage of metrical development which the great G*ri*hya songs of the tenth Ma*nd*ala of the Rig-veda have reached. Let us consider, for instance, the marriage songs and the marriage sayings, X, 85, and see what kind of ending there is at the end of the first pâda. Of the first seventeen verses of this Sûkta sixteen are in Anush*t*ubh metre (verse 14 is Trish*t*ubh); we have therefore thirty-two cases in which the metrical form of these syllables must be investigated. The quantity of the syllable immediately preceding the caesura being a matter of indifference, we have not sixteen but only eight a priori possible combinations for the form of the last four syllables of the pâda ; I give each of these forms below, adding each time in how many of the thirty-two cases it is used :

$- - \smile \overset{\smile}{\smile}$	8
$\smile - \smile \overset{\smile}{\smile}$	5
$- - - \overset{\smile}{\smile}$	5
$\smile - - \overset{\smile}{\smile}$	4
$\smile \smile \smile \overset{\smile}{\smile}$	3
$- \smile \smile \overset{\smile}{\smile}$	3
$\smile \smile - \overset{\smile}{\smile}$	3
$- \smile - \overset{\smile}{\smile}$	1

32

---

[1] Compare the statistics as to the frequency of the different metrical forms at the ending of the first pâda, p. 63 of my above-quoted paper, and Hymnen des Rig-veda, vol. i, p. 28. I have endeavoured in the same paper, p. 65 seq., to make it seem probable that this was the stage of prosody prevailing during the government of the two Kuru kings Parikshit and *G*aname*g*aya.

We see that all the possible combinations are actually represented in these thirty-two cases, and accordingly the metrical build of this Sûkta shows that it belongs to a period to which only the latest songs of the Rig-veda collection can be referred, but the peculiarities of which may be often noticed in the Atharva-veda and in the verses scattered throughout the Brâhma*n*a literature[1].

A hasty glance suffices to show that those verses of the Gr*i*hya ritual which do not appear in the Sa*m*hitâs, but which are quoted at full length in the Gr*i*hya-sûtras, are also in the same stage. For instance, the seven Anush*t*ubh verses which are quoted Sâṅkhâyana-Gr*i*hya I, 19, 5. 6, give us the following relations, if we investigate them as we did those in Rig-veda X, 85:

$$
\begin{array}{cc}
\smile - - \underline{\smile} & 4 \\
- \smile - \underline{\smile} & 3 \\
\smile - \smile \underline{\smile} & 2 \\
- \smile \smile \underline{\smile} & 2 \\
\smile \smile \smile \underline{\smile} & 1 \\
- - \smile \underline{\smile} & 1 \\
- - - \underline{\smile} & 1 \\
\hline
& 14
\end{array}
$$

Thus even the small number of fourteen hemistichs is enough to give us seven of the eight existing combinations, and no single one occurs at all often enough to allow us to call it predominant.

Or we may take the saying that accompanies the performance of the medhâ*g*anana on the new-born child. In the version of Âsvalâyana[2] we have:

$$- \quad - \quad - \quad -\|- \quad \smile\smile-$$
medhâ*m* te deva*h* Savitâ

$$- \quad - \quad \smile \; -\|\smile - \quad - \; -$$
medhâ*m* te A*s*vinau devau.

In the version adopted in the school of Gobhila[3] the

---

[1] For instance, in the verses which occur in the well-known story of *Suna*h*s*epa (Aitareya-Brâhma*n*a VII, 13 seq.).

[2] Â*s*valâyana-Gr*i*hya I, 15, 2.

[3] Mantra-Brâhma*n*a I, 5, 9; cf. Gobhila-Gr*i*hya II, 7, 21.

context of the first line is different, but the metre is the same:

$$- \; - \quad - \quad -\|- \; \cup \cup \; -$$

medhâ*m* te Mitrâvaru*n*au.

Or the saying with which the pupil (brahma*k*ârin) has to lay a log of wood on the fire of the teacher[1]:

$$- \; \cup - \; \cup \cup \| \cup \quad - - \quad \cup$$

Agnaye samidham âhârsham

$$\cup - \quad \cup \quad - \| - \quad - \quad - \; \cup$$

tayâ tvam Agne vardhasva.

There would be no object in multiplying the number of examples; those here given are sufficient to prove our proposition, that the development of the G*ri*hya rites in the form in which they are described to us in the Sûtras, that especially their being accompanied with verses, which were to be recited by their performance, is later than the time of the oldest Vedic poetry, and coincides rather with the transition period in the development of the Anush*t*ubh metre, a period which lies between the old Vedic and the later Buddhistic and epic form.

Besides the formulae intended to be recited during the performance of the various sacred acts, the G*ri*hya-sûtras contain a second kind of verses, which differ essentially from the first kind in regard to metre; viz. verses of ritualistic character, which are inserted here and there between the prose Sûtras, and of which the subject-matter is similar to that of the surrounding prose. We shall have to consider these ya*gñ*agâthâs, as they are occasionally called, later; at present let us go on looking for traces of the G*ri*hya ritual and for the origin of G*ri*hya literature in the literature which precedes the Sûtras.

The Brâhma*n*a texts, which, as a whole, have for their subject-matter the Vaitânika ceremonies celebrated with the three holy fires, furnish evidence that the G*ri*hya fire, together with the holy acts accomplished in connection with it, were also already known. The Aitareya-Brâhma*n*a[2] gives this

---

[1] Âsvalâyana-G*ri*hya I, 21, 1. In Pâraskara and in the Mantra-Brâhma*n*a only the first hemistich has the Anush*t*ubh form.

[2] Aitareya-Brâhma*n*a VIII, 10, 9: etya g*ri*hân pa*sk*âd g*ri*hyasyâgner upa-

fire the most usual name, the same name which is used for
it in the Sûtras, g*ri*hya agni, and describes a ceremony
to be performed over this fire with expressions which agree
exactly with the style of the Gr*i*hya-sûtras [1]. We often
find in the Brâhma*n*a texts also mention of the terminus
technicus, which the Gr*i*hya-sûtras use many times as
a comprehensive term for the offerings connected with
Gr*i*hya ritual, the word pâkaya*gñ*a [2]. For instance, the
*S*atapatha Brâhma*n*a [3], in order to designate the whole
body of offerings, uses the expression : all offerings, those
that are Pâkaya*gñ*as and the others.   It is especially
common to find the Pâkaya*gñ*as mentioned in the Brâhma*n*a texts in connection with the myth of Manu.   The
Taittiriya Sa*m*hitâ [4] opposes the whole body of sacrifices
to the Pâkaya*gñ*as.   The former belonged to the gods, who
through it attained to the heavenly world ; the latter
concerned Manu : thus the goddess I*d*â turned to him.
Similar remarks, bringing Manu or the goddess I*d*â into
relation with the Pâkaya*gñ*as, are to be found Taittirîya
Sa*m*hitâ VI, 2, 5, 4 ; Aitareya-Brâhma*n*a III, 40, 2.   However, in this case as in many others, the *S*atapatha Brâhma*n*a
contains the most detailed data, from which we see how the
idea of Manu as the performer of Pâkaya*gñ*as is connected
with the history of the great deluge, out of which Manu
alone was left.   We read in the *S*atapatha Brâhma*n*a [5] :

vish*t*âyânvârabdhâya *ri*tvig antata*h* ka*m*sena *k*aturgr*i*hîtâs tisra âgyâhutîr
aindrî*h* prapada*m* *g*uhoti, &c.
   [1] Some of the places in which the St. Petersburg dictionary sees names of the
Gr*i*hya fire in Brâhma*n*a texts are erroneous or doubtful. Taittirîya Sa*m*hitâ
V, 5, 9, 2, not gr*i*hya but gahya is to be read. Aupâsana, *S*atapatha
Brâhma*n*a XII, 3, 5, 5, seems not to refer to a sacrificial fire. Following the
identity of aupâsana and sabhya maintained in the dictionary under the
heading aupâsana, one might be tempted in a place like *S*atapatha Brâhma*n*a
II, 3, 2, 3 to refer the words ya esha sabhâyâm agni*h* to the domestic fire.
A different fire is however really meant (Kâtyâyana-*S*rauta-sûtra IV, 9, 20).
   [2] *S*âṅkhâyana I, 1, 1 : pâkaya*gñ*ân vyâkhyâsyâma*h* ; I, 5, 1 = Pâraskara I, 4,
1 : *k*atvâra*h* pâkaya*gñ*â huto ihuta*h* prahuta*h* prâsita iti.
   [3] I, 4, 2, 10 : sarvân ya*gñ*ân . . . ye *k*a pâkaya*gñ*â ye *k*etare.
   [4] I, 7, 1, 3 : sarve*n*a vai ya*gñ*ena devâ*h* suvarga*m* lokam âyan, pâkaya*gñ*ena
Manur asrâmyat, &c.
   [5] I, 8, 1, 6 seq. The translation is that of Prof. Max Müller (India, what
can it teach us ? p. 135 seq.).

'Now the flood had carried away all these creatures, and thus Manu was left there alone. Then Manu went about singing praises and toiling, wishing for offspring. And he sacrificed there also with a Pâka-sacrifice. He poured clarified butter, thickened milk, whey, and curds in the water as a libation.' It is then told how the goddess I*d*â arose out of this offering. I presume that the story of the Pâkaya*g*ñа as the first offering made by Manu after the great flood, stands in a certain correlation to the idea of the introduction of the three sacrificial fires through Purûravas[1]. Purûravas is the son of I*d*â; the original man Manu, who brings forth I*d*â through his offering, cannot have made use of a form of offering which presupposes the existence of I*d*â, and which moreover is based on the triad of the sacred fires introduced by Purûravas; hence Manu's offering must have been a Pâkaya*g*ñа; we read in one of the Gr*i*hya-sûtras[2]: 'All Pâkaya*g*ñаs are performed without I*d*â.'

There are still other passages in the Brâhma*n*a texts showing that the Gr*i*hya offerings were already known; I will mention a saying of Yâ*g*ñаvalkya's reported in the Satapatha Brâhma*n*a[3]: he would not allow that the daily morning and evening offering was a common offering, but said that, in a certain measure, it was a Pâkaya*g*ñа. Finally I would call attention to the offering prescribed in the last book of the Satapatha Brâhma*n*a[4] for the man 'who wishes that a learned son should be born to him;' it is there stated that the preparation of the Â*g*ya (clarified butter) should be performed 'according to the rule of the Sthâlî-pâka (pot-boiling),' and the way in which the offering is to

---

[1] It is true that, as far as I know, passages expressly stating this with regard to Purûravas have not yet been pointed out in the Brâhma*n*a texts; but the words in Satapatha Brâhma*n*a XI, 5, 1, 14-17, and even in Rig-veda X, 95, 18 stand in close connection to this prominent characteristic of Purûravas in the later texts.

[2] Sânkhâyana I, 10, 5.   [3] II, 3, 1, 21.

[4] XIV, 9, 4, 18 = Br*i*hadâra*n*yaka VI, 4, 19 (Sacred Books of the East, vol. xv, p. 220). Cf. Gr*i*hya-sa*m*graha I, 114 for the expression sthâlîpâkâv*ri*tâ which is here used, and which has a technical force in the Gr*i*hya literature.

be performed is described by means of an expression, upaghâtam[1], which often occurs in the Grihya literature in a technical sense.

We thus see that the Brâhmana books are acquainted with the Grihya fire, and know about the Grihya offerings and their permanent technical peculiarities; and it is not merely the later portions of the Brâhmana works such as the fourteenth book of the Satapatha Brâhmana, in which we meet with evidence of this kind; we find it also in portions against the antiquity of which no objections can be raised.

While therefore on the one hand the Brâhmana texts prove the existence of the Grihya ceremonial, we see on the other hand, and first of all by means of the Brâhmana texts themselves, that a literary treatment of this ritualistic subject-matter, as we find it in the Brâhmanas themselves with regard to the Srauta offerings, cannot then have existed. If there had existed texts, similar to the Brâhmana texts preserved to us, which treated of the Grihya ritual, then, even supposing the texts themselves had disappeared, we should still necessarily find traces of them in the Brâhmanas and Sûtras. He who will take the trouble to collect in the Brâhmana texts the scattered references to the then existing literature, will be astonished at the great mass of notices of this kind that are preserved : but nowhere do we find traces of Grihya Brâhmanas. And besides, if such works had ever existed, we should be at a loss to understand the difference which the Hindus make between the Srauta-sûtras based on Sruti (revelation), and the Grihya-sûtras resting on Smriti (tradition) alone[2]. The sacred Grihya acts are regarded as 'smârta,' and when the question is raised with what right they can be considered as a duty resting on the sacrificer alongside of the Srauta acts, the answer is given that they too are based on a Sâkhâ of the Veda, but that this Sâkhâ is

[1] See Grihya-samgraha I, 111. 112.
[2] The Grihya-sûtra of Baudhâyana is called Smârta-sûtra in the best known MS. of this work (Sacred Books of the East, vol. xiv, p. xxx).

hidden, so that its existence can only be demonstrated by reasoning [1].

But the Brâhmana texts furnish us still in another way the most decisive arguments to prove that there have been no expositions of the Grihya ritual in Brâhmana form : they contain exceptionally and scattered through their mass sections, in which they treat of subjects which according to later custom would have been treated in the Grihya-sûtras. Precisely this sporadic appearance of Grihya chapters in the midst of expositions of a totally different contents leads us to draw the conclusion that literary compositions did not then exist, in which these chapters would have occupied their proper place as integral parts of a whole. Discussions of questions of Grihya ritual are found in the Brâhmana literature, naturally enough in those appendices of various kinds which generally follow the exposition of the principal subject of the Srauta ritual. Accordingly we find in the eleventh book of the Satapatha Brâhmana [2], among the manifold additions to subjects previously treated, which make up the principal contents of this book [3], an exposition of the Upanayana, i. e. the solemn reception of the pupil by the teacher, who is to teach him the Veda. The way in which the chapter on the Upanayana is joined to the preceding one, is eminently characteristic ; it shows that it is the merest accident which has brought about in that place the discussion of a subject connected with the Grihya ritual, and that a ceremony such as the Upanayana is properly not in its proper place in the midst of the literature of Brâhmana texts. A dialogue (brahmodya) between Uddâlaka and Saukeya precedes ; the two talk of the Agnihotra and of various expiations (prâyaskitta) connected with that sacrifice. At the end Saukeya, filled with astonishment at the wisdom of Uddâlaka, declares that he wishes to come to him as a pupil (upâyâni bhagavantam), and Uddâlaka

[1] Max Müller, History of Ancient Sanskrit Literature, pp. 94-96.
[2] Satapatha Brâhmana XI, 5, 4.
[3] Max Müller, History of Ancient Sanskrit Literature, p. 359.

accepts him as his pupil. It is the telling of this story and the decisive words upâyâni and upaninyc which furnish the occasion for introducing the following section on the Upanayana [1]. The subject is there treated in the peculiar style of the Brâhmaṇa texts, a style which we need not characterize here. I shall only mention one point, viz. that into the description and explanation of the Upanayana ceremony has been inserted one of those *S*lokas, such as we often find in the Gṛihya-sûtras also, as a sort of ornamental amplification of the prose exposition [2]. 'Here a *S*loka is also sung,' says the Brâhmaṇa [3]:

$$- - - - \ - \ \cup\cup\cup \ \| \ - \cup \ - \ - \cup \ - \ \cup \cup$$
âᵏâryo garbhî bhavati   hastam âdhâya dakshiṇam

$$\cup - - \ - \ \cup \ - \cup - \ \| \ - - \ - \cup - \ - \ \cup \cup$$
tṛitîyasyâṃ sa gâyate   sâvitryâ saha brâhmaṇaḥ [4].

From this passage we see, on the one hand, that the composition of such isolated [5] *S*lokas explaining certain points of the Gṛihya ritual goes back to quite an early period; on the other hand, we are compelled to assume that the *S*lokas of this kind which are quoted in the Gṛihya-sûtras differ nevertheless from the analogous *S*lokas of the early period, or at any rate that the old *S*lokas must have undergone a change which modernized their structure, so as to be received into the Gṛihya-sûtras; for the metre of the *S*loka just quoted, which has the antispast before the caesura in neither of its two halves, and which has even a double iambus before the caesura in one half, is decidedly of an older type than the one peculiar to the *S*lokas quoted in the Gṛihya-sûtras [6].

---

[1] This is also the way in which Sâyaṇa understands the matter; he makes the following remark: taṃ hopaninya ity upanayanasya prastutatvât taddharmâ asmin brâhmaṇe nirûpyante.

[2] Cf. above, p. xiv; below, p. xxxv.

[3] Sect. 12 of the chapter quoted.

[4] 'The teacher becomes pregnant by laying his right hand (on the pupil for the Upanayana); on the third day ḥe (i.e. the pupil) is born as a Brâhmaṇa along with the Sâvitrî (which is repeated to him on that day).'

[5] It is not likely that verses of this kind are taken from more comprehensive and connected metrical texts.

[6] Cf. on this point below, p. xxxv.

Another Gr*i*hya section in the *S*atapatha Brâhma*n*a
seems to have found its place there through a similar accidental kind of joining on to a preceding chapter as the
above-mentioned passage. In XI, 5, 5 a story of the battle
of the gods and Asuras is told: the gods beat the Asuras
back by means of constantly larger Sattra celebrations and
conquer for themselves the world of heaven. It seems to
me that the description of the great Sattras celebrated by
the gods is the occasion of the joining on of a section beginning with the words[1]: ' There are five great sacrifices
(mahâya*g*ñâs); they are great Sattras: the offering to Beings,
the offering to men, the offering to the Fathers (i. e. the
Manes), the offering to the Gods, the offering to the Brahman.' After this introduction follows an account of one of
the five great offerings, namely of the Brahmaya*g*ña, i. e. of
the daily Veda recitation (svâdhyâya). The third Adhyâya
of Âsvalâyana's Gr*i*hya-sûtra begins in exactly the same
way with the sentence : ' Now (follow) the five sacrifices :
the sacrifice to the Gods, the sacrifice to the Beings, the
sacrifice to the Fathers, the sacrifice to the Brahman, the
sacrifice to men,' and then follows here also a discussion
of the Brahmaya*g*ña, which is entirely analogous to that
given in the *S*atapatha Brâhma*n*a. Âsvalâyana here does
not content himself with describing the actual course of
ceremonies as is the rule in the Sûtra texts ; he undertakes,
quite in the way of the Brâhma*n*a texts, to explain their
meaning : ' In that he recites the *R*i*k*as, he thereby satiates
the gods with oblations of milk, in that (he recites) the
Ya*g*us, with oblations of ghee,' &c. It is plain that the
mode of exposition adopted by Âsvalâyana in this passage,
which is different from the usual Sûtra style, finds its
explanation in the supposition that exceptionally in this
case the author of the Gr*i*hya-sûtra had before him a
Brâhma*n*a text, which he could take as his model, whether
that text was the *S*atapatha itself or another similar text.
Among the extremely various prescriptions which we find

[1] *S*atapatha Brâhma*n*a XI, 5, 6, 1.

in the last sections of the *Sa*tapatha Brâhma*n*a, there is a
rather long section, which also really belongs to the G*ri*hya
domain. To quote from this section[1] : 'If a man wishes
that a learned son should be born to him, famous, a public
man, a popular speaker, that he should know all the Vedas,
and that he should live to his full age, then, after having
prepared boiled rice with meat and butter, they should both
eat, being fit to have offspring,' &c. Then follows a description of an Â*g*ya offering, after which the marital cohabitation is to be performed with certain formulas. This,
however, is not the last of the acts through which the father
assures himself of the possession of such a distinguished
son ; certain rites follow, which are to be performed at
birth and after birth, the Âyushya ceremony and the
Medhâ*g*anana. These rites are here prescribed for the
special case where the father has the above-mentioned
wishes for the prosperity of his child ; but the description
agrees essentially with the description of the corresponding
acts in the G*ri*hya-sûtras[2], which are inculcated for all
cases, without reference to a determined wish of the father.
It is a justifiable conjecture that, although this certainly
does not apply to the whole of ceremonies described in the
G*ri*hya-sûtras, many portions of these ceremonies and
verses that were used in connection with them, &c., were
first developed, not as a universal rite or duty, but as the
special possession of individuals, who hoped to attain special
goods and advantages by performing the ceremony in this
way.

It was only later, as I think, that such prescriptions

---

[1] *Sa*tapatha Brâhma*n*a XIV, 9, 4, 17 = B*ri*had Âra*n*yaka VI, 4, 18 (Sacred
Books of the East, vol. xv, p. 219 seq.).

[2] Cf. Prof. Max Müller's notes to the passage quoted from the B*ri*had Âra*n*-
yaka. I must mention in this connection a point touched upon by Prof. Müller,
loc. cit. p. 222, note 1, viz. that Â*s*valâyana, G*ri*hya I, 13, 1, expressly calls
'the Upanishad' the text in which the Pu*m*savana and similar ceremonies are
treated. It is probable that the Upanishad which Â*s*valâyana had in mind
treated these rites not as a duty to which all were bound, but as a secret that
assured the realisation of certain wishes. This follows from the character of
the Upanishads, which did not form a part of the Vedic course which all had to
study, but rather contained a secret doctrine intended for the few.

assumed the character of universality, with which we find
them propounded in the Gr*i*hya-sûtras.

It is scarcely necessary to go through the sections of the
texts of other Vedic schools referring to the Gr*i*hya ritual
in the same way in which we have done it in the case of the
Satapatha Brâhma*n*a. The data which we have produced
from the great Brâhma*n*a of the white Ya*g*ur-veda, will
be sufficient for our purpose, which is to give an idea of
the stage in which the literary treatment of the Gr*i*hya
ritual stood during the Brâhma*n*a period. As we see, there
were then properly no Gr*i*hya texts; but many of the
elements which we find later in the Gr*i*hya texts were
either already formed or were in the process of formation.
Most of the verses which are used for the Gr*i*hya acts—
in so far as they are not verses composed in the oldest
period for the Soma offering and transferred to the Gr*i*hya
ceremonies—bear the formal imprint of the Brâhma*n*a
period; the domestic sacrificial fire and the ritual peculiarities of the Pâkaya*gñ*as which were to be performed at it,
were known; descriptions of some such Pâkaya*gñ*as were
given in prose; there were also already *S*lokas which gave in
metrical form explanations about certain points of the Gr*i*hya
ritual, just as we find in the Brâhma*n*a texts analogous *S*lokas
referring to subjects connected with the *S*rauta ritual.

Thus was the next step which the literary development
took in the Sûtra period prepared and rendered easy. The
more systematic character which the exposition of the
ritualistic discipline assumed in this period, necessarily led to
the taking of this step: the domain of the Gr*i*hya sacrifices was recognised and expounded as a second great
principal part of the ritual of sacrifices alongside of the
*S*rauta domain which was alone attended to in the earlier
period. The Gr*i*hya-sûtras arose which treat, according
to the expression of Âsvalâyana in his first sentence, of the
gr*i*hyâ*n*i[1] as distinguished from the vaitânikâni, or, as
Sânkhâyana says, of the pâkaya*gñ*âs, or, as Pâraskara
says, of the gr*i*hyasthâlîpâkânâ*m* karma. The

---

[1] Similarly Gobhila: gr*i*hyâkarmâ*n*i.

G*ri*hya-sûtras treat their subject of course in exactly the same style in which the sacrifices of the *S*rauta ritual had been treated by the *S*rauta-sûtras, which they constantly assume to be known and which are the works of teachers of the same Vedic schools, and oftentimes even perhaps the works of the same authors. Only certain differences in the character of the two groups of texts are naturally conditioned on the one hand by the greater complexity of the *S*rauta sacrifices and the comparative simplicity of the G*ri*hya sacrifices, on the other hand by the fact that the *S*rauta-sûtras are entirely based on Brâhma*n*a texts, in which the same subjects were treated, while the G*ri*hya-sûtras, as we have seen, possessed such a foundation only for a very small portion of their contents.

It goes without saying that the above-mentioned statement that the subjects treated of in the G*ri*hya-sûtras are Pâkaya*gñ*as[1] or G*ri*hyasthâlipâkas should not be pressed with the utmost strictness, as though nothing were treated in the G*ri*hya-sûtras which does not come under these heads. First of all the term Sthâlipâka is too narrow, since it does not include the offerings of sacrificial butter which constituted a great number of ceremonies. But besides many ceremonies and observances are taught in the G*ri*hya-sûtras, which cannot in any way be characterised as sacrifices at all, only possessing some inner resemblance to the group of sacrifices there treated of, or standing in more or less close connection with them[2].

The Sûtra texts divide the Pâkaya*gñ*as in various ways; either four or seven principal forms are taken up. The

---

[1] I believe with Stenzler (see his translation of Âsvalâyana, pp. 2 seq.) that pâkaya*gñ*a means 'boiled offering.' It seems to me that the expression pâka in this connection cannot be otherwise taken than in the word sthâlîpâka ('pot-boiling'). Prof. Max Müller (History of Ancient Sanskrit Literature, p. 203), following Hindu authorities, explains Pâkaya*gñ*a as 'a small sacrifice,' or, more probably, 'a good sacrifice.' The definition of Lâ*t*yâyana may be also here quoted (IV, 9, 2): pâkaya*gñ*â ity â*k*akshata ekâgnau ya*gñ*ân.

[2] Compare, for instance, the account of the ceremonies which are to be performed for the journey of the newly-married pair to their new home, *S*âṅkhâyana-G*ri*hya I, 15, or the observances to which the Snâtaka is bound, Gobhila III, 5, &c. According to the rule *S*âṅkhâyana I, 12, 13 we are, however, to suppose a sacrifice in many ceremonies where there does not seem to be any.

commonest division is that into the four classes of the
hutas, ahutas, prahutas, prâ*s*itas[1]. The division into
seven classes is doubtless occasioned by the division of the
Haviryag*ñ*as and of the Somayag*ñ*as, which also each include seven classes[2]; for the nature of the sacrifices in
question would hardly of itself have led to such a division.
The seven classes taken up are either those given by Gautama VIII, 15[3]: 'The seven kinds of Pâkayag*ñ*as, viz.
the Ash*t*akâ, the Pârva*n*a (Sthâlipâka, offered on the new and
full moon days), the funeral oblations, the Srâva*n*î, the
Âgrahâya*n*î, the *K*aitrî, and the Âsvayugî.' Or else the
seven classes are established as follows, the fourfold division
being utilised to some extent[4]: 'Huta, Prahuta, Âhuta (sic,
not Ahuta), the spit-ox sacrifice, the Bali offering, the re-
descent (on the Âgrahâya*n*a day), the Ash*t*akâ sacrifice.'
According to the account of Prof. Bühler[5], the exposition
of Baudhâyana, who gives this division, keeps closely to
the course which it prescribes. For the rest, however, the
G*r*ihya texts with which I am acquainted do not follow
any of these divisions, and this is easily accounted for, if
we consider the artificial character of these classifications,
which are undertaken merely for the sake of having a complete scheme of the sacrifices. On the contrary, as a whole
the texts give an arrangement which is based on the nature
of the ceremonies they describe. In many instances we
find considerable variations between the texts of the different schools; often enough, in a given text, the place

---

[1] *S*ânkhâyana I, 5, 1; 10, 7; Pâraskara I, 4, 1. Doubtless Prof. Bühler is
right in finding the same division mentioned also Vasish*th*a XXVI, 10 (Sacred
Books of the East, vol. xiv, p. 128). Âsvalâyana (I, 1, 2) mentions only three
of the four classes.

[2] In Lâ*t*yâyana (V, 4, 22-24) all the sacrifices are divided into seven Haviryag*ñ*a-sa*m*sthâs and into seven Soma-sa*m*sthâs, so that the Pâkayag*ñ*as do not
form a class of their own; they are strangely brought in as the last of the
Haviryag*ñ*as. Cf. Indische Studien, X, 325.

[3] Sacred Books of the East, vol. ii, p. 214.

[4] Baudhâyana G*r*ihya-sûtra, quoted by Bühler, Sacred Books of the East,
vol. xiv, p. xxxi; cf. Sâya*n*a's Commentary on Aitareya-Brâhma*n*a III, 40, 2
(p. 296 of Aufrecht's edition).

[5] Sacred Books of the East, vol. xiv, p. xxxii.

which is assigned to a given chapter is not to be explained
without assuming a certain arbitrariness on the part of the
author. But, as a whole, we cannot fail to recognise in the
arrangement of the different texts a certain agreement,
which we will here merely try to explain in its main traits;
the points of detail, which would complete what we here
say, will occur of themselves to any one who looks at the
texts themselves.

The domestic life of the Hindus represents, so to speak,
a circle, in which it is in a certain measure indifferent what
point is selected as the starting-point. Two especially
important epochs in this life are : on the one hand, the
period of studentship of the young Brahmaḱârin devoted
to the study of the Veda; at the beginning of this period
comes the ceremony of the Upanayana, at the end that of
the Samâvartana; on the other hand, marriage (vivâha),
which besides has a special importance for the Gṛihya ritual,
from the circumstance, that as a rule the cultus of the domestic sacrificial fire begins with marriage. One can just as
well imagine an exposition of the Gṛihya ritual, which proceeds from the description of the studentship to that of the
marriage, as one which proceeds from the description of
the marriage to that of the studentship. The Samâvartana,
which designates the end of the period of studentship,
gives the Hindu the right and the duty to found a household[1]. On the other hand, if the exposition begins with the
marriage, there follows naturally the series of ceremonies
which are to be performed up to the birth of a child, and
then the ceremonies for the young child, which finally lead
up to the Upanayana and a description of the period of
studentship. The Hiraṇyakesi-sûtra alone, of the Sûtras
treated of in these translations, follows the first of the two
orders mentioned[2]; the other texts follow the other order,

---

[1] Hiraṇyakesin says: samâvṛitta âḱâryakulân mâtâpitarau bibhṛiyât, tâbhyâm
anuǵñâto bhâryâm upayaḱḱhet.

[2] The same may be said with regard to two other Gṛihya texts which also
belong to the black Yaǵur-veda, the Mânava and the Kâṭhaka. See Jolly, Das
Dharmasûtra des Vishṇu und das Kâṭhakagṛihyasûtra, p. 75; Von Bradke,
Zeitschrift der Deutschen Morgenländ. Gesellschaft, vol. xxxvi, p. 445.

which has been already described by Prof. Max Müller almost thirty years ago, and we cannot do better than to give his description [1] : 'Then (i. e. after the marriage) follow the Samskâras, the rites to be performed at the conception of a child, at various periods before his birth, at the time of his birth, the ceremony of naming the child, of carrying him out to see the sun, of feeding him, of cutting his hair, and lastly of investing him as a student, and handing him to a Guru, under whose care he is to study the sacred writings, that is to say, to learn them by heart, and to perform all the offices of a Brahmakârin, or religious student.'

In this way we find, as a rule, in the foreground in the first part of the Grihya-sûtras this great group of acts which accompany the domestic life from marriage to the studentship and the Samâvartana of the child sprung from wedlock. We find, however, inserted into the description of these ceremonies, in various ways in the different Sûtras, the exposition of a few ritualistic matters which we have not yet mentioned. In the first place a description of the setting up of the sacred domestic fire, i. e. of the ceremony which in the domain of the Grihya ritual corresponds to the agnyâdheya of the Srauta ritual. The setting up of the fire forms the necessary preliminary to all sacred acts ; the regular time for it is the wedding [2], so that the fire used for the wedding acts accompanies the young couple to their home, and there forms the centre of their household worship. Accordingly in the Grihya-sûtras the description of the setting up of the fire stands, as a rule, at the beginning of the whole, not far from the description of the wedding.

Next the introductory sections of the Grihya-sûtras have to describe the type of the Grihya sacrifice, which is universally available and recurs at all household ceremonies. This can be done in such a way that this type is described for itself, without direct reference to a particular sacrifice. This is the case in Pâraskara, who in the first chapter of his

---

[1] History of Ancient Sanskrit Literature, p. 204.
[2] See, for instance, Pâraskara I, 2, 1 : âvasathyâdhânam dârakâle.

Sûtra describes the rites recurring at each sacrifice, and then remarks : 'This ritual holds good, whenever a sacrifice is offered[1].' Similarly Âsvalâyana, in one of the first chapters of his work, enumerates the rites which are to be performed 'whenever he intends to sacrifice[2].' Other texts give a general description of the Grihya sacrifice by exemplifying it by one special sacrifice. Sâṅkhâyana[3] chooses for this the sacrifice which the bridegroom has to offer, when a favourable answer has been granted to his wooing ; Gobhila[4] gives at least the greater part of the rules in question à propos of the full moon and of the new moon sacrifice ; Hiranyakesin[5], who opens his account at the period of the studentship of the young Brâhmana, describes the sacrificial type à propos of the Upanayana rite.

The sacrifices which are to be offered daily at morning and at evening, those which are celebrated monthly on the days of the new moon and of the full moon—the Grihya copies of the Agnihotra and of the Darsapûrnamâsa sacrifices—and, thirdly, the daily distribution of the Bali offerings : these ceremonies are commonly described along with what we have called the first great group of the Grihya acts, immediately preceding or following the Vivâha.

We find, as a second group of sacred acts, a series of celebrations, which, if the man has founded his household, are to be performed regularly at certain times of the year at the household fire. So the Sravâna sacrifice, which is offered to the snakes at the time when, on account of the danger from snakes, a raised couch is necessary at night. At the end of this period the festival of the re-descent is celebrated : the exchanging of the high couch for the low couch on the ground. Between these two festivals comes the Prishâtaka offering on the full-moon day of the month Âsvayuga ; it receives in the Grihya texts the place corresponding to that which actually belongs to

---

[1] I, 1, 5 : esha eva vidhir yatra kvakid dhomah.
[2] I, 3, 1 : atha khalu yatra kva ka hoshyant syât, &c.
[3] I, 7-10.   [4] I, 6 seqq.   [5] I, 1.

it in the series of the festivals. As a rule [1] the acts we have
just mentioned are followed, in accordance with the natural
series, by the Ash*t*akâ festivals, which are celebrated during
the last months of the year.

Alongside of these acts which are connected with fixed
points of the year we find in the various Gr*i*hya texts
an account of a series of other ceremonies, which, in accordance with their nature, have no such fixed position
in the system of the ritual. Thus, for instance, the rites
which refer to the choice of a piece of ground to build
a house or to the building itself; further, the rites connected with agriculture and cattle raising. In many texts
we find together with this group of acts also an account
of the ceremonies, related to fixed points in the year,
which stand in connection with the annual course of
Vedic study: the description of the opening festival and
of the closing festival of the school term, as well as a point
which generally follows these descriptions, the rules as to
the anadhyâya, i.e. as to the occasions which necessitate an
intermission in the study of the Veda for a longer or for
a shorter period. As a rule, the Gr*i*hya-sûtras bring the
account of these things into the group of acts which refer to
the household life of the Gr*i*hastha; for the Adhyâpana, i.e.
the teaching of the Veda, held the first place among the
rights and duties of the Brâhma*n*a who had completed his
time at school. On the other hand these ceremonies can
naturally also be considered as connected with the school
life of the young Hindu, and accordingly they are placed
in that division by Gobhila [2], between the description of
the Upanayana and that of the Samâvartana.

The sacred acts connected with the burial and the
worship of the dead (the various kinds of *S*râddha rites) may
be designated as a third group of the ceremonies which
are described to us in the Gr*i*hya-sûtras. Finally, a fourth
group comprises the acts which are connected with the
attainment of particular desires (kâmyâni). Among the

[1] Not in *S*âṅkhâyana, who describes the Ash*t*akâs before these sacrifices.
[2] III, 3.

texts here translated we find a somewhat detailed account of these ceremonies in the Gobhila-sûtra and in the Khâdira-G*ri*hya only[1].

These remarks cannot claim to give a complete outline of the contents and arrangement of the G*ri*hya texts; they only aim at giving an idea of the fundamental traits, which in each particular text are modified by manifold variations, but which nevertheless are to these variations as the rule is to the exceptions.

We must now speak of the relations of the G*ri*hya-sûtras to the two other kinds of Sûtra texts, with which they have so many points of contact in the *S*rauta-sûtras and the Dharma-sûtras.

Prof. Bühler, in several places of the excellent introductions which he has prefixed to his translations of the Dharma-sûtras, has called attention to the fact that the relation in which the Sûtra texts of the same school stand to each other is very different in different schools. Many schools possess a great corpus of Sûtras, the parts of which are the *S*rauta-sûtra, the G*ri*hya-sûtra, &c. This is, for instance, the case with the Âpastambiya school[2]; its Sûtra is divided into thirty Pra*s*nas, the contents of which are divided as follows:

I–XXIV: *S*rauta-sûtra.
XXV: Paribhâshâs, &c.
XXVI: Mantras for the G*ri*hya-sûtra.
XXVII: G*ri*hya-sûtra.
XXVIII–XXIX: Dharma-sûtra.
XXX: *S*ulva-sûtra.

In other cases the single Sûtra texts stand more independently side by side; they are not considered as parts of one and the same great work, but as different works. Of course it is the Dharma-sûtras above all which could be freed from the connection with the other Sûtra texts to such an extent, that even their belonging to a distinct Vedic school may be doubtful. The contents

---

[1] Gobhila IV, 5 seq.; Khâd. IV, 1 seq.
[2] Bühler, Sacred Books of the East, vol. ii, pp. xi seq.

of this class of Sûtras indeed have hardly any connection
with the subdivisions and differences of the Vedic texts
handed down in the various schools; there was no reason
why Brahmans, who studied various Sâkhâs of the Veda,
should not learn the ordinances concerning law and morals
given in these Sûtras as they were formulated in the
same texts. The Grihya-sûtras are not so independent of
the differences of the Vedic schools. The close analogy
between the sacrificial ritual of the Grihya acts and that
of the Srauta acts, and the consequent necessity of taking
into account the Srauta ritual in the exposition of the
Grihya ritual, necessarily brought the Grihya-sûtras into
closer connection with and into greater dependence on
the Srauta-sûtras than in the case of the Dharma-sûtras[1].
But above all, the Grihya ceremonies demanded the
knowledge of numerous Mantras, and accordingly as these
Mantras were borrowed from the one or the other Mantra
Sâkhâ[2], there followed in the case of the Grihya text
in question an intimate connection with the corresponding
Mantra school[3]. We find accordingly as a general rule,
that each Grihya-sûtra presupposes a Vedic Samhitâ,
whose Mantras it quotes only in their Pratikas[4], and
that besides each Grihya-sûtra presupposes a previous

---

[1] Professor Jolly in his article on the Dharma-sûtra of Vishnu, p. 71, note 1,
points out that in the eyes of Hindu commentators also the Dharma-sûtras
differ from the Grihya-sûtras in that the former contain rather the universal
rules, while the latter contain the rules peculiar to individual schools. Cf.
Weber, Indische Literaturgeschichte, 2. Aufl., S. 296.

[2] It seems as though the choice of the Mantras which were to be prescribed
for the Grihya ceremonies had often been intentionally made so as to comprise
as many Mantras as possible occurring in the Mantra-Sâkhâ, which served as
foundation to the Grihya texts in question.

[3] When Govindasvâmin (quoted by Bühler, Sacred Books of the East, vol.
xiv, p. xiii) designates the Grihyasâstrâni as sarvâdhikârâni, this should not be
understood literally. In general it is true the Grihya acts are the same for
the disciples of all the Vedic schools, but the Mantras to be used in connection with them differ.

[4] In the introduction to Gobhila I have treated of the special case where a
Grihya-sûtra, besides being connected with one of the great Samhitâs, is connected also with a Grihya-samhitâ of its own, so to speak, with a collection of
the Mantras to be used at the Grihya acts.

knowledge of the ritual which is acquired through the study of the proper *S*rauta-sûtra [1]. It is not necessary to quote the numerous places where the G*ri*hya-sûtras either expressly refer to the *S*rauta-sûtras, or point to them by repeating the same phrases or often even whole Sûtras. It will be sufficient to quote one out of many places, the opening words of the Â*s*valâyana-G*ri*hya, which in a way characterise this work as a second part of the *S*rauta-sûtra : 'The rites based on the spreading (of the three sacred fires) have been declared; we shall declare the G*ri*hya rites [2].'

Thus it is not difficult to perceive the dependence of the G*ri*hya-sûtras on the *S*rauta-sûtras; but there remains the much more difficult question whether in each particular case both texts are to be regarded as by the same author, or whether the G*ri*hya-sûtra is an appendix to the *S*rauta-sûtra composed by another author. Tradition accepts the one alternative for some Sûtras ; for other Sûtras it accepts the other; thus in the domain of the Rig-veda literature Â*s*valâyana and *S*ânkhâyana are credited with the authorship of a *S*rauta-sûtra as well as of a G*ri*hya-sûtra ; the same is true of Âpastamba, Hira*n*yakesin, and other authors. On the other hand, the authorship of the G*ri*hya-sûtras which follow the *S*rauta-sûtras of Kâtyâyana, Lâ*t*yâyana, Drâhyâya*n*a, is not ascribed to Kâtyâyana, Lâ*t*yâyana, Drâhyâya*n*a, but to Pâraskara, Gobhila, and Khâdirâ-*k*ârya.

It seems to me that we should consider the testimony of tradition as entirely trustworthy in the second class of cases. Tradition is very much inclined to ascribe to celebrated masters and heads of schools the origin of works which are acknowledged authorities in their schools, even though they are not the authors. But it is not likely that tradition should have made a mistake in the opposite

---

[1] In the domain of the Atharva-veda literature alone we find this relation reversed ; here the *S*rauta-sûtra (the Vaitâna-sûtra) presupposes the G*ri*hya-sûtra (the Kau*s*ika-sûtra). Cf. Prof. Garbe's preface to his edition of the Vaitâna-sûtra, p. vii. This relation is not extraordinary, considering the secondary character of the Vaitâna-sûtra.

[2] Uktâni vaitânikâni, g*ri*hyâ*n*i vakshyâma*h*.

direction, that e.g. it should designate Pâraskara as author when Kâtyâyana himself was the author.

We shall not be able to trust so implicitly to tradition where it puts down the same author for the Gr*i*hya-sûtra as for the corresponding *S*rauta-sûtra; the possibility that such data are false is so large that we have to treat them as doubtful so long as we have not discovered certain proofs of their correctness. At present, so far as I can see, we are just as little justified in considering that such a proof has been made as we are able to prove the opposite state of things. It is easy to find the many agreements in contents and expression which exist, for instance, between the *S*rauta-sûtra and Gr*i*hya-sûtra of *S*âṅkhâyana, or between the *S*rauta-sûtra and the Gr*i*hya-sûtra of Âsvalâyana[1]. But these agreements cannot be considered as sufficient proof that in each case the Gr*i*hya-sûtra and the *S*rauta-sûtra are by the same author. Even if the author of the Gr*i*hya-sûtra was not Âsvalâyana or *S*âṅkhâyana in person, still he must have been at all events perfectly familiar with the works of those teachers, and must have intended to fit his work to theirs as closely as possible, so that agreements of this kind can in no way astonish us[2]. On the other hand, if the *S*rauta-sûtras and Gr*i*hya-sûtras are read together, it is easy to discover small irregularities in the exposition, repetitions and such like, which might seem to indicate different authors. But the irregularities of this kind which have been detected up to the present are scarcely of such

---

[1] The parallel passages from the *S*rauta-sûtra and the Gr*i*hya-sûtra of the Mânavas are brought together in Dr. Von Bradke's interesting paper, 'Ueber das Mânava-Gr*i*hya-sûtra,' Zeitschrift der Deutschen Morgenländ. Gesellschaft, vol. xxxvi, p. 451.

[2] For this reason I cannot accept the reasoning through which Prof. Bühler (Sacred Books of the East, vol. ii, p. xiv) attempts to prove the identity of the author of the *S*rauta-sûtra and of the Dharma-sûtra of the Âpastambîya school. Bühler seems to assume that the repetition of the same Sûtra, and of the same irregular grammatical form in the *S*rauta-sûtra and in the Dharma-sûtra, must either be purely accidental, or, if this is impossible, that it proves the identity of the authors. But there remains a third possible explanation, that the two texts are by different authors, one of whom knows and imitates the style of the other.

a character as not to be easily ascribable to mistakes and carelessness such as even a careful author may be guilty of in the course of a large work[1]. It seems to me then that until the discovery of further circumstances throwing light on the question of the identity of the authors of the Srautas and of the Grihyas, it would be premature if we were to venture on a decision of this question in one direction or the other.

Prof. Bühler's investigations have made perfectly clear the relation in which the Grihya-sûtras and the Dharma-sûtras stand to each other in those cases, where we have texts of both kinds by the same school. In the case of the Grihya-sûtra and the Dharma-sûtra of the Âpastambîyas he has proved[2] that both texts were the work of the same author according to a common plan, so that the Grihya-sûtra is as short and terse as possible, because Âpastamba had reserved for the Dharma-sûtra a portion of the subject-matter generally treated of in the Grihya-sûtras. Besides there are references in each of the two texts to the other which strengthen the proof of their being written by the same author. In the Sûtra collection of Hiranyakesin the state of things is different. Here, as Prof. Bühler has also shown[3], we find numerous discrepancies between the Grihya and the Dharma-sûtra, which are owing to the fact, that while this teacher took as Dharma-sûtra that of Âpastamba with some unessential changes, he composed a Grihya-sûtra of his own. Of the two Sûtras of Baudhâyana, the same distinguished scholar, to whom we owe the remarks we have just mentioned, has treated in the Sacred Books of the East, vol. xiv, p. xxxi.

I believe that every reader who compares the two kinds of texts will notice that the frame within which the exposition of the Dharma-sûtras is inclosed, is an essentially

---

[1] Cf. my remarks in the introduction to the Sânkhâyana-Grihya, vol. xxix, pp. 5, 6.

[2] Sacred Books of the East, vol. ii, p. xiii seq.

[3] Sacred Books of the East, vol. ii, p. xxiii seq.

broader one than in the case of the Grihya-sûtras. We have
here, I think, the same phenomenon that may also be observed, for instance, in the domain of the Buddhist Vinaya
literature, where the exposition of the life of the community
was at first given only in connection with the explanation of
the list of sins (Pâtimokkha) which was promulgated every
half month at the meetings of the spiritual brethren. It was
not till later that a more comprehensive exposition, touching all the sides of the life of the community was attempted[1],
an exposition which, on the one hand, no longer limited
itself to the points discussed in the Pâtimokkha, and which,
on the other hand, necessarily had much in common with
what was laid down in the Pâtimokkha. The relation of
the Grihya-sûtras and Dharma-sûtras seems to me to be
of a similar nature. The Grihya-sûtras begin to treat of
the events of the daily life of the household, but they do
not yet undertake to exhaust the great mass of this subject-
matter; on the contrary they confine themselves principally
to the ritual or sacrificial side of household life, as is natural
owing to their connection with the older ritualistic literature.
Then the Dharma-sûtras take an important step further;
their purpose is to describe the whole of the rights and
customs which prevail in private, civic, and public life.
They naturally among other things touch upon the ceremonies treated in the Grihya-sûtras, but they generally
merely mention them and discuss the questions of law and
custom which are connected with them, without undertaking
to go into the technical ordinances as to the way in which
these ceremonies are to be performed[2].

Only in a few cases do portions treated of in the domain
of the Dharma-sûtras happen to coincide with portions
treated of in the Grihya-sûtras. Thus especially, apart from
a few objects of less importance, the detailed rules for the
behaviour of the Snâtaka and the rules for the interruptions

---

[1] In the work which has Khandhakâ as its general title and which has been
transmitted to us in two parts, Mahâvagga and Kullavagga.

[2] Compare, for instance, the explanations concerning the Upanayana in the
Dharma-sûtras (Âpastamba I, 1; Gautama I) with the corresponding sections of
the Grihya-sûtras.

of the Veda study (anadhyâya) are generally treated in an exactly similar way in the texts of the one and those of the other category.

We have spoken above of the metrical peculiarities of the Mantras quoted in the Gr*i*hya-sûtras, the metre of which clearly proves what is indubitable from other reasons, that most, if not all, of these verses were composed at a perceptibly older period than the descriptions of the sacred acts in the midst of which they are inserted [1]. A second kind of verses which are quoted in the Gr*i*hya-sûtras must be carefully distinguished from these. It is doubtful whether there are any to be found among them which the authors of the Sûtras have themselves composed; but they were composed at a period decidedly more recent than those Mantras [2], and they therefore exhibit metrical peculiarities which are essentially different. The verses I mean are *S*lokas of ritual contents, which are quoted to confirm or to complete what is stated in the prose, and which are introduced by such expressions as tad apy âhu*h* 'here they say also,' or tad api *s*lo kâ*h* 'here there are also *S*lokas,' and other similar phrases [3].

We called attention above (p. xix) to the fact that a verse of this kind occurs in one of the Gr*i*hya chapters of the *S*atapatha Brâhma*n*a, in a metre corresponding to the peculiarities of the older literary style. On the other hand, the verses appearing in the Gr*i*hya-sûtras differ only in a few cases from the standard of the later *S*loka prosody, as we have it, e. g. in the Mahâbhârata and in the laws of Manu. In the Zeitschrift der Deutschen Morgenländ. Gesellschaft, vol. xxxvii, p. 67, I have given tables for the verses in question out of the Sânkhâyana-Gr*i*hya, and these tables show that the characteristic ending of the first

---

[1] We do not mean to deny that among these verses too a few of especially modern appearance are to be found; e. g. this is true of the verses which Dr. Von Bradke has quoted from the Mânava-Gr*i*hya II, 14, 34 (Zeitschrift der Deutschen Morgenländ. Gesellschaft, vol. xxxvi, p. 429).

[2] Let me here refer to the fact that one of these verses (Â*s*valâyana-Gr*i*hya IV, 7, 16) concludes with the words, ' thus said *S*aunaka.'

[3] Â*s*valâyana-Gr*i*hya I, 3, 10 designates such a verse as ya*g*/*n*agâthâ.

*S*loka Pâda for the later period ᴗ − − ᴗ̆, which, for instance,
in the Nalopâkhyâna of the Mahâbhârata covers precisely
five-sixths of all the cases, occurs in *S*ânkhâyana in thirty
cases out of thirty-nine, that is in about three quarters of
the cases[1]; *S*ânkhâyana has still twice the ending ᴗ − ᴗ ᴗ̆
which is the rule in the Rig-veda, but which is forbidden
by the later prosody: prahuta*h* pit*ri*karma*n*â, uktvâ mantra*m* sp*ri*sed apa*h*[2]. It may be observed that a similar
treatment of the *S*loka metre appears also in the Rig-veda
Prâtisâkhya of *S*aunaka. Here too the modern form of the
ending of the first pâda dominates, although sometimes the
old iambic form is preserved, e. g. II, 5 anta*h*pada*m*vivr*i*t-
taya*h*, III, 6 anudâttodaye puna*h*.

It seems evident that we have in this *S*loka form of the
Sûtra period, the last preparatory stage which the development of this metre had to traverse, before it arrived at
the shape which it assumes in epic poetry; and it is to be
hoped that more exhaustive observations on this point
(account being especially taken of the numerous verses
quoted in the Dharma-sûtras) will throw an important
light on the chronology of the literature of this period lying
between the Vedas and the post-Vedic age.

We add to these remarks on the *S*lokas quoted in the
Gr*i*hya-sûtras, that we come upon a number of passages in
the midst of the prose of the Sûtras, which without being
in any way externally designated as verses, have an un-
mistakable metrical character, being evidently verses which
the authors of the Sûtras found ready made, and which
they used for their own aphorisms, either without changing
them at all, or with such slight changes that the original
form remained clearly recognisable. Thus we read in
Âsvalâyana (Gr*i*hya I, 6, 8), as a definition of the Râkshasa
marriage: hatvâ bhittvâ *k*a *s*irshâ*n*i rudatî*m* rudadbhyo

---

[1] The few verses which are found in Gobhila preserve the same metrical
standard as those quoted in *S*ânkhâyana; it follows that in Gobhila IV, 7, 23,
a*s*vatthâd agnibhaya*m* brûyât, we cannot change brûyât in *k*a, as Prof. Knauer
proposes. The supernumerary syllable of the first foot is unobjectionable, but
the form ᴗ − − − of the second foot should not be touched.

[2] Both passages are to be found in *S*ânkhâyana-Gr*i*hya I, 10.

haret : the approximation of these words to the *Sloka*
metre cannot escape attention, and it is only necessary to
make r u d a d b h y a*h* and r u d a t î *m* change places in order
to obtain a regular *Sloka* hemistich. In Gobhila the
Sûtras I, 2, 21–27 represent three hemistichs, which with
one exception (na *k*a sopânatka*h* kva*k*it) exactly conform
to the laws of the *Sloka* metre. II, 4, 2 gives also a hemistich by slightly changing the order :

Mahâv*ri*kshân *s*ma*s*âna*m* *k*a nadî*s* *k*a vishamâ*ni* *k*a [1].

Somewhat more remote from the original verses is
the wording of the Sûtras I, 6, 8. 9 na pravasann upavased
ity âhu*h*, patnyâ vrata*m* bhavatîti ; we have the metrical
order in one of the *Slokas* quoted by *S*ânkhâyana (G*ri*hya
II, 17) : nopavâsa*h* pravâse syât patnî dhârayate vratam.

The verses which are thus either expressly quoted, or at
any rate made use of by the authors of the G*ri*hya-sûtras,
do not seem to be taken from connected metrical works any
more than the ya*gñ*agâthâs quoted in the Brâhma*n*as ; on
the contrary in a later period of literature, when texts
similar to Manu's Code were composed, they evidently
furnished these texts with some of their materials [2].

Leaving out of consideration the Khâdira-G*ri*hya, which
is evidently a recast of the Gobhilîya-G*ri*hya, and the
Sûtra of Hira*n*yake*s*in, which is, at least in part, based
on that of Âpastamba [3], we are not in regard to the other
G*ri*hya texts in a condition to prove that one of them
borrowed from the other. It often happens that single
Sûtras or whole rows of Sûtras agree so exactly in different
texts that this agreement cannot be ascribed to chance ;
but this does not — so far at least — enable us to tell
which text is to be looked upon as the source of the

---

[1] The text has : nadî*s* *k*a vishamâ*ni* *k*a mahâv*ri*kshân *s*ma*s*âna*m* *k*a.

[2] Cf. Indische Studien, XV, 11. We do not mean to imply anything as to
the metrical portions of other Sûtra texts than the G*ri*hya-sûtras. As regards
some verses quoted in the Baudhâyana-Dharma-sûtra, Prof. Bühler (Sacred
Books of the East, vol. xiv, p. xli) has shown that they are actually borrowed
from a metrical treatise on the Sacred Law.

[3] Cf. Prof. Bühler's remarks, Sacred Books of the East, vol. ii, p. xxiii.

other, or whether they have a common source which has
been lost.

I will content myself with mentioning two such cases of
agreement, in the one of which we can at least prove that a
certain Sûtra cannot originally spring from one of the texts
in which we find it, while in the other case we are able by
means of a possibly not too uncertain conjecture to recon-
struct the opening Sûtras of a lost Grihya-sûtra.

The description of the vrishotsarga (i.e. of the setting a
bull at liberty) agrees almost word for word in the Sûtras
of Sânkhâyana (III, 11), Pâraskara (III, 9), and in the
Kâthaka-Grihya. In Sânkhâyana we read:

§ 15: nabhyasthe·numantrayate mayobhûr ity anuvâkaseshena.

('When the bull is in the midst of the cows, he recites
over them the texts "mayobhûh, &c.," down to the end of
the Anuvâka.')

On the other hand in Pâraskara we have:

§ 7: nabhyastham abhimantrayate mayobhûr ity anuvâkaseshena.

('When the bull is in the midst of the cows, he recites
over it the texts "mayobhûh, &c.," down to the end of the
Anuvâka.')

The quotation mayobhûh is clear, if we refer it to the
Rig-veda. Hymn X, 169, which stands about in the
middle of an Anuvâka, begins with this word[1]. On the
other hand in the Vâgasaneyi Samhitâ there is no Mantra
beginning with Mayobhûh; we find this word in the middle
of the Mantra XVIII, 45, and there follow verses whose use
at the vrishotsarga would seem in part extremely strange.
There can thus be no doubt that Pâraskara here borrowed
from a Sûtra text belonging to the Rig-veda, a Pratîka,
which, when referred to the Vâgasaneyi Samhitâ, results in
nonsense.

The other passage which I wish to discuss here is Pâra-

---

[1] In the Taittirîya Samhitâ (VII, 4, 17) mayobhûh is the beginning of an
Anuvâka; the expression anuvâkaseshena would have no meaning if referred
to this text.

skara I, 4, 1–5. Pâraskara, being just on the point of describing the marriage ritual, prefixes a few sentences, the position of which here it is not very easy to understand. A general division of all Pâkaya*gñ*as—general remarks on the nature of the place for sacrificing : this looks very strange between a discussion of the Arghya and marriage ceremonies. Now these same sentences are found almost word for word and with the same passing on to the marriage ritual in *S*ânkhâyana also (G*ri*hya I, 5, 1–5). Here, as in other cases, we have the borrowing word for word of such portions of text from an older text, and, closely related to this phenomenon, the fact that the sentences in question are awkwardly woven into the context of the G*ri*hya where we read them, and are poorly connected with the surrounding parts. Unless we are much deceived, we have here a fragment from an older source inserted without connection and without change. It would seem that this fragment was the beginning of the original work ; for the style and contents of these Sûtras are peculiarly appropriate for the beginning. Thus, if this conjecture is right, that old lost G*ri*hya began with the main division of all the Pâkaya*gñ*as into four classes, and then proceeded at once to the marriage ritual. Later, when the texts which we have, came into existence, the feeling evidently arose, that in this way an important part of the matter had been overlooked. The supplementary matter was then inserted before the old beginning, which then naturally, as is to be seen in our texts, joins on rather strangely and abruptly to these newly-added portions.

GR*I*HYA-SÛTRA OF
GOBHILA.

INTRODUCTION

TO THE

GR/HYA-SÛTRA OF GOBHILA.

THE Gr*i*hya-sûtra of Gobhila differs from those of .Sâṅkhâyana, Âsvalâyana, Pâraskara, Hira*n*yakcsin in one essential point: while these texts presuppose only the same Vedic Sa*m*hitâs on which also the corresponding *S*rauta-sûtras are based, viz. the Rig-veda-Sa*m*hitâ, the Vâ*g*asancyi-Sa*m*hitâ, and the Taittiriya-Sa*m*hitâ; the Sûtra of Gobhila, on the other hand, presupposes, beside the Sa*m*hitâ of the Sâma-veda[1], another collection of Mantras which evidently was composed expressly with the purpose of being used at Gr*i*hya ceremonies: this collection is preserved to us under the title of the Mantra-Brâhma*n*a, and it has been edited at Calcutta (1873), with a commentary and Bengali trans-lation by Satyavrata Sâma*s*ramin[2].

Prof. Knauer of Kiew, to whom all students of the Gr*i*hya literature are highly indebted for his very accurate edition and translation of Gobhila, has been the first to

---

[1] The term 'Sa*m*hitâ of the Sâma-veda' ought to be understood here in its narrower sense as denoting the so-called first book of the Sa*m*hitâ, the *Kh*anda-âr*k*ika or collection of Yoni verses (see on the relation between this collection and the second book my remarks in the Zeitschrift der Deutschen Morgenländischen Gesellschaft, vol. xxxviii, pp. 464 seq.). Prof. Knauer in his list of the verses quoted by Gobhila (p. 29 of his translation of the Gobhilîya-Gr*i*hya) states that Sâma-veda II, 1138 (=I, 276) and 1139 is quoted in Gobhila III, 9, 6, but an accurate analysis of the words of Gobhila shows that the verse II, 1139 is not referred to, so that only the verse II, 1138 remains, which occurs also in the first book of the Sa*m*hitâ. The 'dvika' of which Gobhila speaks in that Sûtra is not a dv*ri*ka, but, as the commentators rightly understand it (see Knauer's edition of the text, p. xii), it is a dyad of Sâmans or melodies, the two Kâvasha Sâmans which are based on the text I, 276, and are given in the great Sâma-veda edition of Satyavrata Sâma*s*ramin, vol. i, pp. 566, 567.

[2] In the same way the Gr*i*hya-sûtra of Âpastamba stands in connection with a similar collection of Gr*i*hya verses and formulas, the Âpastambîya-Mantra-pâ*th*a.

examine into the relation in which the two texts, the
Mantra-Brâhma*n*a and the Gobhilîya-sûtra, stand to each
other.   He has very kindly enabled me to make use,
before they were published, of the results of his investigations, which he has laid down in the introduction to his
translation of Gobhila. While I wish, therefore, to acknowledge the obligation under which Prof. Knauer has thus
laid me, I must try, on the other side, to state my own
opinion as to the problem in question, which in some
points differs from, or is even opposed to, the theory by
which Prof. Knauer has tried to solve it.

To begin with that side of the question regarding which
there can scarcely be any doubt: it is certain, I believe,
that Gobhila supposes the Mantra-Brâhma*n*a to be known
to the students of his Sûtra.   The reasons which show
this are obvious enough [1].   By far the greater part of the
Mantras of which Gobhila quotes the first words, are not
found in the Sâma-veda nor, for the most part, in any
other Vedic Sa*m*hitâ, except in the Mantra-Brâhma*n*a, in
which they stand in exactly the same order in which
they are referred to by Gobhila.   The descriptions of the
Gr*i*hya sacrifices by Gobhila would have been meaningless
and useless, and the sacrificer who had to perform his
domestic ceremonies according to the ritual of Gobhila,
would have been unable to do so, unless he had known
those Mantras as contained in the Mantra-Brâhma*n*a.
And not only the Mantras, but also the order in which the
Mantras stood, for Sûtras such as, for instance, Gobh. II, 1,
10 ('With the two following verses he should wash,' &c.),
would have no meaning except for one who had studied
the Mantra-Brâhma*n*a which alone could show which 'the
two following verses' were.

There are, consequently, two possibilities : either the
Mantra-Brâhma*n*a existed before the Gobhilîya-sûtra, or
the two works have been composed together and on one
common plan.   It is the first of these alternatives which
Prof. Knauer maintains; I wish, on the other hand, to call

---

[1] Cf. Knauer's Introduction, pp. 24, 31 seq.

the attention of Vedic scholars to some facts which seem to
me to render the second more probable.

A great part of the Mantras which have to be recited,
according to Gobhila, at the performance of the Grihya
ceremonies, are not given in the Mantra-Brâhmana, but
they are either found in the Sâma-veda-Samhitâ and then
their Pratîkas are quoted by Gobhila, or they are cited by
Gobhila in extenso. Thus for the ceremonies described
in the first Prapâthaka of Gobhila, such as the morning and
evening offerings and the sacrifices of the full and new
moon, the Mantra-Brâhmana gives, with one single exception, no Mantras at all [1]; but those Mantras, most of which
consist only of a few words, are given by Gobhila only. It
is scarcely to be believed that in a Samhitâ which had to
contain the Mantras required for the performance of the
Grihya sacrifices, the Mantras belonging to the two daily
and the two fortnightly sacrifices, which occupy one of the
first places among all Grihya ceremonies and are treated
of accordingly in all Grihya-sûtras, should have been
omitted, unless that Samhitâ was intended to stand in
relation to another text by which that deficiency was supplied : and the Gobhilîya-sûtra exactly supplies it. Prof.
Knauer thinks that those Mantras were omitted because
they had already found their place in the Srauta ritual ;
but we must not forget that in the Srauta ritual of the
Sâma-vedins neither the Agnihotra nor the Darsapûrnamâsa sacrifices, which are performed without the assistance
of priests of the Udgâtri class, are treated of. Moreover
the one Mantra to which we have already alluded [2], the
single one which corresponds in the Mantra-Brâhmana to
the first book of Gobhila, seems to me quite sufficient to
show that it was not the intention of the compiler of that
text to disregard that group of sacrifices ; he gave that
Mantra only, because the other Mantras, consisting of but
a few words, were given in extenso in the Gobhila text.
The Mantra of which we speak, belongs to the description

[1] Cf. Knauer's translation, Introduction, p. 25.
[2] Mantra-Brâhmana I, 1, 1.

of the paryukshana of the sacrificial fire. The sacrificer
pours out water to the south, the west, and the north of the
fire, with the Mantras. 'Adite-numanyasva,' 'Anumate
-numanyasva,' 'Sarasvaty anumanyasva'; then he sprinkles
water round the fire once or three times with a longer
Mantra, · Deva Savitah prasuva yagñam prasuva yagñapatim
bhagâya. Divyo gandharvah ketapûh ketam nah punâtu.
Vâkaspatir vâkam nah svadatu.' This last one is the
Mantra given in its entirety in the Mantra-Brâhmana, while
Gobhila [1] has only the first words of it. To assume here
that the author of the Mantra-Brâhmana knew only of that
one Mantra, and that at the time of Gobhila the custom of
the Sâma-vedins had undergone a change, so that they used
four Mantras instead of the one, would be, in my opinion,
an artificial and not very probable way of explaining the
facts ; a much more natural supposition would be, I
believe, that the Sûtra and the Mantra-Brâhmana describe
one and the same form of the ceremony, so that the Brâhmana, by omitting the short Mantras, which were given in
the Sûtra in their entirety, implicitly refers to the Sûtra,
and the Sûtra, on the other hand, by quoting only the first
words of the longer Mantra, refers to the Brâhmana in
which the full text of that Mantra was given.

Among the numerous ceremonies described by Gobhila,
which could ·furnish the occasion for similar remarks, we
select only two : the rites performed in the evening of the
wedding-day [2], and the sacrifice on the full-moon day of
Âsvayuga [3]. The bridegroom, having carried away his
bride from her home, takes her to the house of a Brâhmana,
and when the stars have appeared, he makes six oblations
with the six verses lekhâsandhishu pakshmasu (Mantra-Br. I, 3, 1–6): these are given in the Mantra-Brâhmana,
and Gobhila has only the Pratika. Then follow two short
Mantras: the bride, to whom the polar-star has been
shown, addresses that star with the words : dhruvam asi
dhruvâham patikule bhûyâsam amushyâsâv iti;

---

[1] Gobh. I, 3, 4.   [2] Gobh. II, 3, 17 seq.   [3] Gobh. III, 8.

and when she sees the star Arundhatî, she says, ruddhâham asmi. As the full wording of these Mantras is given
by Gobhila, they are omitted in the Brâhma*n*a. Finally
the bridegroom recites over the bride the *Rik* dhruvâ
dyaur dhruvâ p*ri*thivî, &c.; this we find in the M.-B.
(I, 3, 7), the Pratika only being quoted by Gobhila. If one
were to suppose here that in the two texts two different
stages in the development of this ceremony are represented,
so that only the Mantras lekhâsandhishu and dhruvâ
dyau*h* would belong to the more ancient form of it, while
the Mantras dhruvam asi and ruddhâham asmi would
have been introduced at a later time, it may perhaps not
be possible to disprove, in the strictest sense of the word,
such an opinion. But I think the data we have given point
to another solution of the problem which, if not the only
admissible, is yet the most probable and natural one.
Gobhila gave the full wording of the shorter Mantras with
which the description of the ceremony could be interwoven
without becoming obscure or disproportionate; the longer
Mantras would have interrupted, rather tediously and incon-
veniently, the coherency of his ritual statements; so he
separated them from the rest of his work and made a separate Sa*m*hitâ of them. It is true that there are some
exceptions to the rule that all long Mantras are given in
the Mantra-Brâhma*n*a and all short Mantras only in the
Sûtra: on the one hand, there are some Mantras of considerable extent that are given by Gobhila and omitted in
the Brâhmana, thus, for instance, the Mantra yady asi
saumî used at a preparatory ceremony that belongs to the
Pu*m*savana [1]. On the other hand, a number of short
Mantras which Gobhila gives in extenso, are found nevertheless also in the Mantra-Brâhma*n*a: such is the case, for
instance, with many of the Mantras belonging to the
worship of the Fathers, Gobhila IV, 2. 3, Mantra-Br. II, 3.

---

[1] Gobh. II, 6, 7. It is possible, though we have no positive evidence for this
conjecture, that such statements regarding preparatory or auxiliary ceremonies
may here and there have been added to the Sûtra collection in a later time.
The Khâdira-G*ri*hya (II, 2, 20) has instead of that long Mantra only a few
words which in the Gobhilîya-sûtra stand at the end of it.

It appears then, that allowance must be made for a certain inconsistency or carelessness in the distribution of the material between the two texts: and such an assumption will easily be allowed by any one who does not entertain very exaggerated ideas as to the care and reflection which presided over the composition of the Sûtra texts.

I will add only a few words concerning a second Gṛihya ceremony, which calls for the same sort of comment as the rites which have just been discussed. For the offering on the day of the full moon, Gobhila prescribes (III, 8, 2) first the verse â no mitrâvaruṇâ, second the verse mâ nas toke. The Mantra-Brâhmaṇa (II, 1, 8) has the second of these verses only, not the first: conversely, the first verse alone, and not the second, is to be found in the Saṃ-hitâ of the Sâma-veda (I, 220). We could hardly assume, as I think, that the Mantra-Brâhmaṇa presupposed another form of the rite differing from Gobhila's; we should be much more inclined to consider the leaving out of that matter, which was contained in other texts of the Sâma-veda, as a proof that the compiler of the Mantra-Brâhmaṇa assumed that those texts were known [1].

And this brings me to one of Prof. Knauer's conjectures concerning the Mantra-Brâhmaṇa which I have not yet touched. According to tradition we consider the Mantra-Brâhmaṇa as belonging to the Sâma-veda; in the Calcutta edition it is designated as the 'Sâma-vedasya Mantra-Brâhmaṇam.' Prof. Knauer thinks that it is doubtful whether the Mantra-Brâhmaṇa belonged to the Sâma-veda originally. He conjectures [2] 'that it existed already in the

---

[1] Any one who holds the view that the ritualistic formulas, which are not contained in the Mantra-Brâhmaṇa, represent later extensions of the ceremonies in question, will do well to notice how in any one of the offerings of the Srauta ritual which we possess, both in the old description of the Saṃhitâ and Brâhmaṇa texts, and in the more recent description of the Sûtra texts, Mantras have been added in more recent times to the former ones. I think that it would be difficult to draw from such observations any argument of analogy calculated to support Dr. Knauer's opinion as to the relation of the Mantras in Gobhila and in the Mantra-Brâhmaṇa.

[2] Introduction to his translation, p. 23.

period during which the separate schools were as yet in the
process of sifting, when there were as yet no Sâma-vedists
in the later and stricter sense of the term [1].' For out of
249 Mantras of the Mantra-Brâhma*n*a there are only four
which are found in the Sâma-veda [2], as Prof. Knauer has
shown, while a much greater number of these Mantras
occur in the other Vedic Sa*m*hitâs. I should be inclined
to conclude the other way : just because the author of the
Mantra-Brâhma*n*a presupposed a knowledge of the Sa*m*hitâ
of the Sâma-veda, but not of the other Vedas—or in other
words because he destined his work for Sâma-vedins, he
did not need to repeat what was in the Sâma-veda, but was
compelled to incorporate in his compilation the Mantras
out of the Rig-veda or of the Ya*g*ur-veda [3]. Moreover, I
would draw the same conclusions from the Mantras cited by
Gobhila which are absent in the Mantra-Brâhma*n*a, as I did
from the Mantras which occur in the Mantra-Brâhma*n*a, but
are not to be found in the Sâma-veda. Those Mantras are
all to be found in the Sâma-veda with the exception of those
which Gobhila has in ex tenso, and which therefore could
be omitted in the Mantra-Brâhma*n*a. If we examine the
thirteen Mantras collected by Prof. Knauer (p. 29), we find
that in the case of nine of them the passage of the Sâma-
veda (always of the first Âr*k*ika of the Sâma-veda) where
they are to be found is quoted by Prof. Knauer.

---

[1] Besides the reasons given below in opposition to this conjecture, I may be
permitted to point out that this hypothesis is contrary to the whole chronology
of the G*ri*hya literature which we endeavoured to arrive at in the general
introduction. It is a priori extremely improbable that there was a G*ri*hya
Sa*m*hitâ at a time when there was as yet no Sâma-veda.

[2] Viz. (according to Prof. Knauer's alphabetical list of the Mantras of the
Mantra-Brâhma*n*a) ima*m* stomam arhate, M.-B. II, 4, 2 = Sv. I, 66 ; II, 414 :
tat savitur vare*n*yam, M.-B. I, 6, 29 = Sv. II, 812 ; bharâmedhunam, M.-B. II, 4,
3 = Sv. II, 415 ; *s*akema tvâ, M.-B. II, 4, 4 = Sv. II, 416.

[3] Notice that of the four exceptional cases which we put together in the
previous note, three cases are Mantras which are found only in the second
Âr*k*ika of the Sâma-veda, not in the first (cf. above, p. 3. note 1). The fourth
verse (M.-B. II, 4, 2) is to be found in the first Âr*k*ika, it is true, but it stands
closely related to two verses which are not to be found in that Âr*k*ika (M.-B.
II, 4, 3. 4). This explains why it was put into the Mantra-Brâhma*n*a, as well
as those two verses.

The four other cases are :

> *rikam* sâma yagâmahe, Gobh. III, 2, 48.
> ta*k kakshur* devahitam, III, 8, 5.
> sam anyâ yanti. III, 9, 7.
> pra*gâ*pataye, IV, 7, 36.

Of these Mantras the first is contained in the Sâma-veda (I, 369) just as the nine first-mentioned ones; the second is quoted by Gobhila in extenso; the third is to be found in the Âra*n*yaka division of the Sâma-veda I (vol. ii, p. 292, ed. Bibl. Ind.); in the fourth finally the text is corrupt; it is intended for the verse out of the Mantra-Brâhma*n*a Pra*gâ*pate na tvad etâny anya*h*. Thus the four apparent exceptions all vanish, and we have in the Mantras which are absent in the Mantra-Brâhma*n*a a new proof that this text belongs to the literature of the Sâma-veda[1].

Thus, according to my view, we may describe the origin of the Mantra-Brâhma*n*a as follows. The Sâma-veda contained in its Sa*m*hitâ a much smaller number of Mantras applicable to the G*ri*hya rites than either the Rig-veda or the Ya*g*ur-veda ; the peculiar character of the Sâman texts, intended for musical recitations at the most important sacrificial offerings, was quite remote from the character of formulas suitable for the celebration of a wedding, for the birth of a child, for the consecration of fields and flocks. Hence it is that, to a much greater extent than Âsvalâyana or Pâraskara, Gobhila mentions Mantras for which a reference to the Sa*m*hitâ was not sufficient ; and this led to the compiling of a separate Sa*m*hitâ of such G*ri*hya-mantras, which presupposes the G*ri*hya-sûtra, just as the latter presupposes this Sa*m*hitâ. The almost perfect agreement of the Mantra-Brâhma*n*a with Gobhila furnishes a valuable

---

[1] One will not object that the Mantras in question which are absent in the Mantra-Brâhma*n*a are all to be found in the Rig-veda as well as in the Sâma-veda. Since almost all the verses of the Sâma-ve a are taken from the Rig-veda there is nothing astonishing about this. Before one could conclude from this that the Mantra-Brâhma*n*a belongs to the Rig-veda he would have to answer the question, How is it that the verses in question are always verses of the Rig-veda which are repeated in the Sâma-veda? Why are there not among them verses which are not to be found in the Sâma-veda?

warrant for the good preservation of the two texts: of small discrepancies I have noted only two: Mantra-Brâhmaṇa I, 6, 15, the formula âgantrâ samaganmahi is given for the ceremony of the Upanayana, while Gobhila does not prescribe this Mantra for this ceremony, although other Gṛihya texts do; and secondly, the Mantra-Brâhmaṇa II, 5, 1–7 does not consist of six verses as Gobh. IV, 6, 5–6 allows us to assume, but of seven verses.

In concluding this introduction notice is to be drawn to the fact that the text of Gobhila has preserved for us the traces of a division differing from the one into four Prapâṭhakas which is handed down by tradition: in a number of places certain Sûtras or the last words of certain Sûtras are set down twice, a well-known way of indicating the close of a chapter. This repetition, besides occurring at the end of the first, third, and fourth Prapâṭhaka (not at the end of the second), is to be found in the following places which become more frequent towards the close of the work: I, 4, 31; III, 6, 15; IV, 1, 22; 4, 34; 5, 34; 6, 16.

GR*I*HYA-SÛTRA OF GOBHILA.

1. Now henceforth we shall explain the domestic sacrifices.

2. He should perform (the ceremonies) wearing the sacrificial cord on his left shoulder and having sipped water.

3. During the northern course of the sun, at the time of the increasing moon, on an auspicious day, before noon : this he should know as the (proper) time (for performing the ceremonies).

4. And as the prescription (is stated with regard to the time of the single ceremonies).

5. All (ceremonies) are accompanied by the Anvâhârya (Srâddha).

1, 1–4. Comp. Khâdira-Gr*i*hya I, 1, 1. 2. 5. 7.

5. I cannot give this translation of the words 'sarvâ*ny* evân-vâhâryavanti' without expressing my doubts as to whether the commentator, whom I have followed, is right. He says: 'anu pa*sk*âd âhriyate yasmât prakr*i*ta*m* karma iti, anu pa*sk*âd âhriyate yat prastutât (prakr*i*tât?) karma*na* iti *k*ânvâhârya*m* nândîmu-khasrâddha*m* dakshinâ *k*o*k*yate.' It is evident that the first expla-nation of anvâhârya as a ceremony after which the chief sacrifice follows, is inadmissible. Below, IV, 4, 3. 4, Gobhila himself defines the Anvâhârya Srâddha as a monthly ceremony (comp. Manu III, 123; Max Müller, India, p. 240); it is, consequently, different from a Srâddha accompanying each Gr*i*hya sacrifice. The Sloka which the commentary quotes from a 'gr*i*hyântara' seems to me not to remove the doubt; I think rather that it contains a specu-lation based on this very passage of Gobhila, taken in the sense in

6. At the end (of each ceremony) he should feed worthy (Brâhma*n*as) according to his ability.

7. A student, after he has studied the Veda, when going to put the last piece of wood (on the fire),—

8. Or to seize a wife's hand (i. e. to marry her),—

9. Should fetch water from a hidden place, should sweep a place which is inclined towards north-east, or which is level, and should besmear it (with cow-dung). Beginning from the centre of it he should draw a line from west to east, (another line) from south to north which touches that line at its western end, and three lines from west to east (touching the northwards-turned line at three different points) in its midst (i. e. at neither of its ends). He then should besprinkle (those lines with water).

10. In this way the Laksha*n*a (i. e. the preparation of the place for the sacred fire) is performed everywhere.

11. With the words ‘ Bhûr, bhuva*h*, sva*h*,’ they carry the fire forward (to that place) so that they have it in front of them.

12. Or after the householder has died, the chief

---

which the commentator takes it, and on the Sûtras IV, 4, 3. 4. Thus I rather believe that we ought to understand anvâhârya as a mess of food like that offered after the dar*s*apûr*n*amâsau sacrifices to the officiating priests (Hillebrandt, Neu- und Vollmondsopfer, 133), and I propose to translate : All (sacrifices) are followed by (the offering of) the Anvâhârya food (to the priest).

6. Khâdira-G*ri*hya I, 1, 3.

7. The text goes on to treat of the setting up of the domestic fire. Khâdira-G*ri*hya I, 3, 1.

9. Khâdira-G*ri*hya I, 3, 1 seqq. ; G*ri*hya-sa*m*graha I, 47 seqq. ; Zeitschrift der Deutschen Morgenl. Gesellschaft, XXXV, 557.

12. I have followed in the translation of paramesh*th*ikara*n*am the

(of the family) should do it (i. e. he should set up the sacred fire).

13. In this way, on the coincidence of an (auspicious) Tithi and an (auspicious) Nakshatra, (or of such a Nakshatra) and a Parvan—

14. On the full-moon day or on the new-moon day: then he should celebrate the setting up of his (sacred domestic) fire.

15. He should get fire from a Vaisya's house or from a frying-pan, and should set it up (as his sacred fire) ;

16. Or (he should fetch it) from the house of one who offers many sacrifices, be it a Brâhmana, or a Râganya, or a Vaisya.

17. Or he may kindle another fire by attrition and may set it up.

18. That is pure, but it does not bring prosperity.

19. He may do what he likes (of the things stated as admissible in the last Sûtras).

20. When he puts (at the end of his studentship) the last piece of wood (on the fire), or when he sacrifices when going to seize the hand of a wife, that fire he should keep.

21. That becomes his (sacred) domestic fire.

22. Thereby his morning oblation has been offered.

---

way indicated by the Grihya-samgraha I, 77, and by Sânkhâyana (I, 1, 5): prete vâ grihapatau svayam gyâyân. I think the parameshthî is the same person as the gyâyân. The commentary gives a different explanation: parameshthî agnir ity âkakshate, tasya parameshthino gneh karanam yathoktena vidhinâ svîkaranam.

15–18. Khâdira-Grihya I, 5, 3 seqq.

20, 21. Khâdira-Grihya I, 5, 1. 2. Comp. also above, Sûtras 7 and 8.

22. I. e. in the first of the two cases mentioned in Sûtra 20, the

23. Beginning from that time the sacrificing (of regular morning and evening oblations) in the domestic fire is prescribed, so that he begins with an evening oblation.

24. Before the time has come for setting the fire in a blaze, he should fetch in the evening and in the morning from a hidden place the water with which the different acts (such as sipping water) are performed.

25. Or (he should fetch water only) in the evening.

26. Or he·should draw it out of a water-pot or of a barrel.

27. Before sunset he should set the fire in a blaze, and sacrifice the evening oblation after sunset.

28. In the morning he should set the fire in a blaze before sunrise, and should sacrifice the morning oblation before sunrise or after it.

KÂ*ND*IKÂ 2.

1. He takes as his ya*gñ*opavita (i. e. sacrificial cord) a string, or a garment, or simply a rope of Ku*s*a grass.

---

putting of fuel on the fire, and in the second case, the oblations of fried grain, &c., prescribed for the wedding, are considered as the sacrificer's morning oblation in his newly-established Gr*i*hya fire, so that the regular oblations have to begin with the sâyamâhuti.

23. Khâdira-Gr*i*hya I, 5, 6. Comp. Prof. Bloomfield's note 2, Zeitschrift der Deutschen Morgenl. Gesellschaft, XXXV, 561.

27, 28. Khâdira-Gr*i*hya I, 5, 7–9. As to the two cases regarding the time of the morning oblation, comp. Indische Studien, X, 329.

2, 1–4. Rules regarding the Upavita. Khâdira-Gr*i*hya I, 1, 4–6. Compare the detailed description of the nine threads of which the Upavita-string should consist, in the Gr*i*hya-sa*m*graha II, 48 seqq. A string was evidently considered as the regular and preferable form of the Upavita ; with regard to the second kind of Upavita mentioned in Sûtra 1, the commentary says, 'A garment (is used),

2. Raising his right arm, putting the head into (the upavita), he suspends (the cord) over his left shoulder, so that it hangs down on his right side : thus he becomes ya*gñ*opavîtin.

3. Raising his left arm, putting the head into (the upavita), he suspends it over his right shoulder, so that it hangs down on his left side : thus he becomes prâ*k*inâvîtin.

4. Prâ*k*inâvîtin, however, he is only at sacrifices offered to the Manes.

5. Having gone in a northern direction from the fire, having washed his hands and feet, and having seated himself, he should sip water three times and wipe off (the water) twice.

6. Having besprinkled his feet (with water) let him besprinkle his head.

7. Let him touch the organs of his senses with water :

8. The two eyes, the nose, the two ears.

9. Whatever (limb of his body) requires his consideration (whether it is pure or not), that he should touch with water (i. e. with a wet hand).

10. Here they say :

11. Let him not touch (himself with water, or sip water) while walking,

12. Nor standing,

13. Nor laughing,

14. Nor looking about,

15. Nor without bending down,

---

if the Upavita has been lost, for instance, in a forest, and if it is impossible to get a string.' A similar remark is given with reference to the third kind of Upavita, the rope of Ku*s*a grass.

5–32. Rules regarding the â*k*amana and upaspar*s*ana. Khâdira-G*ri*hya I, 1, 7–10 ; Manu II, 60 seqq.

16. Nor (throwing up the water) with his fingers,

17. Nor except with the (proper) Tîrtha,

18. Nor uttering a sound,

19. Nor without looking (at the water),

20. Nor with his shoulders put back,

21. Nor wearing a part of his under garment as if it were an upper garment,

22. Nor with warm water,

23. Nor with foamy water,

24. And in no case wearing sandals,

25. (Not) with a turban on his head (?),

26. (Not with his garment) tied round his neck,

27. And not stretching out his feet.

28. When he has finally touched (water) again, he becomes pure.

29. Let him, however, sip only water that reaches his heart.

30. For if he does otherwise, he remains impure.

31. Now the cases in which he has to touch (water) a second time.

---

17. As to the Tîrthas (or parts of the hand) sacred to the different deities or beings, comp. Vasish*th*a III, 64 seqq., &c. See also Manu II, 58.

20. According to the commentary he has to hold his hands between his knees. Comp. *S*ânkh.-G*ri*hya I, 10, 8. Thus the shoulders are brought forward.

21–27. These Sûtras form three regular *S*loka hemistichs. Only at the end of the second hemistich there is a metrical irregularity (sopânatka*h* kva*k*it standing at the end of the verse).

25. Kâsaktika*h*, which the commentary explains as a compound of ka, 'the head,' and âsaktikâ = âvesh*th*ikâ.

28. Khâdira-G*ri*hya I, 1, 10.

29. In other texts (for instance, Manu II, 62 ; Vasish*th*a III, 31 seqq.) it is stated that a Brâhma*n*a should sip water that reaches his heart, a Kshatriya water reaching his throat, a Vai*s*ya water that wets his palate ; a *S*ûdra should only touch water with his lips.

32. Having slept, or eaten, or sneezed, or taken a bath, or drunk something, or changed (his garments), or walked on the high road, or gone to a cemetery, he should sip water and then sip water again.

KÂNDIKÂ 3.

1. Having put wood on the (sacred) fire, having swept (the ground) round it, he should, bending his right knee, pour out to the south of the fire his joined hands full of water with (the words), 'Aditi! Give thy consent!'

2. To the west with (the words), 'Anumati! Give thy consent!'

3. To the north with (the words), 'Sarasvati! Give thy consent!'

4. With (the words), 'God Savitri! Give thy impulse!' (Mantra-Brâhmana I, 1, 1) he should sprinkle (water) round the fire once or thrice so as to keep his right side turned towards it—

5. Interchanging the points at which he begins and ends the (sprinkling of water), and sprinkling so as to encompass what he is going to offer (with the streams of water).

6. Let him then make oblations of the sacrificial food, be it prepared or raw, over the fire.

---

32. This Sûtra again forms a Sloka, though a slightly irregular Sloka.

3. Rules regarding the daily morning and evening sacrifice.

1-5. Khâdira-Grihya I, 2, 17-21.

6. The sacrificial food is either krita (prepared) or akrita (unprepared). A mess of boiled rice, for instance, is krita, rice grains are akrita.

7. If it is raw, he should sacrifice after having washed it and having let the water drop off.

8. If it consists in curds or milk or rice gruel, (he should sacrifice it) with a brazen bowl, or with the pot in which the oblations of boiled rice are prepared, or also with the (sacrificial spoon called) Sruva;

9. In the evening the first (oblation) with (the formula), 'To Agni Svâhâ!' the second silently, in the middle and in the north-eastern part (of the fire);

10. In the morning the first (oblation) with (the formula), 'To Sûrya Svâhâ!' the second again silently, again in the middle and in the north-eastern part (of the fire).

11. Having put a piece of wood (on the fire), and having again sprinkled (water) round it, he should pour out again his joined hands full of water in the same way (as prescribed in the Sûtras 1–3); in the Mantras he says, 'Thou hast given thy consent' (instead of 'Give thy consent').

12. Having circumambulated the fire so as to turn his right side towards it, having poured out the remains of water, and filled the vessel again, and put it (in its proper place), (he may do) whatever his business is.

7–12. Khâdira-Grihya I, 5, 10–12. Prodaka in Sûtra 7 is explained by pragatodaka.

9–10. Khâdira-Grihya, l.l. 13–15.

9. The first oblation is made in the middle, the second, sacred to Pragâpati (Sânkhâyana I, 3, 15, &c.), in the north-eastern part of the sacred fire. The tenth Sûtra of course is to be understood in the same way.

12. The water is that mentioned chap. 1, 24. With regard to

13. In that way, from that time (in which he has begun to offer the two daily sacrifices) he should sacrifice, or should have sacrificed, over the (sacred) domestic fire, till the end of his life.

14. Here now they say:

15. 'If they like, his wife may offer the morning and evening oblations over the domestic fire. For his wife is (as it were) his house, and that fire is the domestic fire.'

16. When the morning meal or the evening meal is ready, he should make (his wife) say, 'It is ready!'—

17. In an unbroken voice (?), having made himself pure,

18. He replies in a loud voice, 'Om!' Then in

---

yathârtham the commentary says, 'yathârtham karmâpavargavihitam Vâmadevyagânâdikam prâtarâhutipaskâdvihitam brahmayagñam vâ kuryâd iti vâkyaseshah.' Similarly in the note on II, 4, 11 it is said, 'yathârtham iti karmanah parisamâptir ukyate;' II, 8, 17: 'yathârtham tantrasamâpanam kuryât,' &c. In my translation I have adopted the opinion of Professor Weber (Indische Studien, V, 375), according to whom yathârtham simply means, '(he should behave) as required by circumstances;' '(he should do) what happens to be his business.'

13. The last words are â gîvitâvabhr/thât, which literally means 'till the Avabhr/tha bath of his life.' The Avabhr/tha bath is the bath taken at the end of certain sacrifices, so that the Avabhr/tha of life signifies death.

15. Khâdira-Gr/hya I, 5, 17.

16–18. Khâdira-Gr/hya, l.l. 18, 19. In my translation of Sûtra 17 I have adopted, though not quite without doubt, the conjecture of Professor Roth given in Professor Knauer's note, p. 137. Professor Roth writes r/tebhangayâ vâkâ or r/tebhagayâ vâkâ: he says simply 'om,' and not 'ó-o-ó-o-ó-om.' According to the commentary Sûtra 17 would refer to the wife, not to the husband.

18. The MSS. give mâkhyâ and mâkshâ. We ought to read, tan mâ kshâyîty upâmsu. Comp. Âpastamba II, 2, 3, 11

a low voice: 'To that (food) I bring adoration. May it not fail!'

KÂ*N*DIKÂ 4.

1. He then should silently offer the Balis.

2. Let him speak only what refers to the due preparation of the food. With guests he may converse, if he likes.

3. He then should take some portion of food which is fit for sacrifice, should pour over it some liquid fit for sacrifice (such as ghee, milk, or curds), and should sacrifice it silently in the fire with his hand.

4. The first oblation is sacred to Pra*g*âpati, the second to (Agni) Svish*t*ak*ri*t.

5. He then should offer the Balis, inside or outside (the Agnyagâra), having well cleansed the ground.

6. Let him pour out water once, and put down Balis in four places, and finally sprinkle once (water on the four Balis).

7. Or let him for each Bali which he puts down, sprinkle (water) before and afterwards.

8. What he puts down first, that is the Bali belonging to the Earth. What in the second place, to Vâyu. What in the third place, to the Vi*s*ve devâs. What in the fourth place, to Pra*g*âpati.

9. Then he should offer other Balis (near) the water-pot, the middle (post, and) the door: the first Bali is sacred to the Waters, the second to the Herbs and Trees, the third to the Ether.

4, 1 seqq. The daily Bali offering. Khâdira-G*ri*hya I, 5, 20 seqq.

9. According to the commentary the first of these three Balis has

10. Then he should offer another Bali in the bed or in the privy. That Bali belongs either to Kâma or to Manyu.

11. Then (another Bali) on the heap of sweepings; that (belongs) to the hosts of Rakshas.

12. The remnants of the Balis he should besprinkle with water, and should pour them out towards the south from right to left; they belong to the Fathers.

13. Let him sacrifice in the fire sitting.

14. Let him make the oblation to the Fathers sitting; the other (Balis he may offer) as it happens.

15. He should, however, offer those Balis himself as long as he stays at home.

16. Or another person who must be a Brâhma*n*a (should offer them for him).

17. Both the husband and his wife (should offer them):

18. This is the rule for householders.

19. The wife in the evening, the man in the morning: thus (it is stated).

20. He should offer such Balis of all food whatever, be it prepared for the Fathers, or for auspicious

---

to be offered near the water-pot, the second near the middle door of the house, the third (comp. Gautama V, 16) in the air. With the genitives the word samîpe is supplied. It is difficult to understand why the author, if his intention had been to state three places in which the Balis had to be offered, should have mentioned only two. Thus I believe that the right explanation is that of Professor Knauer, who takes madhyama in the sense of the middle post of the house (comp. III, 3, 31).

11. The commentary explains avasalavi here, as is frequently the case, by pit*r*itîrthena. I agree with the opinion pronounced in the Petersburg Dictionary, in rejecting this explanation.

19. Comp. Manu III, 121.

purposes (for instance, for being offered to Brâhma*n*as), or for (ordinary) purposes.

21. Only in the case of a sacrifice (this rule) ceases.

22. If rice and barley are prepared for one and
the same meal, he should, having offered (Balis) of
the one or the other (kind of food), consider his duty
as fulfilled.

23. If the food is cooked at different times for one
meal, he should perform this Bali ceremony only once.

24. If food is prepared at different places for one
family, he should perform this Bali ceremony only
from (the food which is prepared in) the kitchen
belonging to the householder.

25. However (of the persons belonging to the
family) he whose food becomes ready before (that
of the householder), (that person) should offer the
prescribed portion in the fire, and give to a Brâhma*n*a his share (of the food), and then should eat
himself.

26. He whose (food becomes ready) after (that of
the householder), should only eat.

27. Here they say also:

28. 'At the end of that offering of Balis let him
pronounce a wish.   Then it will be fulfilled to him.'

29. He himself, however, should offer the Âsasya
Bali, from the barley(-harvest) till the rice(-harvest),
and from the rice(-harvest) till the barley(-harvest).
This is called the Âsasya Bali.

_____

22. Kâla I take, as the commentator does, for bhoga nakâla.

23. Here again kâla occurs in the same sense.   Comp. Khâdira-Gr*i*hya I, 5, 34.

29. Khâdira-Gr*i*hya I, 5, 37.   The barley-harvest is in the hot
season, the rice-harvest in autumn (see Zimmer, Altindisches Leben,
243).   The sacrificer offers barley from the barley-harvest till the
rice-harvest; and rice from the rice-harvest till the barley-harvest.

30. Thus he obtains long life.

31. When a donation has been made, he should offer a Bali of chaff, of the scum of boiled rice, and of water. This is sacred to Rudra. This is sacred to Rudra.

KÂNDIKÂ 5.

1. Now at the times of the new moon and of the full moon (the following ceremonies are performed).

2. Let him fast on that full-moon day (when the full moon rises) at the meeting (of day and night).

3. The following day, according to some (teachers).

4. And on that day on which the moon is not seen, (he should fast, considering it) as the new-moon day.

5. The ends of the half-months are the time for fasting, the beginnings for sacrifice.

6. With the sacrificial food of the new-moon

This Bali is called â-sasya, because it is offered until (â) the next crop (sasya) is ripe. As to the regulation that the sacrificer has to offer it himself, compare above, Sûtras 15–19.

31. Khâdira-Grihya I, 5, 30. The repetition of the last words makes it probable that this Sûtra was at one time considered the end of the first book. Comp. Introduction, p. 11.

5. Description of the sacrifices of the full and new moon. Paradigm of the regular Sthâlipâka offering. The first twelve Sûtras of this chapter have been translated by Professor Weber, Ueber den Vedakalender namens Jyotisham, pp. 50 seq.

2. See the note below at Sûtra 10.

3. With these two Sûtras, 'sandhyâm paurnamâsim upavaset; uttarâm ity eke,' a passage should be compared which is identically found in the Aitareya (VII, 11), and in the Kaushîtaka Brâhmana (III, 1): pûrvâm paurnamâsim upavased iti Paingyam, uttarâm iti Kaushîtakam.

6. The month is reckoned here, as is usually done, as beginning with the fortnight of the increasing moon.

sacrifice he celebrates the first half (of the month), with that of the full-moon sacrifice the second.

7. Full-moon is the greatest distance of sun and moon ; new-moon is their nearest approach.

8. That day on which the moon is not seen, that he should take as the day of new-moon.

9. Sometimes he may also while (the moon) is (still) visible (accept it as the day of new-moon) ; for (already then the moon) has made its way.

10. The time of full-moon is reckoned in three ways : (when the full moon rises at) the meeting (of day and night), or when it rises after sunset, or when it stands high (in the sky at sunset).

11. Now on what day it becomes full—

12. The doctrine on this point has to be studied

---

7. Here begins a new exposition of the question of full and new moon which stands independently by the side of the former sections, and which Gobhila has not taken much care to weld together with them.   Comp. Sûtra 10 with Sûtras 2 and 3, and Sûtra 8 with Sûtra 4.

10. The first of the three times is that mentioned in Sûtra 2. It seems to me not very safe to interpret sandhyâ in that modern sense, in which sandhi is used, for instance, in the verse quoted by Mâdhava, Weber, Jyotisha 51, so that it designates the meeting-point of the bright and of the dark fortnight ('âvartane yadâ sandhih parvapratipador bhavet,' &c.).   If sandhyâ were that, we should expect that the same word would occupy a similar position in the definition of amâvâsyâ. I prefer, therefore, with the commentary, to understand sandhyâ in its ancient sense, as the time which divides day from night.   Thus sandhyâ paurnamâsî, the full-moon day, on which the moon rises at the meeting of day and night, stands in opposition to uttarâ paurnamâsî (Sûtra 2), or to astamitoditâ (scil. paurnamâsî, Sûtra 10), exactly in the same way as in the Brâhmana passages quoted above (note on § 3) pûrvâ paurnamâsî is opposed to uttarâ paurnamâsî. The second and third cases are those of the full moon rising (shortly) after sunset, and of the moon becoming full when standing high in the sky.

separately. One should study it, or should ascertain (the exact time of) the Parvan from those who know it.

13. Now on the day which is the fast-day, on that day, in the forenoon, having offered his morning oblation, he besmears that surface on which the fire is placed, on all sides with cow-dung.

14. He then gets the pieces of wood ready (which are to be put on the fire)—of Khadira or of Palâsa wood.

15. If Khadira or Palâsa wood cannot be obtained, it may be wood—as far as it serves the purpose—of any tree, with the exception of Vibhidaka, Tilvaka, Bâdhaka, Nîva, Nimba, Râgavriksha, Salmali, Aralu, Dadhittha, Kovidâra, Sleshmâtaka wood.

16. The Barhis consists of Kusa grass cut off at the points at which the blades diverge from the main stalk.

17. (The blades should be) cut off near the roots at (the ceremonies directed to) the Fathers.

18. If that (i. e. Kusa grass) cannot be obtained, (he may take) any kind of grass, with the exception of Sûka grass, of Saccharum reed, of such grass as is apt to break, of Balbaga grass, of Mutava, of Amphidonax reed, of Suntha.

19. (He should get ready the following things, viz.) Âgya, rice or barley to be cooked for the sacrifice, the pot in which the oblation of cooked rice (or barley) is prepared, the pot-ladle, the Sruva, the water fetched from a hidden place—

20. And the other things which we shall mention in the course of (our exposition of) the ritual.

---

19. As to anuguptâ âpah, see above, chap. 1, 9.

21. On that day he should not go away (from his house on a journey, &c.) ;

22. Even from a distant place he should return to his house.

23. (On that day) he may buy goods from others, but not sell (such goods).

24. Let him not speak much.

25. Let him strive to speak the truth.

26. In the afternoon husband and wife, after having bathed, should eat fast-day food which is pleasant to them. It should contain butter (and should be prepared) in the due way.

KÂNDIKÂ 6.

1. Thus has spoken Mânatantavya : 'Unoffered indeed becomes the offering of a man who does not eat fast-day food.

2. 'He becomes powerless. Hunger will attack him. He does not gain favour among people. His offspring will be perverse.

3. 'But he who eats fast-day food, becomes powerful. Hunger will not attack him. He gains

26. Khâdira-Gr/hya II, 1, 4. 6. The commentary explains kusa-lena : it should be easy to digest. Comp. below, II, 1, 2 : (dârân kurvîta) lakshanaprasastân kusmlena.

6, 1. The teacher's name is spelt elsewhere Mânutantavya, which seems to be the more correct spelling. The Khâdira-Gr/hya (II, 1, 5) has Mânadantavya. Dr. Knauer has called attention to several other blunders of the MSS., which are unusually frequent just in this passage. For I have no doubt that in spite of the unanimous agreement of the MSS. we are to change mânushyâ-hutir into mânushasyâhutir, and I think it very probable, to say the least, that in Sûtra 4 kâmayetaupavasathikam should be corrected into kâmayeyâtâm aupavasathikam, though here the singular could possibly be defended by very faithful believers in the authority of the MSS.

favour among people. His offspring will be still
more blessed.

4. 'Therefore (husband and wife) should eat fast-
day food which is pleasant to them.'

5. Let them sleep that night on the ground.

6. They should spend that night so as to alternate
their sleep with waking, entertaining themselves with
tales or with other discourse.

7. But they should avoid doing anything unholy
(such as cohabiting together).

8. It is said, that when on a journey, he should
not fast.

9. For (say they, in that case) the observance has
to be kept by his wife.

10. Let him do (herein) what he likes.

11. In the same way also one who has set up the
(Srauta) fires should fast—

12. And (he should observe) what is enjoined by
the sacred tradition.

13. Now in the forenoon, after (the sacrificer) has
offered his morning oblation, and has walked round
the fire on its front side, and strewn to the south of
the fire eastward-pointed Darbha grass—

14. (The Brahman) stations himself to the east of
that (grass), facing the west, and with the thumb and
the fourth finger of his left hand he takes one grass
blade from the Brahman's seat and throws it away
to the south-west, in the intermediate direction (between south and west), with (the words), 'Away has
been thrown the dispeller of wealth.'

---

4. Or, which is pleasant to him ? See the note on § 1.

7. Khâdira-Grıhya II, 1, 7.

14. The ceremonies stated in this Sûtra have to be performed
by the Brahman. This is stated in the commentary, and the com-

15. Having touched water, he then sits down on the Brahman's seat, with (the words), ' I sit down on the seat of wealth.'

16. Facing the fire he sits silently, raising his joined hands, till the end of the ceremony.

17. Let him speak (only) what refers to the due performance of the sacrifice.

18. Let him not speak what is unworthy of the sacrifice.

19. If he has spoken what is unworthy of the sacrifice, let him murmur a verse, or a Yagus, sacred to Vishnu.

20. Or let him only say, ' Adoration to Vishnu! '

21. If one wishes, however, to do himself the work both of the Hotri and of the Brahman, he should in the same way place on the Brahman's seat a parasol, or an outer garment, or a water-pot, or a

parison of parallel texts leaves no doubt as to the correctness of this view. Thus Hiranyakesin says (I, 1): etasmin kâle brahmâ yagñopavîtam kritvâpa âkamyâparenâgnim dakshinâtikramya brahmasadanât trinam nirasya, &c. Comp. also the corresponding passages of the Srauta ritual given by Hillebrandt, Neu- und Vollmondsopfer, p. 17. I do not think it probable, however, that we should read brahmâ·sanât, so that it would be distinctly expressed by the text that the Brahman is the subject (comp. Dr. Knauer's Introduction, p. viii). For we read in this same Sûtra brahmâsanât trinam abhisamgrihya; in Sûtra 15, brahmâsana upavisati; in Sûtra 21, brahmâsane nidhâya: of these passages it is in the second made probable by the sense, and it is certain in the third, that brahmâsana is to be understood as a compound equal to brahmasadana. Thus it would, in my opinion, be unnatural not to explain it in the same way also in the first passage. Parâvasu is opposed to Vasu (Sûtra 15) in the same way as some texts, for instance Âpastamba, oppose Parâgvasu to Arvâgvasu.

16 seqq. Khâdira-Grihya I, 1, 19 seqq.

21. ' In the same way ' refers to the ceremonies stated in Sûtras

bolster of Darbha grass, and should return in the
same way (in which he has gone to the Brahman's
seat), and then should perform the other (duties).

KÂNDIKÂ 7.

1. He then washes the mortar, the pestle, and the
winnowing basket, strews to the west of the fire eastward-pointed Darbha grass, and puts (the mortar,
&c.) on (that grass).

2. He then pours out, with a brazen vessel or
with the pot in which the oblations of cooked rice
are prepared, the grain destined for sacrifice, rice or
barley—

3. Once pronouncing the name of the deity (to
whom the offering will be made): 'Agreeable to
such and such (a deity) I pour thee out;' twice (it is
done) silently.

4. Then to the west, with his face turned eastward, he begins to husk the grain, with his right
hand lying over the left.

5. After the grain has three times been winnowed,
he should wash it thrice (if it is destined) for the
gods, they say, twice, if for men, once, if for the
Fathers.

6. Having put a (Darbha) purifier (into the pot

---

13 and 14. On the darbha&alu or, as some MSS. read, dar-
bhavalu, see Bloomfield's note on the G*ri*hya-sa*m*graha, I, 88. 89.
Knauer gives darbhavalu*m* without adding any various readings.
Comp. Khâdira-G*ri*hya I, 1, 23.

7, 2, 3. Khâdira-G*ri*hya II, 1, 9.

4, 5. Comp. Hillebrandt, Neu- und Vollmondsopfer, pp. 29 seqq.
Khâdira-G*ri*hya II, 1, 10–13.

6. Hillebrandt, p. 39.

in which the oblation is to be prepared), he should pour the grain (into it).

7. He should cook the mess of sacrificial food so that it is well cooked, stirring it up (with the pot-ladle) from left to right.

8. When it has been cooked, he should sprinkle (Âgya) on it, should take it from the fire towards the north, and should again sprinkle (Âgya) on it.

9. Having put wood on the fire, he should strew Kusa grass round it on all sides, to the east, to the south, to the north, to the west—

10. On all sides in three layers or in five layers—

11. Thick, so that always an uneven number (of blades) are put together.

12. (He should strew) eastward-pointed grass, covering the roots with the points.

13. Or he should strew it to the west (of the fire), and should draw (some of the grass which he has strewn) from the south end and (some) from the north end, in an easterly direction.

14. He should (arrange the grass so as to) lay the points of the southern blades uppermost.

15. This rule for strewing (grass) round (the fire is valid) for all (ceremonies) at which oblations are made.

16. Some lay also branches of Sami wood or of Parna wood round (the fire).

---

10. Khâdira-Grihya I, 2, 10.

11. This seems to me the most probable translation of ayug-masamhatam, on which expression Dr. Knauer's note on pp. viii seq. of his Introduction should be compared. Comp. Hillebrandt, pp. 64 seq.

13-14. This is the same way of strewing the grass which is described in the Mânava-Grihya I, 10, 4. 5 ; Khâdira-Grihya I, 2, 9.

16. Comp. Grihya-samgraha I, 85. 97.

17. To the north (of the fire) a Sruva full of water (is placed) : this is the Pra*n*îta water ;

18. If there is (such water). Or it may be dispensed with, say some (teachers).

19. Having put the mess of cooked food on the Barhis, and put wood (on the fire), he prepares the Â*g*ya.

20. (He may take) ghee, or oil made from Tila seeds, or curds, or milk, or rice gruel.

21. From that same Barhis (he takes two Darbha blades and) makes purifiers (of them), of the length of one span.

22. Putting an herb between (them and the instrument with which he cuts them), he cuts them off, not with his nail, with (the words), ' Purifiers are ye, sacred to Vish*n*u.'

23. He then wipes them with water, with (the words), ' By Vish*n*u's mind ye are purified.'

24. Having purified (the Â*g*ya by pouring it into the Â*g*ya pot, over which he has laid a Darbha purifier), he purifies it (in the pot) with the two northward - pointed purifiers (in the following way) :

25. Holding them with his two thumbs and fourth fingers, he purifies (the Â*g*ya) three times, from west to east, once with the Ya*g*us : ' May the god Savit*ri* purify thee with this uninjured purifier, with the rays of the good sun ; ' twice silently.

---

20. All the substances which are stated in this Sûtra can be considered as Â*g*ya. G*ri*hya-sa*m*graha I, 106. 107.

21 seqq. Khâdira-G*ri*hya I, 2, 12 seqq.

24. As to sampûyotpunâti, comp. Hira*n*yake*s*in I, 1, 1, 23 : pavitrântarhite pâtre*pa ânîyopabila*m* pûrayitvodagagrâbhyâ*m* pavitrâbhyâ*m* trir utpûya . . .

26. He then should sprinkle them with water and should throw them into the fire.

27. Then, having put that Â*g*ya on the fire, he should take it from (the fire) towards the north.

28. This is the way to prepare the Â*g*ya.

KÂ*N*DIKÂ 8.

1. To the east (is placed) the Â*g*ya, to the west the mess of cooked food.

2. Having sprinkled (water) round (the fire) and poured Â*g*ya on the mess of cooked food, he begins to sacrifice simply with the pot-ladle, picking out portions of the sacrificial food (without 'underspreading' and pouring Â*g*ya over the Havis).

3. If he intends, however, to sacrifice so as to 'underspread' (the Havis with Â*g*ya) and to pour (Â*g*ya) over it, let him sacrifice first the two Â*g*ya portions (in the following way) :

4. He should take four portions of Â*g*ya—five portions (are taken) by the Bh*ri*gus—and should sacrifice from west to east, on the northern side with (the formula), 'To Agni Svâhâ!' on the southern side with (the words), 'To Soma Svâhâ!'

5. He then cuts off (two or three Avadânas) from the Havis, having 'spread under' (Â*g*ya).

6. (Two Avadânas) from the middle and from the east side, if he (belongs to the families who) make

---

8, 2. On the sprinkling of water round the fire, comp. above, chap. 3, 1 seq. On the technical meaning of upaghâtam, see Bloomfield's note on G*ri*hya-sa*m*graha Pari*s*ish*t*a I, 111 (Zeitschrift der Deutschen Morgenländischen Gesellschaft, XXXV, 568).

3 seq. Comp. Khâdira-G*ri*hya II, 1, 17.

6. Khâdira-G*ri*hya II, 1, 19 seq. The Upastara*n*a (Sûtra 5) and

four Avadânas. (Three Avadânas) from the middle, from the east and from the west side, if (he belongs to those who) make five Avadânas.

7. He sprinkles (Âgya) on the cut-off portions.

8. He anoints the places from which he has cut them off (with Âgya) in order that the strength (of the Havis) may not be lost.

9. He should sacrifice over the middle of the fire with (the words), ' To Agni Svâhâ ! '—

10. Once or thrice, in that same way.

11. Now for the Svish/akrit (oblation), after having ' spread under ' (Âgya), he cuts off once a very big (Avadâna) from the eastern part of the northern part (of the Havis). Twice he should sprinkle (Âgya) on it.

12. But if he (belongs to the families who) make five Avadânas, he should ' spread under ' twice, and cut off (the Avadâna), and sprinkle (Âgya) on it twice.

13. He does not anoint the place from which he has cut off, in order that the strength (of the Havis) may be lost.

14. With the words, ' To Agni Svish/akrit

---

the Abhighârana (Sûtra 7) are reckoned as two Avadânas, so that they form together with the two or three portions cut off from the Havis, four or five Avadânas respectively. On the difference of the families regarding the number of Avadânas, comp. Weber, Indische Studien, X, 95.

7 seqq. Comp. Khâdira-Grihya II, 1, 21–24.

11. Comp. the corresponding regulations of the Srauta ritual at Hillebrandt, Neu- und Vollmondsopfer, 117–119.

13. The same rule re-occurs in the Srauta ritual; Hillebrandt, l. l. 117, note 8.

14. The expression used here uttarârdhapûrvârdhe is also found in most of the corresponding passages of the Srauta ritual,

Svâhâ!' he should sacrifice it over the eastern part of the northern part (of the fire).

15. He should sacrifice oblations of Âgya on (the chief oblations of cooked sacrificial food), with the Mahâvyâhr̄itis.

16. The insertion (stands) before the Svish/akr̄it (oblation).

17. If different sacrifices are performed together, there is only one sweeping (of the ground) round (the fire) (chap. 3, 1), one (putting of) fuel (on the fire) (chap. 7, 19), one Barhis, one sprinkling (of water) round (the fire) (chap. 8, 2), one Âgya, and one offering of the two Âgyabhâgas (chap. 8, 3).

18. Having cut off (the Avadânas) for all (the single sacrifices), he sacrifices the Svish/akr̄it oblation only once.

19. After he has sacrificed, he should throw that pot-ladle (which he has used in the preceding ceremonies) into the fire.

20. Or having washed it, he should take with it (the rest of the sacrificial food), and should eat that.

---

given by Hillebrandt, l. l. 119, note 3. The Khâdira-Gr̄ihya has prâgudî/yâm.

15. If the chief oblations consist in Âgya, they are both preceded and followed by the Mahâvyâhr̄iti oblations. See below, chap. 9, Sûtra 27.

16. On the âvâpa (i. e. the special characteristic offerings of each sacrifice) see Sâṅkhâyana-Gr̄ihya I, 9, 12, and the note there (vol. xxix, p. 28).

19. According to the commentary, etad would belong to sauvish/akr̄itam (Sûtra 18): 'After he has sacrificed that, he should throw the pot-ladle into the fire.' The comparison of Baudhâyana I, 17, 23, atraitan meksha𝑛am âhavanîye‿nupraharati (Hillebrandt, p. 119, note 3), shows that the commentary is wrong, and that etad belongs to meksha𝑛am.

21. The Sruva he should not throw into the fire, say some (teachers).

22. By one who has not set up the sacred fires, the mess of cooked food should be offered to Agni at the festivals both of the full and of the new moon.

23. To Agni, or to Agni and Soma, by one who has set them up, at the full-moon (sacrifice) ;

24. To Indra, or to Indra and Agni, or to Mahendra, at the new-moon (sacrifice).

25. Or also one who has set up the sacred fires, should offer it to Agni at the festivals both of the full and of the new moon.

26. Having put a piece of wood (on the fire), and having afterwards sprinkled (water) round (the fire), he performs the Yagñavâstu ceremony (in the following way) :

27. From that same Barhis he should take a handful of Kusa grass, and should dip it thrice into the Âgya or into the Havis, the points, the middle, and the roots, with (the words), 'May the birds come, licking what has been anointed.'

28. He then should besprinkle that (handful of grass) with water, and should throw it into the fire with (the verse), 'Thou who art the lord of cattle, Rudra, who walkest with the lines (of cattle), the manly one: do no harm to our cattle; let this be offered to thee ! Svâhâ ! '

29. This (ceremony) they call Yagñavâstu.

22-25. Comp. Khâdira-Grihya II, 2, 1-4.

26-29. Khâdira-Grihya II, 1, 26 seq.; Grihya-samgraha II, 1 seq.

27. The expression tata eva barhishah has occurred already at chap. 7, 21. The Mantra re-occurs in Vâg. Samhitâ II, 16e, &c.

KÂNDIKÂ 9.

1. He then should take away the remnants of the Havis in a northern direction, should take them out (of the vessel in which they are), and should give them to the Brahman.

2. He should try to satiate him.

3. They say indeed with regard to sacrifice: 'Through the Brâhmana's being satiated (with sacrificial food) I become satiated myself.'

4. Then (he should give to the Brahman) what other food has just become ready.

5. Then he should try to gain the favour of Brâhmanas by (gifts of) food.

6. A full vessel constitutes the fee for the sacrifice; that he should give to the Brahman.

7. A brazen vessel or a wooden cup which has been filled with food, with prepared food or with raw food, or even only with fruits: this they call a full vessel.

8. The Brahman is the only officiating priest at the Pâkayagñas.

9. (The sacrificer) himself is Hotri.

10. A full vessel (see Sûtra 7) is the lowest sacrificial fee at a Pâkayagña.

11. The highest is unlimited.

12. Thus Sudâs Paigavana, after having offered the sacrifice of a mess of cooked food to Indra and

---

9, 1. Khâdira-Grihya II, 1, 29.

6 seqq. Khâdira-Grihya II, 1, 30. 31.

8, 9. The native authorities divide these two Sûtras after *ritvik*; I propose to divide after pâkayagñeshu.

12. The commentary here refers to the rule of the Drâhyâyana-sûtra (=Lâtyâyana VIII, 1, 2): samkhyâmâtre *ka* dakshinâ gâvah.

Agni, gave one hundred thousand (cows as the sacrificial fee).

13. Now if he should not be able to get for the morning or for the evening oblation, or for the sacrifices of the full or of the new moon at his (sacred) domestic fire, any substance fit for sacrifice or a person who could sacrifice (instead of himself, if he is prevented) : what ought he to do ?

14. Until the evening oblation the (time for the) morning oblation is not elapsed, nor the (time for the) evening oblation until the morning oblation. Until the new moon the (time for the) sacrifice of the full moon is not elapsed, nor the (time for the) sacrifice of the new moon until the full moon.

15. During that interval he should try to obtain sacrificial food or to find a sacrificer.

16. Or (if he does not succeed in this) he should cook fruits or leaves of trees or herbs which are sacrificially pure, and should sacrifice them.

17. Or he should at least sacrifice water ; thus has said Pâkayag*ña*, the son of I*d*â. For (even if he offers only water) the sacrifice has been performed.

18. And there is an expiation for one who has not sacrificed.

---

14 seq. Khâdira-Gr*i*hya II, 2, 5 seq. ; Sâṅkhâyana-Gr*i*hya I, 3, 6.

16 seqq. Khâdira-Gr*i*hya II, 2, 10 seqq. In this teacher Pâkayag*ña*, son of I*d*â, whose opinion on the performance of certain Pâkayag*ña*s is here stated, we have of course to see a fictitious sage of the same kind with the well-known *R*i*shi Pragâtha, to whom the authorship of a number of Sûktas in the Pragâtha book (Rigveda, Ma*n*dala VIII) is ascribed.

18, 19. By the repetition of iti these Sûtras seem to be characterised as continuing the statement of Pâkayag*ña*'s opinion ; comp. Dr. Knauer's Introduction, p. xviii. As to Sûtra 18, comp. Sâṅkhâyana-Gr*i*hya I, 3, 9.

19. And, (says Pâkayag̃a,) a Brâhma*n*a should not omit to keep his vow.

20. Here they say also:

21. He should keep (his vow) during that time in which he does not sacrifice, by abstaining from food.

22. When he then has obtained (the necessary substances for sacrificing), he should make up for the (omitted) oblations.

23. For thus also his vow has been duly kept.

24. These rules (which have been given with regard to the sacrifices of the full and new moon) are valid for the Havis oblations which will be stated hereafter.

25. After the end of the Mantra follows the word Svâhâ.

26. At Âg*y*a oblations he should only prepare that Âg*y*a (chap. 7, 28) and should sacrifice it, picking out portions of it. (He should) not (sacrifice) the two Âg*y*a portions nor the Svish*t*ak*r*it.

27. At Âg*y*a oblations he should, if no special rule is given, sacrifice with the Mahâvyâh*r*itis before and after (the chief ceremonies).

---

22. 'He should count the omitted (oblations), should pour the corresponding number of oblations into his vessel, and should sacrifice them in the due way all at once with one Mantra. In the same way also the other oblations (belonging to other gods).' Karmapradîpa.

24. Is Havis here used as opposed to Âg*y*a (Sûtra 26), in the same way in which Kâtyâyana says (*S*raut. I, 9, 1. 20): 'vrîhîn yavân vâ havishi; ubhayata âgya*m* havisha*h*'? Comp. below, III, 8, 10; Âsvalâyana-Gr*i*hya I, 10, 26.

25. Khâdira-Gr*i*hya I, 1, 15.

26. As to upaghâtam, comp. the note on chap. 8, 2.

27. Sânkhâyana-Gr*i*hya I, 12, 13; Khâdira-Gr*i*hya I, 3, 12–13, where the traditional division of the Sûtras differs from that which is supported by tradition in the text of Gobhila. Gobhila has used

28. As at the wedding, thus at the tonsure (of the child's head), the initiation (of the Brahma*k*ârin), and at the cutting of the beard.

29. At the end of the ceremony the Vâmadevya is sung for the sake of averting evil. The Vâmadevya is sung for the sake of averting evil.

End of the First Prapâ*th*aka.

---

the word â*g*yâhutishu in the beginning of Sûtra 26, and it would have been superfluous if he had repeated it in connection with the words nâ*g*yabhâgau na svish*t*akr*i*t. In the corresponding Sûtras of the Khâdira the case was different, and there the words nâ*g*yabhâgau na svish*t*akr*i*t inevitably required the addition of a word like â*g*yâhutishu, by which to show which class of sacrifices it was which required no Â*g*yabhâgas and no Svish*t*akr*i*t. The following word in the Khâdira text, however, anâde*s*e, should be referred, against tradition, to Sûtra 13, as is shown by the comparison of *S*âṅkhâyana-Gr*i*hya I, 12, 13.

28. At the wedding, oblations are made first with the three single Mahâvyâhr*i*tis, afterwards with the Mahâvyâhr*i*tis together; see below, II, 1, 25. 26. The tonsure of the child's head is treated of below, II, 9; the initiation (upanayana), II, 10; the cutting of the beard, III, 1. Comp. Khâdira-Gr*i*hya, I, 3, 10.

29. Apav*ri*tte karma*n*i should be corrected into apav*ri*kte karma*n*i, as has been noticed in the Petersburg Dictionary, s. v. apa-vart. The *S*âṅkhâyana-Gr*i*hya I, 2, 1 says karmâpavarge.

PRAPÂTHAKA II, KÂNDIKÂ 1.

1. Under a propitious Nakshatra let him take a wife—

2. Who should possess the auspicious characteristics in due way.

3. If he can find no such (woman, he should take) earth-clods—

4. From an altar, a furrow, a pool, a cow-stable, a place where four roads meet, a gambling-place, a place where corpses are burnt, and from sterile soil;

5. A ninth (earth-clod) mixed of all.

6. (These he should make) equal (and should) make marks at them.

7. Taking them in his hand he should offer them to the girl, and (reciting the formula): ' Right alone is the first; right nobody oversteps; on right this earth is founded. May N. N. become this universe!' —he should pronounce her name and should say: ' Take one of these.'

8. If she takes one of the first four (clods), he should marry her,

---

1, 1–4. Description of the wedding. Comp. Indische Studien, V, 288, 305 seq.; 312 seq.; 368 seq.

2. In translating kusalena I have been guided by the comparison of I, 5, 26 (comp. Böhtlingk-Roth, s. v. kusala). The commentary understands the Sûtra in a different way. He should take a woman who possesses auspicious characteristics commended by one versed (kusala) in the characteristics of women. If he can find no such person who is able to judge, he should, &c. (Sûtra 3).

4. Comp. Âsvalâyana-Grihya I, 5, 5; Grihya-samgraha II, 21–23.

7. Âsvalâyana-Grihya, l. l. § 4.

9. And according to some (teachers) also, if (she takes) the mixed one.

10. After she has been washed with Klîtaka, barley and beans, a friend should besprinkle her three times at her head, so that her whole body becomes wet, with Surâ of first quality, with (the formula), 'Kâma! I know thy name. Intoxication thou art by name,' &c. (Mantra-Brâhmana I, 1, 2). (In the passage of the formula), ' Bring hither N. N.,' he should pronounce the husband's name. (The Mantras should have) the word Svâhâ at their end. With the two following verses he should wash her private parts.

11. That has to be done by (female) relatives (of the bride).

12. At the wedding wood has been put on the fire to the east of the house, on a surface besmeared (with cow-dung).

13. Then one of the people who assist at the wedding, fills a cup with ' firm ' water, and having walked with the water-pot round the fire on its front side, silent, wrapped in his robe, he stations himself to the south (of the fire), facing the north.

14. Another person with a goad (walks in the same way and stations himself in the same place).

9. See Sûtra 5.

10. 'With Klîtaka,' &c., means, with water into which Klîtaka, &c., has been thrown; comp. Grîhya-samgraha II, 15. ' Surâ of first quality ' is Surâ prepared from molasses; see Grîhya-samgraha II, 16. Comp., however, also Grîhya-samgraha II, 41.

13. Khâdira-Grîhya I, 3, 5 ; Grîhya-samgraha II, 25. 26. 'Firm water' seems to be water which does not dry up. The Grîhya-samgraha says : 'Water that has its smell, its colour, and its taste, which is in great rivers, in wells and other receptacles, and in ponds: such water is called "firm;" this is the fixed meaning.' Comp. Bloomfield's note, Z. D. M. G. XXXV, 574.

15. They place roasted grain mixed with *S*amî leaves, to the amount of four handfuls, in a winnowing basket behind the fire,

16. And an upper mill-stone.

17. Now (the girl) whose hand he is going to seize, has been washed, (her whole body) including her head.

18. The husband should put on her a (new) garment which has not yet been washed, with the verse, 'They who spun' (Mantra-Brâhma*n*a I, 1, 5), and with (the verse), 'Put on her, dress her' (l. l. 6).

19. Leading forward (from the house to the sacred fire, the bride) who is wrapped in her robe and wears the sacrificial cord over her left shoulder, he should murmur (the verse), 'Soma gave her to the Gandharva' (MB. I, 1, 7).

20. While she, to the west of the fire, pushes forward with her foot a rush-mat or something else of that kind, veiled (with clothes), he should make her say: 'May the way which my husband goes, be open to me.'

21. If she does not murmur (these words out of shame, &c.), he should murmur (them, saying), 'To her' (instead of 'To me').

22. She should make the end of the rush-mat (Sûtra 20) reach the end of the Barhis.

23. On the east end of the rush-mat she sits down to the right of the bridegroom.

17–19. Khâdira-Gr*i*hya I, 3, 6. Ya*g*ñopavîtinîm in Sûtra 19 means, according to the commentary, that she wears her outer garment arranged like the sacrificial cord, over her left shoulder; for women are not allowed to wear the sacrificial cord itself.

20. Gr*i*hya-sa*m*graha II, 27 seq.

24. While she touches his right shoulder with her
right hand, he sacrifices six oblations of Âgya with
(the verse), 'May Agni go as the first,' and the
following (verses) (MB. I, 1, 9–14)—

25. And (three oblations) with the Mahâvyâhritis,
one by one ;

26. A fourth with (the four Mahâvyâhritis) together.

KÂNDIKÂ 2.

1. After the sacrifice they both arise.

2. The husband passes behind her back, stations
himself to the south, with his face turned to the
north, and seizes the woman's joined hands.

3. (Standing) to the east (of the girl) her mother
or her brother, having taken the roasted grain,
should make the bride tread on the stone with the
tip of her right foot.

4. The bridegroom murmurs : 'Tread on this
stone' (MB. I, 2, 1).

5. Her brother filling once his joined hands with
roasted grain, pours it into the bride's joined hands.

6. After (Âgya) has been spread under and poured
over (the fried grain), she sacrifices that in the fire
without opening her joined hands, with (the verse
which the bridegroom [?] recites), ' This woman says'
(MB. I, 2, 2).

7. (The verses), 'The god Aryaman,' and, 'Pû-

24–26. Khâdira-Grihya I, 3, 11–13.

2, 1 seqq. Khâdira-Grihya I, 3, 16 seqq.

3. The roasted grain is that mentioned chap. 1, 15, the stone,
Sûtra 16.

6. Comp. Grihya-samgraha II, 34.

7. On the repetitions of the lâgâhoma, see below, Sûtras 9. 10.

shan' (l. l. 3. 4) (are repeated) at the two following (oblations of fried grain).

8. After that sacrifice the husband, passing (behind her back), returns in the same way, and leads her round the fire so that their right sides are turned towards it, or a Brâhmana versed in the Mantras (does the same), with (the verse), 'The maid from the fathers' (MB. I, 2, 5).

9. After she has thus been lead round, she stands as before (Sûtras 1. 2), and treads (on the stone) as before (Sûtra 3), and he murmurs the (Mantra) as before (Sûtra 4), and (her brother) pours (the fried grain into her hands) as before (Sûtra 5), and she sacrifices as before (Sûtra 6).

10. In the same way three times.

11. After (she) has poured the remnants (of the fried grain) into the fire, they make (her) step forward in a north-easterly direction with (the formula), 'For sap with one step' (MB. I, 2, 6. 7).

12. She should put forward her right foot (first) and should follow with the left.

13. (The bridegroom) should say (to her), 'Do not put the left (foot) before the right.'

14. The lookers-on he should address with (the verse), 'Auspicious ornaments wears this woman' (l. l. 8).

15. To the west of the fire the water-carrier follows (their way) and besprinkles the bridegroom on his forehead, and also the other one (i. e. the bride),

---

8. As to the words 'in the same way,' see the second Sûtra of this chapter.

14-16. Khâdira-Grihya I, 3, 27-31.

15. Comp. Sânkhâyana-Grihya I, 12, 5 note (vol. xxix, p. 33). The water-carrier is the person mentioned chap. 1, 13.

with this verse (which the bridegroom murmurs),
' May (the Visve devâs) anoint (or, unite) ' (l. l. 9).

16. After she has been (thus) besprinkled, he
puts up her joined hands with his left hand, seizes
with his right hand her right hand with the thumb,
her hand being turned with the palm upwards, and
murmurs these six verses referring to the seizing of
(a girl's) hand, ' I seize thy hand ' (MB. I, 2, 10–15).

17. When (these verses) are finished, they carry
her away—

KÂNDIKÂ 3.

1. To a convenient house of a Brâhmana, which
is situated in a north-easterly direction.

2. There wood has been put on the (nuptial) fire.

3. To the west of the fire a red bull's hide has
been spread out, with the neck to the east and with
the hair outside.

• 4. On that they make the woman, who has to
keep silence, sit down.

5. And (there) she remains sitting until the stars
appear.

6. When (somebody) has said that a star has
appeared, (the husband) sacrifices six oblations of
Âgya with the (six verses) commencing with (the
verse), ' In the junctions of the lines ' (l. l. I, 3, 1–6).

7. The remnants of each oblation he should pour
out over the bride's head.

8. After the sacrifice they arise, go out (of the
house), and he shows her the ' firm star ' (i. e. the
polar-star).

3, 1 seqq. Khâdira-Grihya I, 4, 1 seqq.

3. This is the standing description of the bull's hide used at the
Srauta or Grihya ceremonies; comp. Sânkhâyana I, 16, 1 note.

9. (Repeating the formula): 'Firm art thou. May I, N. N., become firm in the house of N. N., my husband'—she should pronounce her husband's and her own name.

10. And (he shows her besides the star) Arundhatî.

11. (She says): 'I (N. N.) am held fast,' &c., as above (Sûtra 9).

12. He then addresses her with the verse, 'Firm is the sky' (MB. I, 3, 7).

13. After she has been addressed (thus), she respectfully calls her Guru by his Gotra name.

14. Thus she breaks her silence.

15. From that time through a period of three nights they should both avoid eating saline or pungent food, and should sleep together on the ground without having conjugal intercourse.

16. Here, they say, an Argha reception (should be offered to the young husband).

17. Some say (that this reception should be offered) when (the bridegroom and his companions) have arrived (at the house of the bride's father).

18. The first food which he eats, should be food

---

10. Âsvalâyana-Grihya I, 7, 22.

11. The play on words (Arundhatî—ruddhâ) is untranslatable.

13. 'Her Guru' means, according to the commentary, her husband. The commentary quotes the well-known sentence: patir eko guruh strînâm. Perhaps we may also take the Guru for the Brâhmana in whose house they stay. Comp. also chap. 4, 11.

14. Comp. above, Sûtra 4.

16, 17. Khâdira-Grihya I, 4, 7. 8. Comp. Sânkhâyana-Grihya I, 12, 10 note. The Gobhila commentary states that this Argha reception should be offered by the bride's father. On the different opinions of the Sânkhâyana commentaries see the note quoted.

18. Khâdira-Grihya I, 4, 10.

fit for sacrifice, over which he has murmured (the verses quoted in Sûtra 21).

19. Or he should prepare on the following day a mess of cooked food, of which they eat together.

20. The deities to whom it belongs, are, Agni, Pragâpati, the Visve devâs, and Anumati.

21. Having taken that food out (of the vessel in which it is), and having spread it out, he should touch one part of it with his hand, with (the verses), 'With the tie of food, with the jewel' (MB. I, 3, 8–10).

22. After he has eaten, and has given the rest to the wife, (they may do) what they like.

23. A cow is the sacrificial fee.

KÂNDIKÂ 4.

1. When she mounts the chariot, let him murmur the verse, 'Adorned with Kimsuka flowers, of Sal-mali wood' (MB. I, 3, 11).

2. On the way he should address crossways, rivers and unevennesses (of the soil), big trees, and burial grounds, with (the verse), 'May no waylayers meet us' (ibid. 12).

3. If the axle breaks, or something that is bound gets loose, or if the chariot is overturned, or if some other accident happens, they should put wood on the fire which they carry with themselves, should

22. Khâdira-Grihya I, 4, 11. 14.
23. Khâdira-Grihya I, 4, 6.
4. The way of the bridegroom with the bride to their new home, and their arrival.
2. Perhaps a part of this Sûtra is based on a half Sloka, the two parts of which have been transposed in the prose version, mahâ-vrikshân smasânam ka nadîs ka vishamâni ka.
3. Comp. Pâraskara I, 10.

make oblations (of Âgya) with the Vyâhritis, should
procure a new piece (instead of that which has been
damaged), and should besmear it with the remnants
of the Âgya (that has been offered), with (the verse),
'He who without binding' (Sâma-veda I, 244).

4. Having sung the Vâmadevya, he should mount
(again).

5. When they have arrived, the Vâmadevya (is
sung).

6. When (the bride) has reached the house, Brâhmana women of good character, whose husbands
and sons are living, make her descend (from the
chariot), and make her sit down on a bull's hide
with (the verse which the husband recites), 'Here,
ye cows, bring forth calves' (MB. I, 3, 13).

7. They should place a boy in her lap.

8. Into the joined hands of that (boy) they should
throw lotus-roots (?),

9. Or fruits.

10. After she has made that boy rise, she sacrifices the eight 'firm' Âgya oblations with (the formula), 'Here is steadiness' (MB. I, 3, 14).

11. When she has finished, she puts a piece of
wood (on the fire) and respectfully salutes the Gurus,
according to seniority, with their Gotra names. Then
they may do what they like.

---

8. The explanation of *sakalola* as *sâlûka* is doubtful.   Prof.
Weber believes that we ought to read *sakaloshtân* (lumps of
dung) ; see Indische Studien, V, 371.

10. 'Firm' oblations seem to mean oblations by which the wife
obtains a firm abode in her husband's house.   Comp. Indische
Studien, V, 376.

KÂNDIKÂ 5.

1. Now (follow) the ceremonies of the fourth day.

2. Having put wood on the fire, he four times sacrifices expiatory Âgya oblations with (the formula), 'Agni! Thou art expiation' (MB. I, 4, 1)—

3. (And with the same formula), putting instead of Agni, Vâyu, Kandra, and Sûrya;

4. A fifth oblation (with the names of the four gods) together, changing (in the Mantra the singular) into the plural.

5. The remnants of each oblation he should pour into a water-pot.

6. With that (Âgya) they besmear her body, including her hair and nails, remove (that water and Âgya by rubbing her), and wash her.

7. After three nights have passed, they should cohabit, according to some (teachers).

8. When she has had her monthly illness and the blood has ceased to flow, that is the time for cohabiting.

9. With his right hand he should touch her secret parts with the verse, 'May Vishnu make thy womb

5, 1. The Katurthîkarman.

2, 3. Comp. Sânkhâyana-Grihya I, 18, 3; Khâdira-Grihya I, 4, 12.

4. I. e. instead of prâyaskitte (expiation) he uses the plural prâyaskittayah; and he says, 'you are the expiations of the gods,' &c.

6. Khâdira-Grihya I, 4, 13. Hrâsayitvâ literally means, 'having shortened her.' She is 'shortened' by the removing of the substance with which they have besmeared her (hrâsayitvâ udvartanâdinâ tad abhyanganam apanîya, says the commentary). Comp. on the technical meaning of hrâsana the Grihya-samgraha II, 38, 8–10; Khâdira-Grihya I, 4, 15. 16.

ready' (MB. I, 4, 6), and with that, 'Give conception, Sinîvâlî' (l. l. 7).

10. When those two verses are finished, they cohabit.

KÂ*ND*IKÂ 6.

1. The beginning of the third month of pregnancy is the time for the Pu*m*savana (i. e. the ceremony to secure the birth of a son).

2. In the morning, after she has been washed, sitting on northward-pointed Darbha grass, (all over her body) including her head, she sits down to the west of the fire on northward-pointed Darbha grass, facing the east.

3. Her husband, standing behind her, should grasp down with his right hand over her right shoulder, and should touch the uncovered place of her navel with the verse, 'The two men, Mitra and Varu*n*a' (MB. I, 4, 8).

4. Then they may do what they like.

5. Then afterwards (the following ceremony should be performed).

6. In a north-easterly direction, having bought for three times seven barley corns or beans a Nyag-rodha shoot which has fruits on both sides, which is not dry and not touched by worms, he should set that up.

7. (He buys it with the Mantras) :

6, 1 seq. The Pu*m*savana. Khâdira-G*ri*hya II, 2, 17 seq. On âdisade*s*e the commentary says, âdisadése âdisamîpapradese prathame t*ri*tîyabhâge, ity etat. âdimadesa iti pâ*th*e vyakta evârtha*h*. To me it seems probable that âdimade*s*e is the true reading.

7. The first Mantra consists of seven sections; with each of

'If thou belongest to Soma, I buy thee for the king Soma.

'If thou belongest to Varu*n*a, I buy thee for the king Varu*n*a.

'If thou belongest to the Vasus, I buy thee for the Vasus.

'If thou belongest to the Rudras, I buy thee for the Rudras.

'If thou belongest to the Âdityas, I buy thee for the Âdityas.

'If thou belongest to the Maruts, I buy thee for the Maruts.

'If thou belongest to the Vi*s*ve devâs, I buy thee for the Vi*s*ve devâs.'

8. He should set it up with (the Mantra), 'Ye herbs, being well-minded, bestow strength on this (shoot); for it will do its work.' Then he should put grass around it, should take it, and place it in the open air.

9. Having washed a nether mill-stone, a student or a (wife) addicted (to her husband), a person who is a Brâhma*n*a by birth (only and not by learning), or a girl, pounds (that Nyagrodha shoot) without moving backward (the stone with which she pounds it).

10. In the morning, after she has been washed, sitting on northward-pointed Darbha grass, (all over her body), including her head, she lies down to the west of the fire on northward-pointed Darbha grass, with her head to the east.

11. Her husband, standing behind her, should seize (the pounded Nyagrodha shoot) with the

---

these sections he should, according to the commentary, give three barley corns or beans to the owner of the Nyagrodha tree, or put them down at the root of the tree.

thumb and the fourth finger of his right hand, and should insert it into her right nostril with the verse, 'A man is Agni, a man is Indra' (MB. I, 4, 9).

12. Then they should do what they like.

KÂNDIKÂ 7.

1. Now (follows) the Simantakara*n*a (or parting of the hair), in her first pregnancy,—

2. In the fourth, or sixth, or eighth month (of her pregnancy).

3. In the morning, after she has been washed, sitting on northward-pointed Darbha grass, (all over her body), including her head, she sits down to the west of the fire on northward-pointed Darbha grass, facing the east.

4. Her husband, standing behind her, ties (to her neck) an Udumbara branch with an even number of unripe fruits on it, with (the verse), ' Rich in sap is this tree ' (MB. I, 5, 1).

5. He then parts her hair upwards (i. e. beginning from the front), the first time with Darbha blades, with (the word), ' Bhû*h* !' the second time with (the word), ' Bhuva*h* !' the third time with (the word), ' Sva*h* !'—

6. Then with (a splint of) Vîratara (wood) with this verse, ' With which Aditi's ' (ibid. 2) ;

7, 1 seq. The Sîmantakara*n*a or Sîmantonnayana. Khâdira-G*ri*hya II, 2, 24 seq.

3. This Sûtra is identical with chap. 6, 2.

4. *s*alâ*u*grathnam should be emended, in my opinion, so as to read *s*alâ*u*grapsam. Comp. Pâraskara I, 15, 4: yugmena sa*s*âlugrapsenaudumbare*n*a. Âsvalâyana I, 14, 4: yugmena *s*alâ*u*glapsena. Hira*n*yakesin II, 1 : salâtugrapsam upasa*m*g*ri*hya.

7. Then with a full spindle, with this verse, 'I invoke Râkâ' (ibid. 3. 4);

8. And with a porcupine's quill that has three white spots, with (the verse), 'Which are thy blessings, O Râkâ' (ibid. 5).

9. (There should be prepared) a mess of boiled rice with sesamum seeds, covered with ghee; at that he should make her look.

10. Let him say to her, 'What dost thou see?' and make her answer, 'Offspring!'

11. That (food) she should eat herself.

12. Brâhmana women should sit by her side, pronouncing auspicious words (such as), 'A mother of valiant sons! A mother of living sons! A living husband's wife!'

13. Now (follows) the sacrifice for the woman in labour.

14. When the child is appearing, he strews (Darbha grass) round the fire and sacrifices two Âgya oblations with this verse, 'She who athwart' (MB. I, 5, 6), and with (the verse), 'Vipaskit has taken away' (ibid. 7).

15. 'A male he will be born, N. N. by name'—(in this passage of the last verse) he pronounces a name.

16. What that (name is), is kept secret.

17. When they announce to him that a son has been born, he should say, 'Delay still cutting off the navel-string and giving him the breast.'

18. Let him have rice and barley-grains pounded in the same way as the (Nyagrodha) shoot.

---

13 seq. The soshyantîhoma. Khâdira-Grihya II, 2, 28 seq.

17 seq. Ceremonies for the new-born child (Gâtakarman). Khâdira-Grihya II, 2, 32 seq.

18. See above, chap. 6, 9.

19. Seizing (that pounded substance) with the thumb and the fourth finger of his right hand, he smears it on the tongue of the boy, with the formula, 'This order' (MB. I, 5, 8).

20. In the same way the production of intelligence (is performed). He should give to eat (to the child) clarified butter.

21. Or he takes it with gold (i. e. with a golden spoon) and sacrifices it on the face of the boy with this verse, 'May Mitra and Varuna bestow intelligence on thee' (MB. I, 5, 9), and with (the verse), 'The lord of the seat, the wonderful' (Sâma-veda I, 171).

22. Let him say, 'Cut off the navel-string,' and, 'Give the breast (to the child).'

23. From that time let him not touch (his wife) until ten nights have passed.

KÂNDIKÂ 8.

1. On the third (Tithi) of the third bright fortnight after his birth, in the morning the father has the child washed, including his head, and after sunset, when the evening-red has disappeared, he worships (the moon), holding up his joined hands.

2. Then the mother, having dressed the son in a clean garment, hands him, from south to north, with his face turned to the north, to the father.

---

19. Comp. above, chap. 6, 11.

23. The impurity (asauka) of the mother lasts through ten days after her confinement; comp. the note on Sânkhâyana-Grihya I, 25, 1 (vol. xxix, p. 51).

8, 1 seq. Khâdira-Grihya II, 3, 1 seq.

3. She then passes behind his back and stations herself to the north (of her husband).

4. He then murmurs (the three verses), 'Thy heart, O thou whose hair is well parted' (MB. I, 5, 10–12), and after he has, with the words (standing at the end of verse 12), 'That this son may not come to harm (and thus be torn) from his mother'—

5. Handed him, from south to north, to his mother, they may do what they like.

6. Then in the following bright fortnights (at the time) stated above (Sûtra 1), the father, filling his joined hands with water and turning his face towards the moon, worships it—

7. Letting (the water) flow (out of his joined hands) once with the Yagus, 'What in the moon' (MB. I, 5, 13), and twice silently. Then they may do what they like.

8. When ten nights have elapsed after (the child's) birth, or a hundred nights, or one year, the Nâmadheyakara*n*a (or giving a name to the child, is performed).

9. He who is going to perform (that ceremony—the father or a representative of the father), sits down to the west of the fire on northward-pointed Darbha grass, facing the east.

10. Then the mother, having dressed the son in a clean garment, hands him, from south to north,

---

6. I am not sure about the meaning of prathamoddish*t*a eva. I have translated according to the commentary, which has the following note : prathamoddish*t*a eva prathama*m* ya*h* kâla uddish*t*a*h* kathita*h* tasminn eva kâle t*ri*tîyâyâm ity etat.—The commentary then mentions a reading prathamodita eva, in which udita may either be derived from vad or from ud-i.

8 seq. The Nâmakara*n*a. Khâdira-G*ri*hya II, 3, 6 seq.

10, 11. Comp. above, Sûtras 2. 3.

with his face turned to the north, to the performer (of the ceremony).

11. She then passes behind his back and sits down to the north (of him), on northward-pointed Darbha grass.

12. He then sacrifices to Pragâpati, to the Tithi (of the child's birth), to the Nakshatra (of the child's birth), and to the (presiding) deity (of that Tithi and of that Nakshatra).

13. He then murmurs the Mantra, 'Who art thou? What person art thou?' (MB. I, 5, 14. 15), touching the sense-organs at (the boy's) head.

14. In (the passage of the Mantra), 'Enter upon the month, that belongs to Ahaspati (i. e. the lord of days), N. N.!' and at the end of the Mantra he should give him a name beginning with a sonant, with a semivowel in it, with a long vowel or the Visarga at the end, (and formed with) a K*ri*t (suffix).

15. It should not contain a Taddhita (suffix).

16. (He should give a name with) an odd (number of syllables), ending in -dâ, to girls.

17. And after he has told the name to the mother first, they may do what they like.

18. A cow constitutes the sacrificial fee.

19. Every month (after the birth) of the boy, (or)

---

12. Sânkhâyana-Gr*i*hya I, 25, 5. In the same Gr*i*hya the enumeration of the Nakshatras with their presiding deities is given, I, 26.

· 14. Sânkhâyana-Gr*i*hya I, 24, 4; Âsvalâyana I, 15, 4; Pâraskara I, 17, 2. In the text read dîrghâbhinish*th*ânânta*m* instead of dîrghâbhinish*th*ânânta*m*.

19. Monthly sacrifice in commemoration of the child's birth. Possibly we should translate: Every month (after the birth) of the boy, through one year (comp. Sânkhâyana I, 25, 10. 11), or on the Parvan days, &c.

after one year, or on the Parvan days of the year
(i. e. on the last Tithi of each of the three seasons)
he should sacrifice to Agni and Indra, to Heaven
and Earth, and to the Visve devâs.

20. Having sacrificed to the deity (of the Tithi
and of the Nakshatra respectively), he should sacrifice to the Tithi and to the Nakshatra.

21. When (the father) returns from a journey, or
when (the son) begins to know, 'This is my father,'
or when (the son) has been initiated, (the father)
should grasp with his two hands his son round the
head, and should murmur, 'From limb by limb thou
art produced' (MB. I, 5, 16–18).

22. With (the formula), '.With the cattle's him-
kâra I kiss thee' (l. l. 19) he should kiss him. Then
he may do what he likes.

23. In the same way (he should do) to his
younger sons—

24. According to their age or in the order in
which he meets them.

25. Girls he should silently kiss on their head;
he should silently kiss them on their head.

---

20. Sânkhâyana-Grihya I, 25, 6.

21 seq. The father's returning from a journey. Khâdira-
Grihya II, 3, 13 seq. As to upeta, comp. Sânkhâyana-Grihya II, 1,
1 note. The position of the words in Sûtra 21 is irregular, so as
to raise the suspicion that the words yadâ vâ . . . upetasya vâ
('or when the son begins to know . . . has been initiated') are an
insertion into the text of Gobhila, made by a later compiler, or into
a more ancient text, made by Gobhila himself. Comp. Pâraskara
I, 18.

25. As to the repetition of the last words of this Sûtra, see the
notes on I, 4, 31; II, 10, 50; III, 6, 15.

KÂ*ND*IKÂ 9.

1. Now follows the tonsure of the child's head, in the third year.

2. To the east of the house on a surface besmeared (with cow-dung) wood has been put on the fire.

3. There the following things have been placed:

4. To the south (of the fire) twenty-one Darbha blades, a brass vessel with hot water, a razor of Udumbara wood or a mirror, and a barber with a razor in his hand;

5. To the north, bull's dung and a mess of boiled rice with sesamum seeds which may be more or less cooked.

6. Let them fill vessels separately with rice and barley, with sesamum seeds and beans, and let them place (those vessels) to the east (of the fire).

7. The boiled rice with sesamum seeds (Sûtra 5) and all seeds (mentioned in Sûtra 6) are given to the barber.

8. Then the mother, having dressed the son in a clean garment, sits down to the west of the fire on northward-pointed Darbha grass, facing the east.

9, 1. The *K*û*d*âkara*n*a. Khâdira-Gr*i*hya II, 3, 16 seq. On the literal meaning of *K*û*d*âkara*n*a, see *S*âṅkhâyana I, 28, 1 note.

2. Comp. above, II, 1, 13.

5. Comp. above, chap. 7, 9; Gr*i*hya-sa*m*graha II, 39.

6. I believe that four vessels were filled, one with rice, one with barley, one with sesamum seeds, and one with beans. The Dvandva compounds vrîhiyavais and tilamâshais cannot justify the conclusion that one vessel was filled with rice and barley mixed, and another with sesamum seeds and beans, for the plural pâtrâ*n*i shows that there were more than two vessels. Â*s*valâyana I, 17, 2, says, vrîhiyavamâshatilânâ*m* pr*i*thak pû*rn*asarâvâ*n*i.

9. To the west (of her), facing the east, the person stations himself who is going to perform that (ceremony).

10. He then murmurs, fixing his thoughts on Savit*ri*, looking at the barber, (the Mantra), 'Hither has come Savit*ri* with his razor' (MB. I, 6, 1).

11. And fixing his thoughts on Vâyu, looking at the brass vessel with warm water, (he murmurs the Mantra), 'With warm water, O Vâyu, come hither' (ibid. 2).

12. Drawing water (out of that vessel) with his right hand he moistens the patch of hair on the right side (of the boy's head) with (the Mantra), 'May the waters moisten thee for life' (ibid. 3).

13. With (the Mantra), 'Vish*nu*'s tusk art thou' (ibid. 4) he looks at the razor of Udumbara wood or at the mirror.

14. With (the Mantra), 'Herb! Protect him!' (ibid. 5) he puts seven Darbha blades, with their points turned towards (the boy's) head, into the patch of hair on the right side of his head.

15. Pressing them down with his left hand, and seizing with his right hand the razor of Udumbara wood or the mirror, he touches with it (the Darbha blades), with the (Mantra), 'Axe! Do no harm to him!' (ibid. 6).

16. With (the Mantra), 'With which Pûshan has shaven B*ri*haspati's head' (ibid. 7), he moves forward (that razor or the mirror) three times towards the east without cutting (the hair); once with the Ya*g*us, twice silently.

---

11. I have translated the Mantra according to the reading of Âsvalâyana (G*ri*hya I, 17, 6) and Pâraskara (II, 1, 6): ush*n*ena Vâya udakenehi. Gobhila has udakenaidhi.

17. Then (the barber) with the razor of metal cuts the hair and throws (the cut off hair ends) on the bull's dung.

18. In the same way (after the same rites have been performed), he cuts the patch of hair on the back-side;   •

19. And that on the left side.

20. He should repeat (when going to cut the hair on the back-side, and then again on the left side, the rites stated above), beginning from the moistening of the hair (Sûtra 12).

21. Grasping with his two hands (the boy) round his head he should murmur (the verse), ' The three-fold age of Gamadagni' (MB. I, 6, 8).

22. In the same way (the rites are performed) for a girl,

23. (But) silently.

24. The sacrifice, however, (is performed) with the Mantra.

25. Walking away from the fire in a northerly direction they have the arrangement of (the boy's) hair made according to the custom of his Gotra and of his family.

26. They throw the hair on the bull's dung (mentioned above), take it to the forest, and bury it.

27. Some throw them on a bunch (of grass or the like).

---

20. Thus on the back-side seven Darbha blades are put into the hair, and on the left side seven. This makes, together with the seven blades put into the hair on the right side (Sûtra 14), twenty-one, the number stated in Sûtra 4.

24. In the description of the Kûdâkarana given in this chapter no sacrifice is mentioned. See, however, I, 9, 28.

25. Grihya-samgraha II, 40.

28. Then they may do what they like.

29. A cow constitutes the sacrificial fee.

KÂNDIKÂ 10.

1. In the eighth year after the conception let him initiate a Brâhmana,

2. In the eleventh year after the conception a Kshatriya,

3. In the twelfth year after the conception a Vaisya.

4. Until the sixteenth year the time has not passed for a Brâhmana, until the twenty-second for a Kshatriya, until the twenty-fourth for a Vaisya.

5. After that (time has passed), they become patitasâvitrîka (i. e. they have lost their right of being taught the Sâvitrî).

6. Let them not initiate such men, nor teach them, nor perform sacrifices for them, nor form matrimonial alliances with them.

7. On the day on which the youth is going to receive the initiation, on that day, early in the morning, they give him to eat, and have his hair arranged, and wash him, and deck him with ornaments, and put on him a (new) garment which has not yet been washed.

10, 1 seq. The initiation of the student. Khâdira-Grihya II, 4, 1 seq.

1–4. On the number of years given for the Upanayana of persons of the three castes, see the note on Sânkhâyana-Grihya II, 1, 1.

5, 6. See the note on Sânkhâyana-Grihya II, 1, 9.

8. Their garments are made of linen, of hempen cloth, of cotton, or of wool (according to the caste to which the student belongs).

9. The skins (which they wear), are an antelope-skin, or the skin of a spotted deer, or a goat's skin.

10. Their girdles are made of Muñga grass, of Kâsa grass, of Tâmbala.

11. Their staffs are of Parna wood, of Bilva wood, of Asvattha wood.

12. The garment of a Brâhmana is made of linen, or of hempen cloth, that of a Kshatriya, of cotton, that of a Vaisya, of wool.

13. Thereby also the other articles have been explained.

14. Or if (the proper articles prescribed) cannot be got, all (of them may be used) by (persons of) all castes.

15. To the east of the house on a surface besmeared (with cow-dung) wood has been put on the fire.

16. Having sacrificed with (the Mantras which the student recites) 'Agni! Lord of the vow' (MB. I, 6, 9–13), the teacher stations himself to the west

---

8. There are four kinds of garments indicated, though only persons of three castes are concerned. The explanation of this apparent incongruence follows from Sûtra 12.

10. Tâmbala is stated to be a synonym for sana (hemp).

13. As the garments indicated in Sûtra 8 belong, in the order in which they are stated, to persons of the three castes respectively, thus also of the skins (Sûtra 9), of the girdles (Sûtra 10), and of the staffs (Sûtra 11); the first is that belonging to a Brâhmana, the second, to a Kshatriya, and the third, to a Vaisya.

15. Comp. above, chap. 9, 2.

of the fire, on northward-pointed Darbha grass, facing the east.

17. Between the fire and the teacher the student (stands), raising his joined hands, turning his face towards the teacher, on northward-pointed Darbha grass.

18. Standing on his south side a Brâhmana versed in the Mantras fills (the student's) joined hands with water,

19. And afterwards (those) of the teacher.

20. Looking (at the student the teacher) murmurs (the verse), 'With him who comes to us, we have come together' (MB. I, 6, 14).

21. He causes (the student) to say, ' I have come hither to studentship' (ibid. 16).

22. In (the words), 'What is thy name' (ibid. 17), he asks after his name.

23. The teacher chooses for him a name which he is to use at respectful salutations,

24. (A name) derived from (the name of) a deity or a Nakshatra,

25. Or also of his Gotra, according to some (teachers).

26. Having let the water run out of his joined

22, 23. It is evident that the words tasyâkâryah belong to Sûtra 23, and not to Sûtra 22, to which the traditional division of the Sûtras assigns them. The corresponding section of the Mantra-Brâhmana runs thus: 'What is thy name?'—'My name is N. N.!' It is not clear whether the student, being questioned by the teacher, had to indicate his ordinary name, and then to receive from the teacher his 'abhivâdanîya nâmadheya,' or whether he had to pronounce, on the teacher's question, directly the abhivâdanîya name chosen for him by the teacher. The commentary and the corresponding passage of the Khâdira-Grihya (II, 4, 12) are in favour of the second alternative.

hands (over the student's hands), the teacher with his right hand seizes (the student's) right hand together with the thumb, with (the formula), ' By the impulse of the god Savit*ri*, with the arms of the two A*s*vins, with Pûshan's hands I seize thy hand, N. N. !' (ibid. 18).

27. He then makes him turn round from left to right with (the formula), ' Move in the sun's course after him, N. N. !' (ibid. 19).

28. Grasping down with his right hand over his right shoulder he should touch his uncovered navel with (the formula), ' Thou art the knot of all breath ' (ibid. 20).

29. Raising himself (from the position implied in Sûtra 28, he should touch) the place near the navel with (the formula), ' Ahura ' (ibid. 21).

30. Raising himself (still more, he should touch) the place of the heart with (the formula), ' K*ri*sana ' (ibid. 22).

31. Having touched from behind with his right hand (the student's) right shoulder with (the formula), ' I give thee in charge to Pra*g*âpati, N. N. !' (ibid. 23)—

32. And with his left (hand) the left (shoulder) with (the formula), ' I give thee in charge to the god Savit*ri*, N. N. !' (ibid. 24)—

33. He then directs him (to observe the duties of Brahma*k*arya, by the formula), ' A student art thou, N. N. !' (ibid. 25).

34. ' Put on fuel. Eat water. Do the service. Do not sleep in the day-time ' (ibid. 26).

35. Having gone in a northerly direction from

33, 34. Comp. Sâṅkhâyana-G*ri*hya II, 4, 5 note.

the fire, the teacher sits down to the east, on north-ward-pointed Darbha grass,

36. The student to the west, bending his right knee, turning his face towards the teacher, also on northward-pointed Darbha grass.

37. (The teacher) then ties round (the student) thrice from left to right the girdle made of Mu*ñg*a grass and causes him to repeat (the verse), ' Protecting us from evil word' (ibid. 27), and (the verse), ' The protectress of right' (ibid. 28).

38. Then (the student) respectfully sits down near (the teacher) with (the words), ' Recite, sir! May the reverend one recite the Sâvitrî to me.'

39. He then recites (the Sâvitrî, ibid. 29) to him, Pâda by Pâda, hemistich by hemistich, and the whole verse,

40. And the Mahâvyâh*ri*tis one by one, with the word Om at the end (ibid. 30).

41. And handing over to him the staff, which should be made of (the wood of) a tree, he causes him to repeat (the formula), ' O glorious one, make me glorious' (ibid. 31).

42. Then (the student) goes to beg food,

43. First of his mother, and of two other women friends, or of as many as there are in the neighbour-hood.

44. He announces the alms (received) to his teacher.

45. The rest of the day he stands silently.

46. After sunset he puts a piece of wood on the fire with (the Mantra), ' To Agni I have brought a piece of wood' (ibid. 32).

47. Through a period of three nights he avoids eating pungent or saline food.

48. At the end of that (period) a mess of boiled rice-grains (is offered) to Savit*ri*.

49. Then he may do what he likes.

50. A cow constitutes the sacrificial fee.

End of the Second Prapâ*th*aka.

49, 50. Dr. Knauer very pertinently calls attention to the fact that these Sûtras are not repeated, as is the rule with regard to the concluding words of an Adhyâya or Prapâ*th*aka. Comp. chap. 8, 25 note.

1. Now (follows) the Godâna ceremony (or cutting of the beard), in the sixteenth year.

2. The cutting of the hair (and the beard) has been explained by the (description of the) *Kûdâ-karana* (II, 9).

1, 1. After the description of the regular Upanayana here follow, in chaps. 1 and 2, statements regarding the special Vratas which the Vedic student has to undergo, or rather which he may undergo, in the time of his studentship. Comp. the corresponding statements on the Vratas of the *Rig*vedins, Sânkhâyana-G*ri*hya II, 11 and 12. By the followers of the Sâma-veda the ceremony of the Godâna, or cutting of the beard (comp. Sânkhâyana I, 28, 19 ; Pâraskara II, 1, 7 seq. ; Âsvalâyana I, 18), was put into connection with their system of Vratas ; the undergoing of the Godâna-vrata enabled the student to study the Pûrvâr*k*ika of the Sâma-veda. In the commentary on Gobhila III, 1, 28 we find the following statements with regard to this Vrata as well as to the other Vratas mentioned in Sûtra 28 : 'The Upanayana-vrata has been declared to refer to the study of the Sâvitrî (comp. Bloomfield's notes on G*ri*hya-sa*m*graha II, 42. 43) ; the Godâna-vrata, to the study of the collections of verses sacred to the gods Agni, Indra, and Soma Pavamâna (this is the Pûrvâr*k*ika of the Sâma-veda) ; the Vrâtika-vrata, to the study of the Âra*n*yaka, with the exclusion of the *S*ukriya sections ; the Âditya-vrata, to the study of the *S*ukriya sections ; the Aupanishada-vrata, to the study of the Upanishad-Brâhma*n*a ; the *G*yaish*th*asâmika-vrata, to the study of the Âgya-dohas.' The Vratas were connected with a repetition of the Upanayana ceremony (Sûtras 10 seq.) in the way stated in my note on Sânkhâyana II, 12, 1.—Khâdira-G*ri*hya II, 5, 1 seq.

2. Comp. Sânkhâyana I, 28, 19, 'The Godânakarman is identical with the *Kûdâ*karman.' Pâraskara II, 1, 7, 'At the Kesânta ceremony he says, "Hair and beard" (instead of "hair," as at the *Kûdâ*kara*n*a).'

3. The student has his hair (and beard) cut himself.

4. He has all the hair of his body shaven.

5. The sacrificial fee given by a Brâhma*n*a consists of an ox and a cow,

6. That given by a Kshatriya, of a pair of horses,

7. That given by a Vai*s*ya, of a pair of sheep.

8. Or a cow (is given by persons) of all (castes).

9. A goat (is given) to the person who catches up the hair.

10. The Upanayana (connected with the Godâna-vrata and the other Vratas) has been declared by the Upanayana (treated of above, II, 10).

11. (The use of) a garment, however, which has not yet been washed, is not required (here),

12. Nor the adornment.

13. (One should) not initiate one who does not intend to keep the vow through one year.

14. Handing over to him (i. e. to the student) a staff, which should be made of (the wood of) a tree, he directs him (to observe the duties connected with his vow, in the following words) :

15. ' Obey thy teacher, except in sinful conduct.

16. ' Avoid anger and falsehood,

17. ' Sexual intercourse,

18. ' Sleeping on high (bedsteads),

19. ' Performances of singing, dancing, &c., the use of perfumes and of collyrium,

---

3. At the *K*û*d*âkara*n*a the child sits in the mother's lap and others perform the rites for him.

10. See the note on Sûtra 1.

11. Comp. above, II, 10, 7.

20. ' Bathing,

21. 'Combing the head, cleansing the teeth, washing the feet,

22. ' Shaving,

23. ' Eating honey and flesh,

24. ' Mounting a chariot yoked with cattle,

25. ' Wearing shoes in the village,

26. ' Svayam-indriya-moḱanam.'

27. Wearing the girdle, going the rounds for alms, carrying a staff, putting fuel (on the fire), touching water, reverentially saluting (the teacher) in the morning : these are his standing duties.

28. The Godâna-vrata, the Vrâtika-vrata, the Âditya-vrata, the Aupanishada-vrata, the Gyaish-ṭhasâmika-vrata (last) one year (each).

29. Touching water in the evening and in the morning (is prescribed) for these (Vratas).

30. The Âditya-vrata, however, some do not undergo.

31. They who undergo it, wear one garment.

32. They allow nothing to be between (themselves and) the sun, except trees and (the roofs of) houses.

33. They do not descend into water deeper than knee-deep, except on the injunction of their teacher.

---

28. The meaning of these expressions has been explained in the note on Sûtra 1.

30. According to the commentary some study the Sukriyas as a part of the Âraṇyaka ; these do not undergo the Âditya-vrata. Others, for instance the Kauthumas, separate the Sukriyas from the Âraṇyaka and keep a special vow, the Âditya-vrata, by which they are enabled to study those texts.

KÂNDIKÂ 2.

1. For the Mahânâmnî verses (the Vrata is to be kept) twelve years,

2. (Or) nine, six, three (years).

3. These are the various possibilities.

4. Or also one year, according to some (teachers).

5. (In this case), however, the observances are enhanced.

6. (Keeping the Vrata through one year is allowed only) if (the student's) ancestors have learnt the Mahânâmnî verses.

7. There is also a Brâhma*n*a of the Rauruki (*S*âkhâ, in which it is said) :

8. 'The mothers forsooth say to their sons, when they suckle them :

9. '"Become men, my little sons, who endeavour to accomplish the *S*akvarî-vrata!"'

10. During (the Vrata preparatory to the study of) these (i. e. the Mahânâmnî verses), touching water at the time of each Savana (is prescribed).

11. Let him not eat in the morning before he has touched water.

12. In the evening, after he has touched water, he should not eat, before he has put the piece of wood on the fire.

2, 1. Regarding the Mahânâmnî or *S*akvarî verses and the observances connected with their study, comp. *S*ânkhâyana II, 12 (see especially the note on II, 12, 13) and the sixth Adhyâya of that text. Khâdira-G*ri*hya II, 5, 22 seq.

10. The rules as to 'touching water' have been given above, I, 2, 5 seq. The three Savanas or Soma-pressings of which the Soma sacrifice consists, are the prâta*h*-savana, the mâdhyandina-savana, and the t*ri*tîya-savana, i. e. the morning Savana, the midday Savana, and the third or evening Savana.

12. Comp. above, II, 10, 46; III, 1, 27.

13. He should wear dark clothes.

14. He should eat dark food.

15. Let him be devoted to his teacher.

16. Let him make way for nobody.

17. He should be addicted to austerities.

18. He should stand in day-time.

19. He should sit at night.

20. And when it is raining, he should not retire to a covered place.

21. He should say to (the god) when he sends rain, ' The *S*akvarîs are water.'

22. When (the god) sends lightning, he should say to him, 'Such forsooth is the nature of the *S*akvarîs.'

23. When (the god) thunders, he should say to him, ' The great voice of the great (cow) !'

24. Let him not cross a river without touching water.

25. Let him not ascend a ship.

26. If his life is in danger, however, he may ascend (a ship), after having touched water.

27. In the same way (he should touch water) having disembarked.

28. For in water the virtue of the Mahânâmnîs is contained.

29. If he practises these duties, (the god) Par*g*anya will send rain according to his wish.

30. The rules about dark (clothes), standing, sitting, (making) way, and (dark) food may be considered as optional.

31. After he has kept his vow through one third (of the prescribed time, the teacher) should

---

30. See Sûtras 13. 18. 19. 16. 14.

sing to him the (first) Stotriya verse (of the Mahâ-nâmnîs).

32. In- the same way the two other Stotriya verses (after two-thirds of the time and at the end of the whole time).

33. Or all (the three verses) at the end of the whole (time).

34. He should sing them to (the student) who has fasted and shuts his eyes.

35. Having filled a brass vessel with water, having thrown into it all sorts of herbs, and dipped (the student's) hands into it, the teacher should veil (the student's eyes) from left to right with a (new) garment that has not yet been washed.

36. Or he should sing (the Mahânâmnîs to him) immediately after he has veiled (his eyes).

37. With veiled eyes, keeping silence, he should abstain from food through a period of three nights, or through one day and one night.

38. Or he should stand in the forest till sunset (and spend the night in the village).

39. On the next morning he should put wood on the fire in the forest, should sacrifice with the Mahâvyâhritis, and should cause the student to look at (the following objects, viz.)

40. Fire, Âgya, the sun, a Brahman, a bull, food, water, curds,

41. With (the words), 'The sky have I beheld! Light have I beheld!'

35. Comp. Sânkhâyana-Grihya VI, 3, 7.

36. I. e. the fasting prescribed in Sûtras 34 and 37 may, if they like, follow after the teaching of the sacred song, instead of preceding it.

37. Sânkhâyana-Grihya II, 12, 6 seq.

42. In that way all (the objects stated in Sûtra 40) three times.

43. After the ceremony for averting evil has been performed, the student respectfully salutes the teacher.

44. Thus he has to break the silence (enjoined upon him).

45. A bull, a brass vessel, a garment, an optional gift (of a cow) : this is the sacrificial fee.

46. The first time he may choose (either a bull or a brass vessel).

47. Let him provide his teacher with clothes, according to some (teachers).

48. A mess of cooked food, sacred to Indra, (is prepared). Let him sacrifice of that (food) with this verse, 'To the *Rik*, to the Sâman we sacrifice' (Sâma-veda I, 369), or (with the verse), 'The lord of the seat, the wonderful' (ibid. I, 171), or with both (verses).

49. This (he should do) at (all) the Anuprava-*k*aniya ceremonies.

43. Comp. above, I, 9, 29 ; *Sânkhâyana* VI, 3, 11 seq.

45, 46. The student is to give a fee to his teacher three times, after he has been taught each of the three Stotriya verses (Sûtras 31. 32). To these three occasions the four objects stated in Sûtra 45 correspond, so that the first time either the first or the second of those objects, the bull or the brass vessel, may be chosen ; the second time he gives a garment, the third time a vara (or optional gift). Comp. the similar correspondence of four objects and three cases to which these objects refer, II, 10, 8. 12.

48. This is the Anuprava*k*anîya ceremony (or ceremony to be performed after the study of a Vedic text has been finished) belonging to the Mahânâmnîs ; comp. Khâdira-G*ri*hya II, 5, 34 ; Âsvalâyana-G*ri*hya I, 22, 12 ; *Sânkhâyana* II, 8, 1 note.

49. Perhaps sarvatra ('everywhere') belongs to Sûtra 49, so that we should have to translate : This (should be done) everywhere at

50. The Mantra has to be altered everywhere (so that he has to say), 'I have kept (the vow),' 'I have been able,' 'Thereby I have prospered,' 'I have undergone.'

51. The fee to be given after the study of the Parvans is, a goat for the Agni-Parvan, a ram for the Indra-Parvan, a cow for the Pavamâna-Parvan.

52. After (the student) has returned (from the forest), he should entertain his teacher and his retinue with food,

53. And his fellow-students who have come together.

54. The way to sing the Gyesh*th*asâmans has been explained by (the statements given with regard to) the Mahânâmnî-(vrata).

55. Here the following standing duties are to be observed :

56. He should not have intercourse with a *S*ûdrâ woman.

57. He should not eat bird's flesh.

58. He should avoid (constantly living on) the same grain, and in the same place, and wearing one garment.

59. He should perform the rite of 'touching water' with water drawn out (of a pond, &c.).

---

the Anuprava*k*anîya ceremonies, i. e. also at those Anuprava*k*anîya ceremonies which are connected with the study of the other texts.

50. Instead of 'I will keep the vow,' he says, 'I have kept the vow,' &c.; II, 10, 16.

51. The Parvans are the three great sections, sacred to Agni, Indra, and Soma Pavâmana, into which the first Sâmavedâr*k*ika is divided.

55. According to the commentary he has to keep these observances through his whole life.

58. Or, wearing always the same garment ?

60. From (the time of) his being directed (to observe the duties of his Vrata) he should not eat from an earthen vessel,

61. Nor drink (from such a vessel),

62. (Or rather) from (the time of) his being taught (the *G*yesh*th*asâmans, after the whole preparatory time, or after one third of that time), according to some (teachers).

KÂ*N*DIKÂ 3.

1. On the full-moon day of Praush*th*apada (or) under (the Nakshatra) Hasta the Upâkara*n*a (or opening ceremony of the annual term of Veda-study, is performed).

2. After (the teacher) has sacrificed with the Vyâh*ri*tis, he recites the Sâvitrî to the students as at the Upanayana;

3. And (he chants) the Sâvitrî with its Sâman melody,

---

60. Regarding the directions given to the student by the teacher, see chap. 1, 14.

62. See above, Sûtras 31. 33.

3, 1 seq. The Upâkara*n*a ceremony; Khâdira-G*ri*hya III, 2, 16 seq. Regarding the different terms for this ceremony, comp. Sânkhâyana IV, 5, 2; Âsvalâyana III, 5, 3; Pâraskara II, 10, 2. Hira*n*yakesin says: *sr*ava*n*âpaksha oshadhîshu *g*âtâsu hastena paur*n*amâsyâ*m* vâdhyâyopâkarma.—It seems impossible to me to adopt an explanation of this Sûtra, which gives to praush*th*apadî another meaning than that based on the constant use of these feminines derived from the names of Nakshatras, i.e. the day of the full moon which falls under such or such a Nakshatra. Hastena, therefore, necessarily refers to another day besides the Praush*th*apadî, on which the Upâkara*n*a may be celebrated. Perhaps we may conjecture, praush*th*apadî*m* hastena vopâkara*n*am.

2. Comp. above, II, 10, 39.

4. And (the Bârhaspatya Sâman, with the text), 'Soma, the king, Varu*n*a ' (Sâma-veda I, 91).

5. After they have recited (the first verses) of the *Kh*andas book, from its beginning, they may do what they like.

6. They eat fried barley-grains with (the verse), 'That which is accompanied by grains and by a karambha (i. e. curds with flour)' (Sâma-veda I, 210).

7. They partake of curds with (the verse), 'I have praised Dadhikrâvan' (Sâma-veda I, 358).

8. After they have sipped water, (the teacher) should cause them to repeat the first (?) verses, and to sing the first (?) Sâmans, of the different sections (?).

9. On the day sacred to Savit*ri* they wait.

10. And at (the beginning of) the northerly

---

5. The *Kh*andas book is the first Sâmavedâr*k*ika in which the verses are arranged according to their metre.

6. It is not quite clear from the text, in what connection the rites described in Sûtras 6–8 stand with those treated of in the preceding Sûtras. The expression yathârtham used in Sûtra 5 ('yathârtham iti karma*n*a*h* parisamâptir u*k*yate,' Comm. ; comp. above, I, 3. 12 note) clearly indicates the close of the ceremony ; on the other hand the comparison of Pâraskara II, 10, 15 seq., Sânkhâyana IV, 5, 10 seq., Âsvalâyana III, 5, 10, seems to show that the acts stated in Sûtras 6–8 form part of the ceremony described before.

8. I do not try to translate this very obscure Sûtra according to the commentary, in which khâ*nd*ika is explained as ' the number (of pupils).' Perhaps the word is a misspelling for ka*nd*ikâ or the like, and means sections of the texts. Comp. Khâdira-G*ri*hya III, 2, 23. The construction (â*k*ântodakâ*h* . . . kârayet) is quite irregular.

9. I. e. they do not continue their study. The day sacred to Savit*ri* is the day under the constellation of Hasta, mentioned in Sûtra 1, for Savit*ri* is the presiding deity over that Nakshatra (comp. *S*ânkhâyana I, 26, 11).

10. Comp. the note on Sûtra 16.

course of the sun (they wait) one night with one day before and one day after it,

11. (Or they interrupt their study for) a period of three nights before and afterwards, according to some (teachers).

12. And both times water libations are offered to the Âkâryas.

13. Some perform the Upâkarana on the full-moon day of Srâvana and wait (with studying) the time (from that day) till the day sacred to Savitri (Sûtra 9).

14. On the full-moon day of Taisha they leave off (studying the Veda).

15. They should go out of the village in an easterly or northerly direction, should go to water which reaches higher than to their secret parts, should touch water (in the way prescribed above, I, 2), and should satiate the metres, the Rishis, and teachers (by libations of water).

16. After this second Upâkarana, until the (chief) Upâkarana (has been performed) again for the Vedic texts, an interruption of the study (of the Veda takes place), if clouds rise.

---

12. Regarding the Tarpana ceremony comp. Sânkhâyana IV, 9, 1 note. From the word 'and' the commentator concludes that the libations are offered not only to the Âkâryas, but also to the Rishis, &c. (Sûtra 15).

13. Comp. Gautama XVI, 1; Vasishtha XIII, 1; Âpastamba I, 9, 1, &c.

14. Âpastamba I. 9, 2, &c.

15. This is a description of the Utsarga ceremony; comp. Sânkhâyana IV, 6, 6; Asvalâyana III, 5, 21–23; Pâraskara II, 12.

16. The most natural way of interpreting the text would be, in my opinion, to assume that the 'second Upâkarana' (pratyupâkarana) is identical with the Utsarga. The second Upâkarana thus would in the same time conclude the first term for studying the

17. If lightning (is observed), or if it thunders, or
if it is drizzling, (he shall not study) until the same
time next day.

18. On the falling of a meteor, or after an earth-
quake, or an eclipse of the sun or of the moon (the
study is interrupted until the same time next day),

19. And if a whirlwind occurs.

20. Let them not study on the Ash/akâ days,
and on the days of the new moon,

21. And on the days of the full moon—

22. In the three months Kârttika, Phâlguna, and
Âshâ*dh*a.

23. And (the study is interrupted) for one day and
one night,

24. If a fellow-pupil has died,

25. Or the sovereign of his country;

26. Three days, if his teacher (has died);

27. One day and one night, if somebody (has
died) who has reverentially approached.

28. If singing, or the sound of a musical instrument, or weeping is heard, or if it is storming, (the

Veda, and open a second term. The distinction of two such
periods, which may be called two terms, is frequently met with in
other texts, for instance, in Vasish*th*a XIII, 5–7 (S. B. E. XIV, 63);
Manu IV, 98. According to the commentary, on the other hand,
the second Upâkara*n*a is performed at the beginning of the northerly
course of the sun (comp. Sûtras 10–12); it is stated that after that
ceremony the Uttara (i. e. the Uttarâr*k*ika?) and the Rahasya texts
are studied. It deserves to be noticed that Manu (IV, 96) prescribes the performing of the Utsarga either under the Nakshatra
Pushya (i. e. Tishya), or on the first day of the bright fortnight of
Mâgha, which is considered as coinciding, at least approximately,
with the beginning of the northerly course of the sun.

18. Comp. Manu IV, 105.

22. These are the days of the ancient Vedic *k*âturmâsya
sacrifices.

study of the Veda is discontinued) as long as that (reason of the interruption) lasts.

29. As regards other (cases in which the reading of the Veda should be discontinued), the practice of the *Sish/as* (should be followed).

30. In the case of a prodigy an expiation (has to be performed) by the householder (or) by his wife.

31. If a spar of the roof or the middle (post of the house) breaks, or if the water-barrel bursts, let him sacrifice (Âgya oblations) with the Vyâh*ri*tis.

32. If he has seen bad dreams, let him murmur this verse, ' To-day, O god Savit*ri*' (Sâma-veda I, 141).

33. Now (follows) another (expiation).

34. If he has touched a piled-up (fire-altar) or a sacrificial post, or if he has humming in his ears, or if his eye palpitates, or if the sun rises or sets while he is sleeping, or if his organs of sense have been defiled by something bad, let him sacrifice two Âgya oblations with the two verses, ' May my strength return to me ' (Mantra-Brâhma*na* I, 6, 33. 34).

35. Or (let him sacrifice) two pieces of wood anointed with Âgya.

36. Or let him murmur (those two verses) at light offences.

---

29. The definition of a *Sish/a*, or instructed person, is given in Baudhâyana I, 1, 6 (S. B. E. XIV, 143).

30–36. Different expiations; comp. Khâdira-Gr*i*hya II, 5, 35–37.

34. *K*itya means *K*itya agni, the piled-up fire-altar, the construction of which is treated of, for instance, in the *S*atapatha Brâhma*na* VI–X. Prof. Weber has devoted to the rites connected with the *k*itya agni a very detailed paper, Indische Studien, XIII, 217 seq. That *k*itya does not mean here anything different from *k*itya agni is shown by the Mânava-Gr*i*hya I, 3 : yadi . . . akshi vâ spandet kar*n*o vâ krosed agni*m* vâ *k*ityam ârohet *s*masâna*m* vâ ga*kkh*ed yûpa*m* vopasp*ri*set, &c.

G

KÂ*N*DIKÂ 4.

1. A student, after he has studied the Veda,

2. And has offered a present to his Guru (i. e. to his) teacher,

3. Should, with the permission (of his parents), take a wife,

4. One who does not belong to the same Gotra,

5. And who is not a Sapi*nd*a relation of his mother.

6. The best, however, is a 'naked' girl.

7. Now the bath (which is taken at the end of studentship, will be described).

8. To the north or the east of the teacher's house there is an enclosure.

9. There the teacher sits down, facing the north, on eastward-pointed Darbha grass;

4, 1 seq. The description given in this chapter of the Samâvartana, or of the ceremony performed at the end of studentship, is opened with a few sentences referring to another section of the Gr*i*hya ritual, namely, to marriage. It seems to me that these first Sûtras of this chapter once formed, in a text from which Gobhila has taken them, the introduction to an exposition of the wedding ceremonies, and that Gobhila was induced to transfer them to the description of the Samâvartana, by their opening words, 'A student, after he has studied the Veda, &c.' With Sûtras 1–3, comp. Khâdira-Gr*i*hya I, 3, 1.

3. I prefer to supply, (with the permission) of his parents, and not, of his teacher. Hira*n*yakesin says, samâvr*i*tta â*k*âryakulât mâtâpitarau bibhr*i*yât, tâbhyâm anu*gñ*âto bhâryâm upaya*kkh*et.

5. Regarding the term Sapi*nd*a, see, for instance, Gautama XIV, 13 (S. B. E. II, 247): 'Sapi*nd*a-relationship ceases with the fifth or the seventh (ancestor).' Comp. Manu V, 60.

6. According to the Gr*i*hya-sa*m*graha (II, 17. 18), a 'naked' girl is one who has not yet the monthly period, or whose breast is not yet developed. Comp. Vasish*th*a XVII, 70; Gautama XVIII, 23.

7 seqq. Comp. Khâdira-Gr*i*hya III, 1, 1 seqq.

10. Facing the east the student on northward-pointed Darbha grass.

11. The teacher should besprinkle (him) with lukewarm, scented water, which has been boiled with all kinds of herbs.

12. But as if he (i. e. the student, should do so) himself—

13. (In such a way) he is alluded to in the Mantras; (therefore the besprinkling should be done rather by the student, and not by the teacher [?]).

14. With (the verse), 'The fires which dwell in the waters' (MB. I, 7, 1)—(the student [?]) pours his joined hands full of water (on the ground),

15. And again with (the formula), 'What is dreadful in the waters, what is cruel in the waters, what is turbulent in the waters' (ibid. 2).

16. With (the formula), 'The shining one I take here' (ibid. 3)—he besprinkles himself.

17. And again with (the formula), 'For the sake of glory, of splendour' (ibid. 4).

18. And again with (the verse), 'By which you made the wife (pregnant?') (ibid. 5).

19. A fourth time silently.

20. He then should rise and should worship the sun with the Mantra, 'Rising with (the Maruts) who bear shining spears' (ibid. 6–9), &c.

21. Optionally he may use the single sections of

---

13. In the Mantras prescribed for the besprinkling of the student (Mantra-Brâhmana I, 7, 1 seq.) there occur passages such as, for instance, 'Therewith I, N. N., besprinkle myself.'

21. He may use the first section of the Mantra, which contains the word prâtar, in the morning, &c.

the Mantra separately (in the morning, at noon, and in the evening) as indicated in the text.

22. He should add (the formula), ' The eye art thou' (ibid. 9) after (each of the three sections of the Mantra, 6–8).

23. With the verse, ' Loosen the highest fetter, O Varuna' (ibid. 10), he takes off the girdle.

24. After he has entertained the Brâhmanas with food and has eaten himself, he should have his hair, his beard, the hair of his body, and his nails cut, so as to leave the lock of hair (as required by the custom of his family).

25. Having bathed and adorned himself, and having put on two garments (an under-garment and an upper-garment) which have not yet been washed, he should put a garland (on his head) with (the formula), ' Luck art thou; take delight in me' (ibid. 11).

26. The two shoes (he puts on) with (the formula), ' Leaders are you; lead me' (ibid. 12).

27. With (the formula), ' The Gandharva art thou' (ibid. 13), he takes a bamboo staff.

28. He approaches the teacher together with the assembly (of his pupils) and looks at the assembly of his teacher's (pupils) with (the words), ' Like an eye-ball may I be dear to you' (ibid. 14).

29. Sitting down near (the teacher) he touches the sense-organs at his head with (the verse), ' The she-ichneumon, covered by the lips' (ibid. 15).

30. Here the teacher should honour him with the Argha ceremony.

31. (The student then) should approach a chariot yoked with oxen, and should touch its two side-pieces or the two arms of the chariot-pole with

(the verse), 'O tree, may thy limbs be strong' (ibid. 16).

32. With (the last words of that verse), 'May he who stands on thee, win what can be won'—he mounts it.

33. Having driven (some distance) in an easterly or northerly direction, he turns round from left to right and comes back (to his teacher).

34. When he has come back, the Argha ceremony should be performed (for him by his teacher), say the Kauhaliyas.

KÂNDIKÂ 5.

1. From that time he shall assume a dignified demeanour: this is in short the rule (for his behaviour).

2. Here the teachers enumerate the following (regulations).

3. Nâgâtalomnyopahâsam *ikkhet*.

4. Nor (should he wish for sport) with a girl who is the only child of her mother,

5. Nor with a woman during her courses,

6. Nor with one who descends from the same *Ri*shis.

7. Let him not eat food which has been brought by another door (than the usual),

8. Or which has been cooked twice,

9. Or which has stood over night—

10. Except such as is prepared of vegetables, flesh, barley, or flour.

---

34. Instead of its being performed at the time stated in Sûtra 30.

5, 1 seq. Rules of conduct for the Snâtaka; comp. Khâdira-Gri*hya* III, 1, 33 seq.

11. Let him not run while it is raining.

12. Let him not take himself his shoes in his hands (when putting them on or pulling them off).

13. Let him not look into a well.

14. Let him not gather fruits himself.

15. He should not wear a scentless wreath,

16. If it is not a wreath of gold.

17. (He should not wear a wreath) of which the expression mâlâ (garland) has been used.

18. He should cause the people to call it srag (wreath). (Then he may wear it.)

19. He should avoid using the word bhadra ('blessed') without a reason.

20. He should say (instead of it), mandra ('lovely').

21. There are three (kinds of) Snâtakas:

22. A Vidyâsnâtaka (or a Snâtaka by knowledge), a Vratasnâtaka (or a Snâtaka by the completion of his vow), and a Vidyâvratasnâtaka (i. e. Snâtaka by both).

23. Of these the last ranks foremost; the two others are equal (to each other).

24. (A Snâtaka) should not put on a wet garment.

25. He should not wear one garment.

26. He should not praise any person (excessively).

27. He should not speak of what he has not seen, as if he had seen it,

---

20. As to the reading, comp. Dr. Knauer's remarks in his edition of the text, p. xi of the Introduction.

21, 22. These Sûtras are identical with Pâraskara II, 5, 32. Comp. the definitions of these three kinds of Snâtakas, Pâraskara. l. l. 33–35.

25. Comp. above, chap. 2, 58.

28. Nor of what he has not heard, as if he had heard it.

29. He should give up everything that forms an impediment for his Veda-recitation.

30. He should endeavour to keep himself (pure from every defilement) like a pot of oil.

31. He should not climb a tree.

32. He should not go toward evening to another village,

33. Nor alone,

34. Nor together with V*ri*shalas (or *S*ûdras).

35. He should not enter the village by a by-path.

36. And he should not walk without a companion.

37. These are the observances for those who have performed the Samâvartana,

38. And what (besides) is prescribed by *S*ish*t*as.

KÂ*ND*IKÂ 6.

1. When his cows are driven out, he should repeat (the verse), 'May (Bhava), the all-valiant one, (and Indra protect) these (cows) for me' (MB. I, 8, 1).

2. When they have come back, (he should repeat the verse), 'These which are rich in sweet' (ibid. 2).

---

33. That the Snâtaka is not allowed to go alone to another village, follows from Sûtra 36; thus Sûtra 33 is superfluous. The commentator of course tries to defend Gobhila, but I think he has not succeeded. Probably Gobhila has taken the two Sûtras from different texts on which his own composition seems to be based.

38. Baudhâyana I, 1, 6 (S. B. E. XIV, 144): 'Those are called *S*ish*t*as who, in accordance with the sacred law, have studied the Veda together with its appendages, know how to draw inferences from that, and are able to adduce proofs perceptible by the senses from the revealed texts.'

6, 1 seq. Different ceremonies connected with cattle-keeping. Comp. Khâdira-G*ri*hya III, 1, 45 seq.

3. If he is desirous of thriving (in his cattle), he should lick with his tongue the forehead of the first-born calf, before it is licked by its mother, and should gulp with (the formula), ' Thou art the phlegm of the cows ' (ibid. 3).

4. If he is desirous of thriving (in his cattle), he should, when the cows have calved, at night put wood on the fire in the cow-stable and should sacrifice churned curds with drops of ghee, with (the verse), ' Seizer, seize ' (ibid. 4).

5. If he is desirous of thriving (in his cattle), he makes, when the cows have calved, with a sword of Udumbara wood, marks on a male and on a female calf, first on the male, then on the female, with (the Mantra), ' The world art thou, thousandfold ' (ibid. 5. 6),

6. And after he has done so, he should recite (over the two calves the Mantra), ' With metal, with the butcher's knife ' (ibid. 7).

7. When the rope (to which the calves are bound) is spread out, and (again) when the calves have been bound to it, he should recite over it (the verse), ' This rope, the mother of the cows ' (ibid. 8).

8. Here now the following (rites) have to be performed day by day, (viz.)

9. (The rites at) the driving out (of the cows), at the coming back (of the cows), and at the setting into motion of the rope (with the calves).

10. At the cow-sacrifice (i.e. the sacrifice by which a thriving condition for the cows is obtained), boiled rice-grains with milk (are offered).

---

9. See Sûtras 1. 2. 7.

11. Let him sacrifice to Agni, Pûshan, Indra, and Îsvara.

12. To the bull honour is done (by adorning it, by lavish food, &c.).

13. By the cow-sacrifice also the horse-sacrifice (i.e. the sacrifice by which thriving horses are obtained) has been explained.

14. Of deities Yama and Varu*n*a are added here (to the deities stated above) (Sûtra 11).

15. (After the cow-sacrifice) the cows are besprinkled with scented water; the cows are besprinkled with scented water.

KÂ*N*DIKÂ 7.

1. Now (follows) the *Srava*nâ ceremony.

2. It has to be performed on the full-moon day (of the month Srâva*n*a).

3. Having besmeared (a surface) to the east of the house (with cow-dung), they carry forward (to that place) fire taken from the (sacred) domestic fire.

4. He besmears four spots to the four sides (of the fire),

5. Towards the (four) directions,

6. (To the extent) of more than one prakrama (i.e. step).

7. He puts a dish on the fire and fries (in that

---

15. As to the repetition of the last words of this chapter, see the notes on I, 4, 31; II, 8, 25; 10, 50.

7, 1 seq. The *Srava*nâ ceremony or the Bali-offering to the Serpents. Comp. Khâdira-G*ri*hya III, 2, 1 seq., and the elaborate paper of Dr. Winternitz, Der Sarpabali, ein altindischer Schlangencult (Wien, 1888).

dish) one handful of barley-grains, without burning them.

8. To the west of the fire he places a mortar so that it stands firmly, and husks (the grains), separating (the husked and the unhusked grains ?).

9. After he has carefully ground them to flour, and has thrown (that) into a wooden cup (*k*amasa), and covered it with a winnowing-basket, he puts it up (in the house).

10. Between (the besmeared surface) towards the south, and that towards the east (there should be) a passage.

11. After sunset he takes the wooden cup, (the spoon called) Darvi, and the winnowing-basket, and goes to (the fire) which has been carried forward (Sûtra 3).

12. He throws the flour into the winnowing-basket and fills the wooden cup with water.

13. He takes once a quantity of flour with the Darvi spoon, pours out water on the besmeared place to the east (of the fire), and offers (there) a Bali with (the words), 'O king of Serpents, dwelling towards the east, this is thy Bali!' (MB. II, 1, 1).

14. He pours the rest of the water over (that Bali, taking care) that it does not carry away the Bali.

---

8. As to avahanti, comp. above, I, 7, 4 ; Hillebrandt, Neu- und Vollmondsopfer, p. 30.

11. According to the commentary atipra*n*îta means the fire which has been carried forward (Sûtra 3). Another explanation is then added, which is based on a quotation from a 'tantrântara:' ' After he has established a fire, he should carry forward one firebrand taken from that fire, in a south-eastern direction, with the Mantra ye rûpâ*n*i pratimu*ñk*amânâ*h* &c.; that fire is the atipra*n*îta fire.'

15. Turning round from right to left, he besprinkles the wooden cup and the Darvi spoon, warms them, and (repeats the offering of a Bali) in the same way towards the south, towards the west, and towards the north, as the Mantra (MB. II, 1, 1. 2) runs, without turning away (between the single Bali-offerings).

16. After he has thrown the remnants (of flour) out of the basket into the fire, he goes to that fire which has not been carried forward.

17. To the west of that fire he touches the earth with his two hands turned downwards, and murmurs the Mantra, 'Adoration to the Earth's'— (MB. II, 1, 3).

18. In the evening boiled rice-grains with milk (are prepared).

19. Of that (milk-rice) he should make oblations with (the formulas), ' To *Sravana*, to Vish*n*u, to Agni, to Pra*g*âpati, to the Vi*s*ve devâs Svâhâ ! '

20. The rest (should be performed) according to the Sthâlîpâka rite.

21. To the north of the fire he places a bunch of Darbha grass with roots, and murmurs the Mantra, ' Soma the king' (ibid. 4), and, ' The agreement which you have made ' (ibid. 5).

---

15. Literally, 'turning round, following his left arm.' Comp. *Sâṅkhâyana* II, 3, 2. The Mantra runs thus, ' O king of Serpents, dwelling towards the south (the west, the north), this is thy Bali ! '

16. Comp. Sûtra 11 and the note.

17. Comp. below, IV, 5, 3.

20. Gr*ï*hya-sa*m*graha I, 114: ' Where the technical expression is used, "The rest according to the rite of the Sthâlîpâkas," he should, after he has sacrificed the two Âgyabhâgas, pour (Âgya) into the Sru*k* and cut off (the Avadânas with the Sru*k*).' Comp. Gobhila I, 8, 3 seq.

22. On the following day he has flour of fried barley-grains prepared, and in a new pot, covering (it with another pot), he puts it up (in his house).

23. (Of that flour) he should silently offer Balis day by day in the evening, before the sacrifice, until the Âgrahâya*n*î day.

Kâ*n*dikâ 8.

1. On the full-moon day of (the month) Â*s*vayu*g*a, at the P*r*ishâtaka ceremony, a mess of boiled rice-grains with milk, sacred to Rudra, (is prepared).

2. Of that (milk-rice) let him sacrifice, the first oblation with (the verse), ' To us, O Mitra and Varu*n*a' (Sâma-veda I, 220), the second with (the verse), ' Not in our offspring ' (Rig-veda I, 114, 8),

3. And (eight Â*g*ya oblations) with the ' cow's names ' (i.e. with the formulas), ' The lovely one art thou,' &c., with each (name) separately.

4. The rest (should be performed) according to the Sthâlîpâka rite.

5. Having carried the P*r*ishâtaka around the fire, turning his right side towards (the fire), and having caused the Brâhma*n*as to look at it (i.e. at the P*r*i-shâtaka), he should look at it himself with (the verse

---

23. The sacrifice is that prescribed in Sûtras 18. 19, which should, as well as the offering of Balis, be daily repeated.

8, 1 seq. The P*r*ishâtaka ceremony; comp. Khâdira-G*r*ihya III, 3, 1 seq. A P*r*ishâtaka is a mixture of milk or of curds with Â*g*ya; comp. Khâd. l. l. 3; G*r*ihya-sa*m*graha II, 59; Sâṅkhâyana IV, 16, 3 note.

3. The ' cow's names ' are given in the G*r*ihya-sa*m*graha II, 60; of the nine names given there the last is omitted at the P*r*ishâtaka ceremony.

4. See above, chap. 7, 20 and the note.

repeated by the Brâhmanas and by the sacrificer), 'That bright eye, created by the gods, which rises on the east—may we see it a hundred autumns; may we live a hundred autumns !'

6. After he has entertained the Brâhmanas with food and has eaten himself, (the sacrificer and his family) should tie (to their arms, necks, &c.) amulets made of lac together with all sorts of herbs, for the sake of prosperity.

7. In the evening he should feed the cows with the Prishâtaka, and should let the calves join them.

8. Thus (the cows) will thrive.

9. At the sacrifice of the first fruits a mess of boiled rice-grains with milk, sacred to Indra and Agni, (is prepared).

10. Having sacrificed first a Havis offering of that (milk-rice), he sacrifices over that (oblation) four Âgya oblations with (the verses), ' To him who bears a hundred weapons,' &c. (MB. II, 1, 9–12).

11. The rest (should be performed) according to the Sthâlîpâka rite.

12. The rest of the remnants of the sacrificial food he should give to eat to all (persons present) who have received the initiation (Upanayana).

13. Having 'spread under' water once, he should cut off two portions of the boiled rice-grains.

14. Three (portions are cut off) by descendants of Bhrigu.

15. And over (these portions) water (is poured).

16. (After the food has been prepared in this

---

9 seq. The sacrifice of the first fruits; comp. Khâdira-Grihya III, 3, 6 seq.

11. See chap. 7, 20 and the note.

16, 20. Instead of asamsvâdam, samsvâdayeran, I read

way), he should swallow it without chewing it, with
(the Mantra), 'From the good to the better' (ibid. 13).

17. In the same way three times.

18. Silently a fourth time.

19. After he has cut off a greater portion,

20. They may, if they like, chew that.

21. Having sipped water, they should touch their
mouths, their heads, and their limbs from above
downwards, with (the verse), 'This art thou'
(ibid. 14).

22. In the same way (sacrifices of the first fruits
are performed) of Syâmâka (panicum frumentaceum)
and of barley.

23. (At the sacrifice) of Syâmâka (the Mantra
with which the food is partaken of [comp. Sûtra 16],
is), 'May Agni eat as the first' (ibid. 15).

24. (At the sacrifice) of barley, 'This barley,
mixed with honey' (ibid. 16).

KÂNDIKÂ 9.

1. On the Âgrahâyanî day (or the full-moon day
of the month Mârgasîrsha) Bali-offerings (are made).

2. They have been explained by the Srâvana
sacrifice.

3. He does not murmur (here) the Mantra, 'Adoration to the Earth's.'

---

asamkhâdam, samkhâdayeran. Comp. Khâdira-Grihya III, 3,
13: asamkhâdya pragiret, and the quotations in Böhtlingk-Roth's
Dictionary s. v. sam-khâd and â-svad.

9, 1 seq. The Âgrahâyanî ceremony by which the rites devoted
to the Serpents are concluded. Khâdira-Grihya III, 3, 16 seq.

2. See above, chap. 7.

3. Comp. chap. 7, 17: To the west of that fire he touches the

4. In the morning, after he has sacrificed the (regular) morning oblation, he should have the following (plants and branches of trees) fetched, viz. Darbha grass, a Samî (branch), Vîrina grass, a (Badarî branch) with fruits, Apâmârga, and Sirîsha. He then should silently throw (a portion) of flour of fried barley into the fire, should cause the Brâhmanas to pronounce auspicious wishes, and should circumambulate the house, turning his right side towards it, starting from the room for the (sacred) fire, striking the smoke (of the sacred fire) with those objects (i. e. with the plants and branches mentioned above).

5. He should throw away those objects, after he has made use of them.

6. On solid stones he places a water-barrel with the two (Sâmans belonging to the verse), 'Vâstoshpati' (Sâma-veda I, 275) and with (that) Rik (itself).

7. Let him pour two pots of water into that barrel with this verse, 'Some assemble' (Sâma-veda-Âranyaka, vol. ii, p. 292, ed. Bibl. Indica).

8. In the evening boiled rice-grains with milk (are prepared).

9. Of that (milk-rice) he should make an oblation with (the Mantra), 'She shone forth as the first' (MB. II, 2, 1).

10. The rest (should be performed) according to the Sthâlîpâka rite.

---

earth with his two hands turned downwards, and murmurs the Mantra, 'Adoration to the Earth's.'

6. He sings the two Kâvasha Sâmans of which the verse Sâma-veda I, 275 is considered as the Yoni, and then repeats that verse itself.

8. This Sûtra is identical with chap. 7, 18.

10. Comp. chap. 7, 20 note.

11. To the west of the fire he touches the Barhis with his two hands turned downwards, and murmurs the Vyâh*ri*tis (i. e. the solemn utterances), ' In the Kshatra I establish myself' (ibid. 2. 3).

12. To the west of the fire he should have a layer spread out,

13. Of northward-pointed grass,

14. Inclined towards the north.

15. After they have spread out on that (grass) new rugs, the householder sits down (thereon) on the southern side.

16. Then without an interval the others according to their age,

17. And without an interval their wives, each with her children.

18. When they are seated, the householder touches the layer (of grass) with his two hands turned downwards, and murmurs the verse, ' Be soft to us, O Earth' (ibid. 4).

19. When he has finished that (verse), they lie down on their right sides.

20. In the same way (they lie down on their right sides) three times, turning themselves towards themselves (i. e. turning round forwards, not backwards, and thus returning to their former position ?).

21. They repeat the auspicious hymns as far as they know them ;

22. The complex of Sâmans called Arish*t*a, according to some (teachers).

---

20. The explanation which the commentary gives of this difficult Sûtra can hardly be accepted : trir âv*ri*tya tri*h*k*ri*tvo*h*bhyasya ... abhyâtmam âtmano g*ri*hapater âbhimukhyena, âtmana ârabhyety artha*h*. katha*m* nâma ? yenaiva krame*n*opavish*t*â*h* tenaiva krame*n*a sa*m*vesana*m* trir âvartayeyu*h*.

22. The commentary gives a second name for this Sâman

23. Having touched water, they may do whatever they like.

KÂNDIKÂ 10.

1. The Ash/akâ (is a festival) sacred to the night.

2. It procures prosperity.

3. It is sacred to Agni, or to the Manes, or to Pra*g*âpati, or to the Seasons, or to the Vi*s*ve devâs— thus the deity (to which the Ash/akâ is sacred), is investigated (by different teachers).

4. There are four Ash/akâs in (the four months of) the winter;

5. These all he should endeavour to celebrate with (offerings of) meat;

6. Thus says Kautsa.

7. (There are only) three Ash/akâs (in the winter), says Audgâhamâni,

8. And so say (also) Gautama and Vârkakha*nd*i.

9. The eighth day of the dark fortnight after the Âgrahâya*n*î is called Apûpâsh/akâ (i. e. Ash/akâ of the cakes).

10. Having prepared grains in the way prescribed

---

litany, arish/abhanga.   Nârâya*n*a says: abodhy agnir (Sv. I, 73) mahi tri*n*âm (I, 192) iti dve tvâvata (I, 193) ity âdika*m* sarvaloka-prasiddha*m* prayugya.

10, 1 seq. The Ash/akâ festivals; Khâdira-Gr*i*hya III, 3, 28. Comp. *S*ânkhâyana-Gr*i*hya III, 12, 1 note (S. B. E. XXIX, 102).

4, 7. As to the difference of opinion regarding the number of Ash/akâs, comp. Weber, Naxatra, second article, p. 337.   Gobhila himself follows the opinion of Audgâhamâni, for he mentions only three Ash/akâs in the winter season, the first following after the Âgrahâya*n*î full moon (chap. 10, 9), the second after the Taishî (10, 18), and the third after the Mâghî (IV, 4, 17).

10. See above, I, 7, 2 seq.

for Sthâlipâkas, he cooks (those grains and prepares thus) a *k*aru.

11. And (besides he prepares) eight cakes, without turning them over in the dish (in which he bakes them) ;

12. (Each) in one dish ;

13. Without Mantras, according to Audgâhamâni ;

14. Of the size of the (cakes) sacred to Tryambaka.

15. After he has baked them, he should pour (Â*g*ya) on them, should take them from the fire towards the north, and should pour (Â*g*ya) on them again.

16. In the way prescribed for Sthâlipâkas he cuts off (the prescribed portions) from the mess of boiled grains and from the cakes, and sacrifices with (the words), ' To the Ash*t*akâ Svâhâ !'

17. The rest (should be performed) according to the Sthâlipâka rite.

18. (At the second Ash*t*akâ, on) the eighth day after the full-moon day of Taisha, a cow (is sacrificed).

19. Shortly before the time of junction (of day and night, i. e. before the morning twilight) he should place that (cow) to the east of the fire, and when (that time) has come, he should sacrifice (Â*g*ya) with

11. G*ri*hya-sa*m*graha II, 71 : pr*â*hakkapâlân kurv*i*ta ap*û*pân ash*t*akâvidhau.

14. Regarding the Traiyambaka cakes, comp. Kâtyâyana *S*rautasûtra V, 10, 1 seq.; Vaitâna-sûtra IX, 18, &c.

16. See above, I, 8, 5 seq.

17. Comp. chap. 7, 20 note.

18. With the following paragraphs the *S*rauta rites of the animal sacrifice should be compared; see J. Schwab, Das altindische Thieropfer (Erlangen, 1886).

(the verse), 'What, O beasts, you think' (MB. II, 2, 5).

20. And after having sacrificed, he should recite over (the cow the verse), 'May thy mother give leave to thee' (ibid. 6).

21. Let him sprinkle (the cow) with water in which barley is, with (the words), 'Agreeable to the Ashtakâ I sprinkle thee.'

22. Let him carry a fire-brand round it with (the verse), 'The lord of goods, the sage (goes) round' (Sâma-veda I, 30).

23. Let him give it water to drink.

24. The remainder of what it has drunk he should pour out under (the feet of) the beast with (the formula), 'Away from the gods the Havis has been taken' (MB. II, 2, 7).

25. They then walk in a northerly direction (from the fire) and kill (the cow),

26. The head of which is turned to the east, the feet to the north, if the rite is sacred to the gods,

27. The head to the south, the feet to the west, if the rite is sacred to the Manes.

28. After it has been killed, he should sacrifice (Âgya) with (the verse), 'If the beast has lowed' (ibid. 8).

29. And (the sacrificer's) wife should get water and should wash all the apertures of the cow's body.

30. They lay two purifiers (i. e. grass-blades) on (the cow's body) near its navel, cut it up in the direction of its hairs, and draw the omentum out.

31. He should spit it on two pieces of wood, on one (simple) branch and on another forked branch, should besprinkle it (with water), and should roast it.

32. When it has ceased to drop, he should say, 'Hew the (cow) to pieces—

33. 'So that the blood does not stain the ground to the east of the fire.'

34. After he has roasted (the omentum), he should pour (Âgya) on it, should take it from the fire towards the north, and should pour (Âgya) on it again.

35. After he has cut off (the prescribed portions from) the omentum in the way prescribed for Sthâlî-pâkas, or in the way prescribed for the Svish/akr/t (oblation), he sacrifices with (the words), 'To the Ash/akâ Svâhâ!'

36. The rest (should be performed) according to the Sthâlîpâka rite. The rest according to the Sthâlîpâka rite.

End of the Third Prapâ/Aaka.

---

32. In the text we ought to read vi*a*sata, as Dr. Knauer has observed.

35. The regulations concerning the Avadânas are given for Sthâlîpâkas, I, 8, 5 seq., and for the Svish/akr/t oblation, I, 8, 11 seq.

36. Comp. III, 7, 20 note.

1. He throws the two spits into the fire;

2. That which consists of one (simple) branch, towards the east, the other one towards the west.

3. They cut off the Avadâna portions from all its limbs,

4. With the exception of the left thigh and the lungs.

5. The left thigh he should keep for the Anvash-*t*akya ceremony.

6. On the same fire he cooks one mess of rice-grains and one of meat, stirring up the one and the other separately, from left to right, with two pot-ladles.

7. After he has cooked them, he should pour (Â*g*ya) on them, should take them from the fire towards the north, and should pour (Â*g*ya) on them again.

8. Having poured the juice (of the Avadânas) into a brazen vessel,

9. And having placed the Avadânas on a layer (of grass) on which branches of the Plaksha (tree) have been spread,

10. He cuts off (the prescribed portions) from the

1, 1. Comp. III, 10, 31.

3. Comp. Âsvalâyana-G*ri*hya I, 11, 12; Khâdira-G*ri*hya III, 4, 14 seq.

6. 'He cooks a mess of meat'—i.e. he cooks the Avadânas. Comp. Khâdira-G*ri*hya, l. l. 17; Â*sv*.-G*ri*hya I, 11, 12.

10. See I, 8, 5 seq.

Avadânas in the way prescribed for Sthâlipâkas, (and puts those portions) into (another) brazen vessel ;

11. And (the portion) for the Svish/akr*i*t oblation separately.

12. Taking of the mess of boiled rice-grains (Sûtra 6) a portion of the size of a Bilva fruit, he should mix that, together with the Avadânas (Sûtra 10), with the juice (Sûtra 8).

13. Taking a fourfold portion of Âg*ya* he should sacrifice it with the first of the eight *Ri*/*k*as, ' Entering into fire, the fire ' (MB. II, 2, 9–16).

14. Of the mixture (Sûtra 12) he cuts off the third part and sacrifices it with the second and third (verse).

15. He places the word Svâhâ after the second (of those verses, i.e. after the third verse of the whole Mantra).

16. In the same way he sacrifices the other two-thirds (of that mixture, the one) with the fourth and fifth (verse), and (the other) with the sixth and seventh (verse).

17. Having cut off the rest, he should sacrifice the oblation to (Agni) Svish/akr*i*t with the eighth (verse).

18. Even if he be very deficient in wealth, he should celebrate (the Ash/akâ) with (the sacrifice of) an animal.

19. Or he should sacrifice a Sthâlipâka.

20. Or he should offer food to a cow.

---

20 seq. Regarding these Sûtras, which occur nearly identically in *Sâṅ*khâyana III, 14, 4 seq., Â*s*valâyana II, 4, 8–11, comp. the note, vol. xxix, p. 105.

21. Or he should burn down brushwood in the forest and should say, ' This is my Ashtakâ.'

22. But let him not neglect to do (one of these things). But let him not neglect to do (one of these things).

KÂNDIKÂ 2.

1. On the following day the Anvashtakya (ceremony is performed),

2. Or on the day which follows after that.

3. To the south-east (of the house), in the intermediate direction (between south and east), they partition off (a place with mats or the like).

4. The long-side (of that place should lie) in the same (direction).

5. They should perform (the ceremonies) turning their faces towards the same (direction).

6. (It should measure) at least four prakramas (i.e. steps).

7. (It should have) its entrance from the west.

8. In the northern part of that enclosure they make the Lakshana and carry the fire (to that place).

9. To the west of the fire he places a mortar so that it stands firmly, and husks, holding his left hand uppermost, one handful of rice-grains which he has seized with one grasp.

---

21. I believe that we ought to correct upadhâya into upadahya. Sânkhâyana III, 14, 5: api vâranye kaksham apâdahet. Âsvalâyana II, 4, 9: agninâ vâ kaksham uposhet.

2, 1 seq. The Anvashtakya ceremony; comp. Khâdira-Grihya III, 5, 1 seq.

8. ' They make the Lakshana' means, they prepare the ground on which the fire shall be established, by drawing the five lines. See above, I, 1, 9. 10; Grihya-samgraha I, 47 seq.

10. When (the rice) has been husked,

11. He should once carefully remove the husks.

12. And then he should cut off a lump of flesh from that thigh and should cut it in small pieces on a new slaughtering-bench,

13. (With the intention) that the Pindas (or lumps of food offered to the Manes) should be thoroughly mixed up with flesh.

14. On the same fire he cooks one mess of rice-grains and one of meat, stirring up the one and the other separately, from right to left, with the two pot-ladles.

15. After he has cooked them, he should pour (Âgya) on them, should take them from the fire towards the south, and should not pour (Âgya) on them again.

16. In the southern part of the enclosure (Sûtras 3 seq.) he should have three pits dug, so that the eastern (pit is dug) first,

17. One span in length, four inches in breadth and in depth.

18. Having made the Lakshana to the east of the eastern pit, they carry the fire (to that place).

19. Having carried the fire round the pits on their west side, he should put it down on the Lakshana.

20. He strews (round the fire) one handful of Darbha grass which he has cut off in one portion.

---

12. As to the words 'from that thigh,' comp. above, chap. 1, 5.

14. Comp. chap. 1, 6. The sacrificial food is stirred up here from right to left, not from left to right, because it is sacred to the Manes. The mess of meat consists of the meat treated of in Sûtra 11.

15. Comp. above, chap. 1, 7.

18, 19. As to lakshana, comp. Sûtra 8 note.

21. And (he strews it into) the pits,

22. Beginning with the eastern (pit).

23. To the west of the pits he should have a layer spread out,

24. Of southward-pointed Ku*s*a grass,

25. Inclined towards the south.

26. And he should put a mat on it.

27. To that (layer of grass) they fetch for him (the following sacrificial implements), one by one, from right to left :

28. The two pots in which sacrificial food has been cooked (Sûtra 14), the two pot-ladles (Sûtra 14), one brazen vessel, one Darvî (spoon), and water.

29. (The sacrificer's) wife places a stone on the Barhis and pounds (on that stone the fragrant substance called) Sthagara.

30. And on the same (stone) she grinds some collyrium, and anoints therewith three Darbha blades, including the interstices (between the single blades?).

31. He should also get some oil made from sesamum seeds,

32. And a piece of linen tape.

33. After he has invited an odd number of blameless Brâhma*n*as, whose faces should be turned towards the north, to sit down on a pure spot,

---

27. The last words of the Sûtra, translated literally, would be : 'following the left arm.'   Comp. Sânkhâyana-Gr*i*hya II, 3, 2. They place the different objects apr â daksh i*n*ye na.

29. See chap. 3, 16.   30. See chap. 3, 13.

31. See chap. 3, 15.

32. See chap. 3, 24.

33. As to the two classes of pait*ri*ka and daivika Brâhma*n*as, comp. the note on Sânkhâyana IV, 1, 2.

34. And has given them Darbha grass (in order that they may sit down thereon),

35. He gives them (pure) water and afterwards sesamum-water, pronouncing his father's name, ' N. N.! To thee this sesamum-water, and to those who follow thee here, and to those whom thou followest. To thee Svadhâ !'

36. After he has touched water, (he does) the same for the other two.

37. In the same way (he gives them) perfumes.

38. The words in which he addresses (the Brâh-ma*n*as) when going to sacrifice, are, ' I shall offer it into the fire.'

39. After they have replied, ' Offer it,' he should cut off (the prescribed portions) from the two messes of cooked food (Sûtra 14), (and should put those portions) into the brazen vessel. He then should sacrifice, picking out (portions of the Havis) with the pot-ladle, the first (oblation) with (the words), ' Svâhâ to Soma Pit*ri*mat,' the second with (the words), ' Svâhâ to Agni Kavyavâhana ' (MB. II, 3, 1. 2).

---

34. Comp. the note, p. 932 of the edition of Gobhila in the Bibliotheca Indica.

35. Regarding the sesamum-water (i. e. water into which sesamum seeds have been thrown), comp. Âsvalâyana-G*ri*hya IV, 7, 11.

36. He repeats the same ceremony, pronouncing his grand-father's, instead of his father's, name ; then he repeats it for his great-grandfather.

37. He gives perfumes to the Brâhma*n*as, addressing first his father, then his grandfather and his great-grandfather.

38, 39. Comp. Âsvalâyana-G*ri*hya IV, 7, 18 seq. Regarding the term upa g h â t a *m* g u h u y â t, comp. G*ri*hya-sa*m*graha I, 111 seq. and Professor Bloomfield's note. Regarding the oblation made to Agni Kavyavâhana, comp. Âpastamba VIII, 15, 20 : Agni*m* Kavya-vâhana*m* Svish*t*ak*ri*darthe *ya*gati.

1. From now onwards he has to perform (the rites) wearing his sacrificial cord over his right shoulder and keeping silence.

2. With his left hand he should seize a Darbha blade and should (therewith) draw (in the middle of the three pits) a line from north to south, with (the formula), ' The Asuras have been driven away ' (MB. II, 3, 3.

3. Seizing, again with his left hand, a fire-brand, he should place it on the south side of the pits with (the verse), ' They who assuming (manifold) shapes ' (ibid. 4).

4. He then calls the Fathers (to his sacrifice) with (the verse), ' Come hither, ye Fathers, who have drunk Soma ' (ibid. 5).

5. He then should place pâtra vessels of water near the pits.

6. Seizing, again with his left hand, (the first) vessel, he should pour it out from right to left on the Darbha grass in the eastern pit, pronouncing his father's name, ' N. N.! Wash thyself, and (may) those who follow thee here, and those whom thou followest, (wash themselves). To thee Svadhâ ! '

7. After he has touched water, (he does) the same for the other two.

8. Seizing, again with his left hand, the Darvî spoon, he should cut off one-third of the mixture (of

---

3, 1. Comp. I, 2, 3 seq.
2. Kâtyâyana-*S*rauta-sûtra IV, 1, 8.
3. Kâtyâyana-*S*rauta-sûtra IV, 1, 9.
6. Kâtyâyana-*S*rauta-sûtra IV, 1, 10.
7. See chap. 2, 36.

the different kinds of sacrificial food) and should put
down (that Pinda), from right to left, on the Darbha
grass in the eastern pit, pronouncing his father's
name, ' N. N.! This Pinda is thine, and of those
who follow thee here, and of those whom thou
followest. To thee Svadhâ!'

9. After he has touched water, (he does) the same
for the other two.

10. If he does not know their names, he should
put down the first Pinda with (the formula), 'Svadhâ
to the Fathers dwelling on the earth,' the second
with (the formula), 'Svadhâ to the Fathers dwelling
in the air,' the third with (the formula), 'Svadhâ.to
the Fathers dwelling in heaven.'

11. After he has put down (the three Pindas), he
murmurs, ' Here, O Fathers, enjoy yourselves; show
your manly vigour each for his part' (MB. II, 3, 6).

12. He should turn away, (should hold his breath,)
and turning back before he emits his breath, he
should murmur, ' The Fathers have enjoyed themselves; they have shown their manly vigour each
for his part ' (ibid. 7).

13. Seizing, again with his left hand, a Darbha
blade (anointed with collyrium; chap. 2, 30), he
should put it down, from right to left, on the Pinda
in the eastern pit, pronouncing his father's name,
' N. N.! This collyrium is thine, and is that of
those who follow thee here, and of those whom thou
followest. To thee Svadhâ!'

14. After he has touched water, (he does) the
same for the other two.

15. In the same way (he offers) the oil (to the
fathers);

9, 14. See chap. 2, 36.   15. See chap. 2, 31.

16. In the same way the perfume.

17. Then he performs the deprecation (in the following way) :

18. On the eastern pit he lays his hands, turning the inside of the right hand upwards, with (the formula), 'Adoration to you, O Fathers, for the sake of life! Adoration to you, O Fathers, for the sake of vital breath!' (MB. II, 3, 8) ;

19. On the middle (pit), turning the inside of the left hand upwards, with (the formula), 'Adoration to you, O Fathers, for the sake of terror! Adoration to you, O Fathers, for the sake of sap!' (MB., loc. cit.) ;

20. On the last (pit), turning the inside of the right hand upwards, with (the formula), 'Adoration to you, O Fathers, for the sake of comfort! Adoration to you, O Fathers, for the sake of wrath!' (MB. II, 3, 9).

21. Then joining his hands he murmurs, 'Adoration to you, O Fathers! O Fathers! Adoration to you!' (MB., loc. cit.).

22. He looks at his house with (the words), 'Give us a house, O Fathers!' (MB. II, 3, 10).

23. He looks at the Piṇḍas with (the words), 'May we give you an abode, O Fathers!' (MB. II, 3, 11).

24. Seizing, again with his left hand, the linen thread, he should put it down, from right to left, on the Piṇḍa in the eastern pit, pronouncing his father's

---

16. See chap. 2, 29.

18 seq. Comp. Vâg. Saṃhitâ II, 32.

23. The Vâgasaneyi Saṃhitâ (loc. cit.) has the reading, sato vaḥ pitaro deshma, 'May we give you, O Fathers, of what we possess!'

24. Comp. chap. 2, 32.

name, ' N. N.! This garment is thine, and is that of those who follow thee here, and of those whom thou followest. To thee Svadhâ!' (MB. II, 3, 12).

25. After he has touched water, (he does) the same for the other two.

26. Seizing, again with his left hand, the vessel of water (Sûtra 5), he should sprinkle (water) round the Pi*nd*as from right to left, with (the verse), ' Bringing sap' (MB. II, 3, 13).

27. The middle Pi*nd*a (offered to the grandfather) the wife (of the sacrificer) should eat, if she is desirous of a son, with (the verse), ' Give fruit to the womb, O Fathers' (MB. II, 3, 14).

28. Or of those Brâhma*n*as (that person) who receives the remnants (of the sacrificial food, should eat that Pi*nd*a).

29. Having besprinkled (and thus extinguished) the fire-brand (Sûtra 3) with water, with (the verse), ' *G*âtavedas has been our messenger for what we have offered' (MB. II, 3, 15)—

30. (The sacrificer) should besprinkle the sacrificial vessels, and should have them taken back, two by two.

31. The Pi*nd*as he should throw into water,

32. Or into the fire which has been carried forward (to the east side of the pits, chap. 2, 18),

33. Or he should give them to a Brâhma*n*a to eat,

34. Or he should give them to a cow.

35. On the occasion of a lucky event (such as the birth of a son, &c.) or of a meritorious work (such as the dedication of a pond or of a garden) he should give food to an even number (of Brâhma*n*as).

---

25. See chap. 2, 36.
35. Comp. Sâṅkhâyana-G*ri*hya IV, 4.

36. The rite (is performed) from left to right.

37. Barley is used instead of sesamum.

KÂNDIKÂ 4.

1. By (the description of) the Sthâlîpâka offered at the Anvash/akya ceremony the Pi*nd*apit*riy*ag*ñ*a has been declared ;

2. This is a *S*râddha offered on the day of the new moon.

3. Another (*S*râddha) is the Anvâhârya.

4. (It is performed) monthly.

5. The Havis is prepared (by one who has set up the sacred *S*rauta fires) in the Dakshi*n*âgni (i.e. in that of the three fires which is situated towards the south).

6. And from the same (fire the fire is taken which)

36, 37. *S*âṅkhâyana-G*ri*hya IV, 4, 6. 9. Regarding the use of sesamum seeds, see above, chap. 2, 35.

4, 1. Khâdira-G*ri*hya III, 5, 35. Comp. M. M., 'India, what can it teach us?' p. 240. The word Sthâlîpâka is used here, as is observed in the commentary, in order to exclude the mess of meat (chap. 2, 14) from the rites of the Pi*nd*apit*riy*ag*ñ*a.

3. Anvâhârya literally means, what is offered (or given) after something else, supplementary. In the commentary on Gobhila, p. 666, a verse is quoted :

amâvâsyâ*m* dvit*î*ya*m* yad anvâhârya*m* tad u*ky*ate,

'The second (*S*râddha) which is performed on the day of the new moon, that is called anvâhârya.' First comes the Pi*nd*apit*ri*-yag*ñ*a, and then follows the Anvâhârya *S*râddha ; the last is iden-tical with the Pârva*n*a *S*râddha, which is described as the chief form of *S*râddha ceremonies, for instance in *S*âṅkhâyana-G*ri*hya IV, 1. Comp. Manu III, 122. 123, and Kullûka's note; M. M., 'India, what can it teach us?' p. 240.

5. According to the commentary this and the following Sûtras refer only to the Pi*nd*apit*riy*ag*ñ*a, not to the Anvâhârya *S*râddha. Comp. Khâdira-G*ri*hya III, 5, 36-39.

is carried forward (in order to be used at the cere-monies).

7. In the domestic fire (the Havis is prepared) by one who has not set up the (*S*rauta) fires.

8. One pit (only is made);

9. To the south of it the fire has its place.

10. Here the laying down of the fire-brand is omitted,

11. And (the spreading out of) the layer (of grass),

12. And the anointing (of the bunches of Darbha grass), and the anointing (of the Fathers),

13. And the (offering of) perfume,

14. And the ceremony of deprecation.

15. (The ceremony performed with) the vessel of water forms the conclusion (of the Pi*nd*apit*r*iya*gñ*a).

16. He should, however, put down one garment (for the Fathers in common).

17. On the eighth day after the full moon of Mâgha a Sthâlîpâka (is prepared).

18. He should sacrifice of that (Sthâlîpâka).

19. 'To the Ash*t*akâ Svâhâ!'—with (these words) he sacrifices.

20. The rest (should be performed) according to the Sthâlîpâka rite.

21. Vegetables (are taken instead of meat) as in-gredient to the Anvâhârya (-rice).

22. At animal sacrifices offered to the Fathers let

---

9. See chap. 2, 18.   10. See chap. 3, 3.
11. Chap. 2, 23.   12. Chap. 2, 30; 3, 13.
13. Chap. 3, 16.   14. Chap. 3, 17 seq.
15. Chap. 3, 26.   16. Comp. chap. 3, 24. 25.
17–21. Description of the third Ash*t*akâ festival.
20. Comp. above, III, 7, 20 note.
21. Comp. IV, 1, 12.

him sacrifice the omentum with (the verse), 'Carry the omentum, O *G*âtavedas, to the Fathers' (MB. II, 3, 16) ;

23. At (such sacrifices) offered to the gods, with (the verse), '*G*âtavedas, go to the gods with the omentum' (ibid. 17).

24. If no (god to whom the sacrifice should be offered, and no Mantra with which the oblation should be made) is known, he sacrifices, assigning (his offering to the personified rite which he is performing), thus as (for instance), ' To the Ash*t*akâ Svâhâ !'

25. The rest (should be performed) according to the Sthâlipâka rite.

26. If a debt turns up (which he cannot pay), he should sacrifice with the middle leaf of Golakas, with (the verse), ' The debt which' (MB. II, 3, 18).

27. Now (follows) the putting into motion of the plough.

28. Under an auspicious Nakshatra he should cook a mess of sacrificial food and should sacrifice to the following deities, namely, to Indra, to the Maruts, to Par*g*anya, to A*s*ani, to Bhaga.

29. And he should offer (Â*g*ya) to Sîtâ, Â*s*â, Ara*d*â, Anaghâ.

30. The same deities (receive offerings) at the

25. See III, 7, 20 note.
26. I am not sure about the translation of the words golakâ-nâ*m* madhyamapar*n*ena. The ordinary meaning of golaka is ' ball,' see, for instance, Sânkhâyana-G*ri*hya IV, 19, 4. The commentary says, golakânâ*m* palâ*s*ânâ*m* madhyamapar*n*ena madhya-ma*kkh*adena.

29. The name of the third of those rural deities is spelt differently; Dr. Knauer gives the readings, Ara*d*âm, Ara*t*hâm, Aragam, Ararâm, Aram.

furrow-sacrifice, at the thrashing-floor-sacrifice, at the sowing, at the reaping of the crop, and at the putting of the crop into the barn.

31. And at mole hills he should sacrifice to the king of moles.

32. To Indrâ*nî* a Sthâlipâka (is prepared).

33. Of that he should make an offering with (the verse), 'The Ekâsh*t*akâ, performing austerities' (MB. II, 3, 19).

34. The rest (should be performed) according to the Sthâlipâka ritual. The rest according to the Sthâlipâka ritual.

KÂ*ND*IKÂ 5.

1. At (the sacrifices) for the obtainment of special wishes, which will be henceforth described,

2. And, according to some (teachers), also at (the sacrifices) described above (the following rites should be performed).

3. He should touch the earth, to the west of the fire, with his two hands turned downwards, with (the verse), 'We partake of the earth's' (MB. II, 4, 1).

32–34. Khâdira-G*ri*hya III, 5, 40. I understand that this sacrifice stands in connection with the rural festivals which are treated of in the preceding Sûtras. In the commentary, from the Mantra the conclusion is drawn that the ceremony in question belongs to the day of the Ekâsh*t*akâ. But the Ekâsh*t*akâ is the Ash*t*akâ of the dark fortnight of Mâgha (see S. B. E. XXIX, 102), and the description of the rites belonging to that day has already been given above, Sûtras 17–21. It very frequently occurs in the G*ri*hya ritual that Mantras are used at sacrifices standing in no connection with those for which they have originally been composed.

5, 1 seq. Comp. Khâdira-G*ri*hya I, 2, 6 seq.

4. In the night-time (he pronounces that Mantra so that it ends with the word) 'goods' (vasu), in the day-time (so that it ends) with 'wealth' (dhanam).

5. With the three verses, 'This praise' (MB. II, 4, 2-4) he should wipe along (with his hands) around (the fire).

6. Before sacrifices the Virûpâksha formula (MB. II, 4, 6) (should be recited).

7. And at (ceremonies) which are connected with special wishes, the Prapada formula (MB. II, 4, 5)— (in the following way) :

8. He should murmur (the Prapada formula), 'Austerities and splendour,' should perform one suppression of breath, and should, fixing his thoughts on the object (of his wish), emit his breath, when beginning the Virûpâksha formula.

9. When undertaking ceremonies for the obtainment of special wishes, let him fast during three (days and) nights,

10. Or (let him omit) three meals.

6-8. Khâdira-Grihya I, 2, 23; Grihya-samgraha I, 96. It is stated that the recitation of the Virûpâksha and Prapada formulas and also the parisamûhana (Sûtra 5) should be omitted at the so-called Kshiprahomas, i. e. at sacrifices performed without the assistance of a yagñavid. See Bloomfield's notes on Grihya-samgraha I, 92. 96. Regarding the way in which a prânâyâma ('suppression of breath') is performed, comp. Vasishtha XXV, 13 (S. B. E. XIV, p. 126).

9 seq. Khâdira-Grihya IV, 1, 1 seq.

10. There are two meals a day. The words of this Sûtra, 'Or three meals,' are explained in the commentary in the following way. He should, if he does not entirely abstain from food through three days, take only three meals during that time, i. e. he should take one meal a day. The commentator adds that some read abhaktâni instead of bhaktâni ('or he should omit three meals'), in which case the result would be the same. I prefer the reading

11. At such ceremonies, however, as are repeated regularly, (let him do so only) before their first performance.

12. He should (simply) fast, however, before such ceremonies as are performed on sacrificial days (i. e. on the first day of the fortnight).

13. (At a ceremony) which ought to be performed immediately (after the occurrence by which it has been caused), the consecration follows after (the ceremony itself).

14. Let him recite the Prapada formula (Sûtras 7. 8), sitting in the forest on Darbha grass,

15. Of which the panicles are turned towards the east, if he is desirous of holy lustre,

16. To the north, if desirous of sons and of cattle,

17. To both directions, if desirous of both.

18. One who desires that his stock of cattle may increase, should offer a sacrifice of rice and barley

---

bhaktâni, and propose to supply, not, ' he should eat,' but ' he should omit' ('abhoganam,' Sûtra 9). Possibly the meaning is that three successive meals should be omitted; thus also the compiler of the Khâdira-Gr*i*hya seems to have understood this Sûtra.

11. Comp., for instance, below, chap. 6, 1.

12. Comp. below, chaps. 6, 4 ; 8, 23.

13. My translation of this Sûtra differs from the commentary. There it is said : ' An occurrence which is perceived only when it has happened (sannipatitam eva), and of which the cause by which it is produced is unknown, for instance the appearance of a halo, is called sânnipâtika. Such sânnipâtika ceremonies are upa-rish*t*âddaiksha. The dîkshâ is the preparatory consecration (of the sacrificer), for instance by three days of fasting. A ceremony which has its dîkshâ after itself is called uparish*t*âddaiksha.' Similarly the commentary on Khâdira-Gr*i*hya IV, 1, 3 says, ' upa-rish*t*ât sânnipâtike naimittike karma k*ri*tvâbhoganam.'

with (the verse), 'He who has a thousand arms, the protector of cow-keepers' (MB. II, 4, 7).

19. Having murmured the Kautomata verse (ibid. 8) over fruits of a big tree, he should give them—

20. To a person whose favour he wishes to gain.

21. One (fruit) more (than he gives to that person), an even number (of fruits), he should keep himself.

22. There are the five verses, 'Like a tree' (MB. II, 4, 9–13).

23. With these firstly a ceremony (is performed) for (obtaining property on) the earth.

24. He should fast one fortnight,

25. Or, if he is not able (to do so, he may drink) once a day rice-water,

26. In which he can see his image.

27. This observance (forms part) of (all) fortnightly observances.

28. He then should in the full-moon night plunge up to his navel into a pool which does not dry up, and should sacrifice at the end of (each of those five) verses fried grains with his mouth into the water, with the word Svâhâ.

29. Now (follows) another (ceremony with the same five verses).

30. With the first (verse) one who is desirous of the enjoyment (of riches), should worship the sun, within sight of (that) person rich in wealth (from

---

23. The commentary explains pârthivam, 'prithivyartham kriyate, iti pârthivam, grâmakshetrâdyartham;' similarly the commentary on Khâdira-Grihya IV, 1, 13 says, 'prithivîpatitvaprâptyartham idam uktam karma.'

27. Comp. below, chap. 6, 12.

28. Grihya-samgraha II, 11.

whom he hopes to obtain wealth); then he will obtain wealth.

31. With the second (verse) one who desires that his stock of horses and elephants may increase, should sacrifice fried grains, while the sun has a halo.

32. With the third (verse) one who desires that his flocks may increase, (should sacrifice) sesamum seeds, while the moon (has a halo).

33. Having worshipped the sun with the fourth (verse), let him acquire wealth; then he will come back safe and wealthy.

34. Having worshipped the sun with the fifth (verse) let him return to his house. He will safely return home; he will safely return home.

KÂ*ND*IKÂ 6.

1. Let him daily repeat (the formula), 'Bhû*h*!' (MB. II, 4, 14) in order to avert involuntary death.

2. (He who does so) has nothing to fear from serious diseases or from sorcery.

3. (The ceremony for) driving away misfortune (is as follows).

4. It is performed on the sacrificial day (i. e. on the first day of the fortnight).

5. (Oblations are made with the six verses), ' From the head ' (MB. II, 5, 1 seq.), verse by verse.

6. The seventh (verse is), ' She who athwart' (MB. I, 5, 6).

7. (Then follow) the verses of the Vâmadevya,

6, 1 seq. Comp. Khâdira-G*ri*hya IV, 1, 19 seq.

4. Comp. above, chap. 5, 12.

6. Comp. above, II, 7, 14.

7. The text belonging to the Vâmadevya Sâman, is the T*ri*ka, Sâma-veda II, 32–34.

8. (And) the Mahâvyâhr*i*tis.

9. The last (verse) is, ' Pragâpati ' (MB. II, 5, 8).

10. With the formula, ' I am glory' (MB. II, 5, 9) one who is desirous of glory should worship the sun in the forenoon, at noon, and in the afternoon,

11. Changing (the words), ' of the forenoon' (into ' of the noon,' and ' of the afternoon,' accordingly).

12. Worshipping (the sun) at the time of the morning twilight and of the evening twilight procures happiness, (both times) with (the formula), ' O sun! the ship' (MB. II, 5, 14), and (after that) in the morning with (the formula), ' When thou risest, O sun, I shall rise with thee' (ibid. 15); in the evening with (the formula), ' When thou goest to rest, O sun, I shall go to rest with thee ' (ibid. 16).

13. One who desires to gain a hundred cart-loads (of gold), should keep the vow (of fasting) through one fortnight and should on the first day of a dark fortnight feed the Brâhma*n*as with boiled milk-rice prepared of one Kâ*m*sa of rice.

14. At the evening twilight (of every day of that fortnight), having left the village in a westerly direction, and having put wood on the fire at a place where

---

10. According to the commentary the formula ya*s*o *s*ham bhavâmi comprises five sections; thus it would include the sections II, 5, 9–13 of the Mantra-Brâhma*n*a.   The Mantra quoted next by Gobhila (Sûtra 12) is really MB. II, 5, 14.

13. Comp. chap. 5, 24–27.   One Kâ*m*sa is stated to be a measure equal to one Dro*n*a.   The more usual spelling is ka*m*sa, and this reading is found in the corresponding passage of the Khâdira-G*ri*hya (IV, 2, 1).

14. As to the meaning of ka*n*a (' small grain of rice '), comp. Hillebrandt, Neu- und Vollmondsopfer, p. 32, note 1.

four roads meet, he should sacrifice the small grains
(of that rice), turning his face towards the sun, with
(the words), ' To Bhala Svâhâ ! To Bhala Svâhâ !'
(ibid. 17. 18).

15. (He should repeat those rites) in the same
way the two next dark fortnights.

16. During the time between those dark fortnights he should observe chastity till the end (of the
rite), till the end (of the rite).

KÂNDIKÂ 7.

1. Let him select the site for building his house—

2. On even ground, which is covered with grass,
which cannot be destroyed (by inundations, &c.),

3. On which the waters flow off to the east or to
the north,

4. On which plants grow which have no milky
juice or thorns, and which are not acrid.

5. The earth should be white, if he is a Brâhmana,

6. Red, if he is a Kshatriya,

7. Black, if he is a Vaisya.

8. (The soil should be) compact, one-coloured,
not dry, not salinous, not surrounded by sandy
desert, not swampy.

9. (Soil) on which Darbha grass grows, (should
be chosen) by one who is desirous of holy lustre,

10. (Soil covered) with big sorts of grass, by one
who is desirous of strength,

11. (Soil covered) with tender grass, by one who
is desirous of cattle.

7, 1 seq. Comp. Khâdira-Grihya IV, 2, 6 seq.

12. (The site of the house) should have the form of a brick,

13. Or it should have the form of a round island.

14. Or there should be natural holes (in the ground) in all directions.

15. On such (ground) one who is desirous of fame or strength, should build his house with its door to the east;

16. One who is desirous of children or of cattle, (should build it) with its door to the north;

17. One who is desirous of all (those things), (should build it) with its door to the south.

18. Let him not build it with its door to the west.

19. And a back-door.

20. The house-door.

21. So that (he ?) may not be exposed to looks (?).

19-21. I have translated the words of these Sûtras without trying to express any meaning. According to the commentary the meaning is the following: 19. He should not build a house which has its door on the back-side, or which has one front-door and one back-door. 20. The house-door should not face the door of another house. 21. The house-door should be so constructed that the householder cannot be seen by *Kând*âlas, &c., when he is performing religious acts or when dining in his house. Or, if instead of sa*m*lokî the reading sa*m*loki is accepted, the Sûtra means: the house-door should be so constructed, that valuable objects, &c., which are in the house, cannot be seen by passers-by.— The commentary on Khâdira-G*ri*hya IV, 2, 15 contains the remark: dvâradvaya*m* (var. lectio, dvâra*m* dvâra*m*) parasparam *ri*gu na syâd iti ke*k*it. This seems to me to lead to the right understanding of these Sûtras. I think we ought to read and to divide in this way: (19) anudvâra*m* *k*a. (20. 21) g*ri*hadvâra*m* yathâ na sa*m*loki syât. 'And (let him construct) a back-door, so that it does not face the (chief) house-door.' The Khâdira MSS. have the readings, asallokî, asandraloke, sa*m*loka.

22. 'Let him avoid an Asvattha tree on the east-side (of his house), and a Plaksha on the south-side, a Nyagrodha on the west-side, and on the north-side an Udumbara.

23. 'One should say that an Asvattha brings (to the house) danger from fire; one should say that a Plaksha tree brings early death (to the inhabitants of the house), that a Nyagrodha brings oppression through (hostile) arms, that an Udumbara brings diseases of the eye.

24. 'The Asvattha is sacred to the sun, the Plaksha to Yama, the Nyagrodha is the tree that belongs to Varuna, the Udumbara, to Pragâpati.'

25. He should place those (trees) in another place than their proper one,

26. And should sacrifice to those same deities.

27. Let him put wood on the fire in the middle of the house, and sacrifice a black cow,

28. Or a white goat,

22–24. These are Slokas to which the commentary very appropriately, though not exactly in the sense in which it was originally set down, applies the dictum so frequently found in the Brâhmana texts: na hy ekasmâd aksharâd virâdhayanti. Dr. Knauer's attempts to restore correct Slokas are perhaps a little hazardous; he inserts in the third verse ka after plakshas, and in the second he changes the first brûyât into ka, whereby the second foot of the hemistich loses its regular shape ∪ – – –, and receives instead of it the form ∪ ∪ – ∪.

25. He should remove an Asvattha tree from the east-side, &c.

26. He should sacrifice to the deities to whom the transplanted trees are sacred.

27 seq. Here begins the description of the vâstusamana, which extends to Sûtra 43. As to the animal sacrifice prescribed in this Sûtra, comp. Dr. Winternitz's essay, Einige Bemerkungen über das Bauopfer bei den Indern (Sitzungsbericht der Anthrop. Gesellschaft in Wien, 19 April, 1887), p. 8.

29. (The one or the other) together with milk-rice.

30. Or (only) milk-rice.

31. Having mingled together the fat (of the animal), Âgya, its flesh, and the milk-rice,

32. He should take eight portions (of that mixture) and should sacrifice (the following eight oblations):

33. The first (verse, accompanying the first oblation), is, 'Vâstoshpati!' (MB. II, 6, 1).

34. (Then follow) the (three) verses of the Vâmadevya,

35. (And the three) Mahâvyâhritis.

36. The last (oblation is offered with the formula), 'To Pragâpati (svâhâ).'

37. After he has sacrificed, he should offer ten Balis,

38. In the different directions (of the horizon), from left to right,

39. And in the intermediate points,

40. In due order, without a transposition.

41. (He should offer a Bali) in the east with (the formula), '(Adoration) to Indra!' in the intermediate direction—'To Vâyu!' in the south—'To Yama!' in the intermediate direction—'(Svadhâ) to the Fathers!' in the west—'(Adoration) to Varuna!' in the intermediate direction — 'To Mahârâga!' in the north—'To Soma!' in the intermediate direction — 'To Mahendra!' down-

---

34. Comp. above, chap. 6, 7 note.

36. The commentary says: 'The last oblation should be offered with the formula, "To Pragâpati svâhâ!"' Probably we ought to correct the text, Pragâpata ity uttamâ, 'the last (verse) is, "Pragâpati!" (MB. II, 5, 8);' see above, IV, 6, 9; Khâdira-Grihya IV, 2, 20.

wards—'To Vâsuki!' upwards, in the sky (i. e.
throwing the Bali into the air), with (the formula),
'Adoration to Brahman!'

42. To the east, upwards, and downwards this
should be done constantly, day by day.

43. (The whole ceremony is repeated) every year
or at the two sacrifices of the first fruits.

Kândikâ 8.

1. At the *Sravanâ* and Âgrahâya*nî* sacrifices he
should leave a remainder of fried grains.

2. Having gone out of the village in an easterly
or in a northerly direction, and having put wood on
the fire at a place where four roads meet, he should
sacrifice (those fried grains) with his joined hands,
with the single (verses of the text), 'Hearken, Râkâ!'
(MB. II, 6, 2–5).

3. Walking eastward (he should), looking upwards,
(offer a Bali) to the hosts of divine beings, with (the
formula), 'Be a giver of wealth' (ibid. 6);

4. (Walking?) towards the side, (he should offer
a Bali) to the hosts of other beings, looking downwards.

5. Returning (to the fire) without looking back, he
should, together with the persons belonging to his

---

43. See above, III, 8, 9 seq.

8, 1. See above, III, 7; 9. Comp. Khâdira-G*ri*hya III, 2,
8 seq.

4. The commentary says: Tiryaṅ tiras*kî*na*m* yathâ bhavati
tathâ, iti kriyâvise*sha*na*m* etat. athavâ . . . tiryaṅ tiras*kî*na*h* san.
Arvâṅ ought to be corrected to avâṅ (comp. Khâdira-G*ri*hya III,
2, 13).

5. The commentary explains upetai*h* simply by samîpam
âgatai*h*.

family, as far as they have been initiated (by the Upanayana), eat the fried grains.

6. (This ceremony) procures happiness.

7. (With the two formulas), 'Obeying the will' and 'Sankha' (MB. II, 6, 7. 8), he should sacrifice two oblations of rice and of barley separately,

8. With reference to a person whose favour he wishes to gain.

9. This is done daily.

10. With the Ekâksharyâ verse (MB. II, 6, 9) two rites (are performed) which are connected with the observance (of fasting) for a fortnight.

11. One who is desirous of long life, should sacrifice (with that verse), in the night of the full moon, one hundred pegs of Khadira wood ;

12. Of iron, if he desires that (his enemies) may be killed.

13. Now another ceremony (performed with the same verse).

14. Having gone out of the village in an easterly or in a northerly direction, he should at a place where four roads meet, or on a mountain, set an elevated surface, consisting of the dung of beasts of the forest, on fire, should sweep the coals away, and should make an oblation of butter (on that surface) with his mouth, repeating that Mantra in his mind.

---

7 seq. Khâdira-Grihya IV, 2, 24 seq.

7. I. e. he should sacrifice one oblation of rice, and one of barley.

8. Literally, to a person, &c. The meaning is, he should pronounce the name of that person. The Sûtra is repeated from IV, 5, 20; thus its expressions do not exactly fit the connection in which it stands here.

10 seq. Khâdira-Grihya IV, 3, 1 seq.

15. If (that oblation of butter) catches fire, twelve villages (will be his).

16. If smoke rises, at least three.

17. They call this ceremony one which is not in vain.

18. One who desires that his means of livelihood may not be exhausted, should sacrifice green cow-dung in the evening and in the morning.

19. Of articles which he has bought, he should, after having fasted three (days and) nights, make an oblation with the formula, ' Here this Visvakarman ' (MB. II, 6, 10).

20. Of a garment he should offer some threads (with that formula),

21. Of a cow some hairs (of its tail) ;

22. In the same way (he should offer some part) of other articles which he has bought.

23. The sacrifice of a full oblation (with the verse, ' A full oblation I sacrifice,' MB. II, 6, 11) should be performed on the sacrificial day (i.e. on the first day of the fortnight),

24. And (on such a day let him sacrifice) with (the formula), ' Indrâmavadât (?) ' (MB. II, 6, 12).

25. One who is desirous of glory, (should offer) the first (oblation); one who is desirous of companions, the second.

---

18. Khâdira-Gṛihya IV, 3, 18.   On haritagomayân the com-mentary has the following note: yaiḥ khalu gomayaiḥ saṃkule pradese haritâni triṇâni prasastâny utpadyante tân kila gomayân haritagomayân âkakshate. te khalv ârdrâ ihâbhipreyante. kathaṃ gñâyate. teshv eva tatprasiddheḥ.

19. Khâdira-Gṛihya IV, 3, 7.

23 seq. Khâdira-Gṛihya IV, 3, 8 seq. The Pratîka quoted in Sûtra 24 is corrupt.

KÂNDIKÂ 9.

1. One who desires to become a ruler among men should fast through a period of eight nights.

2. Then he should provide a Sruva spoon, a cup (for water), and fuel, of Udumbara wood,

3. Should go out of the village in an easterly or in a northerly direction, should put wood on the fire at a place where four roads meet,

4. And should sacrifice Âgya, turning his face towards the sun, with (the formulas), ' Food indeed is the only thing that is pervaded by the metres,' and, ' Bliss indeed' (MB. II, 6, 13. 14) ;

5. A third (oblation) in the village with (the formula), ' The food's essence is ghee' (ibid. 15).

6. One who is desirous of cattle, (should offer this oblation) in a cow-stable.

7. If (the cow-stable) is damaged by fire (?), (he should offer) a monk's robe.

8. On a dangerous road let him make knots in the skirts of the garments (of himself and of his companions),

9. Approaching those (of the travellers) who wear garments (with skirts).

9, 1 seq. Khâdira-Grîhya IV, 3, 10 seq.

7. Perhaps we ought to follow the commentary and to translate, ' When (the cow-stable) becomes heated (by the fire on which he is going to sacrifice),' &c. (' goshthe sgnim upasamâdhâyaiva homo na kartavyah, kin tv agnim upasamâdhâyâpi tâvat pratîkshaniyam yâvad goshtham upatapyamânam bhavati '). I have translated kîvaram according to the ordinary meaning of the word ; in the commentary it is taken as equivalent to lauhakûrnam (copper filings).

10. (Let him do so with the three formulas, MB. II, 6, 13–15) with the word Svâhâ at the end of each.

11. This will bring a prosperous journey (to himself) and to his companions. [Or: (He should do the same with the garments) of his companions. This will bring a prosperous journey.]

12. One who desires to gain a thousand cart-loads (of gold), should sacrifice one thousand oblations of flour of fried grains.

13. One who is desirous of cattle, should sacrifice one thousand oblations of the excrements of a male and a female calf;

14. Of a male and a female sheep, if he is desirous of flocks.

15. One who desires that his means of livelihood may not be exhausted, should sacrifice in the evening and in the morning the fallings-off of rice-grains, with (the formulas), 'To Hunger Svâhâ!' 'To Hunger and Thirst Svâhâ!' (MB. II, 6, 16. 17).

16. If somebody has been bitten by a venomous animal, he should murmur (the verse), 'Do not fear, thou wilt not die' (MB. II, 6, 18), and should besprinkle him with water.

17. With (the formula), 'Strong one! Protect' (MB. II, 6, 19), a Snâtaka, when lying down (to sleep), should lay down his bamboo staff near (his bed).

18. This will bring him luck.

19. (The verses), 'Thy worm is killed by Atri' (MB. II, 7, 1–4), he should murmur, besprinkling a place where he has a worm with water.

---

15. Khâdira-Grihya IV, 3, 6.
16 seq. Khâdira-Grihya IV, 4, 1 seq.

4 PRAPÂTHAKA, 10 KÂNDIKÂ, 5.

20. If he intends to do this for cattle, he should fetch in the afternoon an earth-clod taken out of a furrow, and should put it down in the open air.

21. In the morning he should strew the dust of it round (the place attacked by worms),· and should murmur (the same texts).

KÂNDIKÂ 10.

1. To the north of the place (in which the Arghya reception will be offered to a·guest), they should bind a cow (to a post or the like), and should (reverentially) approach it with (the verse), 'Arhanâ putra vâsa' (MB. II, 8, 1).

2. (The guest to whom the Arghya reception is going to be offered) should come forward murmuring, 'Here I tread on this Padyâ Virâg for the sake of the enjoyment of food' (ibid. 2).

3. (He should do so) where they are going to perform the Arghya ceremony for him,

4. Or when they perform it.

5. Let them announce three times (to the guest) separately (each of the following things which are

---

10, 1 seq. The Arghya reception; Khâdira-Grihya IV, 4, 5 seq.; Grihya-samgraha II, 62–65. The first words of the Mantra quoted in Sûtra 1 are corrupt. The Mantra is evidently an adaptation of the well-known verse addressed to the Âgrahâyanî (Gobhila III, 9, 9; Mantra-Brâhmana II, 2, 1), or to the Ash/akâ (Pâraskara III, 3, 5, 8): prathamâ ha vyuvâsa, &c. The first word arhanâ ('duly'), containing an allusion to the occasion of the Arghya ceremony, to which this Mantra is adapted, seems to be quite right; the third word may be, as Dr. Knauer conjectures, uvâsa ('she has dwelt,' or perhaps rather 'she has shone'). For the second word I am not able to suggest a correction.

2. Regarding Padyâ Virâg, comp. Sânkhâyana III, 7, 5 note; Pâraskara I, 3, 12.

[30]   K

brought to him) : a bed (of grass to sit down on),
water for washing the feet, the Argha water, water
for sipping, and the Madhuparka (i.e. a mixture of
ghee, curds, and honey).

6. Let him spread out the bed (of grass, so that
the points of the grass are) turned to the north, with
(the verse), 'The herbs which' (MB. II, 8, 3), and
let him sit down thereon ;

7. If there are two (beds of grass), with the two
(verses) separately (MB. II, 8, 3. 4) ;

8. On the second (he treads) with the feet.

9. Let him look at the water (with which he is to
wash his feet), with (the formula), 'From which side
I see the goddesses' (ibid. 5).

10. Let him wash his left foot with (the formula),
'The left foot I wash;' let him wash his right foot
with (the formula), 'The right foot I wash' (MB.
II, 8, 6. 7) ;

11. Both with the rest (of the Mantra, i.e. with
the formula), 'First the one, then the other' (II, 8, 8).

12. Let him accept the Arghya water with (the
formula), 'Thou art the queen of food' (ibid. 9).

13. The water (offered to him) for sipping he
should sip with (the formula), 'Glory art thou'
(ibid. 10).

14. The Madhuparka he should accept with (the
formula), 'The glory's glory art thou' (ibid. 11).

15. Let him drink (of it) three times with (the

---

8. See Pâraskara I, 3, 9.

11. The commentary says, *seshenâvasish/enodakena.* Comp.,
however, Khâdira-Gr/hya IV, 4, 11.

15. I have adopted the reading *sr î bhaksho*, which is given in
the Mantra-Brâhma*n*a, and have followed the opinion of the com-

formula which he repeats thrice), ' The glory's food art thou ; the might's food art thou ; the bliss's food art thou ; bestow bliss on me ' (MB. II, 8, 12) ;

16. Silently a fourth time.

17. Having drunk more of it, he should give the remainder to a Brâhma*n*a.

18. After he has sipped water, the barber should thrice say to him, ' A cow ! '

19. He should reply, ' Let loose the cow from the fetter of Varu*n*a ; bind (with it) him who hates me. Kill him and (the enemy) of N. N., (the enemies) of both (myself and N. N.). Deliver the cow ; let it eat grass, let it drink water' (MB. II, 8, 13).

20. (And after the cow has been set at liberty), let him address it with (the verse), ' The mother of the Rudras' (MB. II, 8, 14).

21. Thus if it is no sacrifice (at which the Arghya reception is offered).

22. (He should say), ' Make it (ready),' if it is a sacrifice.

23. There are six persons to whom the Arghya reception is due, (namely),

---

mentator that the whole Mantra, and not its single parts, should be repeated each time that he drinks of the Madhuparka. In the Khâdira-G*ri*hya the text of the Mantra differs, and the rite is described differently (IV, 4, 15).

16, 17. Perhaps these two Sûtras should be rather understood as forming one Sûtra, and should be translated as I have done in Khâdira-G*ri*hya IV, 4, 16.

19. Iti after abhidhehi ought to be omitted. Comp. the lengthy discussions on this word, pp. 766 seq. of the edition of Gobhila in the Bibliotheca Indica. ' N. N.' is the host who offers the Arghya; comp. Khâdira-G*ri*hya IV, 4, 18.

21, 22. In the case of a sacrifice the cow is killed ; comp. *S*ânkhâyana II, 15, 2. 3 note ; Pâraskara I, 3, 30.

24. A teacher, an officiating priest, a Snâtaka, a king, the father-in-law, a friend coming as a guest.

25. They should offer the Arghya reception (to such persons not more than) once a year.

26. But repeatedly in the case of a sacrifice and of a wedding. But repeatedly in the case of a sacrifice and of a wedding.

End of the Fourth Prapâ*th*aka.

End of the Gobhila-G*ri*hya-sûtra.

---

24. Vivâhya is explained in the commentary by vivâhayi-tavyo *g*âmâtâ. Comp., however, *S*ânkhâyana II, 15, 1 note.
25, 26. Comp. *S*ânkhâyana II, 15, 10 and the note.

GR*I*HYA-SÛTRA OF
HIRA*N*YAKESIN.

INTRODUCTORY NOTE

TO THE

GR*I*HYA-SÛTRA OF HIRA*N*YAKE*S*IN.

AFTER the excellent remarks of Professor Bühler on the position of Hira*n*yakesin among the Sûtra authors of the Black Ya*g*ur-veda (Sacred Books, vol. ii, p. xxiii seq.), I can here content myself with shortly indicating the materials on which my translation of this G*r*ihya-sûtra, which was unpublished when I began to translate it, is based. For the first half of the work I could avail myself, in the first place, of the text, together with the commentary of Mât*r*i-datta, which the late Dr. Schoenberg of Vienna had prepared for publication, and which was based on a number of MSS. collated by him. It is my melancholy duty gratefully to acknowledge here the kindness with which that prematurely deceased young scholar has placed at my disposal the materials he had collected, and the results of his labour which he continued till the last days of his life. For the second half of the Sûtra his death deprived me of this important assistance; here then Professors Kielhorn of Göttingen and Bühler of Vienna have been kind enough to enable me to finish the task of this translation, by lending me two MSS. of the text and two MSS. of Mât*r*idatta's commentary which they possess.

Finally, Dr. J. Kirste of Vienna very kindly sent me the proof-sheets of his valuable edition before it was published. With the aid of these my translation has been revised.

GR*I*HYA-SÛTRA OF

HIRA*N*YAKE*S*IN.

PR*AS*NA I, PATALA 1, SECTION 1.

1. We shall explain the Upanayana (i.e. the initiation of the student).

2. Let him initiate a Brâhma*n*a at the age of seven years,

3. A Râ*g*anya, of eleven, a Vai*s*ya, of twelve.

4. A Brâhma*n*a in the spring, a Râ*g*anya in the summer, a Vai*s*ya in the autumn.

5. In the time of the increasing moon, under an auspicious constellation, preferably (under a constellation) the name of which is masculine,

6. He should serve food to an even number of Brâhma*n*as and should cause them to say, ' An auspicious day! Hail! Good luck!'—

7. (Then he) should have the boy satiated, should

1, 2. The statement commonly given in the Gr*i*hya-sûtras and Dharma-sûtras is, that the initiation of a Brâhma*n*a shall take place in his eighth year, though there are differences of opinion whether in the eighth year after conception, or after birth (Âsvalâyana-Gr*i*hya I, 19, 1. 2). Mât*ri*datta states that the rule given here in the Gr*i*hya-sûtra refers to the seventh year after birth. In the Dharma-sûtra (comp. Âpastamba I, 1, 18) it is stated that the initiation of a Brâhma*n*a shall take place in the eighth year after his conception. Comp. the remarks of Professor Bühler, S. B. E., vol. ii, p. xxiii.

4. Âpastamba I, 1, 18.

6. Comp. Âpastamba I, 13, 8 with Bühler's note.

have his hair shaven, and after (the boy) has bathed and has been decked with ornaments—

8. He should dress him in a (new) garment which has not yet been washed.

9. In a place inclined towards the east, (or) inclined towards the north, (or) inclined towards north-east, or in an even (place), he raises (the surface on which he intends to sacrifice), sprinkles it with water,

10. Kindles fire by attrition, or fetches common (worldly) fire, puts the fire down, and puts wood on the fire.

11. He strews eastward-pointed Darbha grass round the fire ;

12. Or (the grass which is strewn) to the west and to the east (of the fire), may be northward-pointed.

13. He (arranges the Darbha blades so as to) lay the southern (blades) uppermost, the northern ones below, if their points are turned (partly) towards the east and (partly) towards the north.

14. Having strewn Darbha grass, to the south of the fire, in the place destined for the Brahman,

15. Having with the two (verses), ' I take (the fire) to myself,' and, ' The fire which (has entered)'—taken possession of the fire,

16. And having, to the north of the fire, spread out Darbha grass, he prepares the (following) objects,

9. Pâraskara I, 1, 2 ; 4, 3 ; Âsvalâyana I, 3, 1, &c.
11. Âsvalâyana l. l.; Sânkhâyana I, 8, 1, &c.
13. Gobhila I, 7, 14.
14. Gobhila I, 6, 13 ; Pâraskara I, 1, 2, &c.
15. Taittirîya Samhitâ V, 9, 1. Comp. also the parallel passages, Satapatha Brâhmana VII, 3, 2, 17 ; Kâtyâyana-Sraut. XVII, 3, 27.
16. Gobhila I, 7, 1.

according as they are required (for the ceremony which he is going to perform) :

17. A stone, a (new) garment which has not yet been washed, a skin (of an antelope, or a spotted deer, &c.), a threefold-twisted girdle of Muñga grass if he is a Brâhmana (who shall be initiated), a bow-string for a Râganya, a woollen thread for a Vaisya, a staff of Bilva or of Palâsa wood for a Brâhmana, of Nyagrodha wood for a Râganya, of Udumbara wood for a Vaisya.

18. He binds together the fuel, twenty-one pieces of wood, or as many as there are oblations to be made.

19. Together with that fuel he ties up the (three) branches of wood which are to be laid round the fire, (which should have the shape of) pegs.

20. (He gets ready, besides, the spoon called) Darvî, a bunch of grass, the Âgya pot, the pot for the Pranîta water, and whatever (else) is required;

21. All (those objects) together, or (one after the other) as it happens.

22. At that time the Brahman suspends the sacrificial cord over his left shoulder, sips water, passes by the fire, on its west side, to the south side, throws away a grass blade from the Brahman's seat, touches water, and sits down with his face turned towards the fire.

---

17. Sânkhâyana II, 1, 15 seqq., &c.   As to the stone, comp. below, I, 1, 4, 13.

18. Comp. Âsvalâyana I, 10, 3, and the passages quoted in the note (vol. xxix, p. 173).

20. Regarding the bunch of grass, see below, I, 2, 6, 9.

22. Gobhila I, 6, 14 seq.   Comp. the passages quoted in the note.

23. He takes as 'purifiers' two straight Darbha
blades with unbroken points of one span's length,
cuts them off with something else than his nail, wipes
them with water, pours water into a vessel over
which he has laid the purifiers, fills (that vessel) up
to near the brim, purifies (the water) three times
with the two Darbha strainers, holding their points
to the north, places (the water) on Darbha grass on
the north side of the fire, and covers it with Darbha
grass.

24. Having consecrated the Prokshanî water by
means of the purifiers as before, having placed the
vessels upright, and having untied the fuel, he
sprinkles (the sacrificial vessels) three times with the
whole (Prokshanî water).

25. Having warmed the Darvî spoon (over the
fire), having wiped it, and warmed it again, he puts
it down.

26. Having besprinkled (with water) the Darbha
grass with which the fuel was tied together, he
throws it into the fire.

27. He melts the Âgya, pours the Âgya into the
Âgya pot over which he has laid the purifiers, takes
some coals (from the fire) towards the north, puts
(the Âgya) on these (coals), throws light (on the

---

23. Gobhila I, 7, 21 seq.; Sânkhâyana I, 8, 14 seq.   The water
mentioned in this Sûtra is the Pranîta water.

24. Regarding the Prokshanî water, see Sânkhâyana I, 8, 25
note. The word which I have translated by 'vessels' is bilavanti,
which literally means 'the things which have brims.' Probably this
expression here has some technical connotation unknown to me.
Mâtridatta simply says, bilavanti pâtrâni.—'As before' means, 'as
stated with regard to the Pranîta water.'

25. Pâraskara I, 1, 3.

27. Sânkhâyana I, 8, 18 seq.

Âgya by means of burning Darbha blades), throws
two young Darbha shoots into it, moves a fire-brand
round it three times, takes it (from the coals) towards
the north, pushes the coals back (into the fire), purifies the Âgya three times with the two purifiers,
holding their points towards the north, (drawing
them through the Âgya from west to east and)
taking them back (to the west each time), throws
the two purifiers into the fire,

Patala 1, Section 2.

1. And lays the (three) pegs round (the fire).

2. On the west side (of the fire) he places the
middle (peg), with its broad end to the north,

3. On the south side (of the fire the second peg), so
that it touches the middle one, with its broad end to
the east,

4. On the north side (of the fire the third peg),
so that it touches the middle one, with its broad end
to the east.

5. To the west of the fire (the teacher who is
going to initiate the student), sits down with his face
turned towards the east.

6. To the south (of the teacher) the boy, wearing
the sacrificial cord over his left shoulder, having
sipped water, sits down and touches (the teacher).

7. Then (the teacher) sprinkles water round the
fire (in the following way) :

8. On the south side (of the fire he sprinkles

2, 1. The 'pegs' are the pieces of wood mentioned above, 1, 19.

7–10. Gobhila I, 3, 1 seq.   The vocative Sarasvate instead of
Sarasvati is given by the MSS. also in the Khâdira-Grihya I, 2, 19.

water) from west to east with (the words), 'Aditi!
Give thy consent!'—

9. On the west side, from south to north, with
(the words), 'Anumati! Give thy consent!' On
the north side, from west to east, with (the words),
'Sarasvatî! Give thy consent!'—

10. On all sides, so as to keep his right side
turned towards (the fire), with (the Mantra), 'God
Savit*ri*! Give thy impulse!' (Taitt. Sa*m*h. I, 7, 7, 1).

11. Having (thus) sprinkled (water) round (the
fire), and having anointed the fuel (with Â*g*ya), he
puts it on (the fire) with (the Mantra), 'This fuel is
thy self, *G*âtavedas! Thereby thou shalt be inflamed and shalt grow. Inflame us and make us
grow; through offspring, cattle, holy lustre, and
through the enjoyment of food make us increase.
Svâhâ!'

12. He then sacrifices with the (spoon called)
Darvi (the following oblations):

13. Approaching the Darvi (to the fire) by the
northerly junction of the pegs (laid round the fire),
and fixing his mind on (the formula), 'To Pra*g*âpati,
to Manu svâhâ!' (without pronouncing that Mantra),
he sacrifices a straight, long, uninterrupted (stream
of Â*g*ya), directed towards the south-east.

14. Approaching the Darvi (to the fire) by the
southern junction of the pegs (laid round the fire),

---

11. As to the Mantra, compare *S*ânkhâyana II, 10, 4, &c.

13, 14. The two oblations described in these Sûtras are the
so-called Âghâras; see Sûtra 15, and Pâraskara I, 5, 3; Âsvalâyana I, 10, 13. Regarding the northern and the southern junction of the Paridhi woods, see above, Sûtras 3 and 4. According
to Mât*ri*datta, the words 'long, uninterrupted' (Sûtra 13) are to be
supplied also in Sûtra 14.

(he sacrifices) a straight (stream of Âgya), directed towards the north-east, with (the Mantra which he pronounces), 'To Indra svâhâ!'

15. Having (thus) poured out the two Âghâra oblations, he sacrifices the two Âgyabhâgas,

16. With (the words), 'To Agni svâhâ!' over the easterly part of the northerly part (of the fire); with (the words), 'To Soma svâhâ!' over the easterly part of the southerly part (of the fire).

17. Between them he sacrifices the other (oblations).

18. (He makes four oblations with the following Mantras) : ' Thou whom we have set to work, Gâtavedas! carry forward (our offerings). Agni! Perceive this work (i. e. the sacrifice), as it is performed (by us). Thou art a healer, a creator of medicine. Through thee may we obtain cows, horses, and men. Svâhâ!

'Thou who liest down athwart, thinking, " It is I who keep (all things) asunder :" to thee who art propitious (to me), I sacrifice this stream of ghee in the fire. Svâhâ!

' To the propitious goddess svâhâ!
' To the accomplishing goddess svâhâ!'

---

16. Âsvalâyana I, 10, 13; Sânkhâyana I, 9, 7, &c. As to the expressions uttarârdhapûrvârdhe and dakshinârdhapûrvârdhe, comp. Gobhila I, 8, 14 and the note.

17. I.e. between the places at which the two 'Âgya portions' are offered. Comp. Sânkhâyana I, 9, 8.

18. Satapatha Brâhmana XIV, 9, 3, 3 (=Brihad Âranyaka VI, 3, 1; S. B. E., vol. xv, p. 210); Mantra-Brâhmana I, 5, 6.

PATALA 1, SECTION 3.

1. This is the rite for all Darvi-sacrifices.

2. At the end of the Mantras constantly the word Svâhâ (is pronounced).

3. (Oblations) for which no Mantras are prescribed (are made merely with the words), ' To such and such (a deity) svâhâ!'—according to the deity (to whom the oblation is made).

4. He sacrifices with the Vyâh*ri*tis, ' Bhû*h*! Bhuva*h*! Suva*h*!'—with the single (three Vyâh*ri*tis) and with (the three) together.

5. (The Mantras for the two chief oblations are), the (verse), ' Life-giving, Agni!' (Taitt. Brâhma*n*a I, 2, 1, 11), (and),

' Life-giving, O god, choosing long life, thou whose face is full of ghee, whose back is full of ghee, Agni, drinking ghee, the noble ambrosia that comes from the cow, lead this (boy) to old age, as a father (leads) his son.   Svâhâ!'

6. (Then follow oblations with the verses),

' This, O Varu*n*a' (Taitt. Sa*m*h. II, 1, 11, 6),

' For this I entreat thee' (Taitt. Sa*m*h., loc. cit.),

3, 2. Gobhila I, 9, 25.

3. *S*ânkhâyana I, 9, 18.

4. *S*ânkhâyana I, 12, 12. 13; Gobhila I, 9, 27.   As to suva*h*, the spelling of the Taittirîyas for sva*h*, see Indische Studien, XIII, 105.

5, 6. In the second Mantra we should read v*ri*nâno instead of g*ri*nâno; comp. Atharva-veda II, 13, 1.   As to the Mantras that follow, comp. Pâraskara I, 2, 8; Taittirîya Âra*n*yaka IV, 20, 3.— Regarding the Mantra tvam Agne ayâsi (sic), comp. Taitt. Brâh. II, 4, 1, 9; Âsvalâyana-*S*rauta-sûtra I, 11, 13; Kâtyâyana-*S*rautasûtra XXV, 1, 11; Indische Studien, XV, 125.

' Thou, Agni' (Taitt. Samh. II, 5, 12, 3),

' Thus thou, Agni' (Taitt. Samh., loc. cit.),

' Thou, Agni, art quick. Being quick, appointed (by us) in our mind (as our messenger), thou who art quick, carriest the offering (to the gods). O quick one, bestow medicine on us! Svâhâ!'—(and finally) the (verse),

' Pragâpati!' (Taitt. Samh. I, 8, 14, 2).

7. (With the verse), 'What I have done too much in this sacrifice, or what I have done here deficiently, all that may Agni Svishtakrit, he who knows it, make well sacrificed and well offered for me. To Agni Svishtakrit, the offerer of well-offered (sacrifices), the offerer of everything, to him who makes us succeed in our offerings and in our wishes, svâhâ!'—he offers (the Svishtakrit oblation) over the easterly part of the northerly part (of the fire), separated from the other oblations.

8. Here some add as subordinate oblations, before the Svishtakrit, the Gaya, Abhyâtâna, and Râshtrabhrit (oblations).

9. The Gaya (oblations) he sacrifices with (the thirteen Mantras), 'Thought, svâhâ! Thinking, svâhâ!'—or, 'To thought svâhâ! To thinking svâhâ!' (&c.);

10. The Abhyâtâna (oblations) with (the eighteen Mantras), 'Agni is the lord of beings; may he protect me' (&c.).

11. (The words), 'In this power of holiness, in

---

7. Âsvalâyana-Grihya I, 10, 23; Satapatha Brâhmana XIV, 9, 4, 24.
8. Comp. the next Sûtras and Pâraskara I, 5, 7–10.
9. Taittirîya Samhitâ III, 4, 4.
10. Taittirîya Samhitâ III, 4, 5.
11. See the end of the section quoted in the last note.

this worldly power (&c.)' are added to (each section of) the Abhyâtâna formulas.

12. With (the last of the Abhyâtâna formulas), 'Fathers! Grandfathers!' he sacrifices or performs worship, wearing the sacrificial cord over his right shoulder.

13. The Râsh*t*rabh*ri*t (oblations he sacrifices) with (the twelve Mantras), 'The champion of truth, he whose law is truth.' After having quickly repeated (each) section, he sacrifices the first oblation with (the words), 'To him svâhâ!' the second (oblation) with (the words), 'To them svâhâ!'

14. Having placed a stone near the northerly junction of the pegs (which are laid round the fire), (the teacher)—

PATALA 1, SECTION 4.

1. Makes the boy tread on (that stone) with his right foot, with (the verse), 'Tread on this stone; like a stone be firm. Destroy those who seek to do thee harm; overcome thy enemies.'

---

12. 'He performs worship with that Mantra, wearing the sacrificial cord over his right shoulder, to the Manes. According to others, he worships Agni. But this would stand in contradiction to the words (of the Mantra).' Mât*ri*datta.

13. Taittirîya Sa*m*hitâ III, 4, 7. 'To him' (tasmai) is masculine, 'to them' (tâbhya*h*) feminine. The purport of these words will be explained best by a translation of the first section of the Râsh*t*rabh*ri*t formulas: 'The champion of truth, he whose law is truth, Agni is the Gandharva. His Apsaras are the herbs; "sap" is their name. May he protect this power of holiness and this worldly power. May they protect this power of holiness and this worldly power. To him svâhâ! To them svâhâ!'

14. See above, section 2, § 13.

4, 1. Comp. *Sâṅkhâyana* I, 13, 12; Pâraskara I, 7, 1.

2. After (the boy) has taken off his old (garment), (the teacher) makes him put on a (new) garment that has not yet been washed, with (the verses),

'The goddesses who spun, who wove, who spread out, and who drew out the skirts on both sides, may those goddesses clothe thee with long life. Blessed with life put on this garment.

'Dress him; through (this) garment make him reach a hundred (years) of age; extend his life. Br*i*haspati has given this garment to king Soma that he may put it on.

'Mayst thou live to old age; put on the garment! Be a protector of the human tribes against imprecation. Live a hundred years, full of vigour; clothe thyself in the increase of wealth.'

3. Having (thus) made (the boy) put on (the new garment, the teacher) recites over him (the verse),

'Thou hast put on this garment for the sake of welfare; thou hast become a protector of thy friends against imprecation. Live a hundred long years; a noble man, blessed with life, mayst thou distribute wealth.'

4. He then winds the girdle three times from left to right round (the boy, so that it covers) his navel. (He does so only) twice, according to some (teachers). (It is done) with (the verse),

---

2. Pâraskara I, 4, 13. 12; Atharva-veda II, 13, 2. 3 (XIX, 24). Instead of paridâtavâ u, we ought to read, as the Atharva-veda has, paridhâtavâ u.

3. Atharva-veda II, 13, 3; XIX, 24, 6.

4. Sânkhâyana II, 2, 1; Pâraskara II, 2, 8. The text of the Mantra as given by Hira*n*yakesin is very corrupt, but the corruptions may be as old as the Hira*n*yakesi-sûtra itself, or even older.

'Here she has come to us who drives away sin, purifying our guard and our protection, bringing us strength by (the power of) inhalation and exhalation, the sister of the gods, this blessed girdle.'

5. On the north side of the navel he makes a threefold knot (in the girdle) and draws that to the south side of the navel.

6. He then arranges for him the skin (of an antelope, &c., see Sûtra 7) as an outer garment, with (the Mantras),

'The firm, strong eye of Mitra, glorious splendour, powerful and flaming, a chaste, mobile vesture, this skin put on, a valiant (man), N. N.!

'May Aditi tuck up thy garment, that thou mayst study the Veda, for the sake of insight and belief and of not forgetting what thou hast learnt, for the sake of holiness and of holy lustre!'

7. The skin of a black antelope (is worn) by a Brâhma*n*a, the skin of a spotted deer by a Râ*g*anya, the skin of a he-goat by a Vai*s*ya.

8. He then gives him in charge (to the gods), a Brâhma*n*a with (the verse), 'We give this (boy) in charge, O Indra, to Brahman, for the sake of great learning. May he (Brahman?) lead him to old age, and may he (the boy) long watch over learning.'

---

6. I propose to correct *g*arish*n*u into *k*arish*n*u. See *S*ânkhâyana II, 1, 30.

7. *S*ânkhâyana II, 1, 2. 4. 5, &c.

8. In the first hemistich I propose to correct pari dadhmasi into pari dadmasi. The verse seems to be an adaptation of a Mantra which contained a form of the verb pari-dhâ (comp. Atharva-veda XIX, 24, 2); thus the reading pari … dadhmasi found in the MSS. may be easily accounted for. The second hemistich is very corrupt, but the Atharva-veda (loc. cit.: yathaina*m* *g*arase nayât) shows at least the general sense.

A Râganya (he gives in charge to the gods) with
(the verse), 'We give this boy in charge, O Indra, to
Brahman, for the sake of great royalty.   May he
lead him to old age, and may he long watch over
royalty.'

A Vaisya (he gives in charge) with (the verse),
'We give this boy in charge, O Indra, to Brahman,
for the sake of great wealth.   May he lead him to
old age, and may he long watch over wealth.'

9. (The teacher) makes him sit down to the west
of the fire, facing the north, and makes him eat the
remnants of the sacrificial food, with these (Mantras),
' On thee may wisdom, on thee may offspring ' (Taitt.
Âra*n*yaka, Ândhra redaction, X, 44),—altering (the
text of the Mantras).

10. Some make (the student) eat 'sprinkled
butter.'

11. (The teacher) looks at (the student) while he
is eating, with the two verses, ' At every pursuit we
invoke strong (Indra)' (Taitt. Sa*m*h. IV, 1, 2, 1),
(and), ' Him, Agni, lead to long life and splendour'
(Taitt. Sa*m*h. II, 3, 10, 3).

12. Some make (the boy) eat (that food with
these two verses).

13. After (the boy) has sipped water, (the teacher)
causes him to touch (water) and recites over him (the
verse), ' A hundred autumns are before us, O gods,
before ye have made our bodies decay, before (our)

---

9. The text of those Mantras runs thus, 'On me may wisdom,
&c.'; he alters them so as to say, ' On thee,' &c.

10. Regarding the term 'sprinkled butter,' comp. Âsvalâyana-
Grihya IV, 1, 18. 19.

13. Rig-veda I, 89. 9.

sons have become fathers ; do not destroy us before
we have reached (our due) age.'

End of the First Pa*t*ala.

PRASNA I, PATALA 2, SECTION 5.

1. 'To him who comes (to us), we have come.
Drive ye away death !   May we walk with him
safely ; may he walk here in bliss ; (may he) walk in
bliss until (he returns) to his house '—this (verse the
teacher repeats) while (the boy) walks round the fire
so as to keep his right side turned towards it.

2. (The teacher) then causes him to say, ' I have
come hither to be a student.   Initiate me !   I will
be a student, impelled by the god Savit*ri*.'

3. (The teacher then) asks him :

4. ' What is thy name ? '

5. He says, ' N. N !'—what his name is.

6. (The teacher says), ' Happily, god Savit*ri*, may
I attain the goal with this N. N.'—here he pronounces (the student's) two names.

7. With (the verse), ' For bliss may the goddesses
afford us their protection ; may the waters afford
drink to us.   With bliss and happiness may they
overflow us '—both wipe themselves off.

5, 1. I read, pra su m*ri*tyu*m* yuyotana ; comp. Mantra-Brâhma*n*a
I, 6, 14 (Rig-veda I, 136, 1, &c.).   As to the last Pâda, comp. Rig-
veda III, 53, 20.

2 seq. Comp. Gobhila II, 10, 21 seq. ; Pâraskara II, 2, 6 ; Sânkhâyana II, 2, 4, &c.

5. Mât*ri*datta, 'As it is said below, "he pronounces his two
names" (Sûtra 6), the student should here also pronounce his two
names, for instance, "I am Devadatta, Kârttika."'

6. ' His common (vyâvahârika) name and his Nakshatra name.'
Mât*ri*datta.

7. Rig-veda X, 9, 4.

8. Then (the teacher) touches with his right hand (the boy's) right shoulder, and with his left (hand) his left (shoulder), and draws (the boy's) right arm towards himself with the Vyâhr*i*tis, the Sâvitrî verse, and with (the formula), 'By the impulse of the god Savit*ri*, with the arms of the two A*s*vins, with Pûshan's hands I initiate thee, N. N. !'

9. He then seizes with his right hand (the boy's) right hand together with the thumb, with (the words), 'Agni has seized thy hand; Soma has seized thy hand; Savit*ri* has seized thy hand; Sarasvatî has seized thy hand; Pûshan has seized thy hand; B*ri*haspati has seized thy hand; Mitra has seized thy hand; Varu*n*a has seized thy hand; Tvash*tri* has seized thy hand; Dhât*ri* has seized thy hand; Vish*n*u has seized thy hand; Pra*g*âpati has seized thy hand.'

10. 'May Savit*ri* protect thee. Mitra art thou by rights; Agni is thy teacher.

'By the impulse of the god Savit*ri* become B*ri*haspati's pupil. Eat water. Put on fuel. Do the service. Do not sleep in the day-time'—thus (the teacher) instructs him.

11. Then (the teacher) gradually moves his right

---

8. The word which I have translated 'draws ... towards himself' is the same which is also used in the sense of 'he initiates him' (upanayate). Possibly we should correct the text: dakshi*n*am bâhum anv abhyâtmam upanayate, 'he turns him towards himself from left to right (literally, following his right arm).' Comp. *S*ânkhâyana II, 3, 2.—Regarding the Mantra, comp. *S*ânkhâyana II, 2, 12, &c.

9. *S*ânkhâyana II, 2, 11; 3, 1, &c.

10. *S*ânkhâyana II, 3, 1; 4, 5. We ought to read apo·sâna, instead of apo·sâna*h* as the MSS. have.

11. *S*ânkhâyana II, 4, 1, &c.

hand down over (the boy's) right shoulder and
touches the place of his heart with (the formulas),
'Thy heart shall dwell in my heart; my mind thou
shalt follow with thy mind; in my word thou shalt
rejoice with all thy heart; may Br*i*haspati join thee
to me!

'To me alone thou shalt adhere. In me thy
thoughts shall dwell. Upon me thy veneration
shall be bent. When I speak, thou shalt be silent.'

12. With (the words), 'Thou art the knot of all
breath; do not loosen thyself'—(he touches) the
place of his navel.

13. After (the teacher) has recited over him (the
formula),

'Bhû*h*! Bhuva*h*! Suva*h*! By offspring may I become rich in offspring! By valiant sons, rich in valiant
sons! By splendour, rich in splendour! By wealth,
rich in wealth! By wisdom, rich in wisdom! By
pupils, rich in holy lustre!'

And (again the formulas),

'Bhû*h*! I place thee in the *Ri*k*as, in Agni, on the
earth, in voice, in the Brahman, N. N.!

'Bhuva*h*! I place thee in the Yag*us*, in Vâyu,
in the air, in breath, in the Brahman, N. N.!

'Suva*h*! I place thee in the Sâmans, in Sûrya,
in heaven, in the eye, in the Brahman, N. N.!

'May I be beloved (?) and dear to thee, N. N.!

---

13. The reading of the last Mantra is doubtful. Ish*t*atas
should possibly be ish*t*as, but the genitive analasya, or, as some
of the MSS. have, ana*l*asya (read, analasasya?), points rather to
a genitive like i*kk*hatas. If we write i*kk*hatas and analasasya,
the translation would be: 'May I be dear to thee, who loves me,
N. N.! May I be dear to thee, who art zealous, N. N.!' Comp.
*S*ânkhâyana II, 3, 3.

May I be dear to thee, the fire (?), N. N.! Let us dwell here! Let us dwell in breath and life! Dwell in breath and life, N. N.!'—

14. He then seizes with his right hand (the boy's) right hand together with the thumb, with the five sections, 'Agni is long-lived.'

15. 'May (Agni) bestow on thee long life everywhere' (Taitt. Sa*m*h. I, 3, 14, 4)—

PATALA 2, SECTION 6.

1. (This verse the teacher) murmurs in (the boy's) right ear;

2. (The verse), 'Life-giving, Agni' (Taitt. Sa*m*h. I, 3, 14, 4) in his left ear.

3. Both times he adds (to the verses quoted in the last Sûtras the formula), 'Stand fast in Agni and on the earth, in Vâyu and in the air, in Sûrya and in heaven. The bliss in which Agni, Vâyu, the sun, the moon, and the waters go their way, in that bliss go thy way, N. N.! Thou hast become the pupil of breath, N. N.!'

4. Approaching his mouth to (the boy's) mouth he murmurs, 'Intelligence may Indra give thee, intelligence the goddess Sarasvatî. Intelligence may the two Asvins, wreathed with lotus, bestow on thee.'

5. He then gives (the boy) in charge (to the gods and demons, with the formulas), 'To Kashaka (?) I

14. Comp. above, Sûtra 9.
6, 3. Âsvalâyana I, 20, 8.
4. Âsvalâyana I, 15, 2 ; 22, 26 ; Pâraskara II, 4, 8.
5. Comp. Sânkhâyana II, 3, 1 ; Pâraskara II, 2, 21.   The name

give thee in charge. To Antaka I give thee in charge.
To Aghora ("the not frightful one") I give thee in
charge. To Disease ... to Yama ... to Makha ...
to Va*s*inî ("the ruling goddess") ... to the earth together with Vai*s*vânara ... to the waters ... to the
herbs ... to the trees ... to Heaven and Earth ... to
welfare ... to holy lustre ... to the Vi*s*ve devâs ...
to all beings ... to all deities I give thee in charge.'

6. He now teaches him the Sâvitrî, if he has
(already) been initiated before.

7. If he has not been initiated (before, he teaches
him the Sâvitrî) after three days have elapsed.

8. (He does so) immediately, says Pushkarasâdi.

9. Having placed to the west of the fire a bunch
of grass with its points directed towards the north,
(the teacher) sits down thereon, facing the east, with
(the formula), 'A giver of royal power art thou, a
teacher's seat. May I not withdraw from thee.'

10. The boy raises his joined hands towards the
sun, embraces (the feet of) his teacher, sits down to
the south (of the teacher), addresses (him), 'Recite,
sir!' and then says, 'Recite the Sâvitrî, sir!'

11. Having recited over (the boy the verse), 'We
call thee, the lord of the hosts' (Taitt. Sa*m*h. II, 3,
14, 3), he then recites (the Sâvitrî) to him, firstly
Pâda by Pâda, then hemistich by hemistich, and
then the whole verse (in the following way),

---

in the first section of the Mantra is spelt Ka*s*hakâya and Ka*s*a-
kâya. Comp. Mantra-Brâhma*n*a I, 6, 22: K*r*isana, ida*m* te pari-
dadâmy amum; Atharva-veda IV, 10, 7: Karsanas tvâbhirak-
shatu.

6. 'A repetition of the initiation takes place as a penance.'
Mât*r*idatta.

9–11. Comp. *S*ânkhâyana II, 5, &c.

'Bhûs! Tat Savitur vare*n*ya*m* (That adorable splendour)—

'Bhuvo! Bhargo devasya dhîmahi (of the divine Savit*ri* may we obtain)—

'Suvar! Dhiyo yo na*h* pra*k*odayât (who should rouse our prayers).—

'Bhûr bhuvas! Tat Savitur vare*n*ya*m* bhargo devasya dhîmahi—

'Suvar! Dhiyo yo na*h* pra*k*odayât.—

'Bhûr bhuva*h* suvas! Tat Savitur . . . pra*k*odayât.'

PATALA 2, SECTION 7.

1. He then causes (the student) to put on the fire seven pieces of fresh Palâsa wood, with unbroken tops, of one span's length, which have been anointed with ghee.

2. One (of these pieces of wood he puts on the fire) with (the Mantra), 'To Agni I have brought a piece of wood, to the great *G*âtavedas. As thou art inflamed, Agni, through that piece of wood, thus inflame me through wisdom, insight, offspring, cattle, holy lustre, and through the enjoyment of food. Svâhâ!'—

3. (Then he puts on the fire) two (pieces of wood with the same Mantra, using the dual instead of the

---

7, 1 seq. Comp. Âsvalâyana I, 21, 1; *S*ânkhâyana II, 10, &c. 'The putting of fuel on the fire, and what follows after it, form a part of the chief ceremony, not of the recitation of the Sâvitrî. Therefore in the case of one who has not yet been initiated (see I, 2, 6, 7), it ought to be performed immediately after (the student) has been given in charge (to the gods and demons; I, 2, 6, 5).' Mât*ri*datta.

2. Pâraskara II, 4, 3.

singular), 'To Agni (I have brought) two pieces of wood;'

4. (Then) four (pieces of wood, using the plural), 'To Agni (I have brought) pieces of wood.'

5. He then sprinkles (water) round (the fire) as above.

6. 'Thou hast given thy consent;' 'Thou hast given thy impulse'—thus he changes the end of each Mantra.

7. He then worships the (following) deities (with the following Mantras),

8. Agni with (the words), 'Agni, lord of the vow, I shall keep the vow;'

9. Vâyu with (the words), 'Vâyu, lord of the vow, (&c.);'

10. Âditya (the sun) with (the words), 'Âditya, lord of the vow, (&c.);'

11. The lord of the vows with (the words), 'Lord of the vows, ruling over the vows (&c.).'

12. He then gives an optional gift to his Guru (i. e. to the teacher).

13. (The teacher) makes him rise with (the verse which the student recites), 'Up! with life' (Taitt. Samh. I, 2, 8, 1); he gives him in charge (to the sun) with (the words), 'Sun! This is thy son; I give him in charge to thee;' and he worships the sun with (the Mantra), 'That bright eye created by the gods which rises in the east : may we see it a hundred autumns; may we live a hundred autumns; may we

5. Comp. above, I, 1, 2, 7 seq.

6. He says, 'Anumati! Thou hast given thy consent!' &c.

8 seq. Comp. Gobhila II, 10, 16.

12. Comp. Sânkhâyana I, 14, 13 seq.

13. Pâraskara I, 8, 7; I, 6, 3.

rejoice a hundred autumns; may we be glad a hundred autumns; may we prosper a hundred autumns; may we hear a hundred autumns; may we speak a hundred autumns; may we live undecaying a hundred autumns; and may we long see the sun.'

14. 'May Agni further give thee life.   May Agni further grant thee bliss.   May Indra with the Maruts here give (that) to thee; may the sun with the Vasus give (it) to thee '—with (this verse the teacher) gives him a staff, and then hands over to him a bowl (for collecting alms).

15. Then he says to him, ' Go out for alms.'

16. Let him beg of his mother first;

17. Then (let him beg) in other houses where they are kindly disposed towards him.

18. He brings (the food which he has received) to his Guru (i. e. to the teacher), and announces it to him by saying, '(These are) the alms.'

19. (The teacher accepts it) with the words, ' Good alms they are.'

20. 'May all gods bless thee whose first garment we accept.   May after thee, the prosperous one, the well-born, many brothers and friends be born '—with (this verse the teacher) takes (for himself) the former garment (of the student).

21. When the food (with which the Brâhma*n*as shall be entertained) is ready, (the student) takes some portion of boiled rice, cakes, and flour, mixes

---

14. Sânkhâyana II, 6, 2, &c.

16 seq. Sânkhâyana II, 6, 4 seq.; Âpastamba I, 3, 28 seq.

17. The commentary explains râtikuleshu by *gñâ*tipra-bh*ri*tishu;—comp. yo⸱sya râtir bhavati, I, 3, 9, 18.

20. See above, I, 1, 4, 2, and comp. Atharva-veda II, 13, 5.

(these substances) with clarified butter, and sacrifices with (the formulas), 'To Agni svâhâ! To Soma svâhâ! To Agni, the eater of food, svâhâ! To Agni, the lord of food, svâhâ! To Pragâpati svâhâ! To the Visve devâs svâhâ! To all deities svâhâ! To Agni Svish*t*akr*i*t svâhâ!'

22. Thus (let him sacrifice) wherever (oblations of food are prescribed) for which the deities (to whom they shall be offered) are not indicated.

23. If the deity is indicated, (let him sacrifice) with (the words), 'To such and such (a deity) svâhâ!'— according to which deity it is.

24. Taking (again) some portion of the same kinds of food, he offers it as a Bali on eastward-pointed Darbha grass, with (the words), 'To Vâstu-pati (i. e. Vâstoshpati) svâhâ!'

25. After he has served those three kinds of food to the Brâhma*n*as, and has caused them to say, 'An auspicious day! Hail! Good luck!'—

Patala 2, Section 8.

1. He keeps through three days the (following) vow:

2. He eats no pungent or saline food and no vegetables; he sleeps on the ground; he does not drink out of an earthen vessel; he does not give the remnants of his food to a *S*ûdra; he does not eat honey or meat; he does not sleep in the day-

---

23. Comp. above, I, 1, 3, 3.

24. 'The same,' of course, refers to Sûtra 21.

25. See above, I, 1, 1, 6.

8, 1. This is the Sâvitra-vrata. Comp. I, 2, 6, 7; *S*ânkhâyana, Introduction, p. 8.

2. Regarding the term 'pungent food,' comp. Professor Bühler's notes on Âpastamba I, 1, 2, 23; II, 6, 15, 15.

time ; in the morning and in the evening he brings (to his teacher) the food which he has received as alms and a pot of water ; every day (he fetches) a bundle of firewood ; in the morning and in the evening, or daily in the evening he puts fuel on (the fire, in the following way) :

3. Before sprinkling (water) round (the fire), he wipes (with his wet hand) from left to right round (the fire) with the verse, ' As you have loosed, O Vasus, the buffalo-cow' (Taitt. Sa*m*h. IV, 7, 15, 7), and sprinkles (water) round (the fire) as above.

4. (Then) he puts (four) pieces of wood (on the fire) with the single (Vyâh*ri*tis) and with (the three Vyâh*ri*tis) together, and (four other pieces) with (the following four verses),

' This fuel is thine, Agni ; thereby thou shalt grow and gain vigour. And may we grow and gain vigour. Svâhâ !

' May Indra give me insight ; may Sarasvatî, the goddess, (give) insight ; may both A*s*vins, wreathed with lotus, bestow insight on me. Svâhâ !

' The insight that dwells with the Apsaras, the mind that dwells with the Gandharvas, the divine insight and that which is born from men : may that insight, the fragrant one, rejoice in me ! Svâhâ !

' May insight, the fragrant one, that assumes all shapes, the gold-coloured, mobile one, come to me. Rich in sap, swelling with milk, may she, insight, the lovely-faced one, rejoice in me ! Svâhâ ! '

5. Having wiped round (the fire) in the same way, he sprinkles (water) round (the fire) as above.

---

3. See I, 1, 2, 7 seq.; Âpastamba Dharma-sûtra I, 1, 4, 18.

4. Âpastamba I, 1, 4, 16 ; *S*âṅkhâyana II, 10, 4, &c.

5. See Sûtra 3 and the note.

6. He worships the fire with the Mantras, 'What thy splendour is, Agni, may I thereby' (Taitt. Sa*m*h. III, 5, 3, 2), and 'On me may insight, on me off-spring' (Taitt. Âra*n*yaka X, 44).

7. After the lapse of those three days (Sûtra 1) he serves in the same way the three kinds of food (stated above) to the Brâhma*n*as, causes them to say, 'An auspicious day! Hail! Good luck!' and discharges himself of his vow by (repeating) these (Mantras) with (the necessary) alterations, 'Agni, lord of the vow, I have kept the vow' (see above, I, 2, 7, 8).

8. He keeps the same observances afterwards (also),

9. Dwelling in his teacher's house. He may eat, (however,) pungent and saline food and vegetables.

10. He wears a staff, has his hair tied in one knot, and wears a girdle,

11. Or he may tie the lock on the crown of the head in a knot.

12. He wears (an upper garment) dyed with red Loth, or the skin (of an antelope, &c.).

13. He does not have intercourse with women.

14. (The studentship lasts) forty-eight years, or

---

6. Âsvalâyana-Gr*i*hya I, 21, 4.

7. See I, 2, 7, 21. 25.

8. He keeps the observances stated in Sûtra 2.

9. See above, Sûtra 2. Comp. Âpastamba Dharma-sûtra I, 1, 2, 11, and Sûtra 23 of the same section, which stands in contradiction to this Sûtra of Hira*n*yakesin.

10, 11. Comp. Âpastamba I, 1, 2, 31. 32. Mâtr*i*datta has received into his explanation of the eleventh Sûtra the words, 'he should shave the rest of the hair,' which in the Âpastambîya-sûtra are found in the text.

14. Âsvalâyana-Gr*i*hya I, 22, 3; Âpastamba Dharma-sûtra I, 1, 2, 12 seq.

twenty-four (years), or twelve (years), or until he has learnt (the Veda).

15. He should not, however, omit keeping the observances.

16. At the beginning and on the completion of the study of a Kâ*nd*a (of the Black Ya*g*ur-veda he sacrifices) with (the verse), 'The lord of the seat, the wonderful one, the friend of Indra, the dear one, I have entreated for the gift of insight. Svâhâ!'

In the second place the *Ri*shi of the Kâ*nd*a (receives an oblation).

(Then follow oblations with the verses), 'This, O Varu*n*a;' 'For this I entreat thee;' 'Thou, Agni;' 'Thus thou, Agni;' 'Thou, Agni, art quick;' 'Pra*g*âpati!' and, 'What I have done too much in this sacrifice.' Here some add as subordinate oblations the *G*aya, Abhyâtâna, and Râsh*t*rabh*ri*t (oblations) as above.

End of the Second Pa*t*ala.

PRAS*N*A I, PA*T*AL*A* 3, SECTION 9.

1. After he has studied the Veda, the bath (which signifies the end of his studentship, is taken by him).

2. We shall explain that (bath).

3. During the northern course of the sun, in the time of the increasing moon, under (the Nakshatra) Rohi*n*î, (or) M*ri*ga*s*iras, (or) Tishya, (or) Uttarâ

---

16. Rig-veda I, 18, 6. As the *Ri*shis of the single Kâ*nd*as are considered, *Pra*g*âpati, Soma, Agni, the Vi*s*ve devâs, Svayambhû. Regarding the Mantras quoted in the last section of this Sûtra, see above, I, 1, 3, 5–7.

Phalguni, (or) Hasta, (or) *K*itrâ, or the two Visâkhâs: under these (Nakshatras) he may take the bath.

4. He goes to a place near which water is, puts wood on the fire, performs the rites down to the oblations made with the Vyâh*ri*tis, and puts a piece of Palâ*s*a wood on (the fire) with (the verse), 'Let us prepare this song like a chariot, for *G*âtavedas who deserves it, with our prayer. For his foresight in this assembly is a bliss to us. Agni! Dwelling in thy friendship may we not suffer harm. Svâhâ!'

5. Then he sacrifices with the Vyâh*ri*tis as above,

6. (And another oblation with the verse), 'The threefold age of *G*amadagni, Ka*s*yapa's threefold age, the threefold age that belongs to the gods: may that threefold age be mine. Svâhâ!'

7. (Then follow oblations with the verses), 'This, O Varu*n*a,' &c. (see above, I, 2, 8, 16, down to the end of the Sûtra).

8. After he has served food to the Brâhma*n*as, and has caused them to say, 'An auspicious day! Hail! Good luck!' he discharges himself of his vow by (repeating) these (Mantras), 'Agni, lord of the vow, I have kept the vow.'

9. Having (thus) discharged himself of his vow, he worships the sun with the two (verses), 'Upwards

---

9, 4. Comp. I, 1, 3, 4; Rig-veda I, 94, 1. 'Where the words are used, " He puts wood on the fire " (agnim upasamâdhâya), he should prepare the ground by raising it, &c., should carry the fire to that place, should put wood on it, and then he should sacrifice in the fire. Where those words are not used, he should (only) strew grass round the fire which is (already) established in its proper place, and should thus perform the sacrifice.' Mât*ri*datta.

6. *S*ânkhâyana I, 28, 9.

8. Comp. I, 2, 7, 25; 8, 7.

that (*G*âtavedas)' (Taitt. Sa*m*h. I, 4, 43, 1), and, 'The bright' (ibid.).

10. With (the words), '(Loosen) from us thy highest band, Varu*n*a,' he takes off the upper garment which he has worn during his studentship, and puts on another (garment). With (the words), '(Loosen) the lowest (fetter),' (he takes off) the under garment; with (the words), '(Take) away the middle (fetter),' the girdle. With (the words), 'And may we, O Âditya, under thy law (&c.),' (he deposes) his staff. The girdle, the staff, and the black antelope's skin he throws into water, sits down to the west of the fire, facing the east, and touches the razor (with which he is going to be shaven), with (the formula), 'Razor is thy name; the axe is thy father. Adoration to thee! Do no harm to me!'

11. Having handed over (that razor) to the barber, he touches the water with which his hair is to be moistened, with (the formula), 'Be blissful, (O waters), when we touch you.' [(The barber) then pours together warm and cold water. Having poured warm (water) into cold (water)—]

12. (The barber) moistens the hair near the right ear with (the words), 'May the waters moisten thee for life, for old age and splendour' (Taitt. Sa*m*hitâ I, 2, 1, 1).

---

10. The words quoted in this Sûtra are the parts of a *Rik* which is found in Taittirîya Sa*m*hitâ I, 5, 11, 3.

11. The words which I have included in brackets are wanting in some of the MSS., and are not explained in the commentaries. They are doubtless a spurious addition. Comp. Âsvalâyana I, 17, 6, &c.

12. Pâraskara II, 1, 9. The same expression dakshi*n*a*m* godânam, of which I have treated there in the note, is used in this Sûtra. Comp., besides, Sânkhâyana-G*ri*hya I, 28, 9; Âpa-

13. With (the words), 'Herb! protect him' (Taitt. Sam̃h., loc. cit.), he puts an herb with the point upwards into (the hair).

14. With (the words), 'Axe! do no harm to him!' (Taitt. Sam̃h., loc. cit.), he touches (that herb) with the razor.

15. With (the words), 'Heard by the gods, I shave that (hair)' (Taitt. Sam̃h., loc. cit.), he shaves him.

16. With (the formula), 'If thou shavest, O shaver, my hair and my beard with the razor, the wounding, the well-shaped, make our face resplendent, but do not take away our life'—(the student who is going to take the bath), looks at the barber.

17. He has the beard shaven first, then the hair in his arm-pits, then the hair (on his head), then the hair of his body, then (he has) his nails (cut).

18. A person who is kindly disposed (towards the student), gathers the hair, the beard, the hair of the body, and the nails (that have been cut off), in a lump of bull's dung, and buries (that lump of dung) in a cow-stable, or near an Udumbara tree, or in a clump of Darbha grass, with (the words), 'Thus I

---

stamba-Srauta-sûtra X, 5, 8; Satapatha-Br. III, 1, 2, 6. According to Mâtr̃idatta, there is some difference of opinion between the different teachers as to whether the Mantras for the moistening of the hair and the following rites are to be repeated by the teacher or by the barber.

13. Âsvalâyana I, 17, 8; Pâraskara II, 1, 10; Âpastamba-Sraut., loc. cit.; Kâtyâyana-Sraut. VII, 2, 10. The parallel texts prescribe that one Kusa blade, or three Kusa blades, should be put into the hair.

14. Yâgñikadeva in his commentary on Kâtyâyana (loc. cit.) says, kshuren̄âbhinidhâya kshuradhârâm antarhitatr̃inasyopari nidhâya.

16. Âsvalâyana I, 17, 16. Comp. also Rig-veda I, 24, 11.

hide the sin of N. N., who belongs to the Gotra N. N.'

19. Having rubbed himself with powder such as is used in bathing, he cleanses his teeth with a stick of Udumbara wood—

PATALA 3, SECTION 10.

1. With (the formula), 'Stand in your places for the sake of the enjoyment of food. Stand in your places for the sake of long life. Stand in your places for the sake of holy lustre. May I be blessed with long life, an enjoyer of food, adorned with holy lustre.'

2. Then (the teacher) makes him wash himself with lukewarm water, with the three verses, ' O waters, ye are wholesome' (Taitt. Sa*m*h. IV, 1, 5, 1), with the four verses, 'The gold-coloured, clean, purifying (waters)' (Taitt. Sa*m*h. V, 6, 1), and with the Anuvâka, 'The purifier, the heavenly one' (Taitt. Brâhma*n*a I, 4, 8).

3. Or (instead of performing these rites in the neighbourhood of water) they make an enclosure in a cow-stable and cover it (from all sides); that (the student) enters before sunrise, and in that (enclosure) the whole (ceremony) is performed. 'On that day the sun does not shine upon him,' some say. 'For he who shines (i. e. the sun), shines by the splendour of those who have taken the bath. Therefore the face of a Snâtaka is, as it were, resplendent (?).'

. 4. (His friends or relations) bring him all sorts of

10, 3. Rephâyativa dîpyatîva. Mât*r*/datta. Comp. Âpastamba Dharma-sûtra II, 6, 14, 13, and Bühler's note, S. B. E., vol. ii, p. 135.

4. Comp. above, I, 2, 8, 4.

perfumes, or ground sandal wood; he besprinkles
that (with water), and worships the gods by raising
his joined hands towards the east, with (the formulas), 'Adoration to Graha (the taker) and to
Abhigraha (the seizer)! Adoration to Sâka and
Gangabha! Adoration to those deities who are
seizers!' (Then) he anoints himself with (that
salve of sandal wood) with (the verse), 'The scent
that dwells with the Apsaras, and the splendour that
dwells with the Gandharvas, divine and human
scent: may that here enter upon me!'

5. They bring him a pair of (new) garments that
have not yet been washed. He besprinkles them
(with water) and puts on the under garment with
(the formula), 'Thou art Soma's body; protect my
body! Thou who art my own body, enter upon me;
thou who art a blissful body, enter upon me.' Then
he touches water, (puts on) the upper garment with
the same (Mantra), and sits down to the west of the
fire, facing the east.

6. They bring him two ear-rings and a perforated
pellet of sandal wood or of Badarî wood, overlaid
with gold (at its aperture); these two things he ties
to a Darbha blade, holds them over the fire, and
pours over them (into the fire) oblations (of ghee)
with (the Mantras),

'May this gold which brings long life and splendour and increase of wealth, and which gets through
(all adversities), enter upon me for the sake of long
life, of splendour, and of victory. Svâhâ!

---

6. Regarding the first Mantra, comp. Vâgas. Samhitâ XXXIV,
50. In the fifth Mantra we ought to read oshadhis trâyamânâ.
Comp. below, I, 3, 11, 3; Pâraskara I, 13; Atharva-veda VIII,
2, 6.

'(This gold) brings high gain, superiority in battles, superiority in assemblies; it conquers treasures. All perfections unitedly dwell together in this gold. Svâhâ!

'I have obtained an auspicious name like (the name) of a father of gold. Thus may (the gold) make me shine with golden lustre; (may it make me) beloved among many people; may it make me full of holy lustre. Svâhâ!

'Make me beloved among the gods; make me beloved with Brahman (i. e. among the Brâhmaṇas), beloved among Vaiśyas and Sûdras; make me beloved among the kings (i. e. among the Kshatriyas). Svâhâ!

'This herb is protecting, overcoming, and powerful. May it make me shine with golden lustre; (may it make me) beloved among many people; may it make me full of holy lustre. Svâhâ!'

7. Having thrice washed (the two ear-rings) in a vessel of water with the same five (Mantras), without the word Svâhâ, (moving them round in the water) from left to right—

PATALA 3, SECTION 11.

1. He puts on the two ear-rings, the right one to his right ear, the left one to his left ear, with (the verse which he repeats for each of the two ear-rings), 'Virâg and Svarâg, and the aiding powers that dwell in our house, the prosperity that dwells in the face of royalty: therewith unite me.'

2. With (the Mantra), 'With the seasons and the combinations of seasons, for the sake of long life, of

11, 2. The end of the Mantra is corrupt. We ought to read, as

splendour, with the sap that dwells in the year:
therewith we make them touch the jaws '—he clasps
the two ear-rings.

3. With (the Mantra), 'This herb is protecting,
overcoming, and powerful. May it make me shine
with golden lustre ; (may it make me) beloved among
many people ; may it make me full of holy lustre.
Thou art not a bond '—he ties the pellet (of wood,
mentioned above, Section 10, Sûtra 6) to his neck.

4. He puts on a wreath with the two (verses),
'Beautiful one, elevate thyself to beauty, beauti-
fying my face. Beautify my face and make my
fortune increase'—(and),

'(The wreath) which *G*amadagni has brought to
*S*raddhâ to please her, that I put on (my head)
together with fortune and splendour.'

5. 'The salve coming from the Trikakud (mountain), born on the Himavat, therewith I anoint you
(i. e. the eyes), and with fortune and splendour.
(I put ?) into myself the demon of the mountain (?) '
—with (this verse) he anoints himself with Traikakuda salve, (or) if he cannot get that, with some
other (salve).

6. With (the verse), ' My mind that has fled away'
(Taitt. Sa*m*hitâ VI, 6, 7, 2) he looks into a mirror.

Dr. Kirste has shown, tena sa*m*hanu k*ri*nmasi (Av. V, 28, 13).
Mât*ri*datta says, sa*m*g*ri*h*n*îte = pidhânenâpidadhâti pratigrahasa*m*-
graha*n*ayo*h* sa*m*yuktatvâd ekâpavargatvât.

3. The Mantra, with the exception of the last words, is identical
with the last verse of Section 10, Sûtra 6. Here the MSS. again
have oshadhe for oshadhis.

4. Comp. Atharva-veda VI, 137: yâm *G*amadagnir akhanad
duhitre, &c.; Pâraskara II, 6, 23.

5. Regarding the Traikakuda salve, comp. Zimmer, Altindisches
Leben, p. 69, and see Atharva-veda IV, 9, 9.

7. With (the formula), 'On the impulse of the god,' &c., he takes a staff of reed (which somebody hands him), and with (the formula), 'Thou art the thunderbolt of Indra. O Asvins, protect me!'—he thrice wipes it off, upwards from below.

8. With (the formula), 'Speed! Make speed away from us those who hate us, robbers, creeping things, beasts of prey, Rakshas, Pisâ*k*as. Protect us, O staff, from danger that comes from men ; protect us from every danger; from all sides destroy the robbers '—(and with the verse), 'Not naked (i. e. covered with bark) thou art born on all trees, a destroyer of foes. Destroy all hosts of enemies from every side like Maghavan (Indra)'—he swings (the staff) three times from left to right over his head.

9. With (the formula), 'The divine standing-places are you. Do not pinch me'—he steps into the shoes.

10. With (the formula), 'Pra*g*âpati's shelter art thou, the Brahman's covering '—he takes the parasol.

11. With the verse, 'My staff which fell down in the open air to the ground, that I take up again for the sake of long life, of holiness, of holy lustre '—he takes up his staff, if it has fallen from his hand.

End of the Third Pa*t*ala.

---

7. He takes the staff with the well-known Sàvitra formula, 'On the impulse of the god Savit*ri* . . . I take thee.'

9. Âsvalâyana III, 8, 19; Pâraskara II, 6, 30.

10. Âsvalâyana III, 8, 19; Pâraskara II, 6, 29.

11. Instead of yamâyushe I propose to read âyushe. Comp. Pâraskara II, 2, 12.

PRASNA I, PATALA 4, SECTION 12.

1. They bring him a chariot, (or) a horse, or an elephant.

2. 'Thou art the (Sâman called) Rathantara; thou art the Vâmadevya; thou art the Br*i*hat;' the (verse), 'The two Aṅkas, the two Nyaṅkas' (Taitt. Sa*m*hitâ I, 7, 7, 2); (the verse), 'May this your chariot, O A*s*vins, not suffer damage, neither in pain nor in joy. May it make its way without damage, dispersing those who infest us;' (and the formula), 'Here is holding, here is keeping asunder; here is enjoyment, here may it enjoy itself:' with (these texts) he ascends the chariot, if he enters (the village) on a chariot.

3. 'A horse art thou, a steed art thou'—with these eleven 'horses' names' (Taitt. Sa*m*h. VII, 1, 12) (he mounts) the horse, if (he intends to enter the village) on horseback.

4. With (the formula), 'With Indra's thunderbolt I bestride thee; carry (me); carry the time; carry me forward to bliss. An elephant art thou. The elephant's glory art thou. The elephant's splendour art thou. May I become endowed with the elephant's glory, with the elephant's splendour'—(he mounts) the elephant, if (he intends to proceed to the village) on it.

12, 2. Comp. Pâraskara III, 14, 3-6.

3. In this Sûtra three 'horses' names' are given as the Pratîka of the Ya*g*us quoted, 'Thou art a*s*va, thou art haya, thou art maya.' Mâtr*i*datta observes that the third of them is not found in the Taittirîya Sa*m*hitâ, which gives only ten, and not eleven, horses' names.

4. Pâraskara III, 15, 1 seq.

5. He goes to a place where they will do honour to him.

6. With (the verse), 'May the quarters (of the horizon) stream together with me ; may all delight assemble (here). May all wishes that are dear to us, come near unto us; may (our) dear (wishes) stream towards us '—he worships the quarters of the horizon.

7. While approaching the person who is going to do honour to him, he looks at him with (the words), 'Glory art thou ; may I become glory with thee.'

8. Then (the host who is going to offer the Argha reception to the Snâtaka), having prepared the dwelling-place (for his reception), says to him, ' The Argha (will be offered)!'

9. (The guest) replies, 'Do so !'

10. They prepare for him (the Madhuparka or 'honey mixture') consisting of three or of five substances.

11. The three substances are, curds, honey, and ghee.

12. The five substances are, curds, honey, ghee, water, and ground grains.

13. Having poured curds into a brass vessel, he pours honey into it, (and then the other substances stated above).

14. Having poured (those substances) into a smaller vessel, and having covered it with a larger (cover than the vessel is), (the host) makes (the guest) accept (the following things) separately, one after the other, viz. a bunch of grass (to sit down on),

5. Âsvalâyana III, 9, 3; Sâṅkhâyana III, 1, 14.

10 seq. Pâraskara I, 3, 5; Âsvalâyana I 24, 5 seq.

14. Pâraskara, loc. cit. ; Âsvalâyana, loc. cit., § 7.

water for washing the feet, the Argha water, water for sipping, and the honey-mixture (Madhuparka).

15. Going after (the single objects which are brought to the guest, the host) in a faultless, not faltering (?) voice, announces (each of those objects to the guest).

16. The bunch of grass (he announces by three times saying), ' The bunch of grass ! '

17. (The guest) sits down thereon facing the east, with (the formula), 'A giver of royal power art thou, a teacher's seat; may I not withdraw from thee.'

18. (The host) then utters to him the announcement, ' The water for washing the feet ! '

19. With that (water) a *S*ûdra or a *S*ûdra woman washes his feet; the left foot first for a Brâhma*n*a, the right for a person of the two other castes.

PATALA 4, SECTION 13.

1. With (the formula), ' The milk of Virâ*g* art thou. May the milk of Padyâ Virâ*g* (dwell) in me ' —(the guest) touches the hands of the person that

---

15. The text is corrupt and the translation very doubtful. The MSS. have, anusa*mvr*igin â so*·*nupaki*ñk*ayâ vâkâ. Mât*ri*datta's note, which is also very corrupt, runs thus: anusa*m*vraginâ saha kûr*k*âdinâ dravye*n*a tad agrata*h* k*ri*tvânugantâ. anusa*m*vr*ig*ineti (sic; anuga*kh*a*mn*nusa*m*v°, Dr. Kielhorn's MS.) pramâdapâ*th*a*h*. sampradâtânupaki*ñk*ayâ na vidyata upaghâtikâ vâg yasya [yasyâ, Dr. K.'s MS.] seyam anupaki*ñk*â vâk . . . ke*k*id anusa*mvr*igineti (anusa*m*vragineti, Dr. Kirste) pâ*th*ântara*m* k*ri*tvâ vâgviseshana*m* i*kkh*anti yathâ m*ri*sh*t*â vâk sa*m*sk*ri*tâ vâk tathâ *k*eti. apare yathâpâ*th*am evârtham i*kkh*anti.—Perhaps we may correct, anusa*mvr*iginayânupaki*ñk*ayâ vâkâ. Comp. below, I, 4, 13, 16.

17. See above, I, 2, 6, 9.

19. Pâraskara I, 3, 10. 11 ; Âsvalâyana I, 24, 11.

13, 1. Comp. *S*ânkhâyana III, 7, 5, &c.

washes his feet, and then he touches himself with
(the formula), 'May in me dwell brilliancy, energy,
strength, life, renown, splendour, glory, power!'

2. (The host) then makes to him the announcement, ' The Argha water!'

3. (The guest) accepts it with (the formula), 'Thou
camest to me with glory.   Unite me with brilliancy,
splendour, and milk.   Make me beloved by all creatures, the lord of cattle.'

4. 'To the ocean I send you, the imperishable
(waters); go back to your source.   May I not suffer
loss in my offspring.   May my sap not be shed'—
this (verse the guest) recites over the remainder (of
the Argha water), when it is poured out (by the
person who had offered it to him).

5. Then he utters to him the announcement, 'The
water for sipping!'

6. With (the formula), 'Thou art the first layer
for Ambrosia,' he sips water.

7. Then he utters to him the announcement,
' The honey-mixture!'

8. He accepts that with both hands with the
Sâvitra (formula), and places it on the ground with
(the formula), ' I place thee on the navel of the earth
in the abode of *I*dâ.'   He mixes (the different substances) three times from left to right with his
thumb and his fourth finger, with (the formula),
'What is the honied, highest form of honey which
consists in the enjoyment of food, by that honied,

3. Pâraskara I, 3, 15.   4. Pâraskara I, 3, 14.
6. Âsvalâyana I, 21, 13.
8. Pâraskara I, 3, 18 seq.; Âsvalâyana I, 21, 15 seq.—The
Sâvitra formula is, 'On the impulse of the god Savitri ... I take
thee.' Comp. above, I, 3, 11, 7.

highest form of honey may I become highest,
honied, and an enjoyer of food.' He partakes of
it three times with (the formula), 'I eat thee for the
sake of brilliancy, of luck, of glory, of power, and of
the enjoyment of food,' and gives the remainder to
a person who is kindly disposed towards him.

9. Or he may eat the whole (Madhuparka). Then
he sips water with (the formula), 'Thou art the covering of Ambrosia.'

10. Then he utters to him the announcement,
'The cow!'

11. That (cow) is either killed or let loose.

12. If he chooses to let it loose, (he murmurs),
'This cow will become a milch cow.

'The mother of the Rudras, the daughter of the
Vasus, the sister of the Âdityas, the navel of immor-
tality. To the people who understand me, I say,
"Do not kill the guiltless cow, which is Aditi."

'Let it drink water! Let it eat grass'—

(And) gives order (to the people), 'Om! Let it
loose.'

13. If it shall be killed, (he says), 'A cow art
thou; sin is driven away from thee. Drive away
my sin and the sin of N. N.! Kill ye him who-
ever hates me. He is killed whosoever hates me.
Make (the cow) ready!'

14. If (the cow) is let loose, a meal is prepared
with other meat, and he announces it (to the guest)
in the words, 'It is ready!'

---

9. Âsvalâyana I, 21, 27. 28.

10 seq. Âsvalâyana I, 21, 30 seq.; Pâraskara I, 3, 26 seq.;
Sânkhâyana II, 15, 2. 3 note; Gobhila IV, 10, 18 seq.

13. N. N., of course, means the host's name.

14 seq. Comp. Gobhila I, 3, 16 seq.; Âpastamba II, 2, 3, 11.

15. He replies, 'It is well prepared; it is the Virâg; it is food. May it not fail! May I obtain it! May it give me strength! It is well prepared!' —and adds, 'Give food to the Brâhma*n*as!'

16. After those (Brâhma*n*as) have eaten, (the host) orders blameless (?) food to be brought to him (i. e. to the guest).

17. He accepts that with (the formula), 'May the heaven give it to thee; may the earth accept it. May the earth give it to thee; may breath accept it. May breath eat thee; may breath drink thee.'

18. With (the verse), 'May Indra and Agni bestow vigour on me' (Taitt. Sa*m*h. III, 3, 3, 3) he eats as much as he likes, and gives the remainder to a person who is kindly disposed towards him.

19. If he desires that somebody may not be estranged from him, he should sip water with (the Mantra), 'Whereon the past and the future and all worlds rest, therewith I take hold of thee; I (take hold) of thee; through the Brahman I take hold of thee for myself, N. N.!'—

PATALA 4, SECTION 14.

1. And should, after that person has eaten, seize his right hand.

2. If he wishes that one of his companions, or a pupil, or a servant should faithfully remain with him and not go away, he should bathe in the morning, should put on clean garments, should show

---

16. The meaning of anusa*m*vr*i*ginam (comp. above, I, 4, 12, 15) is uncertain. See the commentary, p. 120 of Dr. Kirste's edition.

14, 2. Mâtr*i*datta: 'The description of the Samâvartana is finished.'

patience (with that servant, &c.) during the day,
should speak (only) with Brâhma*n*as, and by night
he should go to the dwelling-place of that person,
should make water into a horn of a living animal,
and should three times walk round his dwelling-
place, sprinkling (his urine) round it, with (the
Mantra), 'From the mountain (I sever ?) thee, from
thy brother, from thy sister, from all thy relations.
parishîda*h* kleshyati (i. e. kvaishyasi ?) *s*a*s*vat pari-
kupilena sa*m*krâme*n*âvi*kkh*idâ, ûlena parimî*dho* * si
parimî*dho* * sy ûlena.

3. He puts down the horn of the living animal
in a place which is generally accessible.

4. One whose companions, pupils, or servants use
to run away, should rebuke them with (the Mantra),
'May he who calls hither (?), call you hither! He
who brings back, has brought you back (?). May
the rebuke of Indra always rebuke you. If you,
who worship your own deceit, despise me (?), ...
may Indra bind you with his bond, and may he drive
you back again to me.'

Now some ceremonies connected with special wishes of the person
who has performed the Samâvartana and has settled in a house,
will be described.' In my opinion, it would be more correct to
consider Sûtra 18 of the preceding section as the last of the
aphorisms that regard the Samâvartana. With Sûtra 2 compare
Pâraskara III, 7; Âpastamba VIII, 23, 6. It seems impossible
to attempt to translate the hopelessly corrupt last lines of the
Mantra.

4. A part of this Mantra also is most corrupt. In the first line
I propose to write, nivarto vo nyavîv*r*itat. With the last line
comp. Pâraskara III, 7, 3. I think that the text of Pâraskara should
be corrected in the following way: pari tvâ hvalano hvalan nivartas
tvâ nyavîv*r*itat, indra*h* pâsena sitvâ tvâ mahyam . . . (three syllables)
ânayet. The Âpastambîya Mantrapâ*th*a, according to Dr. Winternitz's copy, gives the following text : anupohvad anuhvayo vivartto

5. Then he enters his house, puts a piece of Sidhraka wood on (the fire), and sacrifices with the 'on-drawing verse,' 'Back-bringer, bring them back' (Taitt. Sa*m*h. III, 3, 10, 1).

6. Now (we shall explain) how one should guard his wife.

7. One whose wife has a paramour, should grind big centipedes (?) to powder, and should insert (that powder), while his wife is sleeping, into her secret parts, with the Mantra, ' Indra . . . . from other men than me.'

8. Now (follows the sacrifice for procuring) prosperity in trade.

9. He cuts off (some portion) from (every) article of trade and sacrifices it—

PATALA 4, SECTION 15.

1. With (the verse), ' If we trade, O gods, trying by our wealth to acquire (new) wealth, O gods, may

vo nyavîv*ri*dhat. aindra*h* parikro*s*o tu va*h* parikro*s*atu sarvata*h*, yadi mâm atimanyâdvâ â devâ devavattara indra*h* pâ*s*ena *s*itkvâ vo mahyam id va*s*am ânayât svâhâ.   Comp. Prof. Pischel's remarks, Philologische Abhandlungen, Martin Hertz zum siebzigsten Geburtstage von ehemaligen Schülern dargebracht (Berlin, 1888), p. 69 seq.

7. On sthûrâ dr*i*dhâ[*h*] Mât*ri*datta says, sthûrâ dr*i*dhâh sthûrâh *s*atapadya*h*.   A part of the Mantra is untranslatable on account of the very corrupt condition of the text.   The reading given by most of the MSS. is, Indrâya yâsya *s*epham alikam anye-bhya*h* purushebhyo·nyatra mat.   The Âpastambîya Mantra-pâ*th*a reads, indrâyâsya phaligam anyebhya*h* purushe-bhyonyatra mat.   The meaning very probably is that Indra is invoked to keep away from the woman the *s*epha of all other men except her husband's.

15, 1. Comp. Atharva-veda III, 15, 5; Gobhila IV, 8, 19.

[30]   N

Soma thereon bestow splendour, Agni, Indra, Brÿha-spati, and Îsâna. Svâhâ!'

2. Now (follows) the way for appeasing anger.

3. He addresses the angry person with (the verses), 'The power of wrath that dwells here on thy forehead, destroying thy enemy (?), may the chaste, wise gods take that away.

'If thou shootest, as it were, the thought dwelling in thy face, upwards to thy forehead, I loosen the anger of thy heart like the bow-string of an archer.

'Day, heaven, and earth : we appease thy anger, as the womb of a she-mule (cannot conceive).'

4. Now (follows) the way for obtaining the victory in disputes.

5. He puts wood on the fire at night-time in an inner apartment, performs the rites down to the Vyâhrÿti oblations, and sacrifices small grains mixed with Âgya, with (the verse), 'Tongueless one, thou who art without a tongue! I drive thee away through my sacrifice, so that I may gain the victory in the dispute, and that N. N. may be defeated by me. Svâhâ!'

6. Then in the presence (of his adversary), turned towards him, he murmurs (the verses), 'I take away the speech from thy mouth, (the speech) that dwells in thy mind, (the speech) from thy heart. Out of every limb I take thy speech. Wheresoever thy speech dwells, thence I take it away.

---

3. Pâraskara III, 13, 5. Possibly we ought to correct mrÿd-dhasya into mrÿdhrasya. Avadyâm ought to be ava gyâm; see Atharva-veda VI, 42, 1.

5. The commentary explains kanâs (small grains) as oleander (karavîra) seeds.

6. Comp. Pâraskara III, 13, 6. The text of the Mantras is corrupt.

'Rudra with the dark hair-lock! Hero! At every contest strike down this my adversary, as a tree (is struck down) by a thunderbolt.

'Be defeated, be conquered, when thou speakest. Sink down under the earth, when thou speakest, struck down by me irresistibly (?) with the hammer of . . . (?). That is true what I speak. Fall down, inferior to me, N. N. !'

7. He touches the assembly-hall (in which the contest is going on), and murmurs, 'The golden-armed, blessed (goddess), whose eyes are not faint, who is decked with ornaments, seated in the midst of the gods, has spoken for my good. Svâhâ!'

8. 'For me have the high ones and the low ones, for me has this wide earth, for me have Agni and Indra accomplished my divine aim'—with (this verse) he looks at the assembly, and murmurs (it) turned towards (the assembly).

End of the Fourth Pa/ala.

PRASNA I, PATALA 5, SECTION 16.

1. When he has first seen the new moon, he sips water, and holding (a pot of) water (in his hands) he worships (the moon) with the four (verses), 'Increase' (Taitt. Samh. I, 4, 32), 'May thy milk' (ibid. IV, 2, 7, 4), 'New and new again (the moon) becomes, being born' (ibid. II, 4, 14, 1), 'That Soma which the Âdityas make swell' (ibid. II, 4, 14, 1).

---

7. Probably we should write agîtâkshî.
8. Mâtrĭdatta says, prativâdinam abhigapaty eva.
16. This chapter contains different Prâyaskittas.

2. When he has yawned, he murmurs, '(May) will and insight (dwell) in me.'

3. If the skirt (of his garment) is blown upon him (by the wind), he murmurs, 'A skirt art thou. Thou art not a thunderbolt. Adoration be to thee. Do no harm to me.'

4. He should tear off a thread (from that skirt) and should blow it away with his mouth.

5. If a bird has befouled him with its excrements, he murmurs, 'The birds that timidly fly together with the destroyers, shall pour out on me happy, blissful splendour and vigour.'

Then let him wipe off that (dirt) with something else than his hand, and let him wash himself with water.

6. 'From the sky, from the wide air a drop of water has fallen down on me, bringing luck. With my senses, with my mind I have united myself, protected by the prayer that is brought forth by the righteous ones'—this (verse) he should murmur, if a drop of water unexpectedly falls down on him.

7. 'If a fruit has fallen down from the top of a tree, or from the air, it is Vâyu (who has made it fall). Where it has touched our bodies or the garment, (there) may the waters drive away destruction'—this (verse) he should murmur, if a fruit unexpectedly falls down on him.

8. 'Adoration to him who dwells at the cross-roads,

---

2. Âsvalâyana-Gr*i*hya III, 6, 7.   3. Pâraskara III, 15, 17.

5. I propose to read, nir*ri*thai*h* saha.

6. Atharva-veda VI, 124, 1.   Read su k*ri*tâ*m* k*ri*tena.

7. Atharva-veda VI, 124, 2.   The Atharva-veda shows the way to correct the corrupt third Pâda.

8 seq. Çomp. Pâraskara III, 15, 7 seq.

whose arrow is the wind, to Rudra! Adoration to
Rudra who dwells at the cross-roads!'—this (formula)
he murmurs when he comes to a cross-road;

9. 'Adoration to him who dwells among cattle,
whose arrow is the wind, to Rudra! Adoration to
Rudra who dwells among cattle!'—thus at a dung-
heap;

10. 'Adoration to him who dwells among the
serpents, whose arrow is the wind, to Rudra!
Adoration to Rudra who dwells among the serpents!'—thus at a place that is frequented by
serpents.

11. 'Adoration to him who dwells in the air,
whose arrow is the wind, to Rudra! Adoration to
Rudra who dwells in the air!'—this (formula) let
him murmur, if overtaken by a tornado.

12. 'Adoration to him who dwells in the waters,
whose arrow is the wind, to Rudra! Adoration to
Rudra who dwells in the waters!'—this (formula)
he murmurs when plunging into a river which is full
of water.

13. 'Adoration to him who dwells there, whose
arrow is the wind, to Rudra! Adoration to Rudra
who dwells there!'—this (formula) he murmurs when
approaching a beautiful place, a sacrificial site, or a
big tree.

14. If the sun rises whilst he is sleeping, he shall
fast that day and shall stand silent during that day;

15. The same during the night, if the sun sets
whilst he sleeps.

16. Let him not touch a sacrificial post. By

14, 15. Âpastamba II, 5, 12, 13. 14; Gobhila III, 3, 34, &c.
16. Gobhila III, 3, 34. Should it be esha te vâyur iti?

touching it, he would bring upon himself (the guilt of) whatever faults have been committed at that sacrifice.   If he touches one (sacrificial post), he should say, 'This is thy wind;' if two (posts), 'These are thy two winds;' if many (posts), 'These are thy winds.'

17. 'The voices that are heard after us (?) and around us, the praise that is heard, and the voices of the birds, the deer's running (?) athwart: that we fear (?) from our enemies'—this (verse) he murmurs when setting out on a road.

18. 'Like an Udgâtri, O bird, thou singest the Sâman; like a Brahman's son thou recitest thy hymn, when the Soma is pressed.

'A blessing on us, O bird; bring us luck and be kind towards us!'—(This Mantra) he murmurs against an inauspicious bird;

19. 'If thou raisest thy divine voice, entering upon living beings, drive away our enemies by thy voice. O death, lead them to death!'—(thus) against a solitary jackal.

20. Then he throws before the (jackal, as it were), a fire-brand that burns at both ends, towards that region (in which the jackal's voice is heard), with (the words), 'Fire! Speak to the fire! Death! Speak to the death!'   Then he touches water,

---

17. The Mantra is very corrupt.   Perhaps anihûtam should be corrected into anuhûtam, which is the reading of the Âpastambîya Mantrapâtha.   In the last Pâda bhayâmasi is corrupt; the meaning seems to be, 'that we (avert from ourselves and) turn it to our enemies.'   Probably Dr. Kirste is right in reading bhagâmasi.

18. Comp. Rig-veda II, 43, 2.

19. As to ekasrika, 'solitary jackal,' comp. Bühler's note on Âpastamba I, 3, 10, 17 (S. B. E., II, 38).   Mâtridatta says, srigâlo mrigasabdam kurvâna ekasrika ity ukyate.

21. And worships (the jackal) with the Anuvâka, 'Thou art mighty, thou carriest away' (Taitt. Sam-hitâ I, 3, 3).

PATALA 5, SECTION 17.

1. A she-wolf (he addresses) with (the verse), 'Whether incited by others or whether on its own accord the Bhaye*d*aka (? Bhayo*d*aka, var. lect.) utters this cry, may Indra and Agni, united with Brahman, render it blissful to us in our house.'

2. A bird (he addresses) with (the verse), 'Thou fliest, stretching out thy legs ; the left eye . . .; may nothing here suffer harm (through thee);'

3. An owl (pingalâ) with (the verse), 'The bird with the golden wings flies to the abode of the gods. Flying round the village from left to right portend us luck by thy cry, O owl!'

4. 'May my faculties return into me; may life return, prosperity return; may the divine power return into me; may my goods return to me.

'And may these fires that are stationed on the (altars called) Dhish*n*yâs, be in good order here, each in its right place. Svâhâ!

'My self has returned, life has returned to me; breath has returned, design has returned to me. (Agni) Vaisvânara, grown strong with his rays, may he dwell in my mind, the standard of immortality. Svâhâ!

'The food which is eaten in the evening, that does

17, 2. The commentary explains *s*akuni (bird) by dhvânksha (crow). In the translation of the Mantra (Taitt. Âr. IV, 35) I have left out the unintelligible words nipepi *k*a. The way to correct the last Pâda is shown by Atharva-veda VI, 57, 3 ; X, 5, 23.

4. Comp. Âsvalâyana-Gr*i*hya III, 6, 8.

not satiate in the morning him whom hunger assails.
May all that (which we have seen in our dreams),
do no harm to us, for it has not been seen by day.
To Day svâhâ!'—with these (verses) he sacrifices
sesamum seeds mixed with Âgya, if he has seen a
bad dream.

5. Now the following expiations for portents are
prescribed. A dove sits down on the hearth, or
the bees make honey in his house, or a cow (that is
not a calf) sucks another cow, or a post puts forth
shoots, or an anthill has arisen (in his house): cases
like these (require the following expiation):

6. He should bathe in the morning, should put on
clean garments, should show patience (with every-
body) during the day, and should speak (only) with
Brâhma*n*as. Having put wood on the fire in an
inner apartment, and having performed the rites
down to the Vyâh*ri*ti oblations, he sacrifices with
(the verses), 'This, O Varu*n*a,' &c. (see above I, 2,
8, 16, down to the end of the Sûtra). Then he
serves food to the Brâhma*n*as and causes them to
say, 'An auspicious day! Hail! Good luck!'

PATALA 5, SECTION 18.

1. 'May Indra and Agni make you go. May
the two A*s*vins protect you. B*ri*haspati is your
herdsman. May Pûshan drive you back again'—

---

5. *S*ânkhâyana V, 5. 8. 11; Â*s*valâyana III, 7, &c. Kuptvâ is
corrupt; we should expect a locative. We ought to correct
kuptvâm, as Dr. Kirste has observed, comp. Âpastamba-G*ri*hya
VIII, 23, 9.

6. Comp. above, I, 4, 14, 2; 15, 5; I, 2, 8, 16; I, 3, 9, 7. 8.

18, 1 seq. Comp. *S*ânkhâyana III, 9; Gobhila III, 6; Â*s*valâyana II, 10.

this (verse) he recites over the cows when they go away (to their pasture-grounds), and (the verse), 'May Pûshan go after our cows ' (Taitt. Sa*m*h. IV, 1, 11, 2).

2. With (the verse), ' These cows that have come hither, free from disease and prolific, may they swim (full of wealth) like rivers; may they pour out (wealth), as (rivers discharge their floods) into the ocean'—he looks at the cows, when they are coming back.

3. With (the formula), ' You are a stand at rest; may I (?) become your stand at rest. You are immovable. Do not move from me. May I not move from you, the blessed ones'—(he looks at them) when they are standing still.

4. With (the formula), ' I see you full of sap. Full of sap you shall see me '—(he looks at them) when they are gone into the stable, and with (the formula), ' May I be prosperous through your thousandfold prospering.'

5. Then having put wood on the fire amid the cows, and having performed the rites down to the Vyâh*ri*ti (oblations), he makes oblations of milk with (the verses),

' Blaze brightly, O *G*âtavedas, driving destruction away from me. Bring me cattle and maintenance from all quarters of the heaven. Svâhâ !

' May *G*âtavedas do no harm to us, to cows and horses, to men and to all that moves. Come. hither,

---

3. The Mantra is very corrupt. I think it ought to be corrected somehow in the following way: sa*m*sthâ stha sa*m*sthâ vo bhûyâsam a*k*yutâ stha mâ ma*k* *k*yodhvam mâha*m* bhavatîbhya*s* *k*yoshi. Comp. also Dr. Kirste's note.

5. In the second verse I propose to change abibhrad into

Agni, fearlessly; make me attain to welfare!
Svâhâ!'—

And with (the two verses), ' This is the influx of
the waters,' and ' Adoration to thee, the rapid one,
the shining one' (Taitt. Samh. IV, 6, 1, 3).

6. (Then follow oblations with the verses), ' This,
O Varuna' (&c.; see I, 2, 8, 16, down to the end of
the Sûtra).

End of the Fifth Patala.

PRASNA I, PATALA 6, SECTION 19.

1. After he has returned from the teacher's house,
he should support his father and mother.

2. With their permission he should take a wife
belonging to the same caste and country, a ' naked '
girl, a virgin who should belong to a different Gotra
(from her husband's).

3. Whatever he intends to do (for instance, taking
a wife), he should do on an auspicious day only,
during one of the following five spaces of time, viz.
in the morning, the forenoon, at midday, in the
afternoon, or in the evening.

---

abibhyad; comp. Atharva-veda XIX, 65, 1: ava tâm gahi harasâ
Gâtavedo ı bibhyad ugro ı rkishâ divam â roha sûrya. The last
words of this verse should be sriyam mâ pratipâdaya, or something
similar.

19, 2. sagâtâm savarnâm samânâbhiganâm ka. Mâtridatta. As
to the meaning of ' a naked girl,' (i. e. a girl who has not yet the
monthly illness), comp. Gobhila III, 4, 6 and note.

3. According to Mâtridatta, ' morning' means one Nâdikâ before and one Nâdikâ after sunrise; ' forenoon' means one Nâdikâ
before and one Nâdikâ after the moment at which the first quarter
of the day has elapsed; and thus each of the other three day-times

4. Having put wood on the fire, and having performed (the preparatory rites) down to the laying of (three) branches round (the fire, the bridegroom) looks at the bride who is led to him, with (the verse), 'Auspicious ornaments does this woman wear. Come up to her and behold her.   Having brought luck to her, go away back to your houses.'

5. To the south of the bridegroom the bride sits down.

6. After she has sipped water, she touches him, and he sprinkles (water) round (the fire) as above.

7. After he has performed the rites down to the oblations made with the Vyâh*ri*tis, he sacrifices with (the following Mantras),

'May Agni come hither, the first of gods.   May he release the offspring of this wife from the fetter of death.   That may this king Varu*n*a grant, that this wife may not weep over distress (falling to her lot) through her sons.   Svâhâ!

'May Agni Gârhapatya protect this woman.   May he lead her offspring to old age.   With fertile womb may she be the mother of living children.   May she experience delight in her sons.   Svâhâ!

'May no noise that comes from thee, arise in the house by night.   May the (she-goblins called) the weeping ones take their abode in another (woman)

---

is understood to comprise two Nâ*d*ikâs. As the whole day consists of sixty Nâ*d*ikâs, it is the sixth part of the day (= 10 Nâ*d*ikâs) which is considered as auspicious for such purposes as taking a wife.

4. See I, 1, 2, 1 seq.   Rig-veda X, 85, 33; Pâraskara I, 8, 9, &c.

6. See I, 1, 2, 7 seq.

7. Pâraskara I, 6, 11. With the third verse comp. Atharva-veda XI, 9, 14.

than thee. Mayst thou not be beaten at thy breast
by (the she-goblin) Vike*s*î ("the rough-haired one").
May thy husband live, and mayst thou shine in thy
husband's world, beholding thy genial offspring!
Svâhâ!

'May Heaven protect thy back, Vâyu thy thighs,
and the two A*s*vins thy breast. May Savit*ri* protect
thy suckling sons. Until the garment is put on
(thy sons?), may B*ri*haspati guard (them?), and the
Vi*s*ve devâs afterwards. Svâhâ!

'Childlessness, the death of sons, evil, and distress,
I take (from thee), as a wreath (is taken) from the
head, and (like a wreath) I put all evil on (the head
of) our foes. Svâhâ!

'With this well-disposed prayer which the gods
have created, I kill the Pisâ*k*as that dwell in thy
womb. The flesh-devouring death-bringers I cast
down. May thy sons live to old age. Svâhâ!'

8. After he has sacrificed with (the verses), 'This,
O Varu*na*,' 'For this I entreat thee,' 'Thou Agni,'
'Thus thou, Agni,' 'Thou, Agni, art quick,' 'Pra*g*â-
pati'—he makes her tread on a stone, with (the
verse), 'Tread on this stone; like a stone be firm.
Destroy those who seek to do thee harm; overcome
thy enemies.'

9. To the west of the fire he strews two layers of
northward-pointed Darbha grass, the one more to
the west, the other more to the east. On these
both (the bridegroom and the bride) station themselves, the one more to the west, the other more to
the east.

---

8. See above, I, 1, 3, 5; I, 1, 4, 1.

PRASNA I, PATALA 6, SECTION 20.

1. Facing the east, while she faces the west, or facing the west, while she faces the east, he should seize her hand. If he desires to generate male children, let him seize her thumb ; if he desires (to generate) female children, her other fingers ; if he desires (to generate) both (male and female children), let him seize the thumb together with the other fingers, (so as to seize the hand) up to the hairs (on the hair-side of the hand).

(He should do so with the two Mantras),

'Sarasvatî ! Promote this (our undertaking), O gracious one, rich in studs, thou whom we sing first of all that is.

'I seize thy hand that we may be blessed with offspring, that thou mayst live to old age with me, thy husband. Bhaga, Aryaman, Savit*ri*, Purandhi, the gods have given thee to me that we may rule our house.'

2. He makes her turn round, from left to right, so that she faces the west, and recites over her (the following texts),

'With no evil eye, not bringing death to thy husband, bring luck to the cattle, be full of joy and

---

20, 1. *S*âṅkhâyana I, 13, 2 ; Âsvalâyana I, 7, 3 seq., &c. The text of the first Mantra ought to be corrected according to Pâraskara I, 7, 2 ; in the second Mantra we ought to read yathâsa*h* instead of yathâsat; comp. Rig-veda X, 85, 36 ; Pâraskara I, 6, 3. The bridegroom and the bride, of course, are to face each other ; thus, if the bridegroom stands on the eastern layer of grass (Sûtra 9 of the preceding section), he is to face the west ; if on the western, he is to face the east.

2. The words, agre*n*a dakshi*n*am a*m*sam ... abhyâvartya, evidently have the same meaning which is expressed elsewhere (*S*âṅkhâyana

vigour. Give birth to living children, give birth to heroes, be friendly. Bring us luck, to men and animals.

'Thus, Pûshan, lead her to us, the highly blessed one, into whom men pour forth their sperm, yâ na ûrû u*s*atî vi*s*rayâtai (read, vi*s*rayâtai), yasyâm u*s*anta*h* praharema *s*epam.

'Soma has acquired thee first (as his wife); after him the Gandharva has acquired thee. Thy third husband is Agni; the fourth am I, thy human husband.

'Soma has given her to the Gandharva; the Gandharva has given her to Agni. Agni gives me cattle and children, and thee besides.

'This am I, that art thou; the heaven I, the earth thou; the Sâman I, the *Rik* thou. Come! Let us join together. Let us unite our sperm that we may generate a male child, a son, for the sake of the increase of wealth, of blessed offspring, of strength.

'Bountiful Indra, bless this woman with sons and with a happy lot. Give her ten sons; let her husband be the eleventh.'

3. After he has made her sit down in her proper place (see Sûtra 5 of the preceding section), and has sprinkled Âg*y*a into her joined hands, he twice pours fried grain into them, with (the verse), 'This grain I pour (into thy hands): may it bring prosperity to me, and may it unite thee (with me). May this Agni grant us that.'

II, 3, 2), dakshi*n*am bâhum anvâv*ri*tya. With the first Mantra comp. *Ri*g-veda X, 85, 44; Pâraskara I, 4, 16; with the second, *Ri*g-veda, loc. cit., 37; Pâraskara, loc. cit.; with the following ones, *Ri*g-veda X, 85, 40. 41. 45; Pâraskara I, 4, 16; 6, 3, &c.

3 seq. Comp. *S*âṅkhâyana I, 13, 15 seq.

4. After he has sprinkled (Âg*ya) over (the grain
in her hands), he sacrifices (the grain) with her
joined hands (which he seizes), with (the verse),
'This woman, strewing grain into the fire, prays
thus, "May my husband live long; may my relations
be prosperous. Svâhâ!"'

5. Having made her rise with (the verse which
she recites), 'Up! with life' (Taitt. Sa*m*h. I, 2, 8, 1),
and having circumambulated the fire (with her) so
that their right sides are turned towards it, with (the
verse), 'May we find our way with thee through all
hostile powers, as through streams of water'—he
pours fried grain (into her hands, and sacrifices
them), as before.

6. Having circumambulated (the fire) a second
time, he pours fried grain (into her hands, and sacrifices them), as before.

7. Having circumambulated (the fire) a third
time, he sacrifices to (Agni) Svish*t*akr*i*t.

8. Here some add as subordinate oblations the
*G*aya, Abhyâtâna, and Râsh*t*rabh*ri*t (oblations) as
above.

9. To the west of the fire he makes her step forward in an easterly or a northerly direction the
(seven) 'steps of Vish*n*u.'

10. He says to her, 'Step forward with the right
(foot) and follow with the left. Do not put the left
(foot) before the right.'

---

5. Comp. above, I, 2, 7, 13; Rig-veda II, 7, 3.
8. Comp. I, 2, 8, 16.
9 seq. Comp. Gobhila II, 2, 11 seq.; Sânkhâyana I, 14, 5 seq.

PA*T*ALA 6, SECTION 21.

1. (He makes her step forward, and goes with her himself), with (the Mantras), 'One (step) for sap, may Vish*n*u go after thee; two (steps) for juice, may Vish*n*u go after thee; three (steps) for vows, may Vish*n*u go after thee; four (steps) for comfort, may Vish*n*u go after thee; five (steps) for cattle, may Vish*n*u go after thee; six (steps) for the prospering of wealth, may Vish*n*u go after thee; seven (steps) for the sevenfold Hot*ri*ship, may Vish*n*u go after thee.'

2. After the seventh step he makes her abide (in that position) and murmurs, 'With seven steps we have become friends. May I attain to friendship with thee. May I not be separated from thy friendship. Mayst thou not be separated from my friendship.'

3. He then puts his right foot on her right foot, moves his right hand down gradually over her right shoulder, and touches the place of her heart as above,

4. And the place of her navel with (the formula), 'Thou art the knot of all breath; do not loosen thyself.'

5. After he has made her sit down to the west of the fire, so that she faces the east, he stands to the east (of his bride), facing the west, and besprinkles her with water, with the three verses, 'O waters, ye are wholesome' (Taitt. Sa*m*h. IV, 1, 5, 1), with the four verses, 'The gold-coloured, clean, purifying waters' (V, 6, 1), and with the Anuvâka, 'The purifier, the heavenly one' (Taitt. Brâhma*n*a I, 4, 8).

21, 3. See above, I, 2, 5, 11.   4. See above, I, 2, 5, 12.
5. Comp. I, 3, 10, 2.

6. Now they pour seeds (of rice, &c.) on (the heads of the bridegroom and bride).

End of the Sixth Pa*t*ala.

PRASNA I, PATALA 7, SECTION 22.

1. Then they let her depart (in a vehicle from her father's house), or they let her be taken away.

2. Having put (the fire into a vessel) they carry that (nuptial) fire behind (the newly-married couple).

3. It should be kept constantly.

4. If it goes out, (a new fire) should be kindled by attrition, or it should be fetched from the house of a *S*rotriya.

5. Besides, if (the fire) goes out, the wife or the husband should fast.

6. When (the bridegroom with his bride) has come to his house, he says to her, 'Cross (the threshold) with thy right foot first; do not stand on the threshold.'

7. In the hall, in its easterly part, he puts down the fire and puts wood on it.

8. To the west of the fire he spreads out a red bull's skin with the neck to the east, with the hair outside.

---

6. Mât*r*idatta explains adhi*s*rayanti by vapanti *g*âyâpatyo*h* *s*irasi kshipanti.

22, 4. 'If the fire on which they had put wood, was a fire produced by attrition, (the new fire) should (also) be kindled by attrition. If it was a common (laukika) fire that they had fetched, (the new fire) should be fetched from a *S*rotriya's house. Thereby it is shown that the common fire at the Upanayana ceremony, &c., should be fetched only from a *S*rotriya's house.' Mât*r*idatta.

9. On that (skin) they both sit down facing the east or the north, so that the wife sits behind her husband, with (the verse), ' Here may the cows sit down, here the horses, here the men. Here may also Pûshan with a thousand (sacrificial) gifts sit down.'

10. They sit silently until the stars appear.

11. When the stars have appeared, he goes forth from the house (with his wife) in an easterly or northerly direction, and worships the quarters (of the horizon) with (the hemistich), ' Ye goddesses, ye six wide ones' (Taitt. Samh. IV, 7, 14, 2).

12. (He worships) the stars with (the Pâda), ' May we not be deprived of our offspring;'

13. The moon with (the Pâda), ' May we not get into the power of him who hates us, O king Soma!'

14. He worships the seven Rishis (ursa major) with (the verse), ' The seven Rishis who have led to firmness she, Arundhatî, who stands first among the six Krittikâs (pleiads):—may she, the eighth one, who leads the conjunction of the (moon with the) six Krittikâs, the first (among conjunctions) shine upon us!' Then he worships the polar star with (the formula), ' Firm dwelling, firm origin. The firm one art thou, standing on the side of firmness. Thou art the pillar of the stars; thus protect me against my adversary.

' Adoration be to the Brahman, to the firm, immovable one! Adoration be to the Brahman's son, Pragâpati! Adoration to the Brahman's children,

---

9. Comp. Pâraskara I, 8, 10, and the readings quoted there from the Atharva-veda.

12, 13. These are the two last Pâdas of the verse of which the first hemistich is quoted in Sûtra 11.

to the thirty-three gods! Adoration to the Brahman's children and grandchildren, to the Aṅgiras!

'He who knows thee (the polar star) as the firm, immovable Brahman with its children and with its grandchildren, with such a man children and grandchildren will firmly dwell, servants and pupils, garments and woollen blankets, bronze and gold, wives and kings, food, safety, long life, glory, renown, splendour, strength, holy lustre, and the enjoyment of food. May all these things firmly and immovably dwell with me!'

PATALA 7, SECTION 23.

1. (Then follow the Mantras), 'I know thee as the firm Brahman. May I become firm in this world and in this country.

'I know thee as the immovable Brahman. May I not be moved away from this world and from this country. May he who hates me, my rival, be moved away from this world and from this country.

'I know thee as the unshaken Brahman. May I not be shaken off from this world and from this country. May he who hates me, my rival, be shaken off from this world and from this country.

'I know thee as the unfalling Brahman. May I not fall from this world and from this country. May he who hates me, my rival, fall from this world and from this country.

'I know thee as the nave of the universe. May I become the nave of this country. I know thee as the centre of the universe. May I become the centre of this country. I know thee as the string that holds the universe. May I become the string that holds this country. I know thee as the pillar of the universe. May I become the pillar of this country. I know thee as the navel of the universe. May I become the navel of this country.

'As the navel is the centre of the Prâ*n*as, thus I am the navel. May hundred-and-onefold evil befall him who hates us and whom we hate; may more than hundred-and-onefold merit fall to my lot!'

2. Having spoken there with a person that he likes, and having returned to the house, he causes her to sacrifice a mess of cooked food.

3. The wife husks (the rice grains of which that Sthâlîpâka is prepared).

4. She cooks (that Sthâlîpâka), sprinkles (Â*g*ya) on it, takes it from the fire, sacrifices to Agni, and then sacrifices to Agni Svish*t*akr*i*t.

5. With (the remains of) that (Sthâlîpâka) he entertains a learned Brâhma*n*a whom he reveres.

6. To that (Brâhma*n*a) he makes a present of a bull.

7. From that time he constantly sacrifices (ya*g*ate) on the days of the full and of the new moon a mess of cooked food sacred to Agni.

8. In the evening and in the morning he constantly sacrifices (*g*uhoti) with his hand (and not with the Darvî) the two following oblations of rice or of barley: 'To Agni Svâhâ! To Pra*g*âpati Svâhâ!'

9. Some (teachers) state that in the morning the

5, 6. In the commentary these Sûtras are divided thus : 5. tena brâhma*n*a*m* vidyâvanta*m* parivevesh*t*i ; 6. yo = syâpa*k*ito bhavati tasmâ *r*ishabha*m* dadâti. (5. Therewith he entertains a learned Brâhma*n*a. 6. To one whom he reveres, he presents a bull.) The commentator observes that some authorities make one Sûtra of the two, so that the Brâhma*n*a who receives the food and the one to whom the bull is given, would be the same person.

former (of these oblations) should be directed to Sûrya.

10. Through a period of three nights they should eat no saline food, should sleep on the ground, wear ornaments, and should be chaste.

11. In the fourth night, towards morning, he puts wood on the fire, performs the (regular) ceremonies down to the (regular) expiatory oblations, and sacrifices nine expiatory oblations (with the following Mantras):

PATALA 7, SECTION 24.

1. 'Agni! Expiation! Thou art expiation. I, the Brâhma*n*a, entreat thee, desirous of protection. What is terrible in her, drive that away from here. Svâhâ!

'Vâyu! Expiation! Thou art expiation. I, the Brâhma*n*a, entreat thee, desirous of protection. What is blameful in her, drive that away from here. Svâhâ!

'Sun! Expiation! Thou art expiation. I, the Brâhma*n*a, entreat thee, desirous of protection. What dwells in her that is death-bringing to her husband, drive that away from here. Svâhâ!

'Sun! Expiation! &c.
'Vâyu! Expiation! &c.
'Agni! Expiation! &c.
'Agni! Expiation! &c.
'Vâyu! Expiation! &c.
'Sun! Expiation! &c.'

---

11. According to the commentary he performs the regular ceremonies down to the oblation offered with the Mantra, 'Thus thou, Agni' (see above, I, 3, 5, and compare Pâraskara I, 2, 8). Mât*ri*datta says, prâya*sk*ittiparyanta*m* k*ri*tvâ sa tvam no Agna ity etadanta*m* k*ri*tvâ nava prâya*sk*ittir *g*uhoti . . . vyâhr*ri*tiparyanta*m* k*ri*tvâ imam me Varu*n*eti *k*atasro (I, 3, 5) hutvaitâ *g*uhoti.

2. Having sacrificed (these oblations), he then pours the remainder as an oblation on her head, with (the formulas), ' Bhû*h* ! I sacrifice fortune over thee. Svâhâ! Bhuva*h*! I sacrifice glory over thee. Svâhâ! Suva*h*! I sacrifice beauty over thee. Svâhâ! Bhûr bhuva*h* suva*h*! I sacrifice brightness over thee. Svâhâ!'

3. There (near the sacrificial fire) he places a water-pot, walks round the fire (and that water-pot) keeping his right side turned towards it, makes (the wife) lie down to the west of the fire, facing east or north, and touches her secret parts, with (the formula), 'We touch thee with the five-forked, auspicious, unhostile (?), thousandfoldly blessed, glorious hand that thou mayst be rich in offspring!'

4. He then cohabits with her with (the formula), ' United is our soul, united our hearts, united our navel, united our skin. I will bind thee with the bond of love; that shall be insoluble.'

5. He then embraces her with (the formula), ' Be devoted to me; be my companion. What dwells in thee that is death-bringing to thy husband, that I make death-bringing to thy paramours. Bring luck to me; be a sharp-cutting (destroyer) to thy paramours.'

6. He then seeks her mouth with his mouth, with (the two verses), 'Honey! Lo! Honey! This is honey! my tongue's speech is honey; in my mouth dwells the honey of the bee; on my teeth dwells concord.

' The (magic charm of) concord that belongs to the *k*akravâka birds, that is brought out of the

---

6. With the first verse comp. Taitt. Sa*m*h. VII, 5, 10, 1 ; Kâtyâyana XIII, 3, 21 ; Lâ*t*yâyana IV, 3, 18.

rivers, of which the divine Gandharva is possessed, thereby we are concordant.'

7. A woman that has her monthly courses, keeps through a period of three nights the observances prescribed in the Brâhma*n*a.

8. In the fourth night (the husband) having sipped water, calls (the wife) who has taken a bath, who wears a clean dress and ornaments, and has spoken with a Brâhma*n*a, to himself (with the following verses):

PATALA 7, SECTION 25.

1. (a) 'May Vish*n*u make thy womb ready; may Tvash*tri* frame the shape (of the child); may Pra*g*â-pati pour forth (the sperm); may Dhât*ri* give thee conception!

(b) 'Give conception, Sinîvâlî; give conception, Sarasvatî! May the two A*s*vins, wreathed with lotus, give conception to thee!

(c) 'The embryo which the two A*s*vins produce with their golden kindling-sticks: that embryo we call into thy womb, that thou mayst give birth to it after ten months.

(d) 'As the earth is pregnant with Agni, as the heaven is with Indra pregnant, as Vâyu dwells in the womb of the regions (of the earth), thus I place an embryo into thy womb.

---

7. Taitt. Sa*m*hitâ II, 5, 1, 5. 6: Therefore one should not speak with a woman that has her monthly courses, nor sit together with her, nor eat food that she has given him, &c.

25, 1 (a–c). Rig-veda X, 184, 1–3; comp. S. B. E., vol. xv, p. 221.

(d–f). *S*ânkhâyana-G*ri*hya I, 19. It should be observed that the text of Hira*n*yakesin has in the beginning of (c) quite the same blunder which is found also in the *S*ânkhâyana MSS., yasya instead of vyasya.

(e) 'Open thy womb; take in the sperm; may a male child, an embryo be begotten in the womb. The mother bears him ten months; may he be born, the most valiant of his kin.

(f) 'May a male embryo enter thy womb, as an arrow the quiver; may a man be born here, thy son, after ten months.

(g) 'I do with thee (the work) that is sacred to Praĝâpati; may an embryo enter thy womb. May a child be born without deficiency, with all its limbs, not blind, not lame, not sucked out by Pisâ*k*as.

(h) 'By the superior powers which the bulls shall produce for us, thereby become thou pregnant; may he be born, the most valiant of his kin.

(i) 'Indra has laid down in the tree the embryo of the sterile cow and of the cow that prematurely produces; thereby become thou pregnant; be a well-breeding cow'—

And (besides with the two Mantras), 'United are our names' (above, 24, 4), and, 'The concord of the *k*akravâka birds' (24, 6).

2. (He should cohabit with her with the formulas), 'Bhû*h*! Through Praĝâpati, the highest bull, I pour forth (the sperm); conceive a valiant son, N. N.!—Bhuva*h*! Through Praĝâpati, &c.—Suva*h*! Through Praĝâpati, &c.' Thus he will gain a valiant son.

3. The Mantras ought to be repeated whenever they cohabit, according to Âtreya,

4. Only the first time and after her monthly courses, according to Bâdarâya*n*a.

(g) Comp. Atharva-veda III, 23, 5. The Âpastambîya Mantra-pâ*th*a reads (a)pisâ*k*adhîta*h*.

(h) Sâṅkhâyana-Gri*h*ya I, 19, 6; Atharva-veda III, 23, 4.

(i) Comp. Atharva-veda III, 23, 1.

PATALA 7, SECTION 26 [1].

1. The fire which (the sacrificer keeps) from the time of his marriage, is called the Aupâsana (or sacred domestic fire).

2. With this fire the sacred domestic ceremonies are performed.

3. On account of his worship devoted to this (fire the sacrificer) is considered as an Âhitâgni (i. e. as one who has set up the Srauta fires), and on account of his fortnightly Karu sacrifices (on the days of the new and full moon) as one who offers the sacrifices of the new and full moon (as prescribed in the Srauta ritual); so (is it taught).

4. If (the service at the domestic fire) has been interrupted for twelve days, the sacrificer ought to set the fire up again.

5. Or he should count all the sacrifices (that have been left out), and should offer them.

6. (The punarâdhâna or repeated setting up of the fire is performed in the following way): in an enclosed space, having raised (the surface), sprinkled it (with water), strewn it with sand, and covered it with Udumbara or Plaksha branches, he silently brings together the things belonging to (the sacrifice) according as he is able to get them, produces fire by attrition out of a sacrificially pure piece of wood, or gets a common fire, places it in a big vessel, sets it in a blaze, and puts (fuel) on it with the words, 'Bhûh! Bhuvah! Suvah! Om! Fixity!'

---

[1] This chapter is left out in Mâtridatta's commentary; it seems to be a later addition. The division of the Sûtras is my own.

26, 3. For tasyaupâsanena I think we should read tasyopâsanena.

7. He then puts wood on the fire, performs (the rites) down to the Vyâh*r*iti oblations, and offers two 'mindâ oblations' (i. e. oblations for making up for defects) with (the two Mantras), 'If a defect (mindâ) has arisen in me,' (and), 'Agni has given me back my eye' (Taitt. Sa*m*h. III, 2, 5, 4).

8. He offers three 'tantu oblations' with (the Mantras), 'Stretching the weft (tantu)' (Taitt. Sa*m*h. III, 4, 2, 2), 'Awake, Agni!' (IV, 7, 13, 5), 'The thirty-three threads of the weft' (I, 5, 10, 4).

9. He offers four 'abhyâvartin oblations' with (the Mantras), 'Agni who turns to us (abhyâvartin)!' 'Agni Angiras!' 'Again with sap,' 'With wealth' (Taitt. Sa*m*h. IV. 2, 1, 2. 3).

10. Having made oblations with the single Vyâh*r*itis and with (the three Vyâh*r*itis together), and having made an oblation with the verse, 'Thou art quick, Agni, and free from imprecation. Verily (satyam) thou art quick. Held by us in our quick mind (manas), with thy quick (mind) thou carriest the offering (to the gods). Being quick bestow medicine on us! Svâhâ!'—this (last) oblation contains an allusion to the mind (manas), it refers to Pra*g*âpati, and alludes to the number seven (?),—he quickly repeats in his mind the da*s*a-hot*ri* formula (Taitt. Âra*n*y. III, 1, 1). Then he makes the sagraha oblation (?); (then follow the

---

10. As to the Mantra, 'Thou art quick, &c.,' comp. above, I, 1, 3, 5, and the note on Sânkhâyana I, 9, 12. I cannot see why the oblation made with this Mantra is called saptavatî (alluding to the number seven); possibly we ought to read satyavatî (containing the word satyam, 'verily'). Can the words sagraha*m* hutvâ mean, 'having performed the worship of the planets (graha) at his sacrifice'?

oblations), ' This, O Varu*a* ' (&c.; see I, 2, 8, 16, down to the end of the Sûtra).   Then he serves food to the Brâhma*a*s and causes them to say, ' An auspicious day!   Hail! Good luck!' he then performs in the known way the sacrifice of a mess of cooked food to Agni.

11. Here he gives an optional gift to his Guru: a pair of clothes, a milch cow, or a bull.

12. If he sets out on a journey, he makes the fire enter himself or the two kindling-sticks in the way that has been described (in the *S*rauta-sûtra).

13. Or let him make it enter a piece of wood, in the same way as into the kindling-sticks.

14. A piece of Khadira wood, or of Palâ*s*a, or of Udumbara, or of A*s*vattha wood—

15. With one of these kinds of wood he fetches, where he turns in (on his journey), fire from the house of a *S*rotriya, and puts the (piece of wood) into which his fire has entered, on (that fire), with the two verses, ' He who has received the oblations ' (Taitt. Sa*m*h. IV, 6, 5, 3), and ' Awake!' (IV, 7, 13, 5).

16. The way in which he sacrifices has been explained (in the *S*rauta-sûtra).

17. If one half-monthly sacrifice has been omitted, he should have a sacrifice to (Agni) Pathik*ri*t performed over this (fire).   If two (half-monthly sacrifices), to (Agni) Vai*s*vânara and Pathik*ri*t.   If more than two, (the fire) has to be set up again.

18. If the fire is destroyed or lost, or if it is mixed with other fires, it has to be set up again.

---

12. Comp. *S*ânkhâyana V, 1, 1.

PRASNA I, PATALA 8, SECTION 27.

1. If he will have a house built, he should during the northerly course of the sun, in the time of the increasing moon, under the constellation Rohinî and under the three constellations designated as Uttara (Uttara-Phalgunî, Uttara-Ashâdhâ, Uttara-Proshthapadâh) put wood on the fire, perform the rites down to the Vyâhriti oblations, and should sacrifice with (the verses), ' This, O Varuna ' (&c. ; see I, 2, 8, 16, down to the end of the Sûtra). Then he serves food to the Brâhmanas and causes them to say, ' An auspicious day! Hail! Good luck !' he puts on a garment that has not yet been washed, touches water, takes a shovel with (the formula), ' On the impulse of the god Savitri' (Taitt. Samh. I, 3, 1, 1), draws lines thrice from the left to the right round (the places where the pits for the posts shall be dug) with (the formula), ' A line has been drawn' (Taitt. Samh. I, 3, 1, 1), digs the pits (in which the posts shall be erected) as it is fit, and casts the earth (dug out of those pits) towards the inside (of the building-ground).

2. He erects the southern door-post with (the verse), ' Here I erect a firm house ; it stands in peace, streaming ghee. Thus may we walk in thee, O house, blessed with heroes, with all heroes, with unharmed heroes ; '

3. The northern (door-post) with (the verse), ' Stand here firmly, O house, rich in horses and cows, rich in delight; rich in sap, overflowing with milk be set up, for the sake of great happiness.'

4. With (the verse), 'To thee (may) the young child (go), to thee the calf with its companion, to thee the golden cup; to thee may they go with pots of curds'—he touches the two posts, after they have been erected.

5. In the same way (Sûtras 2. 3) he erects the two chief posts,

6. And touches them as above (Sûtra 4).

7. He fixes the beam of the roof on the posts with (the formula), 'Rightly ascend the post, O beam, erect, shining, drive off the enemies. Give us treasures and valiant sons.'

8. When the house has got its roof, he touches it with (the verse),

'The consort of honour, a blissful refuge, a goddess, thou hast been erected by the gods in the beginning; clothed in grass, cheerful thou art; bring us bliss, to men and animals.'

9. Then, under the constellation Anurâdhâ, the ground (on which the house stands) is expiated (in the following way).

10. By night he puts wood on the fire in an inner room (of the house), performs the rites down to the Vyâh*ri*ti oblations, and sacrifices (with the following Mantras):

PATALA 8, SECTION 28.

1. The two verses commencing 'Vâstoshpati!' (Taitt. Sa*m*h. III, 4, 10, 1).

27, 4. The text has the reading *g*a*g*atâ saha; comp. the note on *S*ânkhâyana III, 2, 9.

8. Comp. Atharva-veda III, 11, 5; this text shows the way to correct the blunders of the Hira*n*yakesin MSS.

28, 1. Comp. Rig-veda VII, 54, 2; Taitt. Brâhm. III, 7, 14, 4; Rig-veda X, 18, 1; Taitt. Brâhm. III, 7, 14, 5.

'Vâstoshpati! Be our furtherer; make our wealth increase in cows and horses, O Indu (i. e. Soma). Free from decay may we dwell in thy friendship; give us thy favour, as a father to his sons. Svâhâ!

'May death go away; may immortality come to us. May Vivasvat's son (Yama) protect us from danger. May wealth, like a leaf (that falls) from a tree, fall down over us. May *Sak*ipati (i. e. Indra) be with us. Svâhâ!

'Go another way, O death, that belongs to thee, separated from the way of the gods. Vâstoshpati! To thee who hears us, I speak: do no harm to our offspring nor to our heroes. Svâhâ!

'To this most excellent place of rest we have gone, by which we shall victoriously gain cows, treasures, and horses. May wealth, like a leaf (that falls) from a tree, fall down over us. May *Sak*ipati be with us. Svâhâ!

'This, O Varu*n*a' (&c.; see chap. 27, Sûtra 1, down to): 'Hail! Good luck!'

2. In this way the ground (on which the house stands) should be expiated every year;

3. Every season, according to some (teachers).

PATALA 8, SECTION 29.

1. 'House, do not fear, do not tremble; bringing strength we come back. Bringing strength, gaining wealth, wise I come back to the house, rejoicing in my mind.

'Of which the traveller thinks, in which much joy

29, 1. Sâṅkhâyana-Gr*i*hya III, 7, 2; Atharva-veda VII, 60.

dwells, the house I call. May it know us as we know it.

'Hither are called the cows ; hither are called goats and sheep ; and the sweet essence of food is called hither to our house.

'Hither are called many friends, the sweet companionship of friends. May our dwellings always be unharmed with all our men.

' Rich in sap, rich in milk, refreshing, full of joy and mirth, free from hunger (?) and thirst, O house, do not fear us'—with (these verses) he approaches his house (when returning from a journey).

2. ' To thee I turn for the sake of safety, of peace. The blissful one! The helpful one! Welfare! Welfare! '—with (this formula) he enters.

3. On that day, on which he has arrived, he should avoid all quarrelling.

4. 'The joyful house I enter which does not bring death to men; most manly (I enter) the auspicious one. Bringing refreshment, with genial minds (we enter the house); joyfully I lie down in it '—with (this verse) he lies down.

5. ' May we find our way with thee through all hostile powers, as through streams of water '—with (this verse) he looks at his wife ; he looks at his wife.

End of the First Prasna.

---

5. Comp. above, chap. 20, Sûtra 5; Rig-veda II, 7, 3.

PRASNA II, PATALA 1, SECTION 1.

1. Now (follows) the Simantonnayana (or parting of the pregnant wife's hair).

2. In the fourth month of her first pregnancy, in the fortnight of the increasing moon, under an auspicious constellation he puts wood on the fire, performs the rites down to the Vyâh*ri*ti oblations, and makes four oblations to Dhât*ri* with (the verse), 'May Dhât*ri* give us wealth' (and the following three verses, Taitt. Sa*m*h. III, 3, 11, 2. 3).

3. 'This, O Varu*n*a' (&c. ; see I, chap. 27, Sûtra 2, down to) : 'Hail! Good luck!'

He then makes the wife who has taken a bath, who wears a clean dress and ornaments, and has spoken with a Brâhma*n*a, sit down to the west of the fire, facing the east, in a round apartment. Standing to the east (of the wife), facing the west he parts her hair upwards (i. e. beginning from the front) with a porcupine's quill that has three white spots, holding (also) a bunch of unripe fruits, with the Vyâh*ri*tis (and) with the two (verses), 'I invoke Râkâ,' (and), 'Thy graces, O Râkâ' (Taitt. Sa*m*h. III, 3, 11, 5). Then he recites over (his wife the formulas), 'Soma alone is our king, thus say the Brâhma*n*a tribes, sitting near thy banks, O Ga*n*gâ,

---

1, 3. The corrupt word viv*ri*tta*k*akrâ(*h*) seems to contain a vocative fem. referring to Ga*n*ge—aviv*ri*tta*k*akra? The Âpastambîya Mantrapâ*th*a reads, viv*ri*tta*k*akra âsînâs tîre*n*a yamune tava. Comp. Â*s*valâyana I, 14, 7 ; Pâraskara I, 15, 8.

whose wheel does not roll back (?)!' (and), 'May we
find our way with thee through all hostile powers, as
through streams of water' (above I, 20, 5).

PATALA 1, SECTION 2.

1. Now (follows) the Pumsavana (i. e. the ceremony for securing the birth of a male child).

2. In the third month, in the fortnight of the
increasing moon, under an auspicious constellation
(&c.; see the preceding section, Sûtras 2 and 3,
down to :) in a round apartment. He gives her a
barley-grain in her right hand with (the formula),
'A man art thou;'

3. With (the formula), 'The two testicles are ye,'
two mustard seeds or two beans, on both sides of
that barley-grain.

4. With (the formula), 'Svâvritat' (? svâvrittat ?)
(he pours) a drop of curds (on those grains). That
he gives her to eat.

5. After she has sipped water, he touches her
belly with (the formula), 'With my ten (fingers) I
touch thee that thou mayst give birth to a child
after ten months.'

6. (He pounds) the last shoot of a Nyagrodha
trunk (and mixes the powder) with ghee, or a silk-
worm (and mixes the powder) with a pap prepared
of panick seeds, or a splinter of a sacrificial post
taken from the north-easterly part (of that post)
exposed to the fire, or (he takes ashes or soot [?] of)

2, 2. Comp. the note on Âsvalâyana I, 13, 2.
6. The translation of this Sûtra should be considered merely as
tentative. Some words of the text are uncertain, and the remarks
of Mâtridatta are very incorrectly given in the MSS.

[30]   P

a fire that has been kindled by attrition, and inserts that into the right nostril of (the wife) whose head rests on the widely spread root (of an Udumbara tree ?).

7. If she miscarries, he should three times stroke (her body), from the navel upwards, with her wet hand, with (the formula), 'Thitherwards, not hitherwards, may Tvash*tri* bind thee in his bonds. Making (the mother) enter upon the seasons, live ten months (in thy mother's womb) ; do not bring death to men.'

8. When her confinement has come, he performs the kshipraprasavana (i. e. the ceremony for accelerating the confinement). Having placed a waterpot near her head and a Tûryanti plant near her feet, he touches her belly.

PATALA 1, SECTION 3.

1. 'As the wind blows, as the ocean waves, thus may the embryo move ; may it come forth together with the after-birth'—with (this verse) he strokes (her body) from above downwards.

2. When the child is born, he lays an axe on a stone, and a piece of gold on that axe; after he has turned these things upside down (so that the stone lies uppermost), he holds the boy over them with (the two verses),

'Be a stone, be an axe, be insuperable gold. Thou indeed art the Veda called son ; so live a hundred autumns.

---

8. Comp. Âpastamba-Gr*ihya* VI, 14, 14 ; Âsvalâyana II, 8, 14 ; IV, 4, 8.

'From limb by limb thou art produced; out of the heart thou art born. Thou indeed art the self (âtman) called son; so live a hundred autumns.'

3. (The contents of this Sûtra are similar to those of Pâraskara I, 16, 2.)

4. They take the Aupâsana (or regular Grihya) fire away, and they bring the Sûtikâgni (or the fire of the confinement).

5. That (fire) is only used for warming (dishes, etc.).

6. No ceremonies are performed with it except the fumigation (see the next Sûtra).

7. He fumigates (the child) with small grains mixed with mustard seeds. These he throws into the coals (of the Sûtikâgni) (eleven times, each time with one of the following Mantras):

(a) 'May Sanda and Marka, Upavira, Sândikera, Ulûkhala, Kyavana vanish from here. Svâhâ!

(b) 'Âlikhat, Vilikhat, Animisha, Kimvadanta, Upasruti. Svâhâ!

(c) 'Aryamna, Kumbhin, Satru, Pâtrapâni, Nipuni. Svâhâ!

(d) 'May Ântrîmukha, Sarshapâruna vanish from here. Svâhâ!

(e) 'Kesinî, Svalominî, Bagâbogâ, Upakâsinî—go away, vanish from here. Svâhâ!

(f) 'The servants of Kuvera, Visvavâsa (?), sent by the king of demons, all of one common origin,

---

3, 7. According to Pâraskara (I, 16, 23) this is done daily in the morning and in the evening, until the mother gets up from childbed.—Comp. the names of the demons, Pâraskara I, 16, 23.—For vikhuram (Mantra i) the Âpastambîya Mantrapâtha has vidhuram ('distress' or 'a distressed one').

walk through the villages, visiting those who
wake (?).   Svâhâ!

(g) '" Kill them!   Bind them!" thus (says) this
messenger of Brahman.   Agni has encompassed
them.   Indra knows them; Br*i*haspati knows them;
I the Brâhma*n*a know them who seize (men), who
have prominent teeth, rugged hair, hanging breasts.
Svâhâ!

(h) ' The night-walkers, wearing ornaments on
their breasts, with lances in their hands, drinking
out of skulls!   Svâhâ!

(i) ' Their father U*kk*ai*hs*râvyakar*n*aka walks (?)
at their head, their mother walks in the rear, seeking
a vikhura (?) in the village.   Svâhâ!

(k) ' The sister, the night-walker, looks at the
family through the rift (?)—she who wakes while
people sleep, whose mind is turned on the wife that
has become mother.   Svâhâ!

(l) ' O god with the black path, Agni, burn the
lungs, the hearts, the livers of those (female demons);
burn their eyes.   Svâhâ!'

8. Then he washes his hands and touches the
ground with (the verses), ' O thou whose hair is well
parted!   Thy heart that dwells in heaven, in the
moon: of that immortality impart to us.   May I
not weep over distress (falling to my lot) through
my sons.

' I know thy heart, O earth, that dwells in
heaven, in the moon: thus may I, the lord of immortality, not weep over distress (falling to my lot)
through my sons.'

9. Now (follows) the medhâ*g*anana (or production

---

8. Pâraskara I, 6, 17.

of intelligence). With (an instrument of) gold over
which he has laid a Darbha shoot tied (to that piece
of gold) he gives to the child, which is held so that
it faces the east, ghee to eat, with the formulas,
'Bhû*h*! I sacrifice the *Ri*kas over thee! Bhuva*h*!
I sacrifice the Ya*g*us over thee! Suva*h*! I sacrifice the Sâmans over thee! Bhûr bhuva*h* suva*h*!
I sacrifice the Atharvan and Angiras hymns over
thee!'

10. He then bathes the child with lukewarm
water with (the following Mantras):

'From chronic disease, from destruction, from
wile, from Varu*n*a's fetter I release thee. I make
thee guiltless before the Brahman; may both
Heaven and Earth be kind towards thee.

'May Agni together with the waters bring thee
bliss, Heaven and Earth together with the herbs;
may the air together with the wind bring thee bliss;
may the four quarters of the heaven bring thee
bliss.

'Rightly have the gods released the sun from
darkness and from the seizing demon; they have
dismissed him from guilt; thus I deliver this boy
from chronic disease, from curse that comes from
his kin, from wile, from Varu*n*a's fetter.'

11. He then places the child in his mother's lap
with (the verse):

PATALA 1, SECTION 4.

1. 'The four divine quarters of the heaven, the
consorts of Wind, whom the sun surveys: to their

---

10. Comp. Atharva-veda II, 10; Taitt. Brâhm. II, 5, 6.

long life I turn thee; may consumption go away
to destruction!'

2. Having placed (him there) he addresses (his
wife with the Mantra), 'May no demon do harm to
thy son, no cow that rushes upon him (?). Mayst
thou become the friend of treasures; mayst thou
live in prosperity in thy own way.'

3. He washes her right breast and makes her
give it to the child with (the formula), 'May this boy
suckle long life; may he reach old age. Let thy
breast be exuberant for him, and life, glory, renown,
splendour, strength.'

4. In the same way the left breast.

5. With (the words), 'He does not suffer, he does
not cry, when we speak to him and when we touch
him'—he touches both breasts. Then he places a
covered water-pot near her head, with (the formula),
'O waters, watch in the house. As you watch with
the gods, thus watch over this wife, the mother of a
good son.'

6. On the twelfth day the mother and the son
take a bath.

7. They make the house clean.

8. They take the Sûtikâgni away, and they bring
the Aupâsana fire.

9. Having put wood on that fire, and having performed the rites down to the Vyâhrti oblations,
they sacrifice twelve oblations with the verses, 'May
Dhâtri give us wealth' (III, 3, 11, 2-5); according
to some (teachers they make) thirteen (oblations).

4, 2. I am not certain about the translation of dhenur atisârini.
The Âpastambîya Mantrapâtha has atyâkârinî. Atisârin means,
suffering from diarrhoea; perhaps we should read abhisârinî.

8. Comp. chap. 3, Sûtra 4.

10. 'This, O Varuna' (&c.; see I, chap. 27, Sûtra 2, down to) : 'Hail ! Good luck !' Then let him give a name to the child, of two syllables or of four syllables, beginning with a sonant, with a semi-vowel in it, with a long vowel (or) the Visarga at its end, or a name that contains the particle su, for such a name has a firm foundation ; thus it is understood.

11. Let the father and the mother pronounce (that name) first. For it is understood, 'My name first, O Gâtavedas.'

12. He should give him two names. For it is understood ('Taitt. Samh. VI, 3, 1, 3), 'Therefore a Brâhmana who has two names, will have success.'

13. The second name should be a Nakshatra name.

14. The one name should be secret; by the other they should call him.

15. He should give him the name Somayâgin (i.e. performer of Soma sacrifices) as his third name ; thus it is understood.

16. When he returns from a journey, or when his son returns, he touches him with (the formula), 'With Soma's lustre I touch thee, with Agni's splendour, with the glory of the sun.'

17. With (the formula), 'With the humkâra (the mystical syllable hum) of the cattle I kiss thee, N. N.! For the sake of long life and of glory ! Hum !' he

---

11. The verse beginning with 'My name,' &c., contains the words, ' which my father and my mother have given me in the beginning' (pitâ mâtâ ka dadhatur yad agre).

13. Comp. Professor Weber's second article, ' Die vedischen Nachrichten von den Naxatra' (Abh. der Berliner Akademie), pp. 316 seq.

17. Comp. above, I, 2, 5, 14.

kisses his head. Then he seizes with his right hand (his son's) right hand together with the thumb, with the five sections, 'Agni is long-lived.'

18. 'May Agni bestow on thee long life every-where' (Taitt. Samh. I, 3, 14, 4)—this (verse) he murmurs in (his son's) right ear as above.

Patala 1, Section 5.

1. Then (follows) in the sixth month the Anna-prâsana (i. e. the first feeding with solid food).

2. In the fortnight of the increasing moon, under an auspicious constellation, he puts wood on the fire, performs the rites down to the Vyâhriti oblations, and sacrifices (with the Mantras), 'This, O Varuna' (&c.; see I, chap. 27, Sûtra 2, down to): 'Hail! Good luck!' Then he gives (to the child) threefold food to eat, curds, honey, and ghee, with (the formula), 'Bhûh I lay into thee! Bhuvah I lay into thee! Suvah I lay into thee!'

3. Then he gives him (other) food to eat with (the formula), 'I give thee to eat the essence of water and of the plants. May water and plants be kind towards thee. May water and plants do no harm to thee.'

Patala 1, Section 6.

1. In the third year (he performs) the Kûdâkarman (i. e. the tonsure of the child's head).

2. In the fortnight (&c., as in the preceding section, Sûtra 2, down to): 'Hail! Good luck!' The boy sits down to the west of the fire, facing the east;

---

18. I, 2, 5, 15; 2, 6, 1.

3. To the north (of the fire) his mother or a student (brahma*k*ârin) holds a lump of bull's dung;

4. Therewith he (or she) receives the (cut-off) hair.

5. He then pours cold and warm water together.

6. Having poured warm water into cold water he moistens the hair near the right ear with (the formula), 'May the waters moisten thee for life' (Taitt. Sa*m*h. I, 2, 1, 1).

7. With (the formula), 'Herb, protect him!' (Taitt. Sa*m*h., loc. cit.) he puts an herb, with its point upwards, into (the hair).

8. With (the formula), 'Axe, do no harm to him!' (Taitt. Sa*m*h., loc. cit.) he touches (that herb) with the razor.

9. With (the words), 'Heard by the gods, I shave that (hair)' (Taitt. Sa*m*h., loc. cit.) he shaves him.

10. In the same way (he moistens, &c.) the other (sides of his head) from left to right.

11. Behind with (the Mantra), 'The razor with which Savit*ri*, the knowing one, has shaven (the beard) of king Soma and Varu*n*a, with that, ye Brâhma*n*as, shave his (head); make that he be united with vigour, with wealth, with glory.'

On the left side with (the Mantra), '(The razor) with which Pûshan has shaven (the beard) of B*ri*haspati, of Agni, of Indra, for the sake of long life, with that I shave thy (head), N. N. !'

6, 3, 4. Some consider, according to Mât*ri*datta, these two Sûtras as one. He says (p. 149 of Dr. Kirste's edition), uttarata ity etadâdi pratig*ri*h*n*âtîty etadanta*m* vâ sûtra*m*, dhârayâm*s* tenâsya kesân pratipa*ll*itavya*m* (read, pratig*ri*h*n*âtîti pa*ll*itavyam).

6. As to dakshi*n*a*m* godânam unatti, comp. the note on Pâraskara II, 1, 9. Comp. also above, I, 3, 9, 12.

7 seq. See above, I, 3, 9, 13 seq.

Before with (the Mantra), 'That he may long live
in joy, and may long see the sun.'

12. After the hair has been shaven, they arrange
the locks (which are left over), according to custom
or according to what family he belongs.

13. A person who is kindly disposed towards him,
gathers the (cut-off) hair and buries it in a cow-
stable, or near an Udumbara tree, or in a clump of
Darbha grass, with (the Mantra), 'Where Pûshan,
Brihaspati, Savitri, Soma, Agni (dwell), they have
in many ways searched where they should depose it,
between heaven and earth, the waters and heaven.'

14. He makes a gift to a Brâhmana according to
his liberality.

15. To the barber (he gives) boiled rice with
butter.

16. In the same way the Godânakarman (or the
ceremony of shaving the beard) is performed in the
sixteenth year.

17. He has him shaven including the top-lock.

18. Some declare that he leaves there the top-
lock.

19. Or he performs the Godâna sacred to Agni.

20. He gives a cow to his Guru.

End of the First Patala.

---

13. Comp. I, 3, 9, 18.

14. Literally, according to his faith (yathâsraddham).

19. Agnigodâno vâ kumâro bhavati upasamâdhânâdi punyâha-
vâkanântam agnikâryam iva vâ bhavatity arthah. Mâtridatta.
Comp., however, the note on Âpastamba-Grihya VI, 16, 13.

PRASNA II, PATALA 2, SECTION 7.

1. Now (follows) the expiation for attacks of the dog-demon (epilepsy) (on the boy).

2. When the attack assails (the boy, the performer of the ceremony) arranges his sacrificial cord over his left shoulder, sips water, and fetches water with a cup that has not yet been used (in order to pour it upon the boy). In the middle of the hall he elevates (the earth at) that place in which they use to gamble; he besprinkles it with water, casts the dice, scatters them (on all sides), makes a heap of them, spreads them out, makes an opening in the thatched roof of the hall, takes the boy in through that (opening), lays him on his back on the dice, and pours a mixture of curds and salt-water upon him, while they beat a gong towards the south. (The curds and water are poured on the sick boy with the following Mantras),

' Kurkura, Sukurkura, the Kurkura with the dark fetter . . . .

' Sârameya runs about, looking, as it were, upon the sea. He, the Suvîri*n*a (?), wears golden ornaments on his neck and on his breast, the most excellent (ornaments) of dogs (?).

'Suvîri*n*a, let him loose ! Let him loose, Ekavrâtya! Let him loose, doggy ! Let him loose, *Kh*at !

' *T*eka and Sasarama*la*m*ka* and Tûla and Vitûla and the white one and the red one. Let him loose ! . . . . the brown and red one.

' On those two single ones the sarasyakâs (?) run

7, 1. *s*vagraho · pasmâra unmatta*h* Sârameya ity eke. Mât*ri*-datta.—Comp. Pâraskara I, 16, 24; Âpastamba VII, 18, 1.

2. The Mantras are partly unintelligible. As to kurkura comp. the note on Pâraskara I, 16, 24.

down in the third heaven from here. *Kh*at! Go away. Sîsarama! Sârameya! Adoration to thee, Sîsara!

'Your mother is called the messenger; your father is the ma*nd*âkaka (ma*nd*ûkaka, the frog?). *Kh*at! Go away, &c.

'Your mother is called dulâ (the staggering one?); your father is the ma*nd*âkaka. *Kh*at! Go away, &c.

'The stallions (stamp with) their feet. Do not gnash (?) thy teeth. *Kh*at! Go away, &c.

'The carpenter hammers at (the chariots) that have wheels (?). Do not gnash (?) thy teeth. *Kh*at! Go away,' &c.

3. Then (the performer of the ceremony) says, 'Choose a boon.'

4. (The father or brother of the boy replies), 'I choose the boy.'

5. They should do so, when the attack assails him, three times in the day, in the morning, at noon, and in the afternoon, and when he has recovered.

End of the Second Pa*t*ala.

PRASNA II, PATALA 3, SECTION 8.

1. Now (follows) the sacrifice of the *s*ûlagava (or spit-ox, for propitiating Rudra and averting plague in cattle).

2. In the fortnight of the increasing moon, under an auspicious constellation, he puts wood on the fire, strews (Darbha grass) on the entire surface around the fire, cooks a mess of sacrificial food with milk,

---

5. There can be little doubt as to the correctness of the reading agada*h* instead of âgata*h*.

8, 1. Comp. Âsvalâyana IV, 8; Pâraskara III, 8; Âpastamba VII, 20.

sprinkles it (with Âgya), takes it from the fire, builds two huts to the west of the fire, and has the spit-ox led to the southerly (hut) with (the verse), ' May the fallow steeds, the harmonious ones, bring thee hither, together with the white horses, the bright, wind-swift, strong ones, that are as quick as thought. Come quickly to my offering, Sarva! Om!'

3. To the northerly (hut he has) the 'bountiful one' (led);—(i. e. the consort of the spit-ox);

4. To the middle (between the two huts) the 'conqueror' (i. e. a calf of those two parents).

5. He gives them water to drink in the same order in which they have been led (to their places), prepares three messes of boiled rice, 'spreading under' and sprinkling (Âgya) on them, and touches (the three beasts with those portions of rice) in the order in which they have been led (to their places), with (the Mantras), 'May he, the bountiful one, touch it. To the bountiful one svâhâ! May she, the bountiful one, touch it. To the bountiful one svâhâ! May the conqueror touch it. To the conqueror svâhâ!'

6. After he has performed (the rites) down to the Vyâhr̩ti oblations, he takes the messes of boiled rice (to the fire) and sacrifices them (the first with the Mantra),

'To the god Bhava svâhâ! To the god Rudra svâhâ! To the god Sarva svâhâ! To the god Îsâna . . . Pasupati . . . Ugra . . . Bhima svâhâ! To the great god svâhâ!'

7. Then he sacrifices the consort's rice to the consort (of Rudra, with the Mantra), 'To the consort

---

3, 4. The text has mid̄h̄ushîm, gayantam.

of the god Bhava svâhâ! To the consort of the god
Rudra . . . Sarva . . . Îsâna . . . Pasupati . . . Ugra . . .
Bhîma . . . of he great god svâhâ!'

8. Then he sacrifices of the middle portion of rice
with (the Mantra), 'To the conqueror svâhâ! To
the conqueror svâhâ!'

9. Then he cuts off from all the three portions of
rice and sacrifices the Svish/akrit oblation with (the
Mantra), 'To Agni Svish/akrit svâhâ!'

10. Around that fire they place their cows so that
they can smell the smell of that sacrifice.

11. 'With luck may they walk round our full
face'—with (these words) he walks round all (the
objects mentioned, viz. the fire, the three beasts, and
the other cows), so as to turn his right side towards
them, and worships (the sûlagava) with the (eleven)
Anuvâkas, 'Adoration to thee, Rudra, to the wrath'
(Taitt. Sa*m*h. IV, 5), or with the first and last of
them.

PATALA 3, SECTION 9.

1. Now follows the distribution of Palâsa leaves
(at different places).

2. 'Protector of the house, touch them! To the
protector of the house svâhâ! Protectress of the

9, 1. The text has bau*dh*yavihâra, on which the commentary
observes, bau*dh*yâni palâsaparnâni, teshâ*m* vihâro vihara*n*a*m* nânâ-
deseshu sthâpana*m* bau*dh*yavihâra*h*, karmanâma vâ. The bau*dh*yavihâra is, as its description clearly shows, a ceremony for propitiating Rudra and his hosts and for averting evil from the cattle
and the fields. The commentary understands it as forming part
of the sûlagava described in chap. 8, and with this opinion it would
agree very well that no indication of the time at which the bau*dh*yavihâra ought to be performed (such as âpûryamâ*n*apakshe pu*n*ye
nakshatre) is given. Comp. also Âpastamba VII, 20, 5 seq.

house, touch them! To the protectress of the house
svâhâ! Protector of the door, touch them! To the
protector of the door svâhâ! Protectress of the door,
touch them! To the protectress of the door svâhâ!'—
with (these formulas) he puts down four leaves; (then
other leaves) with (the formulas), ' Noisy ones, touch
them! To the noisy ones svâhâ! Quivered ones...
ye that run in the rear . . . Minglers (?) . . . Choosers
. . . Eaters, touch them! To the eaters svâhâ!'—

3. Then again ten (leaves) with (the formula),
'Divine hosts, touch them! To the divine hosts
svâhâ!'

4. Then other ten (leaves) with (the formula),
' Divine hosts that are named and that are not
named, touch them! To them svâhâ!'

5. Then he makes a basket of leaves, puts into it
a lump of boiled rice with an ' under-spreading' (of
Âgya) and sprinkling (Âgya) on it, goes outside his
pasture-grounds, and hangs (the basket) up at a tree
with (the formula), ' Quivered ones, touch it! To
the quivered ones svâhâ!'

6. He then performs worship (before that basket)
with (the formula), ' Adoration to the quivered one,
to him who wears the quiver! To the lord of the
thieves adoration!'

7. With sandal salve, surâ and water, unground,
fried grains, cow-dung, with a bunch of dûrvâ grass,
with Udumbara, Palâsa, Samî, Vikankata, and

---

5. I have translated avadhâya (instead of avadâya), as Âpastamba VII, 20, 7 reads.

6. Taittirîya Samhitâ IV, 5, 3, 1. Of course the god to whom
these designations refer is Rudra.

7. The commentary explains surodaka as rain-water, or as rain-
water which has fallen while the sun was shining.

A*s*vattha (branches), and with a cow-tail he besprinkles his cows, the bull first, with (the words), ' Bring luck! Bring luck!' Then (the bull) will bring him luck.

8. He then cooks that mess of sacrificial food, sacred to Kshetrapati (the lord of the field), with milk, sprinkles it (with Âgya), takes it from the fire, and performs a sacrifice to Kshetrapati on the path where his cows use to go, without a fire, on four or on seven leaves.

9. He has him (i. e. the Kshetrapati? an ox representing Kshetrapati?) led (to his place) in the same way as the *s*ûlagava (chap. 8, § 2).

10. He sacrifices quickly, (for) the god has a strong digestion (?).

11. He then performs worship with (the two verses), 'With the lord of the field,' 'Lord of the field' (Taitt. Sa*m*h. I, 1, 14, 2. 3).

12. Of (the remains of that sacrificial food) sacred to Kshetrapati his uterine relations should partake, according as the custom of their family is.

End of the Third Pa*t*ala.

---

8. Mât*ri*datta says, kshaitrapatya*m* kshetrapatidevatâka*m* payasi sthâlîpâkam, &c. The meaning of the expression 'that (enam) mess of sacrificial food' is doubtful; the commentary says, enam iti pûrvâpeksham pûrvavad aupâsana evâsyâpi *s*rapa*n*ârtham.—The last words (on four or on seven leaves) the commentator transfers to the next Sûtra, but he mentions the different opinion of other authorities.

10. nûrtte *s*îghra*m* yagate. kuta*h*. yata*h* sa deva*h* pâka*h* paka-na*s*îlas tîkshmas (read, tîkshnas) tasmât. Mât*ri*datta.—Possibly Dr. Kirste is right in reading tûrta*m*; the corresponding Sûtra of Âpastamba has kshipram (VII, 20, 15), and, as the *S*atapatha Brâhma*n*a (VI, 3, 2, 2) observes, 'yad vai kshipra*m* tat tûrtam.'

PRASNA II, PATALA 4, SECTION 10.

1. On the new-moon day, in the afternoon, or on days with an odd number in the dark fortnight the monthly (*Srâddha* is performed).

2. Having prepared food for the Fathers and having arranged southward-pointed Darbha grass as seats (for the Brâhma*n*as whom he is going to invite), he invites an odd number of pure Brâhma*n*as who are versed in the Mantras, with no deficient limbs, who are not connected with himself by consanguinity or by their Gotra or by the Mantras, (such as his teacher or his pupils).

3. In feeding them he should not look at any (worldly) purposes.

4. Having put wood on the fire and strewn southward pointed and eastward-pointed Darbha grass around it, having prepared the Â*g*ya in an Â*g*ya pot over which he has laid one purifier, having sprinkled water round (the fire) from right to left, and put a piece of Udumbara wood on (the fire), he sacrifices with the (spoon called) Darvi which is made of Udumbara wood.

5. Having performed the rites down to the Â*g*ya-bhâga offerings, he suspends his sacrificial cord over his right shoulder and calls the Fathers (to his sacrifice) with (the verse), 'Come hither, O Fathers, friends of Soma, on your hidden, ancient paths, bestowing on us offspring and wealth and long life, a life of a hundred autumns.'

10, 1. Comp. *Sânkhâyana* IV, 1 ; Â*s*valâyana II, 5, 10 seq.; IV, 7 ; Pâraskara III, 10 ; Gobhila IV, 3.

4. Comp. above, I, 1, 1, 11 seq. 27 ; 2, 7 seq.

6. He sprinkles water in the same direction (i. e. towards the south) with (the verse), 'Divine waters, send us Agni. May our Fathers enjoy this sacrifice. May they who receive their nourishment every month bestow on us wealth with valiant heroes.'

7. Having performed the rites down to the Vyâhriti oblations with his sacrificial cord over his left shoulder, he suspends it over his right shoulder and sacrifices with (the following Mantras) :

'To Soma with the Fathers, svadhâ! Adoration!

'To Yama with the Angiras and with the Fathers, svadhâ! Adoration!

'With the waters that spring in the east and those that come from the north : with the waters, the supporters of the whole world, I interpose another one between (myself and) my father. Svadhâ! Adoration!

'I interpose (another one) through the mountains; I interpose through the wide earth; through the sky and the points of the horizon, through infinite bliss I interpose another one between (myself and) my grandfather. Svadhâ! Adoration!

'I interpose (another one) through the seasons, through days and nights with the beautiful twilight. Through half-months and months I interpose another one between (myself and) my great-grandfather. Svadhâ! Adoration!'

Then he sacrifices with their names : 'To N. N. svadhâ! Adoration! To N.N. svadhâ! Adoration!'

---

6. Comp. Atharva-veda XVIII, 4, 40.

7. Comp. Sânkhâyana III, 13, 5. The translation there given of the words anyam antah pitur dadhe ought to be changed accordingly.—For âbhur anyopapadyatâm read mâtur anyo svapadyatâm as Sânkhâyana has.

'Wherein my mother has done amiss, abandoning her duty (towards her husband), may my father take that sperm as his own; may another one fall off from the mother. Svadhâ! Adoration!'

In the same way a second and a third verse with the alteration of the Mantra, 'Wherein my grandmother,' 'Wherein my great-grandmother.'

PATALA 4, SECTION 11.

1. 'The Fathers who are here and who are not here, and whom we know and whom we do not know: Agni, to thee they are known, how many they are, *G*âtavedas. May they enjoy what thou givest them in our oblation. Svadhâ! Adoration!

'Your limb that this flesh-devouring (Agni) has burnt, leading you to the worlds (of the Fathers), *G*âtavedas, that I restore to you again. Unviolated with all your limbs arise, O Fathers! Svadhâ! Adoration!

'Carry the Â*g*ya, *G*âtavedas, to the Fathers, where thou knowest them resting afar. May streams of Â*g*ya flow to them; may their wishes with all their desires be fulfilled! Svadhâ! Adoration!'

In the same way a second and a third verse with the alteration of the Mantra, 'to the grandfathers,' 'to the great-grandfathers.'

2. In the same way he sacrifices of the food, altering the Mantra, 'Carry the food, &c.'

3. Then he sacrifices the Svish*t*ak*r*it oblation

11, 1. Rig-veda X, 15, 13; Atharva-veda XVIII, 4, 64; Â*s*va-lâyana-G*r*ihya II, 4, 13, &c. Before the verse, 'Carry the Â*g*ya,' the Udî*k*yas, as Mât*r*idatta states, insert the words, 'He then makes oblations of Â*g*ya (with the Mantra, &c.).' According to this reading the words of the second Sûtra, 'In the same way, &c.,' would refer only to these last oblations.

with (the formula), ' To Agni Kavyavâhana Svish-
takrit svadhâ!   Adoration!'

4. He then touches the food with (the formulas),
'The earth is thy vessel, the heaven is the lid.   I
sacrifice thee into the Brahman's mouth.   I sacrifice
thee into the up-breathing and down-breathing of
the Brâhma*n*as.   Thou art imperishable; do not
perish for the Fathers yonder, in yon world!   The
earth is steady; Agni is its surveyor in order that
what has been given may not be lost.

' The earth is thy vessel, the heaven is the lid,
&c.   Do not perish for the grandfathers yonder,
in yon world.   The air is steady; Vâyu is its surveyor, in order that what has been given may
not be lost.

' The earth is thy vessel, the heaven is the lid,
&c.   Do not perish for the great-grandfathers
yonder, in yon world.   The heaven is steady; Âditya
is its surveyor, in order that what has been given
may not be lost.'

5. With (the words), ' I establish myself in the
breath and sacrifice ambrosia,' he causes the Brâhma*n*as to touch (the food).

PATALA 4, SECTION 12.

1. While they are eating, he looks at them with
(the words), 'My soul (âtman) dwells in the Brahman
that it may be immortal.'

2. When they have eaten (and go away), he goes
after them and asks for their permission to take the
remains of their meal (for the rites which he is going

---

5. Comp. Taittirîya Âra*n*yaka X, 34.

to perform). Then he takes a water-pot and a handful of Darbha grass, goes forth to a place that lies in
a south-easterly intermediate direction, spreads the
Darbha grass out with its points towards the south,
and pours out on that (grass) with downward-turned
hands, ending in the south, three handfuls of water,
with (the formulas), 'May the fathers, the friends of
Soma, wipe themselves!   May the grandfathers . . .
the great-grandfathers, the friends of Soma, wipe
themselves!' or, 'N. N.! Wash thyself! N. N.!
Wash thyself!'

3. On that (grass) he puts down, with downward-
turned hands, ending in the south, the lumps (of
food for the Fathers).   To his father he gives his
lump with (the words), 'This to thee, father, N. N.!'
to the grandfather with (the words), 'This to thee,
grandfather, N. N.!' to the great-grandfather with
(the words), 'This to thee, great-grandfather, N. N.!'
silently a fourth (lump).   This (fourth lump) is
optional.

4. Should he not know the names (of the ancestors),
he gives the lump to the father with (the words),
'Svadhâ to the Fathers who dwell on the earth,' to
the grandfather with (the words), 'Svadhâ to the
Fathers who dwell in the air,' to the great-grandfather
with (the words), 'Svadhâ to the Fathers who dwell
in heaven.'

5. Then he gives, corresponding to each lump,
collyrium and (other) salve and (something that
represents) a garment.

---

3. According to the commentary after each formula the words
are added, 'and to those who follow thee;' comp. Taitt. Samh. I,
8, 5, 1 ; III, 2, 5, 5; Kâty.-Sraut. IV, 1, 12.

6. The collyrium (he gives), saying three times, 'Anoint thy eyes, N. N.! Anoint thy eyes, N. N.!'

7. The salve, saying three times, 'Anoint thyself, N. N.! Anoint thyself, N. N.!'

8. With (the formula), 'These garments are for you, O Fathers. Do not seize upon anything else that is ours,' he tears off a skirt (of his garment) or a flake of wool and puts that down (for the Fathers), if he is in the first half of his life.

9. He tears out some hairs of his body, if in the second half.

10. Then he washes the vessel (in which the food was of which he had offered the lumps), and sprinkles (the water with which he has washed it), from right to left round (the lumps) with (the Mantra), 'These honey-sweet waters, bringing refreshment to children and grandchildren, giving sweet drink and ambrosia to the Fathers, the divine waters refresh both (the living and the dead), these rivers, abounding in water, covered with reeds, with beautiful bathing-places; may they flow up to you in yon world!' Then he turns the vessel over, crosses his hands so that the left hand becomes right and the right hand becomes left, and worships (the Fathers) with the formulas of adoration, 'Adoration to you, O Fathers, for the sake of sap' (Taitt. Samh. III, 2, 5, 5).

11. Then he goes to the brink of some water and pours down three handfuls of water (with the following Mantras):

---

6 seq. A fourth time he gives the same thing silently; comp. Sûtra 3.

8, 9. If his age is under fifty years or over fifty years (Mâtri-datta; comp. the commentary on Kâtyâyana-Sraut. IV, 1, 17. 18).

PATALA 4, SECTION 13.

1. 'This is for thee, father, this honey-sweet wave, rich in water. As great as Agni and the earth are, so great is its measure, so great is its might. As such a great one I give it. As Agni is imperishable and inexhaustible, thus may it be imperishable and inexhaustible, sweet drink to my father. By that imperishable (wave), that sweet drink, live thou together with those, N. N.! The *Rik*as are thy might.

'This is for thee, grandfather, &c. . . . As great as Vâyu and the air are . . . As Vâyu is imperishable . . . to my grandfather. . . . The Ya*g*us are thy might.

'This is for thee, great-grandfather, &c. . . . As great as Âditya and the heaven are . . . The Sâmans are thy might.'

2. Returning (from the place where he has performed the Pi*nd*a offerings) he puts the substance cleaving (to the Sthâlî) into the water-pot and pours it out, with (the verse), 'Go away, O Fathers, friends of Soma, on your hidden, ancient paths. After a month return again to our house and eat our offerings, rich in offspring, in valiant sons.'

3. Thereby the (*S*râddha) celebrated in the middle of the rainy season has been declared.

4. There (oblations of) flesh are prescribed;

5. Of vegetables, if there is no flesh.

End of the Fourth Pa*t*ala.

---

3. Mâdhyâvarsham. Comp. the note on *S*ânkhâyana III, 13, 1.

PRASNA II, PATALA 5, SECTION 14.

1. We shall explain (the festival of) the Ash*t*akâ.

2. The eighth day of the dark fortnight that follows after the full moon of Mâgha, is called Ekâsh*t*akâ.

3. On the day before that Ash*t*akâ, under (the Nakshatra) Anûrâdhâs, in the afternoon he puts wood on the fire, strews southward-pointed and eastward-pointed Darbha grass around it, and turns rice out of four shallow cups over which he has laid one purifier, with (the Mantra), 'I turn out, impelled by the god Savit*ri*, this cake prepared from four cups (of rice), which may drive away all suffering from the Fathers in the other world. On the impulse of the god Savit*ri*, with the arms of the two A*s*vins, with Pûshan's hands I turn thee out, agreeable to the fathers, the grandfathers, the great-grandfathers.'

4. With the same purifier he silently strains the Proksha*ni* water; he silently sprinkles (with that water the rice and the vessels), silently husks (the rice), silently bakes it in four dishes like a Puro*d*âsa, sprinkles (Â*g*ya) on it, takes it from the fire, sprinkles (water) round (the fire) from right to left, and puts a piece of Udumbara wood on (the fire). With the (spoon called) Darvi which is made of Udumbara wood, he cuts off in one continual line which is directed towards south-east, (the Avadâna portions)

14, 1. Hira*n*yakesin describes only one Ash*t*akâ, the Ekâsh*t*akâ, while the other texts speak of three or four Ash*t*akâs; comp. the quotations in the note on Sânkhâyana III, 12, 1.

4. The rules of the *S*rauta ritual regarding the baking of the Puro*d*âsa are given by Hillebrandt, Neu- und Vollmondsopfer, p. 43.

one after the other, spreading under and sprinkling over them (Âgya), and sacrifices them, one after the other, in one continual line which is directed towards south-east, with (the Mantras), 'The mortars, the pressing-stones have made their noise, preparing the annual offering. Ekâsh/akâ! May we be rich in offspring, in valiant sons, the lords of wealth. Svadhâ! Adoration!

'God Agni! The cake which is prepared with ghee and accompanied by (the word) svadhâ, that the Fathers may satiate themselves — (this our) offering carry duly, Agni. I, the son, sacrifice an oblation to my fathers. Svadhâ! Adoration!

'Here is a cake, Agni, prepared from four cups (of rice), with ghee, rich in milk, in wealth, in prosperity. May the Fathers gladly accept it all together; may it be well sacrificed and well offered by me. Svadhâ! Adoration!'

5. Then he makes oblations of (other) food with (the verses), 'The one who shone forth as the first,' 'The Ekâsh/akâ, devoting herself to austerities,' 'She who shone forth as the first' (Taitt. Sa*m*hitâ IV, 3, 11, 1. 3. 5).

6. Cutting off (the Avadânas destined for the Svish/akr*i*t oblation) together from the cake and from the (other) food and mixing them with clarified butter, he makes an oblation thereof with (the formula), 'To Agni Kavyavâhana Svish/akr*i*t svadhâ! Adoration!'

7. That (cake) with ghee and honey and with the food (mentioned in Sûtras 5. 6) he touches in the way prescribed for the *S*râddha ceremony and puts

---

7. Comp. above, chap. 11, 4; 12, 2 seq.

down lumps (of it) according to the ritual of the Pinda offerings.

8. (The remains of) that (cake, &c.) he serves to learned Brâhmanas.

9. He gives them food and presents as at the Srâddha ceremony.

10. The known (rites) down to the pouring out of the handfuls of water (are performed here) as at the monthly (Srâddha).

PATALA 5, SECTION 15.

1. On the following day he sacrifices a cow to the Fathers.

2. Having put wood on the fire and strewn southward-pointed and eastward-pointed Darbha grass around it, he sacrifices the oblation for the touching of the animal (see below), with (the verse), 'This cow I touch for the Fathers; may my assembled fathers gladly accept it (which is offered) with fat and ghee, with the word svadhâ; may it satiate my fathers in the other world. Svadhâ! Adoration!' Then he touches (the cow) with one (blade of) sacrificial grass and with an unforked Vapâsrapani of Udumbara wood, with (the formula), 'I touch thee agreeable to the Fathers.'

3. He sprinkles (the cow with water) with (the words), 'I sprinkle thee agreeable to the Fathers.'

4. When it has been sprinkled and fire has been

---

10. See above, chap. 12, 13.

15, 2. On the Vapâsrapani, comp. Kâtyâyana VI, 5, 7; Âsval.-Grihya I, 11, 8. Comp. besides, Taitt. Samh. VI, 3, 6; Âpastamba-Srauta-sûtra VII, 8, 3; 12, 5 seq.

4. The Udikyas read, as Mâtridatta states, 'to the south of the fire.'

carried round it, they kill it to the west of the fire, its head being turned to the west, its feet to the south.

5. After it has been killed, he silently 'strengthens' its sense-organs (by touching them) with water, and silently takes out the omentum, the heart, and the kidneys.

6. With the Vapâsrapanî of Udumbara wood he roasts the omentum; with spits of Udumbara wood the other (parts mentioned in Sûtra 5) separately.

7. After he has roasted them, and has sprinkled Âgya over them, and has taken them from the fire, he sprinkles water round (the fire) from right to left, puts a piece of Udumbara wood on (the fire), and sacrifices with a Darvi spoon of Udumbara wood the omentum, spreading under and sprinkling over it (Âgya), with (the verse), 'Carry the omentum, Gâtavedas, to the Fathers, where thou knowest them resting afar. May streams of fat flow to them; may their wishes with all their desires be fulfilled. Svadhâ! Adoration!'

8. He sacrifices the omentum entirely. The other parts (Sûtra 5) he should offer to the Brâhmanas and should feed them (with those parts of the cow).

9. When the food (for the Brâhmanas) is ready, he cuts off (the Avadânas) together from the mess of boiled rice, and from the pieces of meat, and mixing them with clarified butter he makes oblations

---

5. On the 'strengthening' of the sense-organs of an immolated victim, comp. Âpastamba-Srauta-sûtra VII, 18, 6 seq. Schwab, Thieropfer, 110.—On matasne, see Indische Studien, IX, 248; Schwab 127.

8. Possibly the reading of the Udîkyas indicated by Mâtridatta, vyâkritya instead of upâkritya, is correct. The translation would be, 'With the rest, distributing it, &c.'

thereof with the verses, ' Behold the Ekâsh/akâ, the giver of food with meat and ghee, (which is offered) with (the word) svadhâ. By the Brâhma*n*as that food is purified. May it be an imperishable (blessing) to me ! Svadhâ ! Adoration ! '

' The Ekâsh/akâ, devoting herself to austerities, the consort of the year, exuberant (with milk), has poured forth milk. May you live on that milk, O Fathers, all together. May this (food) be well offered and well sacrificed by me ! Svadhâ ! Adoration !

' The image of the year ' (Taitt. Sam*h*. V, 7, 2, 1).

10. After he has sacrificed, he cuts off (the Avadânas) from the food and from the pieces of meat, and mixing them with clarified butter he makes an oblation with (the formula), ' To Agni Kavyavâhana Svish/akr*i*t svadhâ ! Adoration ! '

11. The known (rites) down to the pouring out of the handfuls of water (are performed here) as at the monthly (*S*râddha).

12. The gifts of food and presents, however, are not necessary here.

13. On the following day, he prepares food for the Fathers with the rest of the meat, and sacrifices with (the two verses), ' Thou, Agni, art quick,' (and), ' Pra*g*âpati ! ' (see above, I, 1, 3, 5).

14. (= Sûtra 11).

End of the Fifth Pa/ala.

---

11. See above, chap. 14, 10.
12. See chap. 14, 9.
13. This is the so-called Anvash/akya ceremony.

PRASNA II, PATALA 6, SECTION 16.

1. Now (follows) the *Sravanâ* ceremony.

2. On the day of that full moon which falls under (the Nakshatra) *Sravana*, after the evening Agnihotra he puts wood on the (third of the three *Srauta* fires, called the) Dakshinâgni. One who has not set up the (*Srauta*) fires, (does the same with) the sacred domestic fire.

3. Then he procures unbroken grains, unbroken fried grains, coarsely ground grains, (leaves and blossoms) of the Kimsuka tree, collyrium and (other) salve, and Âgya.

4. Having 'spread under' (Âgya) in the (spoon called) Darvi, he cuts off (the Avadânas) of those kinds of food (mentioned in Sûtra 3), mixes them with clarified butter, and sacrifices (with the formulas), 'Adoration to Agni the terrestrial, the lord of terrestrial beings! Svâhâ! Adoration to Vâyu the all-pervading, the lord of aerial beings! Svâhâ! Adoration to Sûrya, the red one, the lord of celestial beings! Svâhâ! Adoration to Vishnu, the whitish one, the lord of the beings that dwell in the quarters (of the world). Svâhâ!'

5. He anoints the Kimsuka (flowers and leaves) with Âgya, and sacrifices with (the Mantras), 'Devoured is the gadfly; devoured is thirst (?); devoured is the stinging worm.' 'Devoured is the stinging worm; devoured is thirst; devoured is the gadfly.'

---

5. I am not sure about the translation of vikashti. Perhaps it is only a blunder for vitrishti, which is the reading of the Âpastambiya Mantrapâtha. Comp. Winternitz, Der Sarpabali, ein altindischer Schlangencult (Wien, 1888), p. 28.

'Devoured is thirst; devoured is the gadfly; devoured is the stinging worm.'

6. He takes a water-pot and a handful of Darbha grass, goes forth, his face turned towards the east, spreads the Darbha grass out with its points towards the east, and makes four Bali-offerings on that (grass) with (the formulas), 'To the terrestrial Serpents I offer this Bali,' 'To the aerial, &c.; to the celestial, &c.; to the Serpents dwelling in the quarters (of the world),' &c.

7. Having given there collyrium and (other) salve (to the Serpents), he worships them with the Mantras, 'Adoration be to the Serpents' (Taitt. Saṃhitâ IV, 2, 8, 3).

8. He should take a water-pot and should at that distance in which he wishes the serpents not to approach, three times walk round his house, turning his right side towards it, and should sprinkle water round it with (the formulas), 'Beat away, O white one, with thy foot, with the fore-foot and with the hind-foot, these seven human females and the three (daughters) of the king's tribe.

'Within the dominion of the white one the Serpent has killed nobody. To the white one, the son of Vidarva, adoration!

'Adoration to the white one, the son of Vidarva!'

9. Then he worships the Serpents towards the different regions, one by one with (the corresponding section of) these Mantras, 'The convergent one thou art called, the eastern region' (Taitt. Saṃh. V, 5, 10, 1 seq.).

---

8. Comp. Pâraskara II, 14, 19. In the first Mantra I read râgabândhavîh; comp. the note on Pâr. II, 14, 4.

10. From that time he daily makes the Bali-offerings till the full-moon day of Mârgaṣîrsha.

11. Here the Kiṃsuka offerings (see § 5) are not repeated.

12. The sprinkling (of water) round (the house) does not take place (see § 8).

13. The last Bali he offers with (the words), 'Going to acquit myself, going to acquit myself.'

End of the Sixth Paṭala.

PRASNA II, PATALA 7, SECTION 17.

1. We shall explain the Âgrahâyaṇî ceremony.

2. On the full-moon day of Mârgaṣîrsha he puts wood on the fire, strews (Darbha grass) on the entire surface round the fire, cooks a mess of sacrificial food with milk, sprinkles it (with Âgya), takes it from the fire, performs the rites down to the Vyâhriti oblations, and sacrifices (four oblations) with (the following Mantras):

'This offering, the creeping of Iḍâ, rich in ghee, moving and not moving, accept gladly, O Gâtavedas.

13. Some authorities understand, as Mâtridatta states, that he should offer the Bali only with the words as they stand in the Sûtra, others prescribe the formula (comp. § 6): 'To the terrestrial (aerial, &c.) Serpents I offer this Bali going to acquit myself, going to acquit myself.'

17, 1. Comp. on the Âgrahâyaṇî ceremony Sânkhâyana IV, 17; Pâraskara III, 2, &c.; Winternitz, Sarpabali, 32 seq.

2. The first Mantra is very corrupt; comp. Atharva-veda III, 10, 6. Regarding the legend of Iḍâ, who was procreated out of Manu's Pâka-sacrifice, and 'came forth as if dripping, and clarified butter gathered on her step,' comp. Satapatha Brâhmaṇa I, 8, 1, 7 (M. M., India, what can it teach us? p. 136).

What domestic animals there are, of all shapes, all seven kinds of them : may they gladly dwell here and may they prosper.   Svâhâ !

'The night which men welcome like a cow that comes to them, (the night) which is the consort of the year, may that (night) be auspicious to us. Svâhâ!

'Bringing bliss to the cattle, to the wife, bringing bliss by night and by day, may this (night) which is the consort of the year, be auspicious to us. Svâhâ!

'The full-moon night, bringing abundance, visiting one after another, dividing the months and fortnights : may this (night), the full one, protect us. Svâhâ !'

3. He sacrifices the oblation to Agni Svish*t*akr*i*t with (the verse), 'Agni, make this (sacrifice) full that it may be well offered.   Be victorious, O god, in all battles.   Shine far and wide, showing us a wide path.   Bestow on us long life, full of splendour and free from decay.   Svâhâ !'

4. Then he washes his hands and touches the earth with (the formulas), 'In power I establish myself, in royalty.   Among the horses I establish myself, among the cows.   In the limbs I establish myself, in the self.   In the Prâ*n*as I establish myself, in prosperity.   In Heaven and Earth I establish myself, in sacrifice.

'May the three times eleven gods, the thirty-three, the gracious ones, whose Purohita is B*ri*haspati, on the impulse of the god Savit*ri*—may the gods with (all) the gods give me bliss!'

5. The master of the house sits down at their southerly end,

3. Comp. Taitt. Br. II, 4, 1, 4 ; Pâraskara III, 1, 3.

6. The other persons to the north,

7. According to their seniority.

8. They who know the Mantras among them, murmur the Mantras (which will be stated).

9. With (the verse), ' Be soft to us, O earth, free from thorns; grant us rest; afford us wide shelter' (Taitt. Âr. X, 1, 10), and with the two (verses), 'Verily of the mountains' (Taitt. Sa*m*h. II, 2, 12, 2. 3) they lie down on their right sides.

10. With (the verse), 'Up! with life' (Taitt. Sa*m*h. I, 2, 8, 1) they arise.

11. When they have arisen, they murmur, 'We have arisen; we have become immortal.'

12. In that way they (lie down and) arise that night three times.

13. Having served food to the Brâhma*n*as and having caused them to say, 'An auspicious day! Hail! Good luck!' they rest that night.

End of the Seventh Pa*t*ala.

PRASNA II, PATALA 8, SECTION 18.

1. Now we shall explain the opening and the conclusion (of the annual course of study).

2. During the fortnight that precedes the *S*rava*n*â

---

13. 'Here end the Gr*i*hya ceremonies,' says Mât*ri*datta. Dr. Kirste (Preface, p. viii), accordingly, believes that the three last chapters may be later additions. It may be observed in connection with this, that in the Âpastambîya-Gr*i*hya, which throughout is so closely related to our text, the ceremonies of the Upâkara*n*a and Utsar*g*ana, of which these three chapters treat, are not described.

18, 2. *S*rava*n*âpaksha means, according to Mât*ri*datta, *s*râva-

full moon, when the herbs have appeared, under (the
Nakshatra) Hasta or on the full-moon day (itself),
the opening ceremony of the (annual course of)
study (is performed).

3. Having put wood on the fire and performed
the rites down to the Vyâh*ri*ti oblations, he sacrifices
(with his pupils) to the *Ri*shis of the Kâ*nd*as: ' To
Pra*g*âpati, the *Ri*shi of a Kâ*nd*a, svâhâ! To Soma,
the *Ri*shi of a Kâ*nd*a, svâhâ! To Agni, the *Ri*shi
of a Kâ*nd*a, svâhâ! To the Visve devâs, the *Ri*shis
of a Kâ*nd*a, svâhâ! To Svayambhû, the *Ri*shi of a
Kâ*nd*a, svâhâ!'—these are the *Ri*shis of the Kâ*nd*as.
Or (he sacrifices) to the names of the Kâ*nd*as, to the
Sâvitrî, to the Rig-veda, the Ya*g*ur-veda, the Sâma-
veda, the Atharva-veda, and to Sadasaspati.

4. Having (thus) sacrificed, they repeat the first
three Anuvâkas,

5. Or the beginnings of all Kâ*nd*as.

6. He enters upon (sacrificing) the *G*aya, &c.
(oblations; see above, I, 1, 3, 8).

7. After all rites down to the Svish*t*ak*ri*t oblation
have been performed, they stop studying three days
or one day; then they should go on studying so as
to commence where they have broken off: so say
the teachers.

8. During the fortnight that precedes the Taishî
full moon, under (the Nakshatra) Rohi*nî* or on the
full-moon day (itself), the Utsarga (or conclusion of
the term of study) is celebrated.

_____

*n*apûrvapaksha, and indeed the moon stands in conjunction with the
Nakshatra Hasta only on one day of the first, not of the second,
fortnight of the month *S*râva*na* (comp. the note on Âsvalâyana-
G*ri*hya III, 5, 2. 3). Comp. taishîpakshasya rohi*n*yâm, below, § 8.

8. As to taishîpaksha, comp. the note on Sûtra 2.

9. (The teacher) with his pupils goes in an easterly or northerly direction, and where they find a pleasant water with a pleasant bathing-place, they dive into it and perform three suppressions of the breath with the Agharmarsha*na* hymn (Rig-veda X, 190 = Taitt. Âr. X, 1, 13. 14). Holding purifiers (i. e. Darbha blades) in their hands they bathe with the three (verses), 'Ye waters, ye are wholesome' (Taitt. Sa*m*h. IV, 1, 5, 1), with the four (verses), 'The gold-coloured, pure, purifying waters' (T. S. V, 6, 1, 1 seq.), and with the Anuvâka, '(Soma) which clears itself, the heavenly being' (Taitt. Br. I, 4, 8): giving the Darbha blades to each other and feigning to try to seize (??) each other.

10. Then they arrange on a pure spot that is inclined towards the east, seats of eastward-pointed Darbha grass, so that they end in the north—

PATALA 8, SECTION 19.

1. For Brahman, Pra*g*âpati, B*ri*haspati, Agni, Vâyu, the Sun, the Moon, the Stars, king Indra, king Yama, king Varu*na*, king Soma, king Vai*s*rava*na*, for the Vasus, the Rudras, the Âdityas, the Vi*s*ve devâs, the Sâdhyas, the *Ri*bhus, the Bh*ri*gus, the Maruts, the Atharvans, the Aṅgiras: for these divine beings.

---

9. On the last words of this Sûtra, Mât*ri*datta says, ditsanta iveti dâtum i*kkh*anta ivânyonya*m* prati. athavâ âditsanta iveti pâ*th*a*h*. âditsanto mush*n*anta ivânyonya*m*.—Professor Kielhorn's text MS. has, âtsa*m*ta ivânyonya*m*; Professor Bühler's text MS., ditsa*m*ta ivânyonya*m*.

19, 1. According to Mât*ri*datta, they prepare a seat for Brahman with the words, 'For Brahman I prepare (a seat),' and so on. Comp. chap. 20, 3.

2. Visvâmitra, Gamadagni, Bharadvâga and Gautama, Atri, Vasish*th*a, Kasyapa : these are the seven *Ri*shis.

3. Wearing their sacrificial cords below (round their body) they arrange towards the north, at a place that is inclined towards the north, seats of northward-pointed Darbha grass, so that they end in the east, for Vi*s*vâmitra, Gamadagni, Bharadvâga, Gautama, Atri, Vasish*th*a, Kasyapa.

4. Between Vasish*th*a and Kasyapa they arrange (a seat) for Arundhatî, (the wife of Vasish*th*a) ;

5. Towards the south, in a place inclined towards the east, for Agastya.

6. Then for the (following) teachers, ending with those who teach (only) one Veda (?), viz. for K*ri*sh*n*a Dvaipâyana, Gâtûkar*n*ya, Taruksha, T*ri*nabindu, Varmin, Varûthin, Vâgin, Vâga*s*ravas, Satya*s*ravas, Su*s*ravas, Suta*s*ravas, Soma*s*ushmâya*n*a, Satvavat, B*ri*haduktha Vâmadev(y)a, Vâgiratna, Harya*g*vâyana, Udamaya, Gautama, *Ri*na*ñg*aya, *Ri*ta*ñg*aya, K*ri*ta*ñg*aya, Dhana*ñg*aya, Babhru, Tryaru*n*a, Trivarsha, Tridhâtu, *S*ibinta, Parâ*s*ara, Vish*n*u, Rudra, Skanda, Kâs*i*svara, Gvara, Dharma, Artha, Kâma, Krodha, Vasish*th*a, Indra, Tvash*tri*, Kart*ri*, Dhart*ri*, Dhât*ri*, M*ri*tyu, Savit*ri*, Sâvitrî, and for each Veda, for the Rig-veda, the Ya*g*ur-veda, the Sâma-veda, the Atharva-veda, the Itihâsa and Purâ*n*a.

7. Towards the south, with their sacrificial cords suspended over their right shoulders, in a place inclined towards the south, they arrange seats of southward-pointed Darbha grass, so that they end in the west—

---

2. This is a frequently quoted versus memorialis.

PATALA 8, SECTION 20.

1. For Vaisampâyana, Palingu, Tittira [sic], Ukha, Âtreya, the author of the Pada-text, Kaundinya the author of the commentary, for the authors of the Sûtras, for Satyâshâdha (Hiranyakesin), for the handers-down of the text, for the teachers, the Rishis, the hermits dwelling in the woods, the chaste ones, for those who have only one wife.

2. They prepare (seats) each for his own fathers and maternal ancestors.

3. With (the words), 'For N. N. I prepare (a seat); for N. N. I prepare (a seat)' (he prepares) a seat.

4. With (the words), 'I satiate N. N.; I satiate N. N.' (he makes offerings of) water.

5. With (the words), 'Adoration to N. N.! Adoration to N. N.!' (he offers) perfumes, flowers, incense, and lamps.

6. With (the words), 'To N. N. svâhâ! To N. N. svâhâ!' (he offers) food.

7. With (the words), 'I satiate N. N.; I satiate N. N.' (he offers) water with fruits in it.

8. Having worshipped them with (the words), 'Adoration to N. N.! Adoration to N. N.!'—

9. Having put wood on the fire to the west of the surface (on which he had performed the Tarpana),

---

20, 1. The Kândânukrama of the Âtreyî-sâkhâ, which has been printed by Professor Weber in his edition of the Taittirîya Samhitâ, vol. ii, p. 356, shows that the dative Palingave ought to be corrected to Paingaye. The 'vrittikâra' is there called not Kaundinya, but Kundina.

9. There is only one difference between the text of this Sûtra

and having performed the rites down to the Vyâh*ri*ti oblations (&c., as above, chap. 18, 3-7).

10. With the two (verses), 'From joint to joint,' 'Thou who with a hundred' (Taitt. Sa*m*h. IV, 2, 9, 2) they plant Dûrvâ grass at the shore of the water.

11. They stir up waves in the water and run a race in an easterly or northerly direction until they lose their breath.

12. When they have returned (from that race? or when they have returned from the whole ceremony to the village?) they offer cakes, coarsely ground grain, and boiled rice to the Brâhma*n*as.

13. The same (rites are repeated) when they have finished the study of the whole Veda, with the exception of the planting of Dûrvâ grass, of (stirring up) the water, and of the race.

14. Thus they satiate daily (after the Brahma-yag*ñ*a) the gods, the *Ri*shis, and the Fathers with water; they satiate them with water.

End of the Hira*n*yake*s*i-sûtra.

---

and that of chap. 18, 3-7 : instead of hutvâ trîn âdito ⋆ nuvâkân adhîyate (18, 4) we read here, hutvâ prathamenânuvâkenâdhîyate, which I believe must be translated, ' Having sacrificed with the first Anuvâka, they recite (that Anuvâka).' Mât*ri*datta says, hutvâ prathamottamânuvâkam adhîyate.

13. See Sûtras 10 and 11.

GRIHYA-SÛTRA OF
ÂPASTAMBA.

INTRODUCTORY NOTE

G*R*IHYA-SÛTRA OF ÂPASTAMBA.

THE short treatise of Âpastamba on the G*r*ihya ritual
forms one Pra*s*na of the great corpus of the Âpastambîya-
Kalpa-sûtra (see Sacred Books, vol. ii, p. xii) and stands,
among the G*r*ihya texts, in closest connection with the
Hira*n*yakesi-G*r*ihya-sûtra. The chief difference between
these two Sûtras, both belonging to the Taittirîya School
of the Black Ya*g*ur-veda, consists herein, that Âpastamba,
just as has been stated above[1] with regard to Gobhila,
gives only the rules for the performance of the G*r*ihya
rites without the Mantras, which are contained in a special
collection, the Mantrapâ*th*a, standing by the side of the
Sûtras: Hira*n*yakesin, on the other hand, follows the more
usual practice, as adopted by *S*ânkhâyana, Â*s*valâyana,
Pâraskara, of interweaving the description of the ceremonies
with the text of the corresponding Mantras. As to the
relation in which the Âpastambîya-sûtras stand to the
Mantrapâ*th*a, there is, so far as I can see, no reason why we
should not extend the theory which we have tried to establish with regard to Gobhila, to the evidently parallel case
of Âpastamba : the Sûtras presuppose the existence of the
Mantrapâ*th*a, just as the latter text seems to presuppose
the Sûtras.—The questions regarding the historical relation
of Âpastamba to Hira*n*yakesin have been treated of by
Professor Bühler in his Introduction to Âpastamba's
Dharma-sûtra, S. B. E., vol. ii, pp. xxiii seq.

I have here to thank Dr. Winternitz, to whom we are
indebted for an excellent edition of the Âpastambîya-
G*r*ihya-sûtra, for having placed at my disposal, before publi-

---

[1] See above, pp. 3 seq.

cation, the proof-sheets of his edition, and for lending me his copy of the Mantrapâ*th*a as well as of the commentary of Haradatta. The kindness of the same scholar has enabled me to make use of Professor Eggeling's copy of the first part of Sudar*s*anârya's commentary and of his own copy of the second part of the same work.

GRIHYA-SÛTRA OF ÂPASTAMBA.

PATALA 1, SECTION 1.

1. Now (follow) the ceremonies (the knowledge of) which is derived from practice (and not from the Sruti).

2. They should be performed during the northern course of the sun, on days of the first fortnight (of the month), on auspicious days,

3. With the sacrificial cord suspended over (the sacrificer's) left shoulder.

4. (The rites should be performed) from left to right.

5. The beginning should be made on the east side or on the north side,

6. And also the end.

7. Ceremonies belonging to the Fathers (are performed) in the second fortnight (of the month),

8. With the sacrificial cord suspended over the right shoulder,

9. From right to left,

10. Ending in the south.

11. Ceremonies occasioned by special occurrences (are performed) according as their occasions demand.

1, 1–11. The Paribhâshâs for the Pâkayagñas.

7–10. Comp. 7 with 2, 8 with 3, 9 with 4, 10 with 6.

12. Having set the fire in a blaze, he strews east-ward-pointed Darbha grass around it,

13. Or eastward-pointed and northward-pointed (grass);

14. Southward-pointed at sacrifices to the Fathers,

15. Or southward-pointed and eastward-pointed.

16. To the north of the fire he strews Darbha grass and (on that) he places the vessels (required for sacrifice) upside-down, two by two, if referring to ceremonies directed to the gods,

17. All at once, if to men,

18. One by one, if to the Fathers.

19. The preparation of the (blades used as) 'puri-fiers,' the measure of their length, the preparation of the Prokshanî water, and the sprinkling of the vessels are the same here as at the sacrifices of the new and full moon, (but are performed) in silence.

20. To the west of the fire he pours water into a vessel over which he has laid (two grass blades called) purifiers, purifies (the water) three times with two northward-pointed purifiers, holds it on a level with his nose and mouth, places it to the north of the fire on Darbha grass, and covers it with Darbha grass.

21. On the south side he causes a Brâhmana to sit down on Darbha grass.

22. He melts the Âgya, pours it, to the west of the fire, into the Âgya-pot, over which he has laid two purifiers, draws coals (out of the sacrificial fire) towards the north, puts (the Âgya) on them, throws

---

12 seq. Description of the regular form of a Pâkayagña.

19. Comp. Srauta-sûtra I, 11, 6 seqq.

20. This is the Pranîtâ water.

21. The Brahman.

light on it by means of a burning (grass-blade), throws two Darbha points into it, moves a fire-brand round it three times, takes it from the fire towards the north, sweeps the coals back (into the fire), purifies (the Âgya) three times with two north-ward-pointed purifiers, moving them backward and forward, and throws the purifiers into the fire.

PATALA 1, SECTION 2.

1. He warms at the fire the implement with which he sacrifices, wipes it off with Darbha blades, warms it again, sprinkles it (with water), puts it down, touches the Darbha blades with water, and throws them into the fire.

2. As paridhis (or pieces of wood laid round the fire) yoke-pins are used at the marriage, the Upana-yana, the Samâvartana, the parting of the (wife's) hair, the tonsure of the child's hair, the cutting of the beard, and at expiatory ceremonies.

3. He sprinkles water round the fire, on the south side from west to east with (the words), 'Aditi, give thy consent!' on the west side from south to north with 'Anumati, give thy consent!' on the north side from west to east with 'Sarasvati [sic], give thy consent!' all around with 'God Savitri, give thy impulse!'

4. At ceremonies belonging to the Fathers (water is sprinkled) only all round (the fire), silently.

5. Having put a piece of wood on the fire, he

2, 2. On the paridhi woods, comp. chiefly Hillebrandt, Neu-und Vollmondsopfer, 66 seq.

5. The Srauta rules on the two Âghâras are given Srauta-sûtra II, 12, 7; 14, 1.

offers the two Âghâra oblations as at the sacrifices of the new and full moon, silently.

6. Then he offers the two Âgyabhâga oblations, over the easterly part of the northerly part (of the fire) with (the words), 'To Agni Svâhâ!' over the easterly part of the southerly part (another oblation) exactly like the preceding one, with (the words), 'To Soma Svâhâ!'

7. Having offered the chief oblations (belonging to each sacrifice) according to prescription, he adds the following oblations, viz. the Gaya, Abhyâtâna, Râsh/rabh*ri*t oblations, the oblation to Pragâpati, the Vyâh*ri*tis one by one, the oblation to (Agni) Svish/ak*ri*t with (the following formula), 'What I have done too much in this ceremony, or what I have done here too little, all that may Agni Svish-/ak*ri*t, he who knows, make well sacrificed and well offered. Svâhâ!'

8. The sprinkling (of water) round (the fire is repeated) as above; the Mantras are altered so as to say, 'Thou hast given thy consent,' 'Thou hast given thy impulse.'

9. The designation 'Pâkayag*ñ*a' is used of ceremonies connected with worldly life.

10. There the ritual based on the Brâhma*n*a (holds good),

---

6. Comp. *S*rauta-sûtra II, 18, 5; Hillebrandt, loc. cit., p. 106, note 3.

7. On the Gaya, Abhyâtâna, Râsh/rabh*ri*t formulas, comp. Pâraskara I, 5, 7 seq.; Hira*n*yakesin I, 1, 3, 7 seq.; Taitt. Sa*m*-hitâ III, 4, 4–7.—The last formula occurs also in Â*s*valâyana I, 10, 23; Hira*n*yakesin I, 1, 3, 6, &c.

8. Comp. above, Sûtra 3.

10. According to Haradatta, this Sûtra would imply that where-soever the ritual described in the preceding Sûtras holds good,

11. (To which the words allude), 'He sacrifices twice; he wipes off (his hand) twice; he partakes twice (of the sacrificial food); having gone away he sips (out of the Sru*k*) and licks off (the Sru*k*).'

12. All seasons are fit for marriage with the exception of the two months of the *sisira* season, and of the last summer month.

13. All Nakshatras which are stated to be pure, (are fit for marriage);

14. And all auspicious performances.

15. And one should learn from women what ceremonies (are required by custom).

16. Under the Invakâs (Nakshatra), (the wooers who go to the girl's father) are sent out: such wooers are welcome.

PATALA 1, SECTION 3.

1. Under the Maghâs (Nakshatra) cows are provided;

---

another ritual based on the Brâhma*n*a, and more especially on the treatment of the Agnihotra in the Brâhma*n*a, may be used in its stead.

11. Comp. Taitt. Brâhma*n*a II, 1, 4, 5 ; *S*atapatha Brâhma*n*a II, 3, 1, 18. 21.—At the Agnihotra the sacrificer, having wiped off the Sru*k* with his hand, wipes off the hand on the Barhis or on the earth (Âpast.-*S*raut. VI, 10, 11 ; 11, 4; Kâtyâyana IV, 14, 20). As to the following acts alluded to in this Sûtra, comp. Âpastamba VI, 11, 4. 5; 12, 2.

16. On the Nakshatra Invakâs, comp. Section 3, Sûtra 4. This Sûtra forms a *S*loka-hemistich, on which Haradatta observes, 'This verse has not been made by the Sûtrakâra.'

3, 1, 2. Comp. Rig-veda X, 85, 13; Atharva-veda XIV, 1, 13 ; Kau*s*ika-sûtra 75; Râmâya*n*a I, 71, 24 ; 72, 13 ; Weber, Die vedischen Nachrichten von den Naxatra, II, 364 seq. These parallel passages most decidedly show that in Sûtra 2 we ought to read vyuhyate, not vyûhyate.

2. Under the Phalgunî (Nakshatra) marriage is celebrated.

3. A daughter whom he wishes to be dear (to her husband), a father should give in marriage under the Nish*t*yâ (Nakshatra) ; thus she becomes dear (to her husband); she does not return (to her father's) house: this is an observance based on a Brâhma*n*a.

4. The word Invakâs means M*ri*ga*s*iras ; the word Nish*t*yâ means Svâti.

5. At the wedding one cow ;

6. In the house one cow :

7. With the (first cow) he should prepare an Argha reception for the bridegroom as for a guest,

8. With the other (the bridegroom [?] should do so) for a person whom he reveres.

9. These are the occasions for killing a cow : (the arrival of) a guest, (the Ash*t*akâ sacrifice offered to) the Fathers, and marriage.

10. Let (the wooer) avoid in his wooing a girl that sleeps, or cries, or has left home.

11. And let him avoid one who has been given (to another), and who is guarded (by her relations), and one who looks wicked (?), or who is a most

---

3. Comp. Taittirîya Brâhma*n*a I, 5, 2, 3.

4. Comp. Sûtra 3, and above, Section 2, Sûtra 16.

5-8. Comp. *S*âṅkhâyana-G*ri*hya I, 12, 10. It is clear that with the first cow the bride's father has to receive the bridegroom. The 'house' mentioned in Sûtra 6 seems to be the house of the newly-married couple. In the expression 'whom he reveres,' 'he,' according to the commentaries, is the bridegroom.

10. This Sûtra forms a half-*s*loka.

11. Most expressions in this Sûtra are quite doubtful, and their translation rests on the explanations of the commentators (see pp. 44, 45 of Dr. Winternitz's edition), which are evidently for the most part only guesses.

excellent one (?), or (who is like the fabulous deer) sarabha (?), a hunch-back, a girl of monstrous appearance. a bald-headed girl, a girl whose skin is like a frog's (?), a girl who has gone over to another family (?), a girl given to sensual pleasures (?), or a herdess, or one who has too many friends, or who has a fine younger sister, or one whose age is too near to that of the bridegroom (?).

12. Girls who have the name of a Nakshatra, or of a river, or of a tree, are objectionable.

13. And all girls in whose names the last letter but one is r or l, one should avoid in wooing.

14. If possible, he should place (the following) objects hidden before the girl, and should say to her, ' Touch (one of these things).'

15. (The objects are), different kinds of seeds mixed together, loose earth from (the kind of sacrificial altar called) vedi, an earth-clod from a field, cow-dung, and an earth-clod from a cemetery.

16. If she touches one of the former (objects, this portends) prosperity as characterized (by the nature of what she has touched).

17. The last is regarded as objectionable.

18. Let him marry a girl of good family and character, with auspicious characteristics, and of good health.

19. Good family, a good character, auspicious characteristics, learning, and good health : these are the accomplishments of a bridegroom.

20. A wife who is pleasing to his mind and his

12, 13. These Sûtras would require only slight alterations to make a sloka.

16. The seeds mean offspring, and so on.

eyes, will bring happiness to him ; let him pay no attention to the other things : such is the opinion of some.

PATALA 2, SECTION 4.

1. Let him send out as his wooers friends who have assembled, who are versed in the Mantras.

2. He should recite over them the first two verses (Mantrap. I, 1, 1. 2).

3. When he himself has seen (the bride), let him murmur the third (verse ; M. I, 1, 3).

4. With the fourth (M. I, 1, 4) let him behold her.

5. Let him seize with his thumb and fourth finger a Darbha blade, and let him wipe (therewith) the interstice between her eye-brows with the next Yagus (M. I, 1, 5), and let him throw it away towards the west.

6. If an omen occurs (such as the bride's or her relations' weeping), let him murmur the next (verse ; M. I, 1, 6).

7. With the next (verse ; M. I, 1, 7) let him send an even number of persons who have assembled there, and who are versed in the Mantras, to fetch water.

8. With the next Yagus (M. I, 1, 8) he places a round piece of Darbha net-work on her head; on that, with the next (verse ; M. I, 1, 9) he places a right yoke-hole; on this hole he lays with the next (verse ; M. I, 1, 10), a piece of gold, and washes her with the next five verses (M. I, 2, 1–5), (so that the

---

4, 8. As to the last sentence of this Sûtra, comp. the statements collected by Hillebrandt, Neu- und Vollmondsopfer, p. 59.

water runs over that gold and through the yoke-
hole); with the next (verse; M. I, 2, 6) he causes
her to dress in a fresh garment, and with the next
(M. I, 2, 7) he girds her with a rope.

9. Then he takes hold of her with the next
(verse; M. I, 2, 8) by her right hand, leads her to
the fire, spreads a mat, west of the fire, so that the
points of the blades in it are directed towards the
north, and on this mat they both sit down, the bridegroom to the north.

10. After the ceremonies have been performed
from the putting of wood on the fire down to the
Âgyabhâga oblations, he recites over her the first
two (verses of the third Anuvâka).

11. Then he should take with his right hand,
palm down, her right hand which she holds
palm up.

12. If he wishes that only daughters may be born
to him, he should seize only the fingers (without the
thumb) ;

13. If he wishes that only sons may be born to
him, the thumb.

14. He takes (her hand) so as just to touch her
thumb and the little hairs (on her hand),

15. With the four verses, 'I take thy hand'
(Mantrap. I, 3, 3–6).

16. He then makes her step forward with her
right foot, to the north of the fire, in an easterly or
northerly direction, with (the formula), 'One step
for sap' (M. I, 3, 7).

17. At her seventh step he murmurs, 'Be a
friend' (M. I, 3, 14).

PATALA 2, SECTION 5.

1. Having before the sacrifice gone round the fire, so that their right sides are turned towards it,

2. They sit down in their former position, and while she takes hold of him, he offers the oblations (indicated by the) next (Mantras), with (the Mantras), 'To Soma, the acquirer of a wife, Svâhâ!' (M. I, 4, 1–16), one oblation with each Mantra.

3. He then causes her, to the north of the fire, to tread with her right foot on a stone, with (the verse), 'Tread' (M. I, 5, 1).

4. Having 'spread under' Âgya into her joined hands, he pours roasted grain twice (into them), and sprinkles Âgya over it.

5. Some say that an uterine relation of hers pours the grain (into her hands).

6. He (?) sacrifices (that grain) with (the verse), 'This wife' (M. I, 5, 2).

7. Having gone round the fire, with the right side turned towards it, with the next three (verses; M. I, 5, 3–5) he makes her tread on the stone as above (M. I, 5, 6).

8. And the oblation (is performed) with the next (verse; M. I, 5, 7).

9. (Then follow) again the circumambulation (M. I, 5, 8–10), the injunction to tread on the stone

---

5, 2. See 4, 9.   3. See below, IV, 10, 9.

6. 'The action of sacrificing belongs to the bridegroom; the hands of the wife represent the sacrificial vessel.' Haradatta.—'It is the bridegroom who sacrifices the grain with the verse, "This wife."' Sudarsanârya.

7. See above, Sûtra 3.

(I, 5, 11), and the oblation with the next (verse; I, 5, 12);

10. (Then) the circumambulation again (I, 5, 13-15).

11. He enters upon the performance of the *Gaya* and following oblations.

12. Having performed (the rites) down to the sprinkling (of water) round (the fire), and having untied the rope with the next two verses (I, 5, 16. 17), he should then make her depart (from her father's house in a vehicle), or should have her taken away.

13. Having put that fire (with which the marriage rites have been performed, into a vessel), they carry it behind (the newly-married couple).

14. It should be kept constantly.

15. If it goes out, (a new fire) should be kindled by attrition,

16. Or it should be fetched from the house of a *S*rotriya.

17. Besides, if (the fire) goes out, one of them, either the wife or the husband, should fast.

18. Or he may sacrifice with the next (verse; M. I, 5, 18), and not fast.

19. The next (verse; M. I, 6, 1) is for putting the chariot (on which the young couple is to depart), in position;

20. With the next two (verses; M. I, 6, 2. 3), he puts the two animals to the chariot;

21. First the right one.

22. When she mounts (the chariot), he recites over her the next (verses; M. I, 6, 4-7).

11, 12. See Section 2, Sûtras 7. 8; Section 4, Sûtra 8.

12 seq. Comp. Hira*ny*akesin I, 7, 22, 1 seq.

23. With the next (verse ; M. I, 6, 8), he spreads out two threads in the wheel-tracks (in which the chariot is to go), a dark-blue one in the right (track), a red one in the left.

24. With the next (verses ; M. I, 6, 9-11), he walks on these (threads).

25. And when they pass by bathing-places, posts, or cross-roads, let him murmur the next (verse ; M. I, 6, 12).

PATALA 2, SECTION 6.

1. The next (verse ; M. I, 6, 13), he recites over a boat (with which they are going to cross a river).

2. And let the wife, when she is crossing, not see the crew.

3. When they have crossed, let him murmur the next (verse; M. I, 6, 14).

4. If they have to pass over a cemetery, or if any article (which they carry with them), or their chariot is damaged, the ceremonies from the putting of wood on the fire down to the Âgyabhâga oblations are performed, and while she takes hold of him, he offers the oblations (indicated by the) next (Mantras ; M. I, 7, 1-7), then he enters upon the performance of the Gaya and following oblations, and performs (the rites) down to the sprinkling (of water) round (the fire).

5. If they pass by trees with milky sap or by other trees that serve as marks, by rivers or by deserts, he should murmur the next two (verses ; M. I, 7, 8. 9), according to the characteristics in them (which refer to these different cases).

6. With the next (verse) he shows her the house (M. I, 7, 10).

7. With the next two (verses; M. I, 7, 11. 12) he unyokes the two animals; the right one first.

8. Having, with the next (verse; M. I, 8, 1), spread out, in the centre of the house, a red bull's skin with the neck to the east, with the hair up, he causes her to recite the next (verse; M. I, 8, 2), while he makes her enter the house, (which she does) with her right foot.

9. And she does not stand on the threshold.

10. In the north-east part of the house the cere-monies from the putting of wood on the fire down to the Âgyabhâga oblations are performed, and while she takes hold of him, he offers the oblations (indicated by the) next (Mantras; M. I, 8, 3–15); then he enters upon the performance of the Gaya and following oblations, and performs (the rites) down to the sprinkling (of water) round (the fire). Then they sit down with the next (verse; M. I, 9, 1) on the skin, the bridegroom to the north.

11. He then places with the next (verse; M. I, 9, 2), the son of a wife who has only sons and whose children are alive, in her lap, gives fruits to the (child) with the next Yagus (M. I, 9, 3), and murmurs the next two (verses; M. I, 9, 4–5). Then he (and his wife) observe silence until the stars appear.

12. When the stars have appeared, he goes out (of the house with her) in an easterly or northerly direction, and shows her the polar star and (the star) Arundhatî with the next two verses (M. I, 9, 6–7), according to the characteristics (contained in those verses).

PATALA 3, SECTION 7.

1. He then makes her offer the sacrifice of a Sthâlîpâka sacred to Agni.

2. The wife husks (the rice grains out of which this Sthâlîpâka is prepared).

3. After he has cooked (the Sthâlîpâka), and has sprinkled (Âgya) over it, and has taken it from the fire towards the east or the north, and has sprinkled (Âgya) over it while it stands (there near the fire), (the ceremonies) from the putting of wood on the fire down to the Âgyabhâga oblations (are performed), and while she takes hold of him, he sacrifices of that Sthâlîpâka.

4. The ' spreading under ' and the sprinkling over (of Âgya are done) once; two Avadânas (or cut-off portions are taken).

5. Agni is the deity (of the first oblation); the offering is made with the word Svâhâ.

6. Or he may sacrifice after having picked out, once, a portion (of the sacrificial food with the Darvi spoon).

7. Agni Svishtakrit is the second (deity).

8. (At the Svishtakrit oblation) the ' spreading under ' and taking an Avadâna are done once, the sprinkling over (of Âgya) twice.

9. The Avadâna for the first deity (is taken) out of the middle (of the Sthâlîpâka);

10. It is offered over the centre (of the fire).

7, 1 seq. Hiranyakesin I, 7, 23, 2 seq.

6. As to the technical meaning of upahatya or upaghâtam, comp. the note on Gobhila I, 8, 2 ; Grihya-samgraha I, 111.

11. (The Avadâna) for the second (deity is taken) from the northern part (of the Sthâlîpâka) ;

12. It is offered over the easterly part of the northerly part (of the fire).

13. Having silently anointed (a part of) the Barhis (by dipping it) into the remains both (of the Sthâlîpâka and the Âgya) in the way prescribed (in the Srauta ritual) for the (part of the Barhis called) Prastara, he throws (that part of the Barhis) into the fire.

14. (The rule regarding) the second sprinkling (of water round the fire) is valid (here).

15. He gives (the remains of) that (sacrificial food) with butter to a Brâhmana to eat—

16. Whom he reveres. To that (Brâhmana) he makes the present of a bull.

17. In the same way, with the exception of the sacrificial gift, they should sacrifice a Sthâlîpâka from then onwards, on the days of the new and full moon, after having fasted.

18. Some say that a vessel full (of grain) is the sacrificial gift.

19. From then onwards he should offer morning and evening with his hand these two oblations (to Agni and to Agni Svishtakrit) of (rice) grains or of barley.

---

13. Comp. Srauta-sûtra III, 5, 9 seqq.—On the prastara, see Hillebrandt, Neu- und Vollmondsopfer, 64. 142. 146.

14. See above, I, 2, 8. The upahomas prescribed above, I, 2, 7, are not performed here, but the second parishekana is.

16. I have altered in my translation the division of the two sentences. Comp. Hiranyakesin I, 7, 23, 5–6, and the note there.

19. The two regular daily oblations corresponding to the Agnihotra of the Srauta ritual.

20. The deities are the same as at the Sthâlipâka (just described).

21. Some say that the first oblation in the morning is sacred to Sûrya.

22. Before and after (those oblations) the sprinkling (of water) round (the fire is performed) as stated above.

23. By the sacrifice of the new and full moon the other ceremonies have been explained (the knowledge of) which is derived from practice.

24. The deities (of those rites) are as stated (with regard to each particular case), having their place between Agni (Sûtra 5) and Svish*t*akr*i*t (Sûtra 7).

25. The sacrifice (of a cow) on the arrival of a guest (should be performed as stated below) without alterations.

26. (The deities) of the Vai*s*vadeva ceremony are the Vi*s*ve devâs,

27. Of ceremonies performed on full-moon days, the full-moon day on which they are performed.

PATALA 3, SECTION 8.

1. At the opening and concluding ceremonies of the Vedic study, the *R*ishi who is indicated (as the

---

22. See I, 2, 3. 8.   23. See I, 1, 1.

25. See below, V, 13, 16.

26. See Âpastamba Dharma-sûtra II, 2, 3, 1 (S. B. E., vol. ii, p. 103).

27. For instance, the *S*râva*n*î paur*n*amâsî is the deity of the ceremony described below, VII, 18, 5 seq.

8, 1. Haradatta observes that at the kâ*nd*opâkara*n*a and kâ*nd*a-samâpana the *R*ishi of that kâ*nd*a, at the general adhyâyopâkara*n*a and samâpana all kâ*nd*arshis, should be worshipped.

*Ri*shi of the Kâ*nd*a which they study, is the deity to
whom the ceremony belongs),

2. And in the second place Sadasaspati (cf.
Mantrap. I, 9, 8).

3. They reject a sacrifice performed by a wife or
by one who has not received the Upanayana initiation, and a sacrifice of salt or pungent food, or of
such food as has an admixture of a despised sort
of food.

4. Sacrifices connected with special wishes and
Bali sacrifices (should be performed) as stated (even
against the clauses of the last Sûtra).

5. Whenever the fire flames up of itself, he should
put two pieces of wood on it with the next two
(verses; M. I, 9, 9–10),

6. Or with (the two formulas), ' May fortune reach
me ! May fortune come to me ! '

7. Let him notice the day on which he brings his
wife home.

8. (From that day) through three nights they
should both sleep on the ground, they. should be
chaste, and should avoid salt and pungent food.

9. Between their sleeping-places a staff is inter-
posed, which is anointed with perfumes and wrapped
round with a garment or a thread.

10. In the last part of the fourth night he takes
up the (staff) with the next two (verses; M. I, 10,
1–2), washes it and puts it away; then (the ceremonies) from the putting of wood on the fire down
to the Âg*y*abhâga oblations (are performed), and
while she takes hold of him, he sacrifices the oblations (indicated by the) next (Mantras; M. I, 10,
3–9) ; then he enters upon the performance of the
*G*aya and following oblations, and performs (the

rites) down to the sprinkling (of water) round (the fire). Then he makes her sit down to the west of the fire, facing the east, and pours some Âgya of the remains (of those oblations) on her head with the (three) Vyâhritis and the word Om as the fourth (M. I, 10, 10–13). Then they look at each other with the next two verses (M. I, 11, 1–2), according to the characteristics (contained in those verses); with the next verse (M. I, 11, 3) he besmears the region of their hearts with remains of Âgya; then he should murmur the next three verses (I, 11, 4–6), and should murmur the rest (of the Anuvâka; I, 11, 7–11) when cohabiting with her.

11. Or another person should recite (the rest of the Anuvâka) over her, (before they cohabit).

12. During her (first) monthly illness he instructs her about the things forbidden (to menstruous women), contained in the Brâhmana, in the section, 'A menstruous woman with whom,' &c.

13. After the appearance of her monthly illness, he should, when going to cohabit with her after her illness, recite over her, after she has bathed, the next verses (M. I, 12, 1–13, 4).

PATALA 3, SECTION 9.

1. Each following night with an even number, from the fourth (after the beginning of her monthly illness) till the sixteenth, brings more excellent offspring to them, if chosen for the (first) cohabiting after her illness; thus it is said.

2. If he sneezes or coughs while going about on

12. Taittirîya Samhitâ II, 5, 1, 6 seq.

business, he should touch water and should murmur
the two following (verses; M. I, 13, 5. 6) according
to the characteristics (which they contain).

3. In the same way with the next (Mantras—M. I,
13, 7-10—he should address the following objects),
according to the characteristics (which those Mantras
contain) : a conspicuous tree, a heap of excrements,
the skirt (of his garment) which is blown against him
by the wind, and a shrieking bird.

4. One (for instance, the wife's father) who wishes
that the hearts of both (husband and wife) may be in
accord should observe chastity through at least three
nights and should prepare a Sthâlîpâka.   Then (the
ceremonies) from the putting (of wood) on (the fire)
down to the Âgyabhâga oblations (are performed),
and while the wife takes hold of him, he sacrifices of
the Sthâlîpâka the oblations (indicated by the) next
(Mantras; M. I, 14, 1-7) ; then he enters upon the
performance of the Gaya and following oblations,
and performs (the rites) down to the sprinkling (of
water) round (the fire).   (The remains of) the (sacrificial food) with butter, he should give to eat to an
even number of Brâhmaṇas, at least to two, and
should cause them to pronounce wishes for his
success.

5. When the moon, on the following day, will be
in conjunction with Tishya, she strews three times
seven barley-grains around (the plant) Clypea Her-
nandifolia with (the formula), 'If thou belongest
to Varuṇa, I redeem thee from Varuṇa. If thou
belongest to Soma, I redeem thee from Soma.'

9, 5. Comp. Gobhila II, 6, 6 seq.

6. On the following day she should set upright (the plant) with the next (verse; M. I, 15, 1), should recite the next three (verses; M. I, 15, 2–4) over it, should tie (its root) with the next (verse; M. I, 15, 5) to her hands so that (her husband) does not see it, and should, when they have gone to bed, embrace her husband with her arms, with the verse alluding to the word upadhâna ('putting on;' M. I, 15, 6).

7. Thus he will be subject to her.

8. By this (rite) also (a wife) overcomes her co-wives.

9. For this same purpose she worships the sun daily with the next Anuvâka (M. I, 16).

10. If a wife is affected with consumption or is otherwise sick, one who has to observe chastity, should rub her limbs with young lotus leaves which are still rolled up, and with lotus roots, with the next (formulas, limb by limb) according to the character-istics (contained in those formulas; M. I, 17, 1–6), and should throw away (the leaves and roots) towards the west.

11. With the next (verses; M. I, 17, 7–10) he should give the wife's garment (which she has worn at the wedding [?]) to (a Brâhmana) who knows this (ceremony).

PATALA 4, SECTION 10.

1. We shall explain the Upanayana (or initiation of the student).

2. Let him initiate a Brâhmana in the eighth year after the conception,

3. A Râganya in the eleventh, a Vaisya in the twelfth year after the conception.

4. Spring, summer, autumn : these are the (fit) seasons (for the Upanayana), corresponding to the order of the castes.

5. (The boy's father) serves food to Brâhma*n*as and causes them to pronounce auspicious wishes, and serves food to the boy. (The teacher ?) pours together, with the first Ya*g*us (of the next Anuvâka, warm and cold) water, pouring the warm water into the cold, and moistens (the boy's) head with the next (verse ; M. II, 1, 2).

6. Having put three Darbha blades into his hair (towards each of the four directions) (the teacher [?]) shaves his hair with the next four (verses ; M. II, 1, 3–6) with the different Mantras, towards the different (four) directions.

7. With the following (verse, M. II, 1, 7, somebody) addresses him while he is shaving.

8. Towards the south, his mother or a Brahma-*k*ârin strews barley-grains on a lump of bull's dung ; with this (dung) she catches up the hair (that is cut off), and puts it down with the next (verse; M. II, 1, 8) at the root of an Udumbara tree or in a tuft of Darbha grass.

9. After (the boy) has bathed, and (the cere-monies) from the putting (of wood) on (the fire) down to the Â*g*yabhâga oblations (have been performed), he causes him to put a piece of Palâ*s*a wood on the

---

10, 6, 7. The difference which Haradatta makes between the teacher who begins to shave him (pravapati) and the barber who goes on with shaving (vapantam) seems too artificial.

7. Haradatta : The teacher addresses the barber, &c.—Sudar-*s*anârya : The mother of the boy or a Brahma*k*ârin [comp. Sûtra 8] . . . addresses the teacher who shaves him.

9. Comp. above, II, 4, 3.

fire with the next (verse; M. II, 2, 1), and makes him tread with his right foot on a stone to the north of the fire, with (the verse), 'Tread' (M. II, 2, 2).

10. Having recited the next two (verses; M. II, 2, 3. 4) over a garment that has been spun and woven on one day, and has caused him, with the next three (verses; M. II, 2, 5–7), to put it on, he recites over him, after he has put it on, the next (verse; M. II, 2, 8).

11. He ties thrice around him, from left to right, a threefold-twisted girdle of Mu*ñg*a grass with the next two (verses; M. II, 2, 9. 10), and (gives him) a skin as his outer garment with the next (verse; II, 2, 11).

12. To the north of the fire (the teacher) spreads out Darbha grass; on that he causes (the boy) to station himself with the next (verse; M. II, 3, 1), pours his joined hands full of water into (the boy's) joined hands, makes him sprinkle himself three times with the next (verse; M. II, 3, 2), takes hold of his right hand with the next (formulas; M. II, 3, 3–12), gives him with the next (formulas; M. II, 3, 13–23) in charge to the deities (mentioned in those Mantras), initiates him with the next Ya*g*us (M. II, 3, 24), and murmurs into his right ear the (Mantra), 'Blessed with offspring' (II, 3, 25).

PATALA 4, SECTION 11.

1. The boy says, 'I am come to be a student' (II, 3, 26).

---

11. Comp. Âpast. Dharma-sûtra I, 1, 2, 33; 1, 3, 3 seq.

12. As to the words, 'he initiates him' (upanayati), comp. Sâṅkhâyana II, 2, 11. 12; Â*s*valâyana I, 20, 4 &c.

2. The other (i.e. the teacher) has to ask ; the boy has to answer (II, 3, 27–30).

3. The other murmurs the rest (of the Anuvâka),

4. And causes the boy to repeat (the Mantra) which contains wishes for himself (II, 3, 32).

5. (The rites) down to the Âgyabhâgas have been prescribed.

6. Having then caused him to sacrifice the oblations (indicated in the) next (Mantras; M. II, 4, 1–11), he enters upon (the performance) of the Gaya and following oblations.

7. Having performed (the rites) down to the sprinkling (of water) round (the fire), he puts down, to the west of the fire, a bunch of northward-pointed grass ; on that (the teacher) who performs the initiation, sits down with the next Yagus (M. II, 4, 12).

8. The boy, sitting to the east (of him), facing the west, seizes with his right hand (the teacher's) right foot and says, ' Recite the Sâvitrî, Sir !'

9. He recites (the Sâvitrî) to him, ' That (glorious splendour) of Savit*ri*' (Taitt. Sa*m*h. I, 5, 6, 4; M. II, 4, 13);

10. Pâda by Pâda, hemistich by hemistich, and the whole (verse).

11. (When repeating the Sâvitrî Pâda by Pâda, he pronounces) the Vyâh*ri*tis singly at the beginning or at the end of the Pâdas ;

12. In the same way (the first and the second Vyâh*ri*ti at the beginning or at the end) of the hemistichs ; the last (Vyâh*ri*ti, when he repeats) the whole verse.

13. With the next Mantra (M. II, 4, 14) the boy touches his upper lip ;

11, 5. See above, Section 10, Sûtra 9.

14. With the next (II, 4, 15) both his ears;

15. With the next (II, 5, 1) he takes up the staff.

16. The staff of a Brâhma*n*a is made of Palâ*s*a wood, that of a Râ*g*anya of a branch of the Nyagrodha tree, so that the downward-turned end (of the branch) forms the tip (of the staff), that of a Vai*s*ya of Bâdara or Udumbara wood.

17. Some state (only), without any reference to caste, that the staff should be made of the wood of a tree.

18. After (the teacher) has made him repeat (the formula), ' My memory' (M. II, 5, 2), and he has bestowed an optional gift on his teacher, and (the teacher) has made him arise with (the formula, M. II, 5, 3), ' Up, with life !' (the student) worships the sun with the next (Mantras; II, 5, 4).

19. If (the teacher) wishes, ' May this (student) not be estranged from me,' let him take (the student) by the right hand with the next (verse; II, 5, 6).

20. They keep that fire (used at the Upanayana) three days,

21. And (during that time) salted and pungent food should be avoided.

22. Having wiped (with his hand wet) around (the fire) with (the formula), ' Around thee' (M. II, 6, 1), he should put (twelve) pieces of wood on that (fire) with the next Mantras (II, 6, 2-13).

23. In the same way also on another (fire, when the Upanayana fire is kept no longer),

24. Fetching fuel regularly from the forest.

25. With the next (formula—M. II, 6, 14—the teacher) instructs (the student in his duties).

16, 17. These Sûtras are identical with Dharma-sûtra I, 1, 2, 38 (S. B. E., vol. ii, p. 9).

26. On the fourth day (after the Upanayana the teacher) takes the garment (of the student) for himself with the next (verse; M. II, 6, 15), having made him put on another (garment).

PATALA 5, SECTION 12.

1. Having studied the Veda, when going to take the bath (which signifies the end of his studentship), he enters a cow-shed before sunrise, hangs over its door a skin with the hair inside, and sits there.

2. On that day the sun should not shine upon him.

3. At noon, after (the ceremonies) from the putting (of wood) on the fire down to the Âgya-bhâga oblations (have been performed), he puts a piece of Palâsa wood on (the fire) with the next (verse; M. II, 7, 1), sits down to the west of the fire on a mat or on erakâ grass, recites the next (verse, II, 7, 2) over a razor, and hands it over to the barber with the next Yagus (II, 7, 3). (The rites) beginning with the pouring together of (warm and cold) water down to the burying of the hair are the same as above (comp. M. II, 7, 4).

4. He sits down behind the cow-shed, takes the girdle off, and hands it over to a Brahmakârin.

5. The (Brahmakârin) hides it with the next Yagus (II, 7, 5) at the root of an Udumbara tree or in a tuft of Darbha grass.

6. With water of the description stated above he

---

26. The garment which the teacher takes for himself is that mentioned above, IV, 10, 10.

12, 3. See above, IV, 10, 5–8.

6. See IV, 10, 5.

bathes with the six next (verses; II, 7, 6–11), and with the next (II, 7, 12) he cleanses his teeth with a stick of Udumbara wood.

7. Having bathed and shampooed his body with such ingredients as are used in bathing, (aromatic powder, &c.),

8. He puts on with the next Yagus (M. II, 7, 13) a fresh under garment, and anoints himself, after having given the salve in charge of the deities with the next (Mantras, II, 7, 14), with the next (verse, II, 7, 15) with sandal salve which is scented with all kinds of perfumes. With the next (verse, II, 7, 16) he moves about a gold pellet with its setting, which is strung on a string, three times from left to right in a water-pot ; with the next (verse, II, 7, 17) he ties the (pellet) to his neck ; in the same way, without Mantras, he ties a pellet of Bâdara wood to his left hand, and repeats the rites stated above with a fresh upper garment, with the (verses), ' May the rich' (comp. above, IV, 10, 10 ; M. II, 7, 18).

9. To the skirt (of that garment) he ties two ear-rings, puts them into the (sacrificial spoon called) Darvi, offers the oblations (indicated by the) next (Mantras ; M. II, 8, 1–8), pouring the Âgya over (the ear-rings), and enters upon (the performance of) the Gaya and following oblations.

10. Having performed (the ceremonies) down to the sprinkling (of water) round (the fire), he should tie (one of the ear-rings) with the same (verses) to his right ear, and with the same (verses one) to his left ear.

11. In the same way he should with the following (formulas, M. II, 8, 9–9, 5), according to the characteristics (contained in them), (put) a wreath on his

head, anoint (his eyes), look into a mirror, (put on) shoes, (and should take) a parasol and a staff.

12. He keeps silence until the stars appear.

13. When the stars have appeared, he goes away towards the east or north, worships the quarters (of the horizon) with the next hemistich, and the stars and the moon with the next (M. II, 9, 6).

14. Having spoken with a friend he may go where he likes.

PATALA 5, SECTION 13.

1. Now this (is) another (way for performing the Samâvartana). He bathes silently at a bathing-place and puts silently a piece of wood on (the fire).

2. He sits down on a bunch of grass, as stated above (comp. M. II, 9, 7), at a place where they are going to honour him (with the Argha reception).

3. A king and a chieftain (sit down) in the same way (as a Brâhmana), with the next two (formulas, M. II, 9, 8. 9), according to the characteristics (contained in them).

4. (The host) announces (to the guest), ' The water for washing the feet!'

5. (The guest) should recite the next (verse, II, 9, 10) over (that water) and should stretch out the right foot first to a Brâhmana, the left to a Sûdra.

6. Having touched the person who washes him, he should touch himself (i.e. his own heart) with the next (formula, M. II, 9, 11).

7. (The host, taking the Argha water) in an

13, 2. See above, IV, 11, 7.
5. Comp. Âsvalâyana-Grihya I, 24, 11. 12.

earthen vessel which he holds with two bunches of grass, announces (to the guest), ' The Argha water!'

8. (The guest) should recite the next (formula, II, 9, 12) over (that water) and should murmur the next Yagus (II, 9, 13), while a part (of the water) is poured over his joined hands.

9. Over the rest (of the water) which is poured out towards the east, he recites the next (verse, M. II, 9, 14).

10. (The host) pours together curds and honey in a brass vessel, covers it with a larger (brass cover), takes hold of it with two bunches of grass, and announces (to the guest), ' The honey-mixture!'

11. Some take three substances, (those stated before) and ghee.

12. Some take five, (the three stated before), and grains, and flour.

13. The guest recites the next two (formulas, M. II, 10, 1. 2) over (the honey-mixture) and sips water with the two Yagus (II, 10, 3. 4) before (eating) and afterwards; with the next (verse, II, 10, 5) he should partake three times (of the food) and should give the remainder to a person towards whom he is kindly disposed.

14. A king or a chieftain should only accept it and (give it) to his Purohita.

15. (The host) announces the cow with (the word), ' The cow!'

16. After the guest has recited the next (formula, M. II, 10, 6) over (the cow, the host) cooks its omentum, and having performed the ' spreading under' and the sprinkling over (of Âgya), he sacrifices it with the next (verse, M. II, 10, 7) with a Palâsa leaf from the middle or the end (of the stalk).

17. If the guest chooses to let (the cow) loose, he murmurs the next (formulas, II, 10, 8–11) in a low voice (and says) loudly, 'Om! Let it loose!' (II, 10, 12).

18. (In this case) he recites the next (formulas, M. II, 10, 13–17) in a low voice over the food which is announced to him (instead of the cow), (and says) loudly, 'Om! Make it ready!' (II, 10, 18).

19. For his teacher, for a *Ri*tvig, for his father-in-law, for a king he ought to perform this (Arghya ceremony) as often as they visit his house, if at least one year has elapsed (since they came last).

20. For a renowned teacher (of the Veda the ceremony should be performed) once.

PATALA 6, SECTION 14.

1. The Sîmantonnayana (or parting of the pregnant wife's hair, is performed) in her first pregnancy, in the fourth month.

2. (The husband) serves food to Brâhma*n*as and causes them to pronounce auspicious wishes; then, after (the ceremonies) from the putting (of wood) on the fire down to the Â*g*yabhâga oblations (have been performed), he offers the oblations (indicated in the) next (Mantras, M. II, 11, 1–8), while (the wife) takes hold of him, and enters upon the (performance) of the *G*aya and following oblations.

3. Having performed (the rites) down to the sprinkling (of water) round (the fire), he makes her sit down to the west of the fire, facing the east, and parts her hair upwards (i. e. beginning from the front) with a porcupine's quill that has three white spots,

with three Darbha blades, and with a bunch of unripe Udumbara fruits, with the Vyâhritis or with
the two next (verses, II, 11, 9. 10).

4. He says to two lute-players, 'Sing!'

5. Of the next two (verses, II, 11, 11. 12) the first
(is to be sung on this occasion) among the (people
of the) Sâlvas.

6. The second (is to be used) for Brâhmanas;
and the river near which they dwell is to be named.

7. He ties barley-grains with young shoots (to the
head of the wife); then she keeps silence until the
stars appear.

8. When the stars have appeared, he goes (with
his wife) towards the east or north, touches a calf,
and murmurs the Vyâhritis; then she breaks her
silence.

9. The Pumsavana (i.e. the ceremony to secure
the birth of a male child) is performed when the
pregnancy has become visible, under the constellation Tishya.

10. From a branch of a Nyagrodha tree, which
points eastward or northward, he takes a shoot with
two (fruits that look like) testicles. The putting (of
wood) on the fire, &c., is performed as at the Simantonnayana (Sûtra 2).

11. He causes a girl who has not yet attained
maturity to pound (the Nyagrodha shoot) on an
upper mill-stone with another upper mill-stone, and
to pour water on it; then he makes his wife lie

---

6. Âsvalâyana I, 14, 7; Pâraskara I, 15, 8.   Comp. Zeitschrift
der D. M. Gesellschaft, XXXIX, 88.

7, 8. Sudarsanârya mentions that instead of the singular, 'She
keeps silence, she breaks her silence,' some read the dual, so that
the husband and his wife are referred to.

down on her back to the west of the fire, facing the
east, and inserts (the pounded substance) with his
thumb into her right nostril, with the next Ya*g*us
(II, 11, 13).

12. Then she will give birth to a son.

13. Here follows the ceremony to secure a quick
deliverance.

14. With a shallow cup that has not been used
before, he draws water in the direction of the river's
current; at his wife's feet he lays down a Tûryanti
plant; he should then touch his wife, who is soon to
be delivered, on the head, with the next Ya*g*us
(II, 11, 14), and should sprinkle her with the water,
with the next (three) verses (II, 11, 15–17).

15. Yadi *g*arâyu na pated eva*m*vihitâbhir evâdbhir
uttarâbhyâm (II, 11, 18. 19) avokshet.

PATALA 6, SECTION 15.

1. After he has touched the new-born child with
the Vâtsapra hymn (Taitt. Sa*m*h. IV, 2, 2; M. II,
11, 20), and has taken him on his lap with the next
Ya*g*us (M. II, 11, 21), with the next (three) (verses—
II, 11, 22; 12, 1. 2—one by one) he addresses the
child, kisses him on his head, and murmurs (the third
verse) into his right ear.

2. And he gives him a Nakshatra name.

3. That is secret.

4. He pours together honey and ghee; into this
(mixture) he dips a piece of gold which he has tied
with a noose to a Darbha blade. With the next
(three) formulas (II, 12, 3–5) he gives the boy (by

15, 1. We ought to read uttarâbhir, not uttarâbhyâm. Comp.
below, Sûtra 12.

means of the piece of gold, some of the mixture) to
eat. With the next five (verses, II, 12, 6–10) he
bathes him. Then he pours curds and ghee together and gives him this (mixture which is called)
'sprinkled butter' (prishadâgya) to eat out of a
brass vessel, with the Vyâhritis to which the syllable
'Om' is added as the fourth (II, 12, 11–14). The
remainder he should mix with water and pour out
in a cow-stable.

5. With the next (verse, M. II, 13, 1) he places
(the child) in the mother's lap; with the next (II,
13, 2) he causes her to give him her right breast;
with the next two (verses, II, 13, 3. 4) he touches
the earth, and after (the child) has been laid down,
(he touches him) with the next (formula, II, 13, 5).

6. With the next Yagus (II, 13, 6) he places a
water-pot at (the child's) head, sacrifices mustard
seeds and rice-chaff with his joined hands three
times with each of the next (formulas, II, 13, 7–14, 2),
repeating each time the word Svâhâ, and says (to
the people who are accustomed to enter the room in
which his wife lies), 'Whenever you enter, strew
silently (mustard seeds with rice-chaff) on the fire.'

7. This is to be done until the ten days (after the
child's birth) have elapsed.

8. On the tenth day, after (the mother) has risen
and taken a bath, he gives a name to the son. The
father and the mother (should pronounce that name
first).

9. (It should be a name) of two syllables or of
four syllables; the first part should be a noun; the
second a verb; it should have a long vowel (or) the
Visarga at the end, should begin with a sonant, and
contain a semi-vowel.

10. Or it should contain the particle s u, for such a name has a firm foundation; thus it is said in a Brâhmaṇa.

11. A girl's name should have an odd number of syllables.

12. When (the father) returns from a journey, he should address the child and kiss him on his head with the next two (verses, M. II, 14, 3. 4), and should murmur the next Mantras (II, 14, 5) into his right ear.

13. With the next Yagus (II, 14, 6) he addresses a daughter (when returning from a journey).

PATALA 6, SECTION 16.

1. In the sixth month after the child's birth he serves food to Brâhmaṇas and causes them to pronounce auspicious wishes; then he should pour together curds, honey, ghee, and boiled rice, and should give (the mixture) to the boy to eat, with the next (four) Mantras (II, 14, 7–10);

2. (He should feed him) with partridge, according to some (teachers).

3. In the third year after his birth the Kaula (or tonsure is performed) under (the Nakshatra of) the two Punarvasus.

4. Brâhmaṇas are entertained with food as at the initiation (Upanayana).

5. The putting (of wood) on the fire, &c. (is performed) as at the Simantonnayana.

6. He makes (the boy) sit down to the west of

---

12. Comp. above, Sûtra 1.
16, 4. See above, IV, 10, 5.   5. See above, VI, 14, 2.
6. Comp. VI, 14, 3.

the fire, facing the east, combs his hair silently with
a porcupine's quill that has three white spots, with
three Darbha blades, and with a bunch of unripe
Udumbara fruits ; and he arranges the locks in the
fashion of his ancestral *R*ishis,

7. Or according to their family custom.

8. The ceremonies beginning with the pouring
together of (warm and cold) water and ending with
the putting down of the hair are the same (as above ;
comp. M. II, 14, 11).

9. He puts down the razor after having washed
it off.

10. The ceremony is (repeated) three days with
the (same razor).   (Then) the rite is finished.

11. (The father) gives an optional gift (to the
Brâhma*n*a who has assisted).

12. The Godâna (or the ceremony of shaving the
beard, is performed) in the sixteenth year, in exactly
the same way or optionally under another constellation.

13. Or he may perform the Godâna sacred to
Agni.

14. Some prescribe the keeping of a vow through
one year in connection with the Godâna.

---

8. See IV, 10, 5–8.

10. I translate as if the words tena tryaham and karmani-
v*ritti*h formed two Sûtras.

13. 'Having performed the same rites as at the opening of the
study of the Âgneya-kân*d*a, he performs an Upasthâna to the deities
as taught with regard to the *S*ukriyavrata.' Haradatta.—'After the
ceremonies down to the Âgyabhâgas have been performed, one
chief oblation of Âgya is offered with the formula, "To Agni, the
*R*ishi of the Kân*d*a, svâhâ !"' Sudar*s*anârya.

14. Comp. the statements given in the note on Gobhila III,
1, 1.

15. The difference (between the *K*aula and the Godâna) is that (at the Godâna) the whole hair is shaven (without leaving the locks).

16. According to the followers of the Sâma-veda he should ' touch water.'

PATALA 7, SECTION 17.

1. The ground for building a house should be inclined towards the south-west. He elevates the surface and sweeps (the earth) with a broom of Palâ*s*a wood or of Samî wood, with the next (verse, M. II, 15, 1), in the same (south-west) direction;

2. In the same way three times.

3. He touches the ground, which has thus been prepared, with the next (verse, II, 15, 2). Then he has the pits for the posts dug from left to right, throws the earth (from the pits) towards the inside (of the building-ground), and erects the right door-post with the next two (verses, M. II, 15, 3. 4);

4. In the same way the other (door-post).

5. Having erected after (the door-posts) the other (posts) in the same order in which (the pits) have been dug, he recites the next Ya*g*us (II, 15, 5) over the ridge-pole when it is placed (on the posts),

6. The next (six) (Ya*g*us formulas, II, 15, 6–11) over the (house when it is) finished, according to the characteristics contained in the single formulas.

7. He sets a piece of Palâ*s*a wood or of *S*amî wood on fire, takes the fire up (in a dish) with the next verse (II, 15, 12), carries it to the house with

---

16. The udakopaspar*s*ana according to the rite of the Sâma-vedins is described by Gobhila, I, 2, 5 seqq.

the next Yagus (II, 15, 13), and places the fire in the north-eastern part of the house with the next (II, 15, 14).

8. The place for the water-barrel is to the south of that spot.

9. He strews there Darbha grass, so that its points are turned in every direction, pours rice and barley-grains over the (grass) with the next (verse, II, 15, 15), and thereon he places the water-barrel.

10. With the next (Yagus, II, 15, 16) he pours four potfuls of water into it.

11. If (the barrel) breaks, he recites the next (verse, II, 15, 17) over it.

12. After the ceremonies from the putting of wood on the fire down to the Âgyabhâga oblations have been performed, he offers the (four) oblations (indicated by the) next (Mantras; II, 15, 18–21); then he enters upon the performance of the Gaya and following oblations.

13. Having performed (the rites) down to the sprinkling (of water) round (the fire), he should sprinkle (water) with a water-pot around the house or the resting-place on the inside, with the next Yagus (II, 15, 22) three times from left to right; then he should serve cakes, flour, and boiled rice to the Brâhmanas.

PATALA 7, SECTION 18.

1. When a boy is attacked by the dog-demon (i.e. epilepsy), (the father or another performer of the ceremony), having devoted himself to austerities

---

(such as fasting), covers him with a net. Then he causes a gong to be beaten or a bell to be rung, takes (the boy) by another way than the door into the gambling-hall, raises (the earth in the middle of the hall) at the place in which they gamble, sprinkles it (with water), casts the dice, lays (the boy) on his back on the dice, and besprinkles him with his joined hands with curds and salt, with the next (eleven) (formulas, II, 16, 1–11), in the morning, at noon, and at night.

2. Then he will get well.

3. Over a boy who suffers from the 'Sankha' disease, (the father, &c.) having devoted himself to austerities, should recite the next two (verses, II, 16, 12. 13), and should pour (water) on his head with a water-pot with the next (verse, II, 16, 14), in the morning, at noon, and at night.

4. Then he will get well.

5. On the day of the full moon of (the month) Srâvana after sunset a Sthâlîpâka (is offered).

6. After the ceremonies down to the Âgyabhâga oblations have been performed in the same way as at the fortnightly sacrifices, he sacrifices of the Sthâlîpâka, and with each of the next (formulas, II, 16, 15–17) he offers with his joined hands Kimsuka flowers.

7. With the next (three) verses (II, 17, 1–3) (he offers) pieces of Âragvadha wood (Cathartocarpus fistula);

---

3. 'Sankhin is a person attacked by such a disease that he utters cries like the sound of a conch trumpet (sankha).' Haradatta.

5. Here follows a description of the Sarpabali.

6. Comp. above, III, 7, 2–3.

8. Then the Âgya oblations (indicated by the) next (Mantras, II, 17, 4–7).

9. Then he enters upon the performance of the Gaya and following oblations.

10. Having performed (the rites) down to the sprinkling (of water) round (the fire), he silently takes the objects required (for the rites which he is going to perform), goes out in an easterly or northerly direction, prepares a raised surface, draws on it three lines directed towards the east and three towards the north, pours water on the (lines), and lays (an offering of) flour (for the serpents) on them, with the next (formula, II, 17, 8).

11. Silently (he lays down) unground (?) grain, roasted grain, collyrium, ointment, (the fragrant substance called) Sthagara, and Usira root.

12. With the next (formulas, II, 17, 9–26) he should worship (the serpents), should sprinkle water round (the oblations), should return (to his house) silently without looking back, should sprinkle (water) with a water-pot from left to right, thrice around the house or the resting-place on the inside, with the two verses, 'Beat away, O white one, with thy foot' (II, 17, 27. 28), and should offer food to the Brâhmaṇas.

PATALA 7, SECTION 19.

1. The unground grain (which is left over, see above, VII, 18, 11) they give to the boys to eat.

2. Let him repeat in the same way this Bali-offering of whatever food he has got or of flour, from that day to full moon of (the month) Mârgaśîrsha.

3. On the day of the full moon of Mârga*s*irsha after sunset a Sthâlîpâka (is offered as above, VII, 18, 5).

4. In the Mantra for the Bali-offering he changes (the word ' I shall offer' into) ' I have offered.'

5. Then he does not offer (the Bali) any longer.

6. (Now follows) the Âgraya*n*a sacrifice (or partaking of the first-fruits) of one who has not set up the (*S*rauta) fires.

7. He prepares a Sthâlîpâka of the fresh fruits, sacrifices to the deities of the (*S*rauta) Âgraya*n*a sacrifice with (Agni) Svish*t*akr*i*t as the fourth, fills his mouth with grains, swallows them, sips water, forms a lump of the boiled (sacrificial) food, and throws it up with the next Ya*g*us (II, 18, 1) to the summit of the house.

8. (Now follows) the 'redescent' in the winter.

9. With the next Ya*g*us (II, 18, 2) they 'redescend' (or take as their sleeping-place a layer of straw instead of the high bedsteads which they have used before). With the next Ya*g*us formulas (II, 18, 3–7) they lie down on a new layer (of straw) on their right sides,

10. The father to the south, the mother to the north (of him), and so the others, one after the other from the eldest to the youngest.

11. After he has arisen, he touches the earth with the next two (verses, II, 18, 8. 9).

12. In the same way the lying down, &c., is repeated thrice.

13. Having prepared a Sthâlîpâka for Îsâna and

---

8. Comp. the note on *S*âṅkhâyana IV, 17, 1.

13. The description of the *s*ûlagava sacrifice, which here follows, agrees in most points with the statements of Hira*n*yake*s*in II, 3, 8.

one for Kshetrapati, he goes out in an easterly or northerly direction, prepares a raised surface, (and then follow the ceremonies) beginning with the putting of wood on the fire.

14. To the west of the fire he builds two huts.

PATALA 7, SECTION 20.

1. With the next (verse, II, 18, 10) he has the Îsâna led to the southern (hut),

2. With worldly words the 'bountiful goddess' to the northern (hut),

3. To the middle (between the two huts) the 'conqueror.'

4. He gives them water to drink in the same order in which they have been led (to their places), takes three portions of boiled rice (from the Sthâlî-pâka prepared for Îsâna), takes (these portions of rice) to the fire, makes (the three gods) touch them with the next (formulas, II, 18, 11–13), sacrifices of these portions, to each god of the portion which belongs to him, with the next (formulas, II, 18, 14–30), cuts off (Avadânas) from all (portions), and sacrifices with the next Yagus (II, 18, 31) to Agni Svish*t*akr*i*t.

5. Having worshipped (the god Îsâna) with the next Yagus (II, 18, 32), he distributes with the next (formulas, II, 18, 33–39) leaves together with portions of boiled rice, two (leaves) with each (Yagus), then ten to the divine hosts (II, 18, 40), and ten to the (divine hosts) that follow (and are referred to in the next Yagus, II, 18, 41).

20, 1–3. Comp. Hira*n*yak. II, 3, 8, 2–4. Haradatta explains the Îsâna, the mîd*h*ushî, and the *g*ayanta as images of the three gods.

6. With the next (formulas, II, 18, 42–45) he does the same as before (i.e. he distributes two leaves with each Mantra):

7. Having formed a lump of boiled rice, he puts it into a basket of leaves, and with the next Yagus (II, 18, 46) hangs it up on a tree.

8. Here he should murmur the Rudra texts (Taitt. Sa*m*h. IV, 5),

9. Or the first and last (Anuvâka).

10. He places his cows around the fire so that the smoke (of the sacrifice) may reach them.

11. With his firmly shut fist full of Darbha grass he besprinkles (them) with scents; the bull first.

12. He should perform a sacrifice to Kshetrapati, without a fire, in the path used by his cows.

13. He has (the Kshetrapati) led to his place in the same way as the Îs̄âna (see above, Sûtra 1).

14. He puts (portions of boiled rice) into four or seven leaves, naming (the god).

15. Let him sacrifice quickly; the god has a strong digestion (?).

16. With the next two (verses, II, 18, 47. 48) he does worship (to Kshetrapati).

17. The Sthâlîpâka (belonging to Îs̄âna) he gives to the Brâhma*n*as to eat;

18. That belonging to Kshetrapati his uterine relations eat,

19. Or as is the custom in their family.

---

11. On grumush/i, see the notes of the commentators, p. 93 of Dr. Winternitz's edition, and the commentary on Taitt. Sa*m*hitâ V, 4, 5, 3 (Indische Studien, XII, 60).

15. I have translated here as in Hira*n*yak. II, 3, 9, 11. Haradatta and Sudar*s*anârya give another explanation of the words 'pâko deva*h*;' see p. 93 of the edition.

PATALA 8, SECTION 21.

1. The times for the monthly *Srâddha* are in the second fortnight (of the month), as they are stated.

2. Let him feed, without regard of (worldly) purposes, pure Brâhma*n*as, versed in the Mantras, who are not connected with himself by consanguinity or by their Gotra or by the Mantras (such as his teacher or his pupils), an odd number, at least three.

3. He makes oblations of the food (prepared for the Brâhma*n*as) with the next (verses, II, 19, 1–7);

4. Then the Â*g*ya oblations (indicated by the) next (Mantras, II, 19, 8–13).

5. Or invertedly (i. e. he offers Â*g*ya with the verses referred to in Sûtra 3, and food with those referred to in Sûtra 4).

6. Let him touch the whole (food) with the next (formulas, II, 19, 14–16).

7. Or the (single) prepared (portions of food destined) for the single Brâhma*n*as.

8. Having caused them with the next (formula, II, 20, 1) to touch (the food, he gives it to them to eat).

9. When they have eaten (and gone away), he goes after them, circumambulates them, turning his right side towards them, spreads out southward-pointed Darbha grass in two different layers, pours water on it with the next (formulas, II, 20, 2–7), distributes the Pi*nd*as, ending in the south, with the next (formulas, II, 20, 8–13), pours out water as before with the next (formulas, 14–19), worships (the

---

21, 1. Comp. Dharma*s*âstra II, 7, 16, 8 seq.; Sacred Books, vol. ii, p. 139. Comp. Professor Bühler's remarks, vol. ii, p. xiv.

ancestors) with the next (formulas, II, 20, 20–23),
sprinkles with the next (verse, 24) water three times
from right to left round (the Pi*nd*as) with a water-pot,
besprinkles the vessels, which are turned upside
down, repeating the next Ya*g*us (25) at least three
times without taking breath, sets up the vessels two
by two, cuts off (Avadânas) from all (portions of
food), and eats of the remains at least one morsel
with the next Ya*g*us (26).

10. Of the dark fortnight that follows after the
full moon of Mâgha, the eighth day falls under
(the constellation of) G*y*esh*thâ*: this day is called
Ekâsh*t*akâ.

11. In the evening before that day (he performs)
the preparatory ceremony.

12. He bakes a cake of four cups (of rice).

13. (The cake is prepared) in eight dishes (like a
Puro*dâ*sa), according to some (teachers).

PATALA 8, SECTION 22.

1. After the ceremonies down to the Â*gy*abhâga
oblations have been performed in the same way as
at the fortnightly sacrifices, he makes with his joined
hands oblations of the cake with the next (verse, II,
20, 27).

2. The rest (of the cake) he makes ready, divides
(it) into eight parts and offers it to the Brâhma*n*as.

12, 13. Comp. Hira*n*yak. II, 5, 14, 3 seq.

22, 1. Comp. above, VII, 18, 6.

2. I believe that *s*esha*h* means the rest of the cake. The word
'siddha*h*' possibly refers to such preparations of the food as are
indicated in Hira*n*yak. II, 5, 14, 7. Haradatta understands *s*esha*h*
as the rest of the rites (tantrasya *s*esha*h*): 'The rest of the rites is

3. On the following day he touches a cow with a Darbha blade, with the words, 'I touch thee agreeable to the Fathers.'

4. Having silently offered five Âgya oblations, and having cooked the omentum of the (cow), and performed the 'spreading under' and the sprinkling over (of Âgya), he sacrifices (the omentum) with the next (verse, II, 20, 28) with a Palâsa leaf from the middle or the end (of the stalk).

5. (He sacrifices) boiled rice together with the meat (of the cow) with the next (verses, II, 20, 29-35),

6. Food prepared of meal with the next (verse, II, 21, 1),

7. Then the Âgya oblations (indicated by the) next (Mantras, II, 21, 2-9).

8. (The rites) from the Svish/akr/t down to the offering of the Pindas are the same (as at the Srâddha).

9. Some (teachers) prescribe the Pinda offering for the day after the Ash/akâ.

10. Here (follows) another (way for celebrating the Ash/akâ sacrifice). He sacrifices curds with his joined hands in the same way as the cake.

11. Having left over from the meat of the (cow, see above, 3. 4) as much as is required, on the day after (the Ash/akâ) (he performs) the rite of the Anvash/akâ.

12. This rite has been explained in the description of the monthly Srâddha.

13. If he goes out in order to beg for something,

---

the regular one, without alterations:' it must be admitted that the expressions used by Hira*n*yak. II, 5, 14, 10 would agree well with this explanation.

4. See above, V, 13, 16.

let him murmur the next (Mantras, II, 21, 10-16) and then state his desire.

14. If he has obtained a chariot, he has the horses put to it, lets it face the east, and touches with the next (verse, II, 21, 17) the two wheels of the chariot or the two side-pieces.

15. With the next Yaǵus (II, 21, 18) he should mount, and drive with the next (verse, II, 21, 19) towards the east or north, and should then drive off on his business.

16. Let him mount a horse with the next (formulas, II, 21, 20-30),

17. An elephant with the next (formula, II, 21, 31).

18. If any harm is done him by these two (beasts), let him touch the earth as indicated above.

19. If he is going to a dispute, he takes the parasol and the staff in his left hand.

PATALA 8, SECTION 23.

1. Having sacrificed, with his right hand, a fist full of chaff with the next (verse, II, 21, 32), he should go away and murmur the next (verse, 33).

2. Over an angry person let him recite the two next (formulas, II, 22, 1. 2); then his anger will be appeased.

3. One who wishes that his wife should not be touched by other men, should have big living centipedes ground to powder, and should insert (that powder) with the next (formula, II, 22, 3), while she is sleeping, into her secret parts.

4. For success (in the generation of children)

---

18. See VII, 19, 11. On reshane, comp. below, 23, 9.
23, 3. Comp. Hiraṇyak. I, 4, 14, 7.

let him wash (his wife) with the urine of a red-brown cow.

5. For success (in trade) let him sacrifice with the next (verse—II, 22, 4—some portion) from the articles of trade which he has in his house.

6. If he wishes that somebody be not estranged from him, let him pour his own urine into the horn of a living animal, and sprinkle (it) with the next two (verses, II, 22, 5. 6) three times from right to left around (the person) while he is sleeping.

7. In a path which servants or labourers use to run away, he should put plates (used for protecting the hands when holding a hot sacrificial pan) on (a fire), and should offer the oblations (indicated by the) next (Mantras, II, 22, 7–10).

8. If a fruit falls on him from a tree, or a bird befouls him, or a drop of water falls on him when no rain is expected, he should wipe that off with the next (Mantras, II, 22, 11–13), according to the characteristics (contained in these Mantras).

9. If a post of his house puts forth shoots, or if honey is made in his house (by bees), or if the footprint of a dove is seen on the hearth, or if diseases arise in his household, or in the case of other miracles or prodigies, let him perform in the new-moon night, at dead of night, at a place where he does not hear the noise of water, the rites from the putting (of wood) on the fire down to the Âgya-bhâga oblations, and let him offer the oblations (indicated in the) next (Mantras, II, 22, 14–23), and enter upon the performance of the Gaya and following oblations.

6, 7. Comp. Pâraskara III, 7; Hira*n*yak. I, 4, 13, 19 seqq.

10. Having performed (the ceremonies) down to the sprinkling (of water) round (the fire), he puts up towards the south with the next (verse, II, 22, 24) a stone as a barrier for those among whom a death has occurred.

End of the Âpastambiya-G*ri*hya-sûtra.

SYNOPTICAL SURVEY

OF THE

CONTENTS OF THE GR*I*HYA-SÛTRAS.

----

1. The sacred Gr*i*hya fire. *S.* I, 1; Â. I, 9; P. I, 2; G. I, 1; Kh. I, 5, 1 seq.; H. I, 22, 2 seq.; 26; Âp. 5, 13 seq.
2. General division of Gr*i*hya sacrifices. *S.* I, 5; 10; Â. I, 1, 2 seq. (comp. III, 1); P. I, 4, 1.
3. Regular morning and evening oblations. *S.* I, 3, 8 seq. (comp. V, 4); Â. I, 2, 1 seq.; 9; P. I, 9; G. I, 1, 22 seq.; 3; 9, 13 seq.; Kh. I, 5, 6 seq.; H. I, 23, 8 seq.; Âp. 7, 19 seq.
4. The Bali oblations. *S.* II, 14; Â. I, 2, 3 seq.; P. II, 9 (comp. I, 12); G. I, 4; Kh. I, 5, 20 seq.; Âp. 8, 4.
5. Sacrifices on the days of the new and full moon. *S.* I, 3 (comp. V, 4); Â. I, 10; P. I, 12; G. I, 5 seq.; Kh. II, 1; 2, 1 seq.; H. I, 23, 7; Âp. 7, 17.

----

6. General outline of Gr*i*hya sacrifices. *S.* I, 7 seq.; Â. I, 3; P. I, 1; G. I, 3 seq.; Kh. I, 1 seq.; H. I, 1, 9 seq.; Âp. 1, 1 seq.
   a. The yag*n*opavîta, the prâ*k*înâvîta, the touching of water. G. I, 2; Kh. I, 1, 4 seq.; Âp. 1, 3. 8.
   b. Besmearing of the surface with cow-dung, drawing of the lines. *S.* I, 7, 2 seq.; Â. I, 3, 1; P. I, 1, 2; G. I, 1, 9; 5, 13; Kh. I, 2, 1 seq.
   c. The fire is carried forward. *S.* I, 7, 9; Â. I, 3, 1; P. I, 1, 2; G. I, 1, 11; Kh. I, 2, 5; H. I, 1, 10.
   d. The samûhana. *S.* I, 7, 11; Â. I, 3, 1; G. IV, 5, 5; Kh. I, 2, 6.
   e. The strewing of grass around the sacred fire. *S.* I, 8, 1 seq.; Â. I, 3, 1; P. I, 1, 2; G. I, 5, 16 seq.; 7, 9 seq.; Kh. I, 2, 9 seq.; H. I, 1, 11 seq.; Âp. 1, 12 seq.
   f. The purifiers. *S.* I, 8, 14 seq.; Â. I, 3, 2 seq.; P. I,

1, 2; G. I, 7, 21 seq.; Kh. I, 2, 12 seq.; H. I, 1,
23; Âp. 1, 19.

g. Preparation of the Âgya for sacrifice. S. I, 8, 18 seq.;
Â. I, 3, 3; P. I, 1, 2 seq.; G. I, 7, 19 seq.; Kh. I,
2, 14 seq.; H. I, 1, 27; Âp. 1, 22.

h. The Âgya oblations. S. I, 9; Â. I, 3, 4 seq.; P. I,
1, 4; 5, 3 seq.; G. I, 8; 9, 26 seq.; Kh. I, 3.
12 seq.; H. I, 2, 12 seq.; 3; Âp. 2, 5 seq.

7. Sacrifices of cooked food. S. I, 3; Â. I, 10; G. I, 6,
13 seq.; 7 seq.; Kh. II, 1; Âp. 7.

8. Animal sacrifice (comp. Ash/akâ, Anvash/akya, Sûlagava).
Â. I, 11; P. III, 11; G. III, 10, 18–IV, 1; Kh. III, 4;
H. II, 15.

a. The omentum. Â. I, 11, 10 (comp. II, 4, 13); IV, 8.
18; P. III, 11, 4. 6; G. III, 10, 30 seq.; IV, 4,
22 seq.; Kh. III, 4, 9 seq. 25 seq.; H. II, 15,
6 seq.

b. The Avadânas. Â. I, 11, 12 (comp. II, 4, 14); P.
III, 11, 6 seq.; G. IV, 1, 3. 9 &c.; Kh. III, 4,
14 seq.; H. II, 15, 9 seq.

9. Marriage. S. I, 5 seq.; Â. I, 5 seq.; P. I, 4 seq.; G. II, 1
seq.; Kh. I, 3 seq.; H. I, 19 seq.; Âp. 2, 12 seq.

a. Different kinds of marriage (brâhma, daiva, &c.). Â.
I, 6.

b. Election of the bride. S. I, 5. 5 seq.; Â. I, 5; G. II,
1, 1 seq.; III, 4, 4 seq.; H. I, 19, 2; Âp. 3,
10 seq.

c. The wooers go to the girl's house. S. I, 6; Âp. 2,
16; 4, 1 seq.

d. Sacrifice when the bride's father has declared his
assent. S. I, 7 seq.

e. The bride is washed. S. I, 11; G. II, 1, 10. 17;
Kh. I, 3, 6.

f. Dance of four or eight women. S. I, 11, 5.

g. The bridegroom goes to the girl's house. S. I, 12.

h. He gives her a garment, anoints her, gives her a
mirror, &c. S. I, 12, 3 seq.; P. I, 4, 12 seq.; G.
II, 1, 18; Kh. I, 3, 6; Âp. 4, 8.

i. Argha at the wedding. S. I, 12, 10; G. II, 3, 16
seq.; Kh. I, 4, 7 seq.; Âp. 3, 5 seq.

k. Sacrifice with the Mahâvyâhritis and other formulas
(Gaya, Abhyâtâna, &c., formulas). S. I, 12, 11;

Â. I, 7, 3; P. I, 5, 3 seq.; G. II, 1, 24; Kh. I, 3, 8. 11; H. I, 19, 7 (comp. 3, 8 seq.; 20, 8); Âp. 5, 2. 11 (comp. 2, 7).

l. Seizing of the bride's hand. *S.* I, 13, 2; Â. I, 7, 3 seq.; P. I, 7, 3; G. II, 2, 16; Kh. I, 3, 17. 31; H. I, 20, 1; Âp. 4, 11 seq.

m. The formula, 'This am I, that art thou.' *S.* I, 13, 4; Â. I, 7, 6; H. I, 20, 2.

n. The treading on the stone. *S.* I, 13, 10 seq.; Â. I, 7, 7; P. I, 7, 1; G. II, 2, 3; Kh. I, 3, 19; H. I, 19, 8; Âp. 5, 3.

o. Circumambulation of the fire. *S.* I, 13, 13; Â. I, 7, 6; P. I, 5, 1; 7, 3; G. II, 2, 8; Kh. I, 3, 24; H. I, 20, 5; Âp. 5, 1. 7.

p. Sacrifice of fried grain. *S.* I, 13, 15 seq.; Â. I, 7, 8; P. I, 6, 1 seq.; G. II, 2, 5 seq.; Kh. I, 3, 20 seq.; H. I, 20, 3 seq.; Âp. 5, 4 seq.

q. The seven steps. *S.* I, 14, 5 seq.; Â. I, 7, 19; P. I, 8, 1; G. II, 2, 11; Kh. I, 3, 26; H. I, 20, 9 seq.; 21, 1 seq.; Âp. 4, 16.

r. The bride is carried away to her new home. *S.* I, 15; Â. I, 7, 21; 8; P. I, 8, 10; 10; G. II, 2, 17 seq.; 4; Kh. I, 4, 1 seq.; H. I, 22, 1; Âp. 5, 12 seq.

s. Ceremonies on entering the new home; looking at the polar star. *S.* I, 16, 17, comp. Â. I, 7, 22; comp. P. I, 8, 19; comp. G. II, 3, 5 seq.; 4, 6 seq.; comp. Kh. I, 4, 3; H. I, 22, 6 seq.; Âp. 6, 8 seq.

t. The rites of the fourth day; the cohabitation. *S.* I, 18. 19; P. I, 11, 13; G. II, 5; Kh. I, 4, 12; H. I, 23, 11; 24, 25; Âp. 8, 8 seq.

10. The Pu*m*savana (i. e. the ceremony to secure the birth of a male child). *S.* I, 20; Â. I, 13; P. I, 14; G. II, 6; Kh. II, 2, 17 seq.; H. II, 2; Âp. 14, 9 seq.

11. A ceremony for the protection of the embryo. *S.* I, 21 (comp. Â. I, 13, 1).

12. The Sîmantonnayana (or parting of the pregnant wife's hair). *S.* I, 22 (comp. V, 4); Â. I, 14; P. I, 15; G. II, 7, 1 seq.; Kh. II, 2, 24 seq.; H. II, 1; Âp. 14, 1 seq.

Song of lute-players. *S.* I, 22, 11 seq.; Â. I, 14, 6 seq.; P. I, 15, 7 seq. (comp. H. II, 1, 3); Âp. 14, 4 seq.

13. Ceremony before the confinement. *S.* I, 23; P. I, 16, 1 seq.; G. II, 7, 13 seq.; Kh. II, 2, 28 seq.; H. II, 2, 8 seq.; Âp. 14, 13 seq.

14. The *G*âtakarman (or ceremony for the new-born child) and similar rites. *S.* I, 24 (comp. V, 4); Â. I, 15; P. I, 16, 3 seq.; G. II, 7, 17 seq.; 8, 1 seq.; Kh. II, 2, 32; 3, 1 seq.; H. II, 3, 2 seq.; Âp. 15.

    a. Name given to the child. *S.* I, 24, 4 seq.; Â. I, 15, 4 seq.; P. I, 17; G. II, 7, 15; 8, 8 seq.; Kh. II, 2, 30 seq. 3, 6 seq.; H. II, 4, 10 seq.; Âp. 15, 2 seq. 8 seq.

    b. The 'production of intelligence.' *S.* I, 24, 9; Â. I, 15, 2; P. I, 16, 3; G. II, 7, 20; Kh. II, 2, 34; H. II, 3, 9.

    c. Driving away demons and goblins from the child. P. I, 16, 23; H. II, 3, 7.

15. The getting up of the mother from childbed. *S.* I, 25 (with enumeration of the Nakshatras and their presiding deities, chap. 26); P. I, 17, 1; comp. H. II, 4, 6; Âp. 15, 8.

16. How the father should greet his children when returning from a journey. Â. I, 15, 9; P. I, 18; G. II, 8, 21; Kh. II, 3, 13; H. II, 4, 16; Âp. 15, 12.

17. The feeding of the child with solid food (Annaprâsana). *S.* I, 27; Â. I, 16; P. I, 19; H. II, 5; Âp. 16, 1 seq.

18. The tonsure of the child's head (*K*û*d*âkarman). *S.* I, 28; Â. I, 17; P. II, 1; G. II, 9; Kh. II, 3, 16 seq.; H. II, 6; Âp. 16, 3 seq.

19. The ceremony of shaving the beard (Godâna-Karman, Ke-*s*ânta). *S.* I, 28, 18 seq.; Â. I, 18; P. II, 1, 3 seq.; G. III, 1; Kh. II, 5, 1 seq.; H. II, 6, 16 seq.; Âp. 16, 12 seq.

20. The initiation of the student. Studentship. The Samâvartana. *S.* II, 1 seq.; III, 1; IV, 5 seq.; VI; Â. I, 19 seq.; III, 5; 8–10; P. II, 2–6; 8; 10–12; G. II, 10–III, 4; Kh. II, 4–III, 1, 32; III, 2, 16–33; H. I, 1 seq.; II, 18–20; Âp. 10 seq.

    a. Time of the initiation. The patitasâvitrika. *S.* II, 1, 1 seq.; Â. I, 19, 1 seq.; P. II, 2, 1 seq.; 5, 36 seq.; G. II, 10, 1 seq.; Kh. II, 4, 1 seq.; H. I, 1, 2 seq.; Âp. 10, 1 seq.

    b. The skin, the girdle, and the staff belonging to the different castes. *S.* II, 1, 1 seq. 15 seq.; II, 13; Â. I, 19, 10 seq.; P. II, 5, 16 seq.; G. II, 10, 8 seq.; H. I, 1, 17; 4, 7; Âp. 11, 16 seq.

    a. Election of the ground. Â. II, 7 seq.; G. IV, 7, 1 seq.;
       Kh. IV, 2, 6 seq.

    b. Entering the new house. S. III, 4; Â. II, 9. 9; P.
       III, 4, 5 seq., 18.

    c. The putting up of the water-barrel. P. III, 5; Âp.
       17, 8 seq.

    d. Leaving the house when travelling and returning to it.
       S. III, 5-7; Â. II, 10, 1 seq.; H. I, 29.

23. Ploughing. S. IV, 13; Â. II, 10, 3. 4; P. II, 13; G. IV,
    4, 27 seq.

24. Partaking of the first-fruits (Âgrayana). S. III, 8; Â. II, 2,
    4 seq.; P. III, 1; G. III, 8, 9 seq.; Kh. III, 3, 16 seq.;
    Âp. 19, 6 seq.

25. Sacrifice to Sîtâ. P. II, 17; comp. G. IV, 4, 29.

26. Ceremonies referring to cattle (comp. also the Âsvayuga sacri-
    fice, below, No. 30).

    a. The driving out of the cows, and other rites referring
       to the cows. S. III, 9; Â. II, 10, 5 seq.; G. III,
       6; Kh. III, 1, 45 seq.; H. I, 18.

    b. Making marks on the cattle. S. III, 10.

    c. The Vrishotsarga. S. III, 11; P. III, 9.

    d. The Sûlagava ('spit-ox' offered to Rudra). Â. IV,
       8; P. III, 8; H. II, 8-9; Âp. 19, 13-20, 19.

       α. Distribution of Palâsa leaves. P. III, 8, 11;
         H. II, 9, 1 seq.; Âp. 20, 5 seq.

       β. Sacrifice to Kshetrapati. H. II, 9, 8 seq.;
         Âp. 20, 12 seq.

27. The Kaitra offerings. S. IV, 19.

28. The Srâvana sacrifice to the Serpents. S. IV, 15; Â. II, 1; P.
    II, 14; G. III, 7 (comp. IV, 8, 1); Kh. III, 2, 1 seq.; H.
    II, 16; Âp. 18, 5-19, 2.

29. The Praushthapada sacrifice. P. II, 15.

30. The Âsvayuga sacrifice. S. IV, 16; Â. II, 2. 1-3; P. II,
    16; G. III, 8, 1 seq.; Kh. III, 3, 1 seq.

31. The rites of the Âgrahâyanî (concluding ceremonies of the
    rites devoted to the Serpents). S. IV, 17. 18; Â. II, 3;
    P. III, 2; G. III, 9 (comp. IV, 8, 1); Kh. III, 3, 6 seq.;
    H. II, 17; Âp. 19, 3 seq. 8 seq.

32. The Ashtakâs. S. III, 12-14; Â. II, 4, 5; P. III, 3; G.

S. II, 15, 4 seq.; 16, 3; Â. I, 24, 1 seq.; P. I, 3, 1; G. IV, 10, 23 seq.; Kh. IV, 4, 21 seq.; Âp. 13, 2 seq.; 14. 19. 20.

b. The cow offered to the guest. S. II, 15, 1 seq.; 16, 1; Â. I, 24, 30 seq.; P. I, 3, 26 seq.; G. IV, 10, 18 seq.; Kh. IV, 17 seq.; H. I, 13, 10 seq.; Âp. 13, 15 seq.

c. Miscellaneous rules about the reception of guests. S. II, 17.

RITES FOR THE OBTAINMENT OF SPECIAL WISHES, FOR AVERTING MISFORTUNE ; DIFFERENT EXPIATIONS.

36. Longer sections are devoted to the description of ceremonies for the obtainment of special wishes by G. IV, 5–6; 8–9; Kh. IV, 1–4, 4. Comp. Â. III, 6, 1 seq.; Âp. 8, 4.

a. Rites for procuring success and averting evil in disputes and on different other occasions. H. I, 14, 7–15, 8; Âp. 22, 19 seq.; 23, 2 seq. Entering a court of justice. P. III, 13.

b. Mounting a chariot and similar acts. Â. II, 6; P. III, 14–15, 6; Âp. 22, 14.

c. Rites when going out on business or on dangerous ways. Â. III, 7, 8–10.

d. Sacrifice of a person menaced by unknown danger. Â. III, 11.

e. Going out and begging. Âp. 22, 13 seq.

f. Formulas to be pronounced on receiving gifts. P. III, 15, 22 seq.

g. Crossing a river. S. IV, 14.

h. Formulas to be pronounced at cross-roads and other different places. P. III, 15, 7 seq.; H. I, 16, 8 seq.

i. Rites referring to battles. Â. III, 12.

k. Rites in order that friends may not be estranged and servants may not run away. P. III, 7; H. I, 13, 19–14, 5; Âp. 23, 6. 7.

l. Rite when first seeing the new moon. H. I, 16, 1.

m. Rite for establishing concord between husband and wife. Âp. 9, 4 seq.

n. Rite if one cannot pay a debt. G. IV, 4, 26.

o. Oblations for sick persons. Â. III, 6, 3 seq.; for a

sick child. P. I, 16, 24 seq.; for a boy suffering
from epilepsy. H. II, 7; Âp. 18, 1 seq.   Cure for
headache. P. III, 6.

p. Penance of a student who has broken his vow of
chastity. P. III, 12.

q. Different expiations. *S.* V, 1, 8. 9; 5-6; 8; 10:
11; Â. III, 6, 5-7, 2; 7, 7; 10, 9 seq.; G. III, 3,
30 seq.; Kh. II, 5, 35 seq.; H. I, 16, 2 seq.
14 seq.-chap. 17, 6; Âp. 8, 5 seq.; 9, 2 seq.; 23,
9 seq.

MISCELLANEOUS MATTER.

37. Qualities of a Brâhma*n*a on whom gifts should be bestowed.
S. I, 2.
38. The choosing of priests for officiating at a sacrifice. Â. I, 23.
39. The *K*aitya sacrifice. Â. I, 12, 1 seq. (comp. Pâr. III, 11,
10 seq.).
40. The Dhanvantari sacrifice. Â. I, 12, 7.
41. Consecration of ponds. *S.* V, 2.
42. Consecration of gardens. *S.* V, 3.
43. Sandhyâ or twilight devotion. *S.* II, 9; Â. III, 7, 3 seq.
44. The sacrificer setting out on a journey makes the sacred fire
enter him. *S.* V, 1, 1 seq.; H. I, 26, 12 seq.

ÂPASTAMBA'S
YAG*Ñ*A-PARIBHÂSHÂ-SÛTRAS.

INTRODUCTION.

As Professor Oldenberg was unable to find any other texts connected with the Gr*i*hya-sûtras, I have tried to bring this volume to its proper size by adding a translation of Âpastamba's Ya*g*ña-Paribhâshâ-sûtras. These Sûtras give some general information about the performance of sacrifices, and may prove useful to the students both of the *S*rauta and the Gr*i*hya sacrifices. Paribhâshâ is defined as a general rule or definition applicable throughout a whole system, and more binding than any particular rule. How well this sense of paribhâshâ was understood in India, we may see from a passage in the *S*i*s*upâlavadha XVI, 80 :

> Parita*h* pramitâksharâpi sarva*m*
> vishayam prâptavatî gatâ pratish*thâ*m
> na khalu pratihanyate kuta*s*it
> paribhâsheva garîyasî yadâg*ñ*â.

'Whose (the king's) command, though brief, having reached the whole kingdom round about and obtained authority, is never defeated, being of the highest weight, like a Paribhâshâ.'

These Paribhâshâs are a very characteristic invention of ancient Indian authors, particularly during the Sûtra period. We find them as early as the Anukrama*n*is, and even at that early time they had been elaborated with many purely technical contrivances. Thus we are told in the Index to the Rig-veda that, as a general rule, if no deity is mentioned in the index of the hymns, Indra must be supposed to be the deity addressed ; when no metre is mentioned, the metre must be understood to be the Trish*t*ubh ; at the beginning of each Ma*nd*ala the hymns must be taken to be addressed to Agni, till we come to hymns distinctly addressed to Indra. Now it is clear that in this case these Paribhâ-shâs or general instructions must have been laid down before the whole work was carried out. The same applies to other Paribhâshâs, such as those of the metrical Sûtras, but I feel more doubtful as to the Paribhâshâs in the grammatical Sûtras of Pâ*n*ini. To judge from the Paribhâshendusekhara, it would seem that the Paribhâshâ-sûtras to Pâ*n*ini's grammar also had been settled before a single Sûtra of Pâ*n*ini was composed, and yet it seems almost incredible that this gigantic web of Sûtras should have been woven on so complicated a warp. This question ought to be settled once for all, as it would throw considerable light on the workmanship of Pâ*n*ini's Sûtras, and there is no one better qualified to settle it for us than the learned editor of the Paribhâshendusekhara. It is different with our Paribhâshâs. There is no necessity to suppose that they were worked out first, before the Sûtras were composed. They look more like useful generalisations than like indispensable preliminary instructions. They give us a general idea of the sacrifice, and inculcate rules that ought to be observed throughout. But I doubt whether they are as essential for enabling the priest to carry out the instructions of the Sûtras in performing a sacrifice as the grammatical paribhâshâs are in carrying out the grammatical rules of Pâ*n*ini.

The Âpastamba-sûtras for which our Paribhâshâs are intended are said to have comprised thirty Prasnas (see Burnell, Catalogue, p. 19, and p. xxix in Professor Oldenberg's Introduction). Burnell mentions that sometimes two Prasnas, treating of the Pait*ri*medhika rites, were counted as the thirty-first and thirty-second of the whole work. Of these thirty Prasnas fifteen have been edited with Rudradatta's commentary by Professor Garbe in the Bibliotheca Indica, 1882–1885. Rudradatta's commentary does not seem to have extended beyond the fifteenth Prasna ; some authorities, however, suppose that Haradatta, to whom commentaries on the later Prasnas are ascribed, was only another name for Rudradatta. According to *K*au*nd*appa's Prayogaratnamâlâ (see Burnell, Classified Index, I, p. 17 a), the Paribhâshâ-sûtras formed part of the twenty-fourth Prasna (*k*aturvi*m*se tata*h* prasne nyâyaprâvarahautrakam). Here Nyâya in the sense of method, way, plan, seems to stand for Paribhâshâ. Another name is Sâmânya-sûtra (see Burnell, Classified Index, p. 15 b, where it is mentioned as § 4 of Prasna XXIV). *Kaunda*ppâ-*k*ârya himself, who is said to have been minister of Vira-bhûpati, the son of the famous king Bukka of Vi*g*ayanagara, begins his work with a paribhâshâ-pari*kkh*eda.

I published a German translation of these Sûtras with notes many years ago, in the Zeitschrift der Deutschen Morgenländischen Gesellschaft, 1855. I here give the same translation, but I have shortened the notes and compared the translation once more with the MSS.

The principal MSS. used are MS. I. O. L. 1676 b, 259, and 1127. MS. 1676 b, now 308, is described in Professor Eggeling's Catalogue of the Sanskrit MSS. in the Library of the India Office, vol. i, p. 58 b. It is written in Devanâ-garî, contains thirty leaves, and is called at the end iti *S*rîkapardinâ bhâshye uddh*ri*tasâram paribhâshâpa*t*alam. MS. 259, now 309, contains twenty-seven leaves in Devanâ-garî, and is called at the end iti Kapardisvâmi-bhâshye paribhâshâpa*t*alam. MS. 1127, now 307, in Devanâgarî, is dated Samvat 1691, *S*âka 1556, and contains on 220 leaves portions of Tâlav*ri*ndanivâsin's manual, the Âpastambasûtra-prayoga-v*ri*tti, and on pp. 75 a–116 a Kapardisvâmin's commentary on Âpastamba's Paribhâshâ-pa*t*alam. Burnell mentions another copy of this work in his Classified Index, I, p. 17 b, and he states (Catalogue, p. 24) that, according to tradition, the author was a native of Southern India, called A*nd*appi*ll*ai, and that tâlav*ri*nda or tâlav*ri*nta is a translation of the Tamil panai-kkâ*t*u, a very common name for villages among palmyra trees (panai = palmyra, kâ*t*u = forest).

While preparing my new translation for the Press, I received a printed edition of the text and commentary published by *S*rî Satyavratasâma*s*ramibha*tt*â*k*ârya in his valuable Journal, the Ushâ, beginning in the eighth fasci-culus. He gives also a Bengâli translation, and some commentaries in the same language, which have proved useful in certain difficult passages.

ÂPASTAMBA'S

YAG*Ñ*A-PARIBHÂSHÂ-SÛTRAS.

GENERAL RULES OF THE SACRIFICE.

Sûtra I.
We shall explain the sacrifice.

Commentary.

Yag*ñ*a, sacrifice, is an act by which we surrender some-thing for the sake of the gods. Such an act must rest on a sacred authority (âgama), and serve for man's salvation (*s*reyo*r*tha). The nature of the gift is of less importance. It may be puro*d*â*s*a, cake; *k*aru, pulse; sâ*m*nâyya, mixed milk; pa*s*u, an animal; soma, the juice of the Soma-plant, &c.; nay, the smallest offerings of butter, flour, and milk may serve for the purpose of a sacrifice.

Yag*ñ*a, yâga, yagana, and ish*t*i are considered as synonymes.

Sûtra II.
The sacrifice is for the three colours or castes (var*n*a), for Brâhma*n*as and Râ*g*anyas, also for the Vai*s*ya.

Commentary.

Though the sacrifice is meant for the three castes, here called var*n*a, i.e. colour, the third caste, that of the Vai*s*ya or citizen, is mentioned by itself, while the two castes, the Brâhma*n*as and Râ*g*anyas (the Kshatriyas or nobles), are mentioned together. This is done because there are certain sacrifices (bahuya*g*amâna), performed by Brâhma*n*as and Râ*g*anyas together, in which Vai*s*yas take no part. In the *S*ânk*h*âyana-sûtras, I, 1, 3, also the Vaisya is mentioned by himself. In Kâtyâyana's Sûtras, however, no such distinction is made, and we read, I, 6, Brâhmana-râganya-vaisyânâm srutch. Women, if properly married, are allowed to participate in sacrifices, but no one is allowed to be accompanied by a Sûdrâ woman, even though she be his wife. Properly a Brâhmana should marry a wife of his own caste only. A Kshatriya may marry a woman of his own or of the Brâhmana caste. A Vaisya's proper wife should be taken from his own caste. See, however, Manu III, 12 seq.

The four castes, with the Sûdra as the fourth, are mentioned once in the Rig-veda, X. 90, 12. The opposition between Âryas and Sûdras occurs in the Atharva-veda, XIX, 62, &c., and in most of the Brâhmanas. In the Satapatha Brâhmana we read of the four castes, Brâhmana, Râganya, Vaisya, and Sûdra, and we are told that none of them vomits the Soma. Kâtyâyana excludes from the sacrifice the angahîna, cripple, shanda, eunuch, and all asrotriyas, persons ignorant of the Veda, which would bar, of course, the whole class of the Sûdras, but they are also specially excluded. Concessions, however, had to be made at an early time, for instance, in the case of the Rathakâra, who is admitted to the Agnyâdhâna, &c. This name means chariot-maker, but Âpadeva, in his Mîmâmsâ-nyâya-prakâsa, remarks that, though rathakâra means a chariot-maker etymologically, it should be taken here as the name of a clan, namely that of the Saudhanvanas (MS. Mill 46, p. 13ᵇ). Deva, in his commentary on the Kâtyâyana-sûtras, makes the same remark. See also Weber, Ind. Stud. X, 12 seq. These Saudhanvanas, often identified with the Ribhus, are evidently the followers of Bribu, mentioned RV. VI, 45, 31; 33, and wrongly called Bridhu in Manu X, 107; see M. M., Hist. of A. S. L., p. 494. In the Sânkhâyana-Srauta-sûtras, XVI, 11, 11 (ed. Hillebrandt), he is rightly called Bribu. In later times Rathakâra is the name of a caste, and its members are supposed to be the offspring of a marriage between a Mâhishya and a Karanî. A Mâhishya is the son of a Kshatriya and a Vaisyâ,

a Kara*n*î the daughter of a Vai*s*ya and a *S*ûdrâ.
Sudhanvan also is used in Manu, X, 23, as the name of
a caste. namely the offspring of fallen (vrâtya) Vai*s*yas.

Another exception is made in favour of a Nishâda-
sthapati, a Nishâda chieftain. If it meant a chieftain of
Nishâdas, it might be meant for a Kshatriya who
happens to be a chieftain of Nishâdas. Here it is meant
for a chieftain who is himself a Nishâda, a native settler.
He is admitted to the Gavedhuka sacrifice.

Again, although, as a rule, the sacrificer must have
finished his study of the Veda and be married, a sacrifice
is mentioned which a Brahma*k*ârin, a student, may
perform. The case thus provided for is, yo brahma*k*ârî
striyam upeyât, sa gardabham pa*s*um âlabheta.
As these sacrificers are not upanîta, and therefore
without the sacred fires, their sacrifices have to be performed with ordinary fires, and the sacrificial offerings,
the puro*d*âsas, are not cooked in kapâlas, jars, but on
the earth, while the avadânas (cuttings), heart, tongue,
&c., are sacrificed in water, and not in fire. The Nishâda
chieftain has to learn the necessary Vedic verses by heart,
without having passed through a regular course of Vedic
study. The same applies to women, who have to recite
certain verses during the sacrifice.

That certain women are admitted to the sacrifice, is
distinctly stated by Kâtyâyana, I, 1, 7, strî *k*âvi*s*eshât.

SÛTRA III.

The sacrifice is prescribed by the three Vedas.

Commentary.

In order to know the whole of the sacrifice, one Veda is
not sufficient, still less one *s*âkhâ (recension) only. The
sacrifice is conceived as a whole, and its members (aṅgas)
are described in different parts of the three Vedas.

SÛTRA IV.

By the *R*ig-veda, the Ya*g*ur-veda, the Sâma-
veda (is the sacrifice prescribed).

SÛTRA V.

The Darsa-pûrnamâsau, the new and full-moon sacrifices, are prescribed by the *Rig*-veda and the Yagur-veda.

SÛTRA VI.

The Agnihotra is prescribed by the Yagur-veda.

SÛTRA VII.

The Agnish*t*oma is prescribed by all.

Commentary.

By saying all, the Atharva-veda is supposed to be included, at least according to one commentator.

The Agnish*t*oma requires sixteen priests, the Pa*s*u sacrifices six, the *K*âturmâsyas five, the Darsa-pûrnamâsas four.

SÛTRA VIII.

With the *Rig*-veda and Sâma-veda the performance takes place with a loud voice (u*kk*ai*h*).

Commentary.

Even lines of the Yagur-veda, if they are contained in the *Rig*-veda and Sâma-veda, would have to be pronounced with a loud voice. Certain mantras, however, are excepted, viz. the *g*apa, abhimantra*n*a, and anumantra*n*a-mantras.

SÛTRA IX.

With the Yagur-veda the performance takes place by murmuring (upâ*ms*u).

Commentary.

This murmuring, upâ*ms*u, is described as a mere opus operatum, the words being repeated without voice and without thought. One may see the movements of the vocal organs in murmuring, but one should not hear them at a distance. If verses from the *Rig*-veda or Sâma-veda

occur in the Ya*g*ur-veda, they also have to be murmured.
See Kâty. I, 3, 10.

SÛTRA X.

With the exception of addresses, replies, choosing
of priests (prava ra), dialogues, and commands.

Commentary.

As all these are meant to be understood by others, they
have therefore to be pronounced in a loud voice. The
address (â*s*ruta) is o*m s*râvaya ; the reply (pratyâ*s*ruta)
is astu *s*rausha*t*[1]; the choosing of priests (pravara) is
agnir devo hotâ ; a dialogue (sa*m*vâda) is brahman
prokshishyâmi, om proksha ; a command (sampresha)
is proksha*n*îr âsâdaya.

SÛTRA XI.

In the Sâmidhenî hymns the recitation is to be
between (the high and the low tone).

Commentary.

The Sâmidhenîs are the hymns used for lighting the
fire. One commentator explains antarâ, between, as between high tone (krush*t*a) and the murmuring (upâ*m s*u).
Another distinguishes three high tones, the krush*t*a (also
called târa or krau*ñk*a), the madhyama, and the
mandra, and assigns the madhyama to the Sâmidhenî
hymns. The mandra notes come from the chest, the
madhyama notes from the throat, the uttama notes
from the head.

SÛTRA XII.

Before the Â*g*yabhâgas (such as the Â*g*ya-por-
tions at the Dar*s*a-pûr*n*amâsa), and at the morning
Savana (oblation of Soma), the recitation is to be
with the soft (mandra) voice.

---

[1] See Hillebrandt, Das Altind. Neu- und Vollmondsopfer, p. 94.

Commentary.

The pronunciation is loud, u*kk*ai*h*, but soft, mandra. Satyavrata restricts this rule to the passages mentioned in Sûtra X. He also treats the second part of Sûtras XII. XIII, and XIV as separate Sûtras.

SÛTRA XIII.

Before the Svish*t*ak*ri*t (at the Dar*s*a-pûr*n*a-mâsa) sacrifice, and at the midday Savana, the recitation is to be with the middle voice.

SÛTRA XIV.

In the remainder and at the third Savana with the sharp (krush*t*a) voice [1].

Commentary.

The remainder refers to the Dar*s*a-pûr*n*amâsa sacrifice, the three Savanas to the Soma sacrifice. Satyavrata takes all these rules as referring to the cases mentioned in Sûtra X.

SÛTRA XV.

The movement of the voice is the same.

Commentary.

In the three cases mentioned before, the voice moves quickly, when the words are to be pronounced high; slowly, when low; and measuredly, when neither loud nor low.

SÛTRA XVI.

The Hot*ri*-priest performs with the *Ri*g-veda.

SÛTRA XVII.

The Udgât*ri*-priest with the Sâma-veda.

---

[1] See on this, Rig-veda Prâtisâkhya 13, 17; Âsval. I, 5, 27: Sânkh. I, 14; Hillebrandt, l. c. p. 103.

Sûtra XVIII.

The Adhvaryu-priest with the Ya*g*ur-veda.

Sûtra XIX.

The Brahma-priest with all.

Commentary.

'With all' means with the three Vedas, because the Brahma-priest, or superintendent of the whole sacrifice, must be acquainted with the three Vedas. Others would include the Atharva-veda.

Sûtra XX.

When it is expressly said, or when it is rendered impossible, another priest also may act.

Commentary.

Vipratishedha is explained by asambhava and a*s*akti.

Sûtra XXI.

The priestly office (ârtvi*g*ya) belongs to the Brâhma*n*as.

Commentary.

Sacrifices may be performed for Kshatriyas, Vai*s*yas, and, in certain cases, even for others, but never by any but Brâhma*n*as. The reason given for this is curious,— because Brâhma*n*as only are able to eat the remains of a sacrifice. See *S*atap. Br. II, 3, 1, 39 ; Kâtyâyana IV, 14, 11 ; also I, 2, 8, com.

Sûtra XXII.

For all sacrifices the fires are laid once.

Commentary.

The sacrificial fires have to be arranged for the first time

[30]   Y

by a peculiar ceremony, called the Agnyâdhâna. They
are generally three (Tretâ), the Gârhapatya, the father;
the Dakshi*n*a, the son; and the Âhavanîya, the grand-
son. The first laying of the Gârhapatya fire-altar takes
place in spring for a Brâhma*n*a, in summer for a Râ*g*anya,
in winter for a Vai*s*ya.

Sûtra XXIII.

If it is said, *g*uhoti, 'he sacrifices,' it should be
known that sar pir â*g*ya, melted butter, is meant.

Commentary.

Sarpis is here taken as an adjective, running; yad
asarpat tat sarpir abhavat.   Â*g*ya is explained as
navanîtavikâradravyagâtîyavaka*n*a*h* sabda*h*, i. e. a
word signifying any kind of substance made of fresh butter.

In the Aitareya-Brâhma*n*a I, 3, we read â*g*ya*m* vai
devânâ*m* surabhi, gh*ri*tam manushyâ*n*âm, ayutam
pit*ri*nâm, navanîta*m* garbhâ*n*âm, 'Â*g*ya is sweet or
fragrant to the gods, gh*ri*ta to men, ayuta to the manes,
navanîta to children.'   Here the commentator explains
that â*g*ya is butter, when melted (vilîna*m* sarpis), gh*ri*ta,
when hardened.   Ayuta, sometimes called astu, is butter,
when slightly melted, nishpakva, when thoroughly melted.
According to Kâtyâyana I, 8, 37, â*g*ya is of different
kinds.   It may be simple gh*ri*ta, which, as a rule, should
be made of the milk of cows.   But in the absence of â*g*ya,
the milk of buffaloes (mâhisha), or oil (taila), or sesam-oil
(gârtila), or linseed oil (atasisneha), &c., may be taken.

Sûtra XXIV.

If it is said, *g*uhoti, it should be known that the
Adhvaryu is meant as performer.

Commentary.

Though there is a man who offers the sacrifice, yet the
actual homa, the throwing of butter &c. into the fire, has
to be performed by the Adhvaryu priest.

SÛTRA XXV.

Likewise, the spoon (*g*uhû) as the vessel.

Commentary.

*G*uhû, the spoon, is so called because it is used for pouring out (*g*uhoti, homa).

SÛTRA XXVI.

If the *g*uhû has been elsewhere employed, let it be done with a ladle (sruva).

Commentary.

The *g*uhû is a sru*k*, a spoon, the sruva, a ladle.

SÛTRA XXVII.

The offering is made in the Âhavanîya fire.

SÛTRA XXVIII.

The sacrificial vessels are kept from the first laying of the fires (âdhâna) for the whole life.

Commentary.

All sacrificial vessels and instruments are to be kept, and most of them are burnt with the sacrificer at his death.

SÛTRA XXIX.

At every sacrifice these vessels are to be purified.

SÛTRA XXX.

The rule for the sacrifice are the Mantras and Brâhma*n*as.

SÛTRA XXXI.

The name Veda belongs both to the Mantras and Brâhma*n*as.

SÛTRA XXXII.

The Brâhmaṇas are the precepts for the sacrifice.

SÛTRA XXXIII.

The rest of the Brâhmaṇa, that which does not contain precepts, consists of explanations, i. e. reproof, praise, stories, and traditions.

Commentary.

It is difficult to find words corresponding to technical terms in Sanskrit. Arthavâda, which I have translated by explanation, means not only the telling of the meaning, but likewise the telling of the object; parakṛiti, story, means literally the action of another; purâkalpa, traditions, means the former state. The difference between the two is stated to be that parakṛiti refers to the act of one person, purâkalpa to that of several. This subject is fully treated in the Pûrva-mîmâmsâ. Satyavrata begins a new Sûtra with 'reproof' (nindâ).

SÛTRA XXXIV.

All the rest are Mantras.

SÛTRA XXXV.

But passages which are not handed down, are not to be classed as Mantras, as, for instance, the pravara, the words used in choosing priests, divine or human; ûha, substitution of one word for another; and nâmadheya-grahaṇa, the mentioning of the names of particular sacrificers.

Commentary.

The reason why such passages are not to be treated as Mantras is that they should not be subject to some of the preceding rules, as, for instance, the murmuring, enjoined in Sûtra IX. Those passages naturally vary in each sacrifice. With regard to the names a distinction is made

between the gârhyam nâma, the domestic name of a
person, such as Yagñaśarman, and the astrological name,
such as Rauhina, derived from the star Rohinî.

Sôtra XXXVI.

Likewise the sound of a carriage and the sound
of a drum.

Commentary.

These sounds, though serving for the sacrifice, are not
to be considered as liable to the rules given for the recitation of Mantras.

Sôtra XXXVII.

The prohibition of reciting Mantras in the Svâdhyâya does not apply to the sacrifice, because there
is then a different object.

Commentary.

Svâdhyâya, i. e. self-reading, is the name given to the
study of the Veda, both in first learning and in afterwards
repeating it. This study is under several restrictions, but
these restrictions cease when the Veda is used for sacrificial
purposes.

Sôtra XXXVIII.

Sacrificial acts are accompanied by one Mantra.

Commentary.

If it is said that the priest cuts the plants with fourteen
verses, that means that there are fourteen plants to be cut
and that one verse is used for each plant.

Sôtra XXXIX.

This applies also to sacrificial acts which have
a number and are to be carried out by separate
(repeated) acts.

Commentary.

If a rule is given, such as tri*h* prokshati, he sprinkles thrice, the mantra which accompanies the act, is recited once only. Again in the case of acts that require repetitions, such as rubbing, pounding, &c., the hymns are recited once only.

Sûtra XL.

The same applies to rubbing, sleeping, crossing a river, down-pours of rain, the conjuring of unlucky omens, unless they happened some time ago.

Commentary.

If several members of the body are to be rubbed, the verses required for the purpose are recited once only. A prayer is enjoined if one wakes during the night. If one wakes more than once that prayer is not to be repeated. In crossing a river the necessary verse is not to be repeated at every wave, nor during a down-pour, at every drop of rain. If some unlucky sight has to be conjured, the conjuring verse is spoken once and not repeated, unless some time has elapsed and a new unlucky sight presents itself.

Sûtra XLI.

In case of a journey, however, one hymn is used till the object (of the journey) has been accomplished.

Commentary.

I read prayâ*n*e tu-â-arthanirv*ri*tte*h*. Another reading is arthaniv*ri*tti*h*.

Sûtra XLII.

It is the same also with regard to acts which do not produce an immediate effect.

Commentary.

The commentators distinguish between acts which

produce a visible effect, such as pounding or sprinkling, and acts which do not, such as addressing, approaching, looking. The latter are called asa*mm*nipâtin. Thus when the stones used for the preparation of Soma are addressed, the hymn which is used for addressing them, is not repeated for each single stone, the same as in Sûtra XL. Sûtras XLI and XLII are sometimes joined.

Sûtra XLIII.

Repetition takes place in the case of the Havish-kr*i*t, Adhrigu, Puronuvâkyâ, and Manotâ hymns, (because they have to be used) at different times.

Commentary.

Havishkr*i*t-adhrigu-puronuvâkyâ-manotam is to be taken as a Dvandva compound.

The Havishkr*i*t hymn is an invocation when the havis is made. The Adhrigu hymn is 'Daivyâ*h* samitâra*h*,' &c. The Puronuvâkyâ hymn is that which precedes the Yâ*g*yâ, immediately after the Sampraisha. The Manotâ hymn is 'Tva*m* hy agne prathamo manotâ,' &c. These hymns are to be repeated, if the act which they accompany has to be repeated after a certain interval.

Sûtra XLIV.

When it is expressly stated, one sacrificial act may be accompanied by many hymns.

Commentary.

Thus we read, 'He takes the Abhri, the hoe, with four Mantras.'

Sûtra XLV.

One ought to let the beginnings of a sacrificial act coincide with the end of the Mantras.

Commentary.

The mantra which indicates the nature and purpose of a sacrificial act should come first, and as soon as it has been finished the act should follow.   See Kâty. I, 3, 5.

SÛTRA XLVI.

In the case of the âghâra, sprinkling of clarified butter, and of dhârâ, pouring out of Soma, the beginning of the mantra and the act takes place at the same time.

SÛTRA XLVII.

Mantras are indicated by their first words.

Commentary.

These first words are often called Pratîkas, and rules are given in Âsvalâyana's Srauta-sûtras I, 1, 17–19, as to the number of words that should form such a pratîka, if it is meant for one verse, for three verses, or for a whole hymn.   According to Âsvalâyana, if one foot is quoted, it is meant for a verse ; if an imperfect foot of an initial verse is quoted, it is meant for a whole hymn ; if more than a foot is quoted, it is meant for three verses.

SÛTRA XLVIII.

One should know that with the beginning of a following mantra, the former mantra is finished.

SÛTRA XLIX.

In the case of Hotrâ and Yâ*g*amâna-mantras, an aggregation takes place.

Commentary.

Hotrâs are mantras recited by the Hotri-priest, Yâ*g*amânâs are mantras recited by the sacrificer himself. They are hymns which accompany, but do not enjoin any sacrificial act.

SÛTRA L.

In the case of the Yâ*g*yâs and Anuvâkyâs this (the aggregation) is optional.

Commentary.

The Yâ*g*yâ is explained by praya*kkh*ati yâ*g*yayâ, the Anuvâkyâ by âhvayaty anuvâkyayâ. Sometimes more than one are mentioned, but in that case the priest is free to do as he likes. According to the same principle, when we read that one should sacrifice with rice or with barley, that means that rice should be used after the rice-harvest, barley after the barley-harvest, and not that rice and barley should be used at the same time.

SÛTRA LI.

It is the same with numbers.

Commentary.

If we read that, as in the case of fees to be given to priests, two, seven, eleven, twelve, twenty-one, sixty, or a hundred, this means that either one or the other, not that all should be given at the same time.

SÛTRA LII.

But accumulation is meant in the buying (of Soma), in the redemption, and in initiation.

Commentary.

When it is said that Soma is bought for a goat, gold, &c., that it is re-bought from the priests by means of a fee, or that at the time of the Dîkshâ, the purification and initiation of a sacrificer, clothes, gold, grain, &c., should be given, these are cases not of aut-aut but of et-et.

The Soma-plant, which is supposed to be bought from northern barbarians, is botanically described in an Âyur-vedic extract, quoted in the Dhûrtasvâmi-bhâshya*t*ikâ (MS. E. I. H. 531, p. 3[b]), as

*s*yâmâlâmlâ *k*a nishpatrâ kshîri*n*î tva*k*i mâ*m*salâ, *s*lesh-
malâ vamanî vallî somâkhyâ *khy*âgabho*g*anam. 'The creeper
called Soma is dark, sour, without leaves, milky, fleshy on
the surface, producing phlegm and vomiting, food for goats.'

This passage, quoted from some Âyur-vedic text, is still
the only one which gives an approximative description of
the Soma-plant. Dr. Hooker says that the predicates 'sour
and milky' point to Sarcostemma, but the question is not
decided yet. For further information see George Watt,
The Soma Plant, an extract from the third volume of the
Dictionary of Economic Products of India, and Hillebrandt,
Vedische Mythologie, pp. 14 seq.

Sûtra LIII.

If one has performed an offering to Rudra, to the
Râkshasas, to Nir*r*iti, or to the Pit*ri*s, if one
has cut or broken or thrown away anything, or
rubbed oneself, &c., one should touch water.

Commentary.

The touching of water is for the sake of purification.
Nirasana is left out in some MSS. The *k*a, inserted after
abhimar*s*anâni, is explained, as usual, as including other
acts also, corresponding to our etc.

Sûtra LIV.

All priestly performances take place on the northern side of the Vihâra.

Commentary.

Uttarata-upa*k*âra*h* has to be taken as a compound.
Vihâra is explained as vihriyante=gnaya*h* pâtrâ*n*i *k*a
yasmin de*s*e, i.e. the sacrificial ground. Upa*k*âra is
explained as adhvaryvâdînâ*m* sa*m*kara*h*, and this sa*m*kara,
according to Kâtyâyana I, 3, 42, is the path between the
*K*âtvâla and Utkara, the Utkara being on the west, the
pra*n*îtâs on the east of the Vihâra. Kâtyâyana I, 8, 26,
expresses the same rule by uttarata-upa*k*âro yag*ñ*a*h*,
the vihâra being the place where the yag*ñ*a takes place.

SÛTRA LV.

The priest should never turn away from the fire, i. e. should never turn his back on the altar.

SÛTRA LVI.

Nor from the Vihâra.

SÛTRA LVII.

Sacrificial utensils should be turned inside, the performers being outside.

Commentary.

The meaning is that the priest should carry such things as spoons, vessels, &c., holding them towards the altar. The sacrificer and his wife should likewise be on the inside of the priest, and the priests should take precedence sideways according to their rank.

SÛTRA LVIII.

After a sacrificial object has been hallowed by a Mantra, the priest should not toss it about.

SÛTRA LIX.

Sacrificial acts intended for the gods, should be performed by the priest towards the east or towards the north, after he has placed the Brahmanic cord over the left and under the right arm (ya*gñ*opavi-tin), and turning towards the right.

SÛTRA LX.

Sacrificial acts intended for the Fathers should be performed by the priest towards the south, after he has placed the Brahmanic cord over the right and under the left arm (prâ*k*înâvîtin), and turning towards the left.

Sûtra LXI.

Ropes which have to be joined, should be joined by the priest from left to right, after having tied them from right to left.

Sûtra LXII.

Ropes which are not joined (single ropes), should be tied by the priest from left to right.

Commentary.

The exact process here intended is not quite clear. The ropes seem to have been made of vegetable fibres. See Kâty. I, 3, 15–17.

Sûtra LXIII.

Let a man sacrifice with the Amâvâsyâ sacrifice at the time of the Amâvâsyâ, new moon.

Commentary.

Amâ-vâsyâ is the dwelling together, i.e. the conjunction, of sun and moon, an astronomical expression which was adopted in the common language of the people at a very early time. It does not occur, however, in the Rig-veda. In our Sûtra amâvâsyâ is used in the sense both of new moon and new-moon sacrifice.

Sûtra LXIV.

And let a man sacrifice with the Paur*n*amâsyâ sacrifice at the time of the Paur*n*amâsî, full moon, thus it is said.

Commentary.

Here the full moon is called paur*n*amâsî, the sacrifice paur*n*amâsyâ. Satyavrata joins the two Sûtras in one, and leaves out yag*e*teti, which may have belonged to the commentary.

SÛTRA LXV.

Let a man observe that full-moon day as a day of abstinence on which the moon comes out full before.

Commentary.

The full moon (paur*n*amâsî) is really the very moment on which the moon is full and therefore begins to decrease. That moment on which sun and moon are, as the Hindus said, at the greatest distance from each other, is called the parva-sandhi, the juncture of the two phases of the moon. Thus the name of paur*n*amâsî belongs to the last day of the one and to the first day (pratipad) of the other phase, and both days might be called paur*n*amâsî. If therefore the moon is full on the afternoon, the evening, or the twilight of one day, that day should be observed as a fast-day, and the next day should be the day of sacrifice.

The meaning of purastâd, which I have translated by before, is doubtful. One commentator says it has no object, and should be dropped, purastâd ity etat padam asmin sûtra idânîm anvaya*m* na labhate prayo-*g*anâbhâvât. Purastâd, before, may, however, mean before the second day, on which the real sacrifice takes place, and the commentator mentions purastât-paur*n*a-mâsî as a name of the *k*aturda*s*î-yuktâ, i.e. the full moon beginning on the fourteenth day. The same kind of full moon is also called Anumati, Pûrvâ-paur*n*amâsî, and Sandhyâ-paur*n*amâsî, while that which takes place on the pratipad, the first day of the lunar phase, is called Râkâ, Uttarâ-paur*n*amâsî, Astamitoditâ, and *Sva*h-pûritâ.

Corresponding to these two kinds of Paur*n*amâsî there are also two kinds of Amâvâsyâ. That which falls on the fourteenth day is called Pûrvâ-amâvâsyâ, or Sinîvâlî, the ἔνη καὶ νέα; that which falls on the pratipad, the first day of the new phase, is called Kuhû, Uttarâ-amâvâsyâ, *S*voyuktâ. See also Ait.-Brâhm. II, 4; Nir. XI, 31–32.

Sûtra LXVI.

Or the day when one says, To-morrow it will be full.

Commentary.

In that case the day before should be observed as a day of abstinence. The real full moon would then take place in the fore-noon, pûrvâh*n*e, of the next day. Abstinence, upavâsa, consists in abstaining from meat and from mai-thuna, in shaving beard and head, cutting the nails, and, what seems a curious provision, in speaking the truth. See Kâty.-*S*rauta-sûtras II, 1, 8-12.

Sûtra LXVII.

The Vâ*g*asaneyins mention a third, the Kharvikâ full moon.

Commentary.

Kharva means small. If one divides the night into twelve parts, and if in a portion of the twelfth part the greatest distance of sun and moon takes place, then the full moon is called kharvikâ, also kshi*n*â. Or, if on the sixteenth day, the full moon takes place before noon, that also is called kharvikâ paur*n*amâsî. In that case absti-nence or fasting takes place on the sixteenth day (tasyâ*m* sho*d*ase•hany upavâsa*h*). Both paur*n*amâsîs are also called sadyaskâlâ.

Sûtra LXVIII.

Let a man observe that new-moon day (amâ-vâsyâ) as a day of abstinence, on which the moon is not seen.

Commentary.

This Sûtra has to be connected with Sûtra LXV. The abstinence takes place on the day, if the actual new moon, the nearest approach of sun and moon, falls on the afternoon, at night, or at twilight. And this new moon, the junction of the fifteenth day and the pratipad, is called Kuhû. We should read amâvâsyâm.

SÛTRA LXIX.

Or the day when one says, To-morrow they will not see it.

Commentary.

In that case, when the real new moon takes place in the fore-noon, abstinence is observed on the day before, and the new moon is called Sinîvâli. Satyavrata reads svo yukta iti vâ instead of svo na drash*t*âra iti vâ. Dra-sh*t*ara*h* should be explained as îkshitâra*h*, 'they will not see it.' There is much difference of opinion on this subject among different *S*âkhâs, Sûtrakâras, and their commentators; see Taitt. Sa*m*h. III, 4, 9; Weber, Ind. Stud., V, p. 228.

SÛTRA LXX.

The principal acts (pradhâna), prescribed in one (typical) performance, follow the same special rules (vidhâna).

Commentary.

This Sûtra is variously explained : Satyavrata's commentary, which I have followed in the translation, explains pradhânâni as âgncyâdîni, i.e. the chief parts of such a sacrifice as the Dar*s*a-pûr*n*amâsa; vidhânâni as angâni. Kapardisvâmin's commentary also explains vidhânâni as the angâni of a pradhânam; pradhâ-nam as pûr*n*amâsa, &c. It would therefore mean that such ceremonies as the Âgneya (ash*t*a-kapâla), âgnî-shomiya (ekâda*s*a-kapâla), and upâ*m*su, which form the pradhânas of the Dar*s*apûr*n*amâsa, retain through-out the same vidhânas or angas as prescribed in one Prakara*n*a, viz. the Dar*s*apûr*n*amâsa. The Angas or members are all the things used for sacrificial purposes, milk, butter, grains, animals, &c.

SÛTRA LXXI.

The special rules are limited by (the purpose of) the (typical) performance (prakara*n*a).

Commentary.

Here the rules (vidhis) are again the Aṅgas, which belong to a sacrifice, as the members belong to the body.

Sûtra LXXII.

If no special instruction is given (in the Sruti), the acts are general.

Sûtra LXXIII.

If a special instruction is given, they are restricted.

Commentary.

Nirdesa is explained as visesha-sruti, and the meaning is supposed to be that unless such a special rule is given, the Aṅgas of all the Pradhâna acts remain the same, as, for instance, the Paryagnikaraṇa, the Prayâgas, &c. Special instructions are when it is said: payasâ maitravaruṇam srînâti, sruveṇa puroḍâsam anakti, he cooks the Maitravaruṇa with milk, he anoints the Puroḍâsa with the spoon, &c.

Sûtra LXXIV.

The Ashṭâ-kapâla for Agni, the Ekâdasa-kapâla for Agni-Shomau, and the Upâṃsu-yâga (the muttered offering of butter), form the principal acts at the Paurṇamâsî, the full moon.

Commentary.

The Ashṭâ-kapâla is the cake baked in eight cups, the Ekâdasa-kapâla that baked in eleven cups, and respectively destined for Agni and Soma. What is meant are the sacrificial acts for which these cakes are used.

Sûtra LXXV.

The other Homas are Aṅga.

Commentary.

The other acts, such as the prayâgas and anuyâgas, are auxiliary, and have no promise of reward by themselves.

SÛTRA LXXVI.

The Ash*t*â-kapâla for Agni, the Ekâda*s*a-
kapâla or Dvâda*s*a-kapâla for Indra-Agnî,
form the principal acts at the Amâvâsyâ, the new
moon, in the case of one who does not sacrifice with
Soma.

SÛTRA LXXVII.

In the case of one who sacrifices with Soma, the
second principal act is the Sâ*m*nâyya (both at the
full-moon and new-moon sacrifices).

Commentary.

The Sâ*m*nâyya is a mixture of dadhi and payas, sour
and sweet milk, and is intended for Indra or Mahendra[1].
It takes the place of the second Puro*d*â*s*a at the new-moon
sacrifice.

SÛTRA LXXVIII.

In the case of a Brâhma*n*a, who does not sacrifice with Soma, the Agnîshomîya cake is omitted.

Commentary.

This rule does not seem to be accepted by all schools.
It is not found in Kâtyâyana, and Hira*n*yakesin observes:
Nâsomayâ*g*ino brâhma*n*asyâgnîshomîya*h* puro*d*â*s*o vidyata
ity ekeshâm. See Hillebrandt, l. c. p. iii.

SÛTRA LXXIX.

Without distinction of caste, the Aindrâgna
offering is omitted for one who offers the Sâ*m*-
nâyya.

Commentary.

Even though he be not a Somayâ*g*in, says the commentary.

---

[1] Vaidya in his Dictionary explains it, however, as any substance
mixed with clarified butter and offered as a burnt offering, which
can hardly be right.

This whole matter is summed up in Kapardin's commentary: Amâvâsyâyâm asomayâgina aindrâgna-sâmnâyyayor vikalpa*h.* Paur*n*amâsyâ*m* tv asomayâgino brâhma*n*asyâgnîshomîyayâgâbhâva*h.* Tadrahitâpi paur*n*amâsî purushârtha*m* sâdhayati. Tatra dvayor eva hi yâgayo*h* paur*n*amâsîsabdavâ*k*yatvam asti, pratyeka*m* nâmayogât. Tasmâd agnishomîyayâgarahitâv evetarau purushârtha*m* sâdhayata*h.*

Sûtra LXXX.

The Pit*ri*-yag*ñ*a, the sacrifice to the fathers, is not A*ṅ*ga (auxiliary) because its own time is prescribed.

Commentary.

The text should be pit*ri*yag*ñah* svakâlavidhânâd ana*ṅ*ga*h* syât. This sacrifice for the Manes, called also the Pi*nd*a-pit*ri*yag*ñ*a, falls under the new-moon sacrifice, but is to be considered as a prad hâna, a primary sacrifice, not as an a*ṅ*ga, a member of the Dar*s*a.

Sûtra LXXXI.

Also, because it is enumerated like the Dar*s*a-pûr*n*amâsa sacrifice.

Commentary.

This refers to such passages from the Brâhma*n*as as: There are four great sacrifices, the Agnihotram, the Dar*s*apûr*n*amâsau, the *K*âturmâsyâni, and the Pi*nd*a-pit*ri*yag*ñah*.

Sûtra LXXXII.

Also, because, when the Amâvâsyâ sacrifice is barred, the Pit*ri*yag*ñ*a is seen to take place.

Sûtra LXXXIII.

A principal act (pradhâna) is accompanied by auxiliary acts (a*ṅ*ga).

Commentary.

This Sûtra forms sometimes part of the preceding Sûtra, and would then refer to the Pit*r*iyag*ñ*a only.

Sûtra LXXXIV.

A principal act is what has its own name, and is prescribed with special reference to place, time, and performer.

Commentary.

This Sûtra is sometimes divided into two; the first, dese kâle kartariti nirdi*s*yate, the second, asva*s*abda*m* yat. The following are given as illustrations. If it is said that 'he should sacrifice with the Vai*s*vadeva on a slope inclined to the East,' we have the locality. If it is said that 'he should sacrifice with the Vâ*g*apeya in autumn,' we have the time. If it is said that 'the sacrificer himself should offer the Agnihotra on a parvan (change of the moon),' we have the performer. In each of these cases, therefore, the prescribed sacrificial act is a pradhâna sâṅgam, a principal act with auxiliary members.

Sûtra LXXXV.

The Darvi-homa (libation from a ladle) stands by itself.

Commentary.

Apûrva is explained by the commentator, not in its usual sense of miraculous, but as not being subject to the former regulations.

Sûtra LXXXVI.

They are ordered by the word *g*uhoti, he pours out.

Sûtra LXXXVII.

They are offered with the word Svâhâ.

Commentary.

According to Kâtyâyana I, 2, 6–7, the *g*uhotis are

offered sitting, the *yagatis* standing. See Sûtra XCII. The *guhoti* acts consist in pouring melted butter into the fire of the Âhavanîya altar, which is so called because 'âhû-yante-sminn âhutaya*h* kshipyanta iti.'

Sûtra LXXXVIII.

Taking (the butter) once.

Sûtra LXXXIX.

Or, if there are several Âhutis, taking (the butter) for each Âhuti.

Sûtra XC.

Or, doing as he likes in dividing (the butter).

Commentary.

These three Sûtras belong together. They teach that one slice (avadâna) of butter should be taken, melted, and poured on the Âhavanîya fire; or, if there are more than one âhuti, then one slice should be taken for each. This, however, is made optional again by the last Sûtra.

Sûtra XCI.

There is no fuel (in the Darvi-homa), except at the Agnihotra.

Commentary.

In the case of the Agnihotra it is distinctly stated, dve samidhâv âdadhyât, let him lay down two sticks.

Sûtra XCII.

One pours out (*guhoti*) the Darvi-homas, sitting west of the Âhavanîya fire, and bending the right knee, or not bending it.

Sûtra XCIII.

If it is distinctly stated, it is done in a different way.

Commentary.

The vidhi, contained in Sûtra XCII, is therefore called autsargika, general, and liable to exceptions, as when it is said, that he turns to the east.

Sûtra XCIV.

One pours out (*g*uhoti) all âhutis, west of the Âhavanîya fire, passing (the altar) southward, and then turning to the north.

Sûtra XCV.

The Â*s*ruta and Pratyâ*s*ruta, the Yâ*g*yâ and Anuvâkyâ, the Upastara*n*a and Abhighâra*n*a, with the slicings, the *K*aturg*ri*hita also, and the Vasha*t*kâra constitute the Darvi-homas.

Commentary.

The Â*s*ruta is â *s*râvaya; the Pratyâ*s*ruta, astu *s*rausha*t*; Anuvâkyâ and Yâ*g*yâ are verses, the first inviting the deity, the second accompanying the sacrifice. Whenever vegetable, animal, or sâ*m*nâyya offerings have to be sliced, upastara*n*a, spreading, and abhighâra*n*a. sprinkling with fat, take place. With â*g*ya offerings there is *K*aturg*ri*hîta (taking four times), and the Vasha*t*kâra.

Sûtra XCVI.

With âhutis one should let the act (the pouring out) take place after the Vasha*t*kâra has been made, or while it is being made.

Commentary.

The Vasha*t*kâra consists in the word Vasha*t*, to be uttered by the Hot*ri*-priest. The five sacrificial interjections are, svâhâ, *s*rausha*t*, vausha*t*, vasha*t*, and svadhâ.

Sûtra XCVII.

With the Grahas the act should be made to coincide with the Upayâma.

Commentary.

Grahas are offerings of Soma, and likewise the vessels (*k*amasa) in which the Soma is offered. The Soma is offered with the words upayâma-gr*i*hîto*si, and while these words are being uttered, the fluid should be poured out (dhârâ*m* srâvayet).

SÛTRA XCVIII.

With the Ish*t*akâs, the act should be made to coincide with the words tayâ deva tena.

Commentary.

When the different ish*t*akâs or bricks are placed to-gether for building an altar, &c., the act itself begins with the first and ends with the last words of the accompanying verse.

SÛTRA XCIX.

When there is a number of Puro*d*â*s*as, one should slice off one after another, saying for each portion vyâvartadhvam (separate) !

Commentary.

Puro*d*â*s*a is a cake made of meal (pakva*h* pish*t*api*nd*a*h*), different from *k*aru, which is more of a pulse consisting of grains of rice or barley, and clarified butter (ghr*i*tata*nd*ulo-bhayâtmakam). This puro*d*â*s*a cake has to be divided for presentation to different deities. If there are more than two deities, the plural vyâvartadhvam, separate, has to be used.

SÛTRA C.

When the two last are sliced off, he should say for each portion, vyâvartethâm, separate ye two !

Commentary.

Each slice, avadâna, is said to be about a thumb's breadth. In the case of sâ*m*nâyya, the mixture of sour and sweet milk, a kind of coagulated sour milk, each por-tion is to be of the same breadth, but, as it is fluid, it is

taken out with a ladle (sruva) of a corresponding size; see
Kâtyâyana I, 9, 7.

SÛTRA CI.

For these two last portions he makes the indication of the deity.

Commentary.

With the earlier portions, there is a rule which of two
gods should have the first or the second portion. With the
last couple, however, the priest may himself assign which-
ever portion he likes to one or the other god. The commentary says, svayam eva idam asyâ iti saṅkalpayet.

SÛTRA CII.

When there is a number of *K*arus and Puro-
*d*âsas, one separates what belongs to the *K*arus
and what belongs to the Puro*d*âsas, before the
strewing.

Commentary.

Prâg adhivapanât, before the strewing, is explained
by prâg adhivapanârthakr*ish*n*âg*inâdânât, before
one takes the black skin which is used for the strewing.

SÛTRA CIII.

One then marks the two (the materials for the
*K*arus and the Puro*d*âsas) according to the deities
(for whom they are intended).

SÛTRA CIV.

Let the word idam be the rule.

Commentary.

This means that the offering (havis) intended for each
deity should be pointed out by the words idam, this,
Agne*h*, is for Agni, &c. Thus we read with regard to
the offerings intended for certain gods and goddesses:
ida*m* Dhâtur, idam Anumatyâ, Râkâyâ*h* Sinîvâlyâ*h*,
Kuhvâ*h*.

Sûtra CV.

All this applies also to *K*arus and Puro*d*âsas which are separated.

Commentary.

The commentary explains vyatishikta by anyonya*m* vyavahita, though it is difficult to see how it can have that meaning. It is said that in the Vai*s*vadeva the *K*arus and Puro*d*âsas are vyatishikta, but that they also have to be divided before the adhivapana, and to be marked for each deity. Thus we read : Idam Agne*h*, Savitu*h*, Pûsh*n*o, Marutâ*m*, Dyâvâp*r*ithivyo*h*, &c.

Sûtra CVI.

At the time when the Kapâlas are put on the fire, one puts on the *k*aru with the first kapâla verse.

Commentary.

*K*aru is here used for the vessel for boiling the *k*aru, the *k*arusthâlî. The first of these verses is dh*r*ish*t*ir asi. Kapâlas are the jars in which the rice is cooked.

Sûtra CVII.

The verse is adapted and changed to dhruvo·si.

Commentary.

Sa*m*nâma means the same as ûha, i.e. the modification of a verse so as to adapt it to the object for which it is used. In our case, *k*aru, being a masculine, dh*r*ish*t*i, a feminine, is replaced by dhruva, a masculine.

Sûtra CVIII.

At the time when the meal is to be cleansed, one cleanses the grains.

Commentary.

This takes place after the *k*aru-pot has been put on. The ta*nd*ulas are the unhusked grains, pish*t*a is the ground flour. In Sanskrit a distinction is made between *s*asya, the corn in the field, dhânya, corn with the husk, ta*nd*ula, grains without husks, anna, roasted grains.

Sûtra CIX.

At the time of cooking (adhi*s*rapa*n*a) one throws the grains in with the cooking verse.

Commentary.

This verse is gharmo*si.

Sûtra CX.

Without taking the *k*aru (out of the sthâlî) one puts it down.

Sûtra CXI.

At the Dar*s*a-pûr*n*amâsa sacrifices there are fifteen Sâmidhenîs.

Commentary.

Sâmidhenîs are particular verses recited while the fire is being kindled. The first and last verses are repeated thrice, so as to make fifteen in all.

Sûtra CXII.

At the Ish*t*i and Pa*s*ubandha sacrifices there are seventeen Sâmidhenîs, when they are so handed down.

Sûtra CXIII.

When it is said that wishful ish*t*is are performed in a murmur, this means that the names of the chief deities are pronounced in a murmur (likewise the yâ*g*yâ and anuvâkyâ).

Sûtra CXIV.

The Dar*s*a-pûr*n*amâsa sacrifice is the Prak*r*iti or norm for all ish*t*is.

Commentary.

The Sûtras, in describing the performance of certain sacrifices, treat some of them in full detail. These are called prakriti. Prakriyante‑smin dharmâ iti prakara*n*am prakriti*h*. They form the type of other sacrifices, which are therefore looked upon as mere modifications, vikriti, and in describing them those points only are fully described in which they differ from their prakriti. A sacrifice which is a vikriti, may again become the prakriti of another sacrifice. This system is no doubt compendious, but it is not free from difficulty, and, in some cases, from uncertainty. It shows how much system there is in the Indian sacrifices, and how fully and minutely that system must have been elaborated, before it assumed that form in which we find it in the Brâhma*n*as and Sûtras. It must not be supposed that the sacrifices which serve as prakriti, are therefore historically the most ancient.

Sûtra CXV.

It is also the norm for the Agnishomîya Pa*s*u, the animal sacrifice for Agni-Shomau.

Sûtra CXVI.

And this is the norm for the Savanîya.

Sûtra CXVII.

And the Savanîya is the norm for the Aikâda*s*inas.

Sûtra CXVIII.

And the Aikâda*s*inas are the norm for the Pa*s*uga*n*as.

Commentary.

The rules for the Pa*s*uga*n*as are therefore to be taken over from the Aikâda*s*inas, the Savanîya, the Agnishomîya-pa*s*u, and the Dar*s*a-pûr*n*amâsa, so far as they have been modified in each particular case, and are finally determined by the rules of each Pasuga*na*, as, for instance, the Âditya-pa*s*u.

SÛTRA CXIX.

The Vai*s*vadeva is the norm for the Varu*na*-praghâsa, Sâkamedha, and Sîra.

Commentary.

The Vai*s*vadeva, beginning, like the Dar*s*a-pûr*na*-mâsa, with an Âgneya ash*t*akapâla, takes certain rules from the Dar*s*a-pûr*na*mâsa, and transfers these, together with its own, as, for instance, the nine prayâ*g*as, to the Varu*na*-praghâsa, &c.

SÛTRA CXX.

The Vai*s*vadevika Ekakapâla is the norm for all Ekakapâlas.

Commentary.

The Ekakapâla is a puro*d*âsa cake, baked in one kapâla. It is fully described in the Vai*s*vadeva, and then becomes the norm of all Ekakapâlas. An ekaka-pâla cake is not divided.

SÛTRA CXXI.

The Vai*s*vadevî Âmikshâ is the norm for the Âmikshâs (a preparation of milk).

SÛTRA CXXII.

Here the Vikâra, the modification, is perceived from similarity.

Commentary.

If it has once been laid down that the Dar*s*a-pûr*na*-mâsa is the prak*r*iti or norm for all ish*t*is, then similarity determines the modification in all details, such as the offerings and the gods to whom offerings are made. Thus *K*aru, being a vegetable offering, would rank as a vikâra of puro*d*âsa, which occurs in the Dar*s*a-pûr*na*mâsa sacrifice, and is likewise vegetable. Honey and water would be looked upon as most like the Âgya in the Darsa-pûrṇamâsa. Âmikshâ, a preparation of milk, would come nearest to the Sâmnâyya, which is a mixture of sour and sweet milk.

SÛTRA CXXIII.

Offerings for one deity are vikâras of the Âgneya.

Commentary.

In the Darsa-pûrṇamâsa, which is the prakṛiti of the ishṭis, the puroḍâsa for Agni is meant for one deity. Hence all offerings to one deity in the vikṛitis follow the general rules of the Âgneya puroḍâsa, as described in the Darsa-pûrṇamâsa, for instance, the karu for Sûrya, the Dvâdasa-kapâla for Savitṛi.

SÛTRA CXXIV.

Offerings for two deities are vikâras of the Agnîshomîya.

Commentary.

They must, however, be vegetable offerings, because the puroḍâsa for Agnî-Shomau is a vegetable offering. As an instance, the Âgnâvaishṇava Ekâdasakapâla is quoted. Agnîshomîya has a short a, but the first a in âgnavaishṇava is long.

SÛTRA CXXV.

Offerings for many deities are vikâras also of the Aindrâgna.

Commentary.

The ka in bahudevatâs ka is explained by the commentary as intended to include the Âgnâvaishṇava also. Any offering intended for more than one deity may be considered as intended for many deities.

SÛTRA CXXVI.

They are optionally vikâras of the Aindrâgna.

Commentary.

Sometimes these two Sûtras are combined into one. The commentator, however, sees in the vâ of aindrâgnavikârâ vâ a deeper meaning. Agnî-Shomau, he says, consists of four, Indrâgnî of three syllables. Therefore if the name of more than one deity consists of four syllables, it should be treated as a vikâra of the Agnîshomîya, if of less than four syllables, as a vikâra of the Aindrâgna.

SÛTRA CXXVII.

An exception must be made in the case of the gods of the prakriti, as, for instance, the Aindra purodâsa, the Saumya karu.

Commentary.

The exception applies to cases where the offering in a vikriti sacrifice is meant for the same principal deities as those of the prakriti offering. For instance, in the Darsa-pûrnamâsa Agni and Soma are the deities of the Agnîshomîya, Indra and Agni of the Aindrâgna. If then in one of the secondary or vikriti sacrifices there occurs an Aindra purodâsa, or a Saumya karu, then the Aindra purodâsa is treated as a vikâra of the Aindrâgna, the Saumya karu as a vikâra of the Agnîshomîya. The Somendra karu also, as its principal deity is Soma, would follow the Agnîshomîya, the Indrâsomîya purodâsa, as its principal deity is Indra, would follow the Aindrâgna.

SÛTRA CXXVIII.

If there is sameness both in the offering and in the deity, then the offering prevails.

Commentary.

If a karu for Pragâpati occurs in a vikriti sacrifice, it would follow that, being offered to Pragâpati, it should be offered with murmuring, but, as it is a vegetable offering, it follows the norm of the purodâsa, though the purodâsa is intended for Agni.

SÛTRA CXXIX.

If there is contradiction with regard to the substance and the preparation of an offering, the substance prevails.

Commentary.

A puro*d*âsa may be made of vrihi, rice, or of nîvâra, wild growing rice. The wild rice has to be pounded, but not the good rice. The preparation, however, has to yield in a vik*r*iti, the important point being the substance.

SÛTRA CXXX.

If there is contradiction with regard to the substance, the object prevails.

Commentary.

An example makes the meaning of this Sûtra quite clear. Generally the yûpa or sacrificial post for fastening sacrificial animals is made of Khadira wood. But if a post made of wood is not strong enough to hold the animal, then an iron post is to be used, the object being the fastening of the animal, while the material is of less consequence.

SÛTRA CXXXI.

In a Prak*r*iti sacrifice there is no Ûha, modification of the mantras.

Commentary.

Certain mantras of the Veda have to be slightly altered, when their application varies. In the normal sacrifices, however, no such alteration takes place.

SÛTRA CXXXII.

In a Vik*r*iti sacrifice modification takes place, according to the sense, but not in an arthavâda.

Commentary.

Some mantras remain the same in the Vik*r*iti as in the Prak*r*iti. Others have to be modified so as to be adapted to anything new that has to be. If, for instance, there is a Puro*d*âsa for Agni in the Prak*ri*ti, and in its place a Puro*d*âsa for Sûrya in the Vik*ri*ti, then we must place Sûrya instead of Agni in the dedicatory mantra.

SÛTRA CXXXIII.

When we hear words referring to something else, that is arthavâda.

Commentary.

Arthavâda is generally explained as anything occurring in the Brâhma*n*as which is not vidhi or command. Here, however, it refers to Mantras or passages recited at the sacrifice. We saw how such passages, if they referred to some part of the sacrifice, had to be modified under certain circumstances according to the sense. Here we are told that passages which do not refer to anything special in the sacrifice, are arthavâda and remain unmodified. All this is expressed by the words paravâkyas*r*ava*n*ât. Vâkya stands for padâni, words, such as are used in the nivâpa-mantra, &c. Some of these words are called samavetârthâni, because they tell of something connected with the performance of the sacrifice, as, for instance, Agnaye *g*ush*t*a*m* nirvapâmi, I offer what is acceptable to Agni; others are asamavetârthâni, as, for instance, Devasya tvâ Savitu*h* prasave. When such passages which are not connected with some sacrificial act occur (*r*ava*n*ât), they naturally remain unaltered.

SÛTRA CXXXIV.

If what is prescribed is absent, a substitute is to be taken according to similarity.

Commentary.

Here we have no longer modification, but substitution (pratinidhi). In cases where anything special that has been prescribed is wanting, a substitute must be chosen, as similar as possible, and producing a similar effect.

According to Ma*n*ḍana's Trikâ*n*ḍa, the degrees of similarity
are to be determined in the following order:

Kâryai rûpais tathâ par*n*ai*h* kshîrai*h* pushpai*h* phalair
api,

Gandhai rasai*h* sad*r*ig grâhyam pûrvâlâbhe param param.

'What is similar by effect, by shape, by leaves, by milk,
by flowers, and by fruit, By smell, or by taste is to be taken
one after the other, if the former cannot be found.'

Sûtra CXXXV.

If there is nothing very like, something a little
like may be substituted, only it must not be prohibited.

Commentary.

If in a *k*aru of mudgas, kidney-beans, phaseolus
mungo, these kidney-beans should fail, a substitute may
be taken, but that substitute must not be mâshas, phaseolus radiatus, because these mâshas are expressly forbidden; for it is said, Aya*g*ñiyâ vai mâshâ*h*, 'Mâshas
are not fit for sacrifice.'

Sûtra CXXXVI.

The substitute should take the nature of that for
which it is substituted.

Commentary.

Taddharma, having the same qualities. If, for instance,
nîvâra has been substituted for vrîhi, it should be treated
as if it were vrîhi. The name vrîhi should remain, and
should not be replaced by nîvâra, just as Soma, if replaced
by pûtikâ, is still called Soma. Thus, when in the course
of a sacrifice vrîhi has once been replaced by nîvâra, and
vrîhi can be procured afterwards, yet nîvâra is then to be
retained to the end. If, however, the substituted nîvâra
also come to an end, and afterwards both nîvâra and vrîhi
are forthcoming, then vrîhi has the preference. If neither
be forthcoming, then some substitute is to be taken that
approaches nearest to the substitute, the nîvâra, not to the

original vrîhi. Further, if a choice has been allowed between vrîhi, rice, and yava, barley, and vrîhi has been
chosen, and afterwards, as substitute for vrîhi, nîvâra,
then, if nîvâra come to an end, and in the absence of
vrîhi, when a new supply of both nîvâra and yava has
been obtained, the yava is to be avoided, and the original
substitute for vrîhi, the nîvâra, must be retained. In most
of these cases, however, a certain penance also (prâya-
s*k*itta) is required.

Sûtra CXXXVII.

If something is wanting in the measure, let him
finish with the rest.

Commentary.

If it is said that a puro*d*âsa should be as large as a
horse's hoof, and there is not quite so much left, yet whatever is left should be used to finish the offering.

Sûtra CXXXVIII.

Substitution does not apply to the master, the
altar-fire, the deity, the word, the act, and a prohibition.

Commentary.

The master is meant for the sacrificer himself and his
wife. Their place cannot, of course, be taken by anybody
else. The altar-fire is supposed to have a supernatural
power, and cannot be replaced by any other fire. Nothing
can take the place of the invoked deities, nor of the words
used in the mantras addressed to them, nor can the sacrifice
itself be replaced by any other act. Lastly, when it is said
that mâshas, varakas, kodravas are not fit for sacrifice,
or that a man ought not to sacrifice with what should not be
eaten by Âryas, nothing else can be substituted for what is
thus prohibited.

Sûtra CXXXIX.

The Prak*r*iti stops from three causes, from a
corollary, from a prohibition, and from loss of purpose.

[30]   A a

Commentary.

A corollary (pratyâmnâna) occurs, when it is said, 'instead of Kusa grass, let him make a barhis of reeds.' A prohibition (pratishedha) occurs, when it is said, 'he does not choose an Ârsheya.' Loss of purpose (arthalopa) occurs, when peshana, pounding, would refer to *k*aru, a pulse, that cannot be pounded, while grains can be.

Sûtra CXL.

The Agnish*t*oma is the Prak*r*iti of the Ekâha sacrifices.

Commentary.

The Ekâha are sacrifices accomplished in one day.

Sûtra CXLI.

The Dvâda*s*âha is the Prak*r*iti of the Aharga*n*as.

Commentary.

The Dvâda*s*âha lasts twelve days and is a Soma sacrifice. It is either an Ahîna or a Sattra. An Aharga*n*a is a series of daily and nightly sacrifices. Those which last from two nights to eleven nights are called Ahîna. Those which last from thirteen to one hundred nights or more are called Sattras.

Sûtra CXLII.

The Gavâmayana is the Prak*r*iti of the Sâ*m*vatsarikas.

Commentary.

The Gavâmayana lasts three years, and it is the type of all Sâ*m*vatsarika sacrifices, whether they last one, two, three or more years. They all belong to the class of Sattras.

Sûtra CXLIII.

Of the Nikâyi sacrifices the first serves as Prak*r*iti.

Commentary.

Among the Nikâyi sacrifices, lit. those which consist of a number, all having the same name, but different rewards, the first is the prak*ri*ti of the subsequent ones. The commentator calls them sâdyaskra &c., and mentions as the first the Agnish*to*ma. See Sûtra CXLVI, and Weber, Ind. Stud. XIII, p. 218.

SÛTRA CXLIV.

At the Agnish*to*ma there is the Uttara-vedi.

Commentary.

The commentator explains this by saying that at the Soma sacrifices, i. e. at the Agnish*to*ma, Ukthya, Sho-*da*sin, and Atirâtra, the fire is carried from the Âhavanîya to the Uttara-vedi, which is also called the Soma altar.

SÛTRA CXLV.

The fire is valid for the successive sacrifices.

Commentary.

This fire refers to the fire on the Uttara-vedi, mentioned in the preceding Sûtra, and the object of the Sûtra seems to be to include the act of lighting the fire on the Uttara-vedi in the Prak*ri*ti, though properly speaking it does not form part of the Agnish*to*ma. But I cannot quite understand the argument of the commentator.

SÛTRA CXLVI.

This does not apply to the Sâdyaskras, the Vâ*g*apeya, the Sho*da*sin, and the Sârasvata Sattra.

Commentary.

With regard to the Sho*da*sin and its vikâra, the Vâ*g*a-peya, the laying of the fire is not mentioned. In the case of the Sâdyaskras, it becomes impossible, because they have to be quickly finished. In the case of the Sârasvata Sattra, there is the same difficulty on account of not remaining in the same place (anavasthâpân nâgni*s ki*yate).

Sûtra CXLVII.

A sacrificer wishes the object of his sacrifice at the beginning of the sacrifice.

Commentary.

Some MSS. read kâmayeta, 'he should wish,' but the commentator explains that such a command (vidhi) is unnecessary, because it is natural to form a wish (svata*h* siddhatvât).

Sûtra CXLVIII.

At the beginning of a special part of the sacrifice, one should wish the object of that part of the sacrifice.

Commentary.

The commentary, though objecting, and objecting rightly, to kâmayeta, 'he should wish,' in the preceding Sûtra, accepts kâmayeta as determining the present Sûtra, saying kâmayetety anuvartate. One should read yag*ñ*âṅgakâmam, not yag*ñ*akâmam, for the commentary explains it by yag*ñ*âṅgaphalasaṅkalpa*h*. Whether it was really intended that there should be a special wish for each part or subsidiary act of a sacrifice (yag*ñ*âṅga), is another question, but the commentator evidently thought so.

Kâtyâyana, who treats the same subject (1, 2, 10 seq.), states that there should be this desire for a reward for certain sacrifices which are offered for a certain purpose, as, for instance, the Dvâda*s*âha, but that there are no such motives for other sacrifices, and parts of sacrifices. He mentions, first of all, a niyama, a precept for the sacrifice, such as 'Speak the truth.' Then a nimitta, a special cause, as when some accident has taken place that must be remedied, for instance, when the house has been burnt down, &c. Thirdly, the Agnihotra, the morning and evening Homa; fourthly, the Dar*s*a-pûr*n*amâsau; fifthly, the Dâkshâya*n*a, a vik*r*iti of the Dar*s*a-pûr*n*amâsau, the Âgraya*n*a; sixthly, the Nirû*dh*a-pa*s*u, the animal sacrifice. All these have to be performed as a sacred duty, and without any view to special rewards. Thus we read in Vâsish*th*a :

Ava*s*yam brâhma*n*o¸gnin âdadhîta, dar*s*apûr*n*amâsâgra-ya*n*esh*ti*kâturmâsyapa*s*usomai*s* *k*a ya*g*eta, 'A Brâhma*n*a should without fail place his fires, and offer the Dar*s*a-pûr*n*amâsa, the Âgraya*n*esh*t*i, the *K*âturmâsyas, the Pa*s*u, and the Soma sacrifices.'

Hârîta says: Pâkaya*gñ*ân ya*g*en nitya*m* havirya*gñ*â*m*s *k*a nitya*s*a*h*, Somâ*m*s *k*a vidhipûrve*n*a ya i*kkh*ed dharmam avyayam, 'Let a man offer the Pâkaya*gñ*as always, always also the Haviryag*ñ*as, and the Soma sacrifices, according to rule, if he wishes for eternal merit.' The object of these sacrifices is aparimitani*h*sreyasarûpa-moksha, eternal happiness, and hence they have to be performed during life at certain seasons, without any special occasion (nimitta), and without any special object (kâma). According to most authorities, however, they have to be performed during thirty years only. After that the Agnihotra only has to be kept up. The proper seasons for these sacrifices are given by Manu, IV, 25-27:

'A Brâhma*n*a shall always offer the Agnihotra at the beginning or at the end of the day and of the night, and the Dar*s*a and Paur*n*amâsa (ish*t*is) at the end of each half-month ;

'When the old grain has been consumed the (Âgraya*n*a) Ish*t*i with new grain ; at the end of the (three) seasons the (*K*âturmâsya) sacrifices ; at the solstices an animal (sacrifice) ; at the end of the year Soma offerings ;

'A Brâhma*n*a, who keeps sacred fires, shall, if he desires to live long, not eat new grain or meat, without having offered the (Âgraya*n*a) Ish*t*i with new grain and an animal (sacrifice)[1].'

These Pâkayag*ñ*as, Haviryag*ñ*as or ish*t*is, and Soma sacrifices are enumerated by Gautama[2], as follows :

---

[1] See Manu, transl. by Bühler, S. B. E., XXV, who quotes to the same purpose Gaut. VIII, 19–20 ; Vâs. XI, 46 ; Vi. LIX, 2–9 ; Baudh. II, 4, 23 ; Yâg*ñ*. I, 97, 124–125.

[2] Kâtyâyana, p. 34.

Seven Pâkasa*m*sthâs :	Seven Haviry*ag*ñasa*m*sthâs :	Seven Somasa*m*sthâs :
(1) Ash*t*akâ,	(1) Agnyâdheyam,	(1) Agnish*t*oma*h*,
(2) Pârva*n*am,	(2) Agnihotram,	(2) Atyagnish*t*oma*h*,
(3) *S*râddham,	(3) Darsapûr*n*amâsau,	(3) Ukthya*h*,
(4) *S*râva*n*î,	(4) *K*âturmâsyâni [1],	(4) Sho*d*asî [2],
(5) Âgrahâya*n*î,	(5) Âgraya*n*esh*t*i*h*,	(5) Vâgapeya*h*,
(6) *K*aitrî,	(6) Nirû*dh*apa*s*ubandha*h*,	(6) Atirâtra*h*,
(7) Â*s*vayugî.	(7) Sautrâma*n*î.	(7) Aptoryâma*h*.

In a commentary on Dhûrtasvâmin's Âpastambasûtra-bhâshya (MS. E. I. H. 137) another list is given :

Pâkaya*g*ñas :	Haviry*ag*ñas :	Somaya*g*ñas :
(1) Aupâsanahoma*h*,	Agnihotram,	Agnish*t*oma*h*,
(2) Vaisvadevam,	Darsapûr*n*amâsau,	Atyagnish*t*oma*h*,
(3) Pârva*n*am,	Âgraya*n*am,	Ukthya*h*,
(4) Ash*t*akâ,	*K*âturmâsyâni,	Sho*d*asî,
(5) Mâsisrâddham,	Nirû*dh*apa*s*ubandha*h*,	Vâgapeya*h*,
(6) Sarpabali*h*,	Sautrâma*n*î,	Atirâtra*h*,
(7) Îsânabali*h*.	Pi*nd*apit*r*iya*g*ña*h*.	Aptoryâma*h*.

This list is nearly the same as one given by Satyavrata Sâmâsrami in the Ushâ. He gives, however, another list, which is :

Seven Pâkasa*m*sthâs :	Seven Havi*h*sa*m*sthâs :	Seven Somasa*m*sthâs :
(1) Sâya*m*homa*h*,	Agnyâdheyam,	Agnish*t*oma*h*,
(2) Prâtarhoma*h*,	Agnihotram,	Atyagnish*t*oma*h*,
(3) Sthâlîpâka,	Darsa-,	Ukthya*h*,
(4) Navaya*g*ña*h*,	Paur*n*amâsau,	Sho*d*asî,
(5) Vaisvadevam,	Âgraya*n*a,	Vâgapeya*h*,
(6) Pit*r*iya*g*ña*h*,	*K*âturmâsyâni,	Atirâtra*h*,
(7) Ash*t*akâ.	Pa*s*ubandha*h*.	Aptoryâma*h*.

According to the substances offered, sacrifices are some-

---

[1] Vaisvadevam parva, Varu*n*apraghâsâ*h*, sâkamedhâ*h*.

[2] Agnish*t*oma, Ukthya, Atirâtra, sometimes Sho*d*asin, are the original Soma sacrifices; Atyagnish*t*oma, Vâgapeya, and Aptoryâma are later. See Weber, Ind. Stud. X, pp. 352, 391.

times divided into vegetable and animal sacrifices. The
vegetable substances are, ta*nd*ulâ*h*, pish*t*âni, phalikara*n*â*h*,
puro*d*â*s*a*h*, odana*h*, yavâgû*h*, pr*i*thukâ*h*, lâ*g*â*h*, dhânâ*h*,
and aktava*h*. The animal substances are, paya*h*, dadhi,
â*g*yam, âmikshâ, vâ*g*inam, vapâ, tva*k*a*h*, mâ*m*sam, lohitam,
and pa*s*urasa*h*.

SÛTRA CXLIX.

If there are fewer Mantras and more (sacrificial)
acts, then after dividing them into equal parts, let
him perform the former with the former, the latter
with the latter.

Commentary.

It happens, for instance, in certain ish*t*is that a pair
of Yâ*g*yâ and Anuvâkyâ mantras is given, but six acts.
In that case one half of the mantras is used for one half of
the acts, and the other half of the mantras for the other
half of the acts.

SÛTRA CL.

If there are fewer acts and more Mantras, let him
perform and act with one mantra, those which remain are optional, as the materials for the sacrificial
post.

Commentary.

Kapardisvâmin seems to have divided this Sûtra into
three, the second being ava*s*ish*t*â vikalpârthâ*h*, the third
yathâ yûpadravyâ*n*iti. But it is better to take it as one, as
it is in MS. 1676.

If there are, for instance, fourteen vapanas, while there
are many more mantras, let him select fourteen mantras
and use them for each vapana, while the rest will be
useful for another performance. A similar case occurs
when different kinds of wood are recommended for making
the sacrificial post, or when rice or barley are recommended
for an offering. Here a choice has to be made. The iti
at the end is explained as showing that there are other
instances of the same kind.

SÛTRA CLI.

From the end there takes place omission or addition.

Commentary.

This refers again to the same subject, namely what has to be done if there are either more or less mantras than there are acts which they are to accompany. In that case it is here allowed to use as many mantras as there are acts, and to drop the rest of the mantras. Or, if there are less mantras than there are acts, then, after the mantras have been equally divided, the last verse is to be multiplied. For instance, in the Dvikapâla sacrifice for the two Asvins, the placing of the two kapâlas is accompanied by two mantras. The rest of the mantras enjoined in the prakriti is left out. But if there are, for instance, twelve or more ishtakâs, bricks, to be placed, while there are only ten mantras, then the mantras are equally divided, and the fifth and tenth to be repeated, as many times as is necessary to equal the number of the ishtakâs.

SÛTRA CLII.

As the Prakriti has been told before, anything that has not been told before, should be at the end.

Commentary.

This seems to mean that anything new, peculiar to a Vikriti, and not mentioned in the Prakriti, should come in at the end, that is, after those portions of the sacrifice which are enjoined in the Prakriti.

SÛTRA CLIII.

The rule should stand on account of the fitness of the Kumbhî, a large pot, the Sûla, the spit for boiling the heart, and the two Vapâsrapanis, the spits for roasting the vapâ.

Commentary.

Kumbhî is explained by sronyâdipâkasamarthâ

b*ri*hatî sthâlî; *Sû*la by h*ri*dayapâkârthâ yash*ti*h, and Vapâ*s*rapa*nî* by vapâ*s*rapa*nârthe yash*tî* dve. The exact object of the Sûtra is not quite clear. Pra-bhutva is explained by samarthatva, that is, fitness. This would mean, that on account of their fitness, or because they can be used for the object for which they are intended, or, so long as they can be used, the rule applying to them should remain. The commentary explains tantram by tantratâ or ekatâ. It may mean that the same pots and spits should be used, so long as they fulfil their purpose. The next Sûtra would then form a natural limitation.

SÛTRA CLIV.

But if there is a different kind of animal, there is difference (in pots and spits), owing to the diversity of cooking.

Commentary.

If different animals are to be cooked, then there must be different pots for each (pratipa*s*um), because each requires a different kind of cooking. The commentary adds that, as the reason for using different pots is given, that reason applies also to young and old animals of the same kind (*gâ*ti), i. e. the young and small animal would require a different pot and a different kind of cooking.

SÛTRA CLV.

At the Vanaspati sacrifice, which is a modifica-tion (vikâra) of the Svish*t*akr*i*t, the addresses (nigama) of the deities should take place in the Yâ*g*yâ, because they are included in the Prakr*i*ti.

Commentary.

These nigamas of the deities are not mentioned in the rules of the Vanaspati sacrifice, but they are mentioned in the rules for the Svish*t*akr*i*t sacrifice of the Dar*s*a-pûr*n*amâsa, which is the Prakr*i*ti, and should therefore be taken over. Here again, because a reason is given, it is understood that the same reason would apply to other portions of Svish*t*ak*ri*t also, such as the Dvir abhi-ghâra*n*a, which is to be retained in the Vanaspati sacrifice.

SÛTRA CLVI.

The Anvârambha*n*îyâ or initiatory ceremony does not take place in a Vik*ri*ti, because the Vik*ri*tis would fall within the time of the Pra-k*ri*ti, and the Anvârambha*n*îyâ has but one object, namely (the initiation of) the Da*r*sa-pûr*n*a-mâsa sacrifice.

Commentary.

The Anvârambha*n*îyâ ceremony has to be performed by those who begin the Da*r*sa-pûr*n*amâsa sacrifice. It has thus one object only, and is never enjoined for any other cause. It is not therefore transferred to any Vik*ri*ti, such as the Saurya ceremony, &c. The Da*r*sa-pûr*n*a-mâsa sacrifice having to be performed during the whole of life, or during thirty years, the Vik*ri*tis would necessarily fall within the same space of time. The initiatory ceremony has reference to the Da*r*sa-pûr*n*amâsa sacrifice only, and thus serves as an introduction to all the Vik*ri*tis, without having to be repeated for each.

SÛTRA CLVII.

Or (according to others) the Anvârambha*n*îyâ should take place (in the Vik*ri*tis also), because the time (of the Da*r*sa-pûr*n*amâsa) does not form an essential part.

Commentary.

This Sùtra is not quite clear. It shows clearly enough that, according to some authorities, the Anvârambha*n*îyâ or initiatory ceremony of the Da*r*sa-pûr*n*amâsa sacrifice should take place in the Vik*ri*tis also; but why? Because the time has not the character of a *s*esha, which is said to be a synonym of a*n*ga, an essential part of a sacrifice.

When it is said that the Darṣa-pûrṇamâsa should be performed during life, this is not meant as determining the time of the sacrifice. It only means that so long as there is life a man should perform these sacrifices, and that their non-performance would constitute a sin. The former argument, therefore, that the time of the Vikṛiti sacrifices would fall within the time of the Prakṛiti sacrifice is not tenable.

SÛTRA CLVIII.

And again, because there is difference in the undertaking.

Commentary.

Ârambha, the beginning, is explained as the determination to perform a certain sacrifice (darṣapûrṇamâsâbhyâm yakshya iti niṣḱayapuraḥsaraḥ saṅkalpaḥ). The object of the undertaking in the case of the Darṣa-pûrṇamâsa sacrifice, as the Prakṛiti, is simply svarga, in the Vikṛitis it may be any kind of desire. Therefore the Anvârambhaṇîyâ ceremony of the Darṣa-pûrṇamâsas should be transferred to its Vikṛitis. This seems to have been the opinion of the same authorities who are referred to in Sûtra CLVII. The final outcome of the whole controversy, however, is clearly that our Âḱârya is in favour of omitting the Anvârambhaṇîyâ in the Vikṛitis. Anayoḥ pakshayor anvârambhaṇîyâbhâvapakshasyaiva balavattvam âḱâryâbhilashitam iti manyâmahe. The Anvârambhaṇîyâ is not to be considered as an ordinary Aṅga, but as a special act to fit the sacrificer to perform the Darṣa-pûrṇamâsa and to perform it through the whole of his life.

SÛTRA CLIX.

For every object (new sacrifice) let him bring forward the fire (let him perform the Agnipraṇayana, the fetching of the Âhavanîya from the Gârhapatya fire). When the sacrifice is finished the fire becomes again ordinary fire, as when the (divine) fire has returned (to the firesticks).

Commentary.

The fire for a sacrifice is supposed to be set apart or consecrated (*sâstrîya*), but it is so for a special sacrifice only, and when that sacrifice is ended, it is supposed to become like ordinary fire again. A rtha is prayo*g*ana, the sacrifice for which the fire is intended (agnisâdhyavihitakarmânush*th*ânam; tasya tasya vihitasya karma*n*o-nush*th*ânârtha*m* gârhapatyâdibhya âhavanîyâdyagnim pra*n*ayet). The commentator remarks that there are two Agnis, the one who is visible, the other who is the god. Now while the divine Agni leaves the coals and ascends or is absorbed again in the two firesticks (ara*n*i), the other remains like ordinary kitchen fire. See on Samârohâ*n*a, Weber, Ind. Stud. IX, p. 311; Âsvalâyana-*S*rauta-sûtra III, 10, 4–5.

INDEX.

ekâda*s*akapâla, cake baked in eleven
cups (at the full-moon and new-
moon sacrifices), 74, 76, 124ᶜ.
ekâha, sacrifice accomplished in one
day, 140.

aikâda*s*ina, the Aikâda*s*inas, 117, 118.
aindra, intended for Indra, 127.
aindrâgna, intended for Indra and
Agni, 76, 79, 125, 126, 127ᶜ.

autsargika (vidhi), general (rule), 93ᶜ.
aupâsanahoma, p. 344.

ka*nd*ûyana, rubbing, 40.
kapâla, jar in which the rice is
cooked, 106.
kapâlamantra, verse used for the
Kapâla, 106.
kart*ri*, the performer, 24, 57, 84.
karma*k*odanâ, precept for the sacrifice, 32.
karman, sacrifice, sacrificial act, 37,
38, 44, 45 (karmâdi), 59 (daivâ-
ni karmâ*n*i), 138, 149, 150, 159.
kâma, object, 147, 148.
kâmay, to wish, 147.
kâmya, wishful, 113 (kâmyâ ish*t*a-
ya*h*).
kâla, time, 80, 84, 157.
kumbhî, a large pot, 153.
Kuhû, the new moon on the first
day of the lunar phase, 65ᶜ, 68ᶜ.
k*rish*nâgina, black skin used for the
strewing (adhivapana), 102ᶜ.
kratu, sacrifice, 22, 145, 147 (kratvâ-
dau).
kratukâma, object of the sacrifice,
147.
kraya, buying (of Soma), 52.
krush*t*a, sharp voice, high tone, 11ᶜ,
14.
krau*ñk*a, high tone, 11ᶜ.
kshî*n*â=kharvikâ, 67ᶜ.

kharvikâ, the Kharvikâ full moon,
67.

gavâmayana, 142.
gârhapatya, the Gârhapatya fire (the
father), 22ᶜ.
gârhya (nâman), the domestic name,
35ᶜ.
grah, to take (the butter), 88, 89.
graha, offering of Soma, also Soma
vessel, 97.

ghr*i*ta, butter when hardened, 23ᶜ.

*k*aturgr*i*hîta, the taking four times,
95.
*k*aturda*s*îyuktâ, the full moon beginning on the fourteenth day,
65ᶜ.
*k*andramas, moon, 65.
*k*aru, a pulse consisting of grains of
rice or barley, and clarified
butter, 99ᶜ, 102, (103, 105), 110,
122ᶜ, 123ᶜ, 127, 128ᶜ.
*k*aru=*k*arusthâlî, 106, 108ᶜ.
*k*arupuroda*s*iya, belonging to the
*K*arus and Puroda*s*as, 102.
*k*arusthâlî, vessel for boiling the
*k*aru, 106ᶜ, (110).
*k*âturmâsya, one of the seven Haviryag*ñ*as, 7ᶜ, 148ᶜ; p. 344.
*k*âtvâla, a hole in the ground for the
sacrifices, 54ᶜ.
*k*esh*t*âp*ri*thaktvanirvartin, to be carried out by separate (repeated)
acts, 39.
*k*aitrî, p. 344.
*k*odanâ, precept, 32, 86.

*kh*edana, cutting, 53.

*g*apa, the *G*apa-mantras, 8ᶜ.
*g*âtibheda, difference of the kind (of
animal), 154.
*g*ânu, knee, 92.
*g*uhû, spoon, 25, 26ᶜ.
*g*uhoti, see hu.
*g*uhoti*k*odana, ordered by the word
*g*uhoti, he pours out, 86.

ta*nd*ula, grain, 108, 109.
taddharma, having the same qualities, 136.
tantra, rule, 104, 153. See prati-
tantram.
tayâ-deva-tena, the words for placing
the bricks together, 98.
târa, high tone, 11ᶜ.
tulyavat, like, 81.
tr*i*tîyasavana, the third oblation of
Soma, 14.

dakshi*n*a, the Dakshi*n*a fire (the son),
22ᶜ.
dakshi*n*a, right, 92 (*g*ânu).
dakshi*n*â, southward, 94.
dakshi*n*âpavarga, towards the south,
60.

[30]

B b

TRANSLITERATION OF ORIENTAL ALPHABETS ADOPTED FOR THE TRANSLATIONS OF THE SACRED BOOKS OF THE EAST.

CONSONANTS.	MISSIONARY ALPHABET.			Sanskrit.	Zend.	Pehlevi.	Persian.	Arabic.	Hebrew.	Chinese.
	I Class.	II Class.	III Class.							
Gutturales.										
1 Tenuis	k	…	…	क	ꭓ	ꭇ	ک	ک	ה ה	k
2 „ aspirata	kh	…	…	ख	ᔓ	ꭒ	ک	…	ה ה	kh
3 Media	g	…	…	ग	ꭒ	ꭇꭓ	…	…	ה ה	…
4 „ aspirata	gh	…	…	घ	ꭒ	ꭒꭓ	…	…	ה ᑦ	…
5 Gutturo-labialis	q	…	…	…	…	…	…	…	…	…
6 Nasalis	ḣ (ng)	…	…	ङ	{ ʒ (ng) } ꭓ (ṅ)	…	…	…	…	h, hs
7 Spiritus asper	h	…	…	ᨡ	ᔐ (ᔐhᵥ)	ꭇ	‑	‑	ר	…
8 „ lenis	'	…	…	…	…	…	—	—	צ	…
9 „ asper faucalis	ʻh	…	…	…	…	…	ں	ں	ר	…
10 „ lenis faucalis	ʼh	'h	…	…	…	…	س	س	ᔓ	…
11 „ asper fricatus	…	ʼh	…	…	…	…	ن	ن	ר	…
12 „ lenis fricatus	…	…	…	…	…	…	…	…	…	…
Gutturales modificatae (palatales, &c.)										
13 Tenuis	…	k	…	च	ꭇ	ꭒ	ᔓ	…	…	k
14 „ aspirata	…	kh	…	छ	ᔓ	ꭇꭓ	ᔓꭓ	ں	…	kh
15 Media	…	g	…	ज	…	…	…	…	…	…
16 „ aspirata	…	gh	…	झ	…	…	…	…	…	…
17 „ Nasalis	…	ñ	…	ञ	…	…	…	…	…	…

CONSONANTS (continued).	MISSIONARY ALPHABET. I Class.	MISSIONARY ALPHABET. II Class.	MISSIONARY ALPHABET. III Class.	Sanskrit.	Zend.	Pehlevi.	Persian.	Arabic.	Hebrew.	Chinese.
18 Semivocalis	y			म	३ ख्यु init.	ʋ	ی	ی	י	y
19 Spiritus asper										
20 " lenis		(j̈)								
21 " asper assibilatus		(j̈)		ष	२ ९	⸢२ ⸣	۳ ؞	۳		
22 " lenis assibilatus		s				ᶜ				z
23 Tenuis	t	z								
24 " aspirata	th		TH	ए ष	२ ९	⸢२ ⸣	ﯪ	ﯪ	⸢ ⸣	t
Dentales.										th
25 " assibilata										
26 Media	d			ण ष	ᶜ ᶜ	ᶜ	ﯬ ﯬ	ﯬ ﯬ	ᶜ ᶜ	
27 " aspirata	dh		DH							
28 " assibilata										n
29 Nasalis	n			त ऌ	ᶜ	ᶜ	ﯗ	ﯗ	ᶜ ᶜ	ī
30 Semivocalis	l	l	L							
31 " mollis 1										
32 " mollis 2										
33 Spiritus asper 1	s		s S	स	ᶜ	ᶜ	ᶜ	ᶜ	ᶜ ᶜ ᶜ	s
34 " asper 2										
35 " lenis	z						⸢(j̈)	⸢		z
36 " asperrimus 1			z (ẕ)		ᶜ	ᶜ	ж (ẕ)	ж	ᶜ	b, ǵh
37 " asperrimus 2			ž (ẕ)							

(linguales, &c.) Dentales modificatae		
38 Tenuis	l	
39 " aspirata	th	
40 Media	d	
41 " aspirata	dh	
42 Nasalis	n	
43 Semivocalis	r	
44 " fricata		
45 " diacritica		
46 Spiritus asper	sh	
47 " lenis	zh	
Labiales.		
48 Tenuis	p	
49 " aspirata	ph	
50 Media	b	
51 " aspirata	bh	
52 Tenuissima	p	
53 Nasalis	m	
54 Semivocalis	w	
55 " aspirata	hw	
56 Spiritus asper	f	
57 " lenis	v	
58 Anusvâra	m	
59 Visarga	h	

VOWELS.	MISSIONARY ALPHABET. I Class.	II Class.	III Class.	Sanskrit.	Zend.	Pehlevi.	Persian.	Arabic.	Hebrew.	Chinese.
1 Neutralis	0								⁻	ᴈ
2 Laryngo-palatalis	ĕ					⟩ fin.				
3 „ labialis	ŏ					ᴈ init.				
4 Gutturalis brevis	a	(a)		अ	⟨⟩	⟩	ᵎ	ᵎ	׀׀	a
5 „ longa	â			आ	ᴀᴀ		ᴌ	ᴌ	׀⊦	â
6 Palatalis brevis	i	(ĕ)		इ	⟩	⟩	⊦	⊦	׀•⊦׀	—
7 „ longa	î			ई	⟩		✓	✓		⌐
8 Dentalis brevis	ĭ									
9 „ longa	ī									
10 Lingualis brevis	ri			ऋ						u
11 „ longa	rî			ॠ						⊲
12 Labialis brevis	u	(u)		उ	∧	⟩	ᵎ⌐ᴦ	ᵎ⌐ᴦ	׀⸗ᴦ	e
13 „ longa	û			ऊ	ℰ(e)ℇ(e)					ê
14 Gutturo-palatalis brevis	e	(e)		ऌ	℈, ℥	⟩	÷⊘ᴎ	÷⊘ᴎ	׀⊦	âi
15 „ longa	ê (ai)			ॡ						ei, ĕï
16 Diphthongus gutturo-palatalis	âi	(ai)								
17 „	ei (ĕï)			ᴈ /ᴈ	↷		⸗ᴐᴎ	⸗ᴐᴎ		
18 „	oï (ŏü)				ℰꙋ(au)					o
19 Gutturo-labialis brevis	o	(o)				⟩			׀⸗	âu
20 „ longa	ô (au)			ओ		⟩				
21 Diphthongus gutturo-labialis	âu	(au)		औ						
22 „	eu (ĕü)									
23 „	ou (ŏü)									
24 Gutturalis fracta	ä									
25 Palatalis fracta	ï									ü
26 Labialis fracta	ü									
27 Gutturo-labialis fracta	ö									

SACRED BOOKS OF THE EAST

TRANSLATED BY

VARIOUS ORIENTAL SCHOLARS

AND EDITED BY

F. MAX MÜLLER

₊ *This Series is published with the sanction and co-operation of the Secretary of State for India in Council.*

REPORT presented to the ACADÉMIE DES INSCRIPTIONS, May 11, 1883, by M. ERNEST RENAN.

'M. Renan présente trois nouveaux volumes de la grande collection des "Livres sacrés de l'Orient" (Sacred Books of the East), que dirige à Oxford, avec une si vaste érudition et une critique si sûre, le savant associé de l'Académie des Inscriptions, M. Max Müller. . . . La première série de ce beau recueil, composée de 24 volumes, est presque achevée. M. Max Müller se propose d'en publier une seconde, dont l'intérêt historique et religieux ne sera pas moindre. M. Max Müller a su se procurer la collaboration des savans les plus éminens d'Europe et d'Asie. L'Université d'Oxford, que cette grande publication honore au plus haut degré, doit tenir à continuer dans les plus larges proportions une œuvre aussi philosophiquement conçue que savamment exécutée.'

EXTRACT from the QUARTERLY REVIEW.

'We rejoice to notice that a second series of these translations has been announced and has actually begun to appear. The stones, at least, out of which a stately edifice may hereafter arise, are here being brought together. Prof. Max Müller has deserved well of scientific history. Not a few minds owe to his enticing words their first attraction to this branch of study. But no work of his, not even the great edition of the Rig-Veda, can compare in importance or in usefulness with this English translation of the Sacred Books of the East, which has been devised by his foresight, successfully brought so far by his persuasive and organising power, and will, we trust, by the assistance of the distinguished scholars he has gathered round him, be carried in due time to a happy completion.'

Professor E. HARDY, Inaugural Lecture in the University of Freiburg, 1887.

' Die allgemeine vergleichende Religionswissenschaft datirt von jenem grossartigen, in seiner Art einzig dastehenden Unternehmen, zu welchem auf Anregung Max Müllers im Jahre 1874 auf dem internationalen Orientalistencongress in London der Grundstein gelegt worden war, die Übersetzung der heiligen Bücher des Ostens' (*the Sacred Books of the East*).

Oxford
AT THE CLARENDON PRESS
LONDON: HENRY FROWDE
OXFORD UNIVERSITY PRESS WAREHOUSE, AMEN CORNER, E.C.

FIRST SERIES.

Vol. I. The Upanishads.

Translated by F. Max Müller. Part I. The *Kh*ândogya-upanishad, The Talavakâra-upanishad, The Aitareya-âra*n*yaka, The Kaushîtaki-brâhma*n*a-upanishad, and The Vâgasaneyi-sa*m*hitâ-upanishad. 8vo, cloth, 10s. 6d.

The Upanishads contain the philosophy of the Veda. They have become the foundation of the later Vedânta doctrines, and indirectly of Buddhism. Schopenhauer, speaking of the Upanishads, says : ' In the whole world there is no study so beneficial and so elevating as that of the Upanishads. It has been the solace of my life, it will be the solace of my death.'

[See also Vol. XV.]

Vol. II. The Sacred Laws of the Âryas,

As taught in the Schools of Âpastamba, Gautama, Vâsish*th*a, and Baudhâyana. Translated by Georg Bühler. Part I. Âpastamba and Gautama. 8vo, cloth, 10s. 6d.

The Sacred Laws of the Âryas contain the original treatises on which the Laws of Manu and other lawgivers were founded.

[See also Vol. XIV.]

Vol. III. The Sacred Books of China.

The Texts of Confucianism. Translated by James Legge. Part I. The Shû King, The Religious Portions of the Shih King, and The Hsiâo King. 8vo, cloth, 12s. 6d.

Confucius was a collector of ancient traditions, not the founder of a new religion. As he lived in the sixth and fifth centuries B.C. his works are of unique interest for the study of Ethology.

[See also Vols. XVI, XXVII, XXVIII, XXXIX, and XL.]

Vol. IV. The Zend-Avesta.

Translated by James Darmesteter. Part I. The Vendîdâd. 8vo, cloth, 10s. 6d.

The Zend-Avesta contains the relics of what was the religion of Cyrus, Darius, and Xerxes, and, but for the battle of Marathon, might have become the religion of Europe. It forms to the present day the sacred book of the Parsis, the so-called fire-worshippers. Two more volumes will complete the translation of all that is left us of Zoroaster's religion.

[See also Vols. XXIII and XXXI.]

VOL. V. Pahlavi Texts.

Translated by E. W. WEST. Part I. The Bundahis, Bahman Yast, and Shâyast lâ-shâyast. 8vo, cloth, 12s. 6d.

The Pahlavi Texts comprise the theological literature of the revival of Zoroaster's religion, beginning with the Sassanian dynasty. They are important for a study of Gnosticism.

VOLS. VI AND IX. The Qur'ân.

Parts I and II. Translated by E. H. PALMER. 8vo, cloth, 21s.

This translation, carried out according to his own peculiar views of the origin of the Qur'ân, was the last great work of E. H. Palmer, before he was murdered in Egypt.

VOL. VII. The Institutes of Vishnu.

Translated by JULIUS JOLLY. 8vo, cloth, 10s. 6d.

A collection of legal aphorisms, closely connected with one of the oldest Vedic schools, the Kathas, but considerably added to in later time. Of importance for a critical study of the Laws of Manu.

VOL. VIII. The Bhagavadgîtâ, with The Sanatsugâtîya, and The Anugîtâ.

Translated by KÂSHINÂTH TRIMBAK TELANG. 8vo, cloth, 10s. 6d.

The earliest philosophical and religious poem of India. It has been paraphrased in Arnold's 'Song Celestial.'

VOL. X. The Dhammapada,

Translated from Pâli by F. MAX MÜLLER; and

The Sutta-Nipâta,

Translated from Pâli by V. FAUSBÖLL; being Canonical Books of the Buddhists. 8vo, cloth, 10s. 6d.

The Dhammapada contains the quintessence of Buddhist morality. The Sutta-Nipâta gives the authentic teaching of Buddha on some of the fundamental principles of religion.

VOL. XI. Buddhist Suttas.

Translated from Pâli by T. W. RHYS DAVIDS. 1. The Mahâ-parinibbâna Suttanta; 2. The Dhamma-kakka-ppavattana Sutta. 3. The Tevigga Suttanta; 4. The Âkankheyya Sutta; 5. The Ketokhila Sutta; 6. The Mahâ-sudassana Suttanta; 7. The Sabbâsava Sutta. 8vo, cloth, 10s. 6d.

A collection of the most important religious, moral, and philosophical discourses taken from the sacred canon of the Buddhists.

Vol. XII. The *Satapatha-Brâhmana*, according to the Text of the Mâdhyandina School.

Translated by Julius Eggeling. Part I. Books I and II. 8vo, cloth, 12s. 6d.

A minute account of the sacrificial ceremonies of the Vedic age. It contains the earliest account of the Deluge in India.

[See also Vol. XXVI.]

Vol. XIII. Vinaya Texts.

Translated from the Pâli by T. W. Rhys Davids and Hermann Oldenberg. Part I. The Pâtimokkha. The Mahâvagga, I–IV. 8vo, cloth, 10s. 6d.

The Vinaya Texts give for the first time a translation of the moral code of the Buddhist religion as settled in the third century B.C.

[See also Vols. XVII and XX.]

Vol. XIV. The Sacred Laws of the Âryas,

As taught in the Schools of Âpastamba, Gautama, Vâsishtha, and Baudhâyana. Translated by Georg Bühler. Part II. Vasishtha and Baudhâyana. 8vo, cloth, 10s. 6d.

Vol. XV. The Upanishads.

Translated by F. Max Müller. Part II. The Katha-upanishad, The Mundaka-upanishad, The Taittirîyaka-upanishad, The Brihadâranyaka-upanishad, The Svetâsvatara-upanishad, The Prasña-upanishad, and The Maitrâyana-brâhmana-upanishad. 8vo, cloth, 10s. 6d.

Vol. XVI. The Sacred Books of China.

The Texts of Confucianism. Translated by James Legge. Part II. The Yî King. 8vo, cloth, 10s. 6d.

Vol. XVII. Vinaya Texts.

Translated from the Pâli by T. W. Rhys Davids and Hermann Oldenberg. Part II. The Mahâvagga V–X. The Kullavagga, I–III. 8vo, cloth, 10s. 6d.

Vol. XVIII. Pahlavi Texts.

Translated by E. W. West. Part II. The Dâdistân-î Dinik and The Epistles of Mânûskîhar. 8vo, cloth, 12s. 6d.

Vol. XIX. The Fo-sho-hing-tsan-king.

A Life of Buddha by Asvaghosha Bodhisattva, translated from Sanskrit into Chinese by Dharmaraksha, A.D. 420, and from Chinese into English by Samuel Beal. 8vo, cloth, 10s. 6d.

This life of Buddha was translated from Sanskrit into Chinese, A.D. 420. It contains many legends, some of which show a certain similarity to the Evangelium infantiae, &c.

VOL. XX. Vinaya Texts.

Translated from the Pâli by T. W. RHYS DAVIDS and HERMANN OLDENBERG. Part III. The *K*ullavagga, IV–XII. 8vo, cloth, 10s. 6d.

VOL. XXI. The Saddharma-pu*nd*arîka ; or, The Lotus of the True Law.

Translated by H. KERN. 8vo, cloth, 12s. 6d.

' *The Lotus of the true Law,' a canonical book of the Northern Buddhists, translated from Sanskrit. There is a Chinese translation of this book which was finished as early as the year* 286 *A.D.*

VOL. XXII. *G*aina-Sûtras.

Translated from Prâkrit by HERMANN JACOBI. Part I. The Â*k*ârâṅga-Sûtra and The Kalpa-Sûtra. 8vo, cloth, 10s. 6d.

The religion of the Gainas was founded by a contemporary of Buddha. It still counts numerous adherents in India, while there are no Buddhists left in India proper.

VOL. XXIII. The Zend-Avesta.

Translated by JAMES DARMESTETER. Part II. The Sîrôzahs, Yasts, and Nyâyis. 8vo, cloth, 10s. 6d.

VOL. XXIV. Pahlavi Texts.

Translated by E. W. WEST. Part III. Dînâ-î Maînôg-î Khira*d*, *S*îkand-gûmânîk Vi*g*âr, and Sad Dar. 8vo, cloth, 10s. 6d.

———••———

SECOND SERIES.

VOL. XXV. Manu.

Translated by GEORG BÜHLER. 8vo, cloth, 21s.

This translation is founded on that of Sir William Jones, which has been carefully revised and corrected with the help of seven native Commentaries. An Appendix contains all the quotations from Manu which are found in the Hindu Law-books, translated for the use of the Law Courts in India. Another Appendix gives a synopsis of parallel passages from the six Dharma-sûtras, the other Sm*ri*tis, the Upanishads, the Mahâbhârata, &c.

VOL. XXVI. The *S*atapatha-Brâhma*n*a.

Translated by JULIUS EGGELING. Part II. Books III and IV. 8vo, cloth, 12s. 6d.

VOLS. XXVII AND XXVIII. The Sacred Books of China.

The Texts of Confucianism. Translated by JAMES LEGGE. Parts III and IV. The Lî Kî, or Collection of Treatises on the Rules of Propriety, or Ceremonial Usages. 8vo, cloth, 12s. 6d. each.

VOL. XXIX. The Grihya-Sûtras, Rules of Vedic Domestic Ceremonies.

Part I. Sânkhâyana, Âsvalâyana, Pâraskara, Khâdira. Translated by HERMANN OLDENBERG. 8vo, cloth, 12s. 6d.

These rules of Domestic Ceremonies describe the home life of the ancient Âryas with a completeness and accuracy unmatched in any other literature. Some of these rules have been incorporated in the ancient Law-books.

VOL. XXX. The Grihya-Sûtras. Part II. [*In the Press.*]

VOL. XXXI. The Zend-Avesta.

Part III. The Yasna, Visparad, Âfrinagân, Gâhs, and Miscellaneous Fragments. Translated by L. H. MILLS. 8vo, cloth, 12s. 6d.

VOL. XXXII. Vedic Hymns.

Translated by F. MAX MÜLLER. Part I. 8vo, cloth, 18s. 6d.

VOL. XXXIII. The Minor Law-books.

Translated by JULIUS JOLLY. Part I. Nârada, Brihaspati. 8vo, cloth, 10s. 6d.

VOL. XXXIV. The Vedânta-Sûtras, with the Commentary by Sankarâkârya.

Translated by G. THIBAUT. 8vo, cloth, 12s. 6d.

VOL. XXXV. The Questions of King Milinda. Translated from the Pâli by T. W. RHYS DAVIDS. 8vo, cloth, 10s. 6d.

VOL. XXXVII. The Contents of the Nasks, as stated in the Eighth and Ninth Books of the Dînkard. Translated by E. W. WEST. [*In the Press.*]

VOLS. XXXIX AND XL. The Sacred Books of China. The Texts of Tâoism. Translated by JAMES LEGGE. 8vo, cloth, 21s.

** The Second Series will consist of Twenty-four Volumes in all.

SOME ORIENTAL WORKS

RECENTLY PUBLISHED BY THE CLARENDON PRESS.

A Practical Arabic Grammar. Part I.
> Compiled by A. O. GREEN, Brigade Major, Royal Engineers. *Second Edition, Enlarged.* Crown 8vo, 7s. 6d.

First Lessons in Tamil; or, an Introduction to the Common Dialect of that Language. With an easy Catechism in Tamil of both the Colloquial and Classical Dialects. By the Rev. G. U. POPE, M.A., D.D. Crown 8vo, 7s. 6d.

Grammar of the Bengali Language, Literary and Colloquial. By JOHN BEAMES. Crown 8vo, 4s. 6d.

A Catalogue of the Chinese Translation of the Buddhist Tripiṭaka, *the Sacred Canon of the Buddhists in China and Japan.*
> Compiled by order of the Secretary of State for India by BUNYIU NANJIO, Priest of the Temple, Eastern Hongwanzi, Japan; Member of the Royal Asiatic Society. 4to, 32s. 6d.
> 'An immense service rendered to Oriental scholarship.'—*Saturday Review.*

The Chinese Classics: with a Translation, Critical and Exegetical Notes, Prolegomena, and Copious Indexes. By JAMES LEGGE, D.D., LL.D. In Seven Volumes. Royal 8vo.
> Vol. I. *Confucian Analects, &c.* [*Out of print.*]
> Vol. II. *The Works of Mencius.* 1l. 10s.
> Vol. III. *The Shoo-King, or the Book of Historical Documents.* In two Parts. 1l. 10s. each.
> Vol. IV. *The She-King, or the Book of Poetry.* In two Parts. 1l. 10s. each.
> Vol. V. *The Ch'un Ts'ew, with the Tso Chuen.* In two Parts. 1l. 10s. each.

Record of Buddhistic Kingdoms; being an Account by the Chinese Monk FÂ-HIEN of his Travels in India and Ceylon (A.D. 399–414) in search of the Buddhist Books of Discipline. Translated and annotated, with a Corean recension of the Chinese Text, by JAMES LEGGE, M.A., LL.D. Crown 4to, boards, 10s. 6d.

Anecdota Oxoniensia.

ARYAN SERIES.

Buddhist Texts from Japan. I. Vagrakkhedikâ; *The Diamond-Cutter.*

Edited by F. Max Müller, M.A. Small 4to, 3s. 6d.

One of the most famous metaphysical treatises of the Mahâyâna Buddhists.

Buddhist Texts from Japan. II. Sukhâvatî-Vyûha : *Description of Sukhâvatî, the Land of Bliss.*

Edited by F. Max Müller, M.A., and Bunyiu Nanjio. With two Appendices: (1) Text and Translation of Saṅghavarman's Chinese Version of the Poetical Portions of the Sukhâvatî-Vyûha; (2) Sanskrit Text of the Smaller Sukhâvatî-Vyûha. Small 4to, 7s. 6d.

The *editio princeps* of the Sacred Book of one of the largest and most influential sects of Buddhism, numbering more than ten millions of followers in Japan alone.

Buddhist Texts from Japan. III. *The Ancient Palm-Leaves containing the* Pragñâ-Pâramitâ-Hridaya-Sûtra *and the* Ushnisha-Vigaya-Dhârani.

Edited by F. Max Müller, M.A., and Bunyiu Nanjio, M.A. With an Appendix by G. Bühler, C.I.E. With many Plates. Small 4to, 10s.

Contains facsimiles of the oldest Sanskrit MS. at present known.

Dharma-Samgraha, *an Ancient Collection of Buddhist Technical Terms.*

Prepared for publication by Kenjiu Kasawara, a Buddhist Priest from Japan, and, after his death, edited by F. Max Müller and H. Wenzel. Small 4to, 7s. 6d.

Kâtâyana's Sarvânukramani of the *Rig*veda.

With Extracts from Shadgurusishya's Commentary entitled Vedârthadîpikâ. Edited by A. A. Macdonell, M.A., Ph.D. 16s.

Oxford

AT THE CLARENDON PRESS

LONDON: HENRY FROWDE

OXFORD UNIVERSITY PRESS WAREHOUSE, AMEN CORNER, E.C.

www.ingramcontent.com/pod-product-compliance
Lightning Source LLC
Chambersburg PA
CBHW021337110726
47900CB00005B/1511